K-Love

by

Devon Atwood & Alice Cornwall

K-Rom Publishing

Cover design by Kaye Studios
Edited by Clare Wood, Self-Publishing Services LLC
Formatted by Self-Publishing Services LLC

Dedication

We dedicate this book to EXO, Hyun Bin, Kim Soo Hyun, our bestie San, and our husbands for putting up with this.

Chapter One

The ocean slipped in and out of view as the car followed the winding road along the coast, the sun sparkling off the water. Sitting in the passenger seat, Hyun Tae stopped thinking of all the reasons he was in California and let the scenery lull him into a trance as it blurred past.

The flight from Korea had been seventeen hours, a long time to be on a plane fighting boredom with headphones and movies. He'd coped with long travel many times to various places around the world, but this was the first time it wasn't for a vacation.

The road straightened out, and Daniel hit the accelerator, making the Z4 jump forward, its engine growling. The speedometer needle crept up, and Hyun Tae glanced over at his friend. Daniel wore aviator sunglasses and a ball cap, as did Hyun Tae, but they hid Daniel's face better, which was a shame because he'd had a few plastic surgeries to perfect his already perfect features. Born to an American mother and a Korean father, Daniel was a good-looking combination of both.

Hyun Tae had known Daniel since they were five years old. Both of them had lived privileged lives, but for different reasons. Hyun Tae's family owned one of the biggest biotech companies in South Korea, and he was due to take his father's place. Daniel's choices were dictated by something far more unpredictable.

As the car went around the bend, they both saw the police cruiser at the same time and swore in unison. Lights flashed in the rearview mirror as Daniel braked around the hill and pulled over so fast the tires spit up dust, his hands shaking on the wheel.

Hyun Tae didn't hesitate, unclicking his seatbelt and shoving his seat back. "Switch."

Daniel obeyed without protest, and they climbed over each other as the police car pulled up behind them.

Daniel opened the glove box ad searched for the temporary registration on the new car, purchased only a few days ago. Hyun Tae pulled his wallet out of his back pocket and found his Korean driver's license, fear flooding through him. They couldn't take the risk of Daniel getting a ticket.

From the rearview mirror, Hyun Tae watched the officer approach the car. The officer's gaze went over every detail of the new car, and then he turned to look at the two passengers with flat, bored eyes. Hyun Tae's heart was nearly exploding out of his chest as he took off his sunglasses. He hoped they had succeeded in changing seats before they were seen, and that the officer wouldn't be able to tell one from the other from that distance.

"Do you know why I pulled you over?" the officer asked.

"I was speeding," Hyun Tae said.

"Do you know how fast you were going?"

"Seventy, sir."

"Do you know what the speed limit is?"

"Sixty-five?" he asked. He hadn't been paying attention.

"Thirty-five on this road."

"Oh." Twice the speed limit. Hyun Tae knew that was serious enough to get his license suspended or worse, but it was better for him to suffer the inconvenience than for Daniel's name to be on any record.

"That's twice as fast as the speed limit," the officer said, stating the obvious, and then paused, as if for effect.

"I'm sorry; I shouldn't have done that. I'm really sorry."

"Way too fast."

"Yes, it is," Hyun Tae said, wondering what this was leading to.

The officer asked to see the registration and took Hyun Tae's license without comment. He went back to his vehicle.

Daniel stared out at the rocky hillside, and Hyun Tae did the same, trying not to think about everything they were jeopardizing. A cool breeze blew in, and he realized he was sweating. If Daniel's name got on any public records, their semester together at Bates University would be over, and Hyun Tae really didn't want that. Neither of them did.

Footsteps crunched on the dirt and gravel, and Hyun Tae fixed his gaze on the outside mirror, watching the officer walk slowly back to them. When he reached their car, the officer held out the registration and license, as well as a citation, which Hyun Tae took, looking up at the officer.

"You have ten days to pay the fine or contest it. The instructions are on the back, if you want to contest. Keep your speed down from now on."

"Thank you, Officer," Hyun Tae said, barely able to believe their luck. Only a ticket?

Daniel kept his eyes down, but the officer didn't seem to notice him, wishing them a good day and walking away.

Hyun Tae rolled up the window and started the car, handing the paperwork to Daniel.

"*Mian*," Daniel apologized in Korean, his voice subdued.

Hyun Tae pulled back onto the road, driving at a grandfatherly pace until they were out of sight of the police car, and then he found the freeway taking them back to Riverside.

"If you get caught, I'm staying here without you," Hyun Tae said.

"I know. But I'll be careful from now on."

Hyun Tae's phone buzzed, and he answered it. "*Yoboseyo*," he said in greeting, knowing it would be Joon Suh.

"*Hyung*," Joon Suh replied, using the Korean term for "brother" or "best friend."

"Were you able to access his e-mails?"

"Yeah."

"Anything?"

"He likes caviar, and he has no tolerance for late homework. Maybe you should take a different class."

Hyun Tae ignored the suggestion. That wasn't an option. Hyun Tae had come to California, so he could find out more about Professor Kruljac, not to pursue a college degree.

Joon Suh cleared his throat. "And I couldn't register you for his class this morning. Their system is down or something."

"Well, I have to have the class." This was an unfortunate glitch.

"You can go to the registration office and see if they can do it for you, if you don't want to wait. You've still got two weeks until classes start."

"Yeah, I don't want to wait."

Hyun Tae ended the call and looked over at Daniel. "We have to go to the registration office before we go home."

"Couldn't get the class?"

"Their system was down." Hyun Tae wanted nothing more than to get to the house they'd rented and take a shower, but that would have to wait.

They were in Riverside within an hour, driving past sprawling tract developments, some of which looked like they were on a downward slide, and then along tree-lined streets to a wide boulevard that led to the campus and the student housing of Bates University.

The afternoon was pleasant as they drove around the campus, the hot sun relieved by cool breezes. Bates wasn't a top school, but it had an irresistible Southern California vibe. The people were casual and eclectic, with a lot of tanned beachgoers who looked like they'd been marinating in nothing but chill for most of their lives. The campus had a lot of wide lawns, and the main building had Spanish architecture, with a white stucco exterior and archways leading into a shaded entryway.

Hyun Tae parked in front, and they made their way to the registration office. It wasn't too crowded, for which Hyun Tae was thankful.

"Next!" a woman called from one of several desks stationed throughout the registration office.

Hyun Tae and Daniel went to the desk of a petite, middle-aged woman. She had sharp blue eyes and a gray streak that looked like silver ribbon in her hair.

"How can I help you?" she asked. Her nameplate read Marie Bryant.

Hyun Tae answered, "I need to sign up for a class. Biology 332, with Professor Kruljac."

"Sure," she said, her eyes going to her screen. "Can I have your name and date of birth please?"

"Hyun Tae Kim, August 23rd, 1994."

Her fingers hesitated for a moment, her eyes going to his face, and he had the curious feeling she was assessing him.

"This should only take a second. The system went down this morning, but they should have it back up soon if you want to make other changes," she said, her voice taking on a conversational tone, as if she were a dentist distracting a patient from a root canal.

He wasn't one for small talk, but he felt obligated to say something. "That happens."

"Oh, sure," she said, clicking away on the keyboard. "Hmm. I see you are a transfer . . . from Seoul National. Bates is a great school, very friendly. How are you liking it so far?"

"I just got here this afternoon, actually. So far it's nice."

"Oh good, and it looks like most of your classes transferred. That's great."

"Yes," he said, wondering why any of that mattered, since she wasn't an advisor. He only needed her to register him for a class.

"I have a 332 class with Professor Simmons at eleven thirty on Wednesdays and Fridays. That would fit nicely with your others."

"No, I would prefer Professor Kruljac," Hyun Tae said.

"Oh, I see," she said, clicking away. "All right, I can add you on Tuesdays and Thursdays then, but you'll have to run across campus pretty fast."

"That's fine." The seconds ticked away in silence as he waited.

"I love Korea!" she said, blurting out the words.

He looked up at her, surprised by the unexpected and random turn of the conversation. "You've been there?"

A faint hint of pink showed in her cheeks. "Oh no, but I watch K-dramas."

Daniel exchanged a quick look with him, and Hyun Tae stifled the urge to laugh. Comparing Korean life to Korean television shows was like comparing American life to a romantic comedy.

"My mom likes them too," Hyun Tae answered, just to be friendly.

She turned her chair to her printer and looked back at him, smiling brightly and clearing her throat. "I have a daughter. Are you single?"

He could almost feel Daniel shaking with silent laughter next to him, but he didn't dare look. "No, I mean, yes, but I'm not dating right now."

Instead of handing him the schedule she had printed out, she reached over and swiped through her phone. Her fingers were shaking, and he softened. They had an amateur matchmaker on their hands.

She held up her phone. A very pretty girl with blond hair smiled back at him, her outstretched hands holding a baby duck. Her eyes were as blue as her mother's, and there was something infectious about her smile.

"She is beautiful," he said honestly.

Daniel peered over his shoulder. "Yes, she is."

The woman looked up at Daniel. "Are you single?"

He laughed. "Yes, I am."

She took a deep breath, and Hyun Tae realized she was about to try and snag Daniel. "Would you take her on a blind date?"

"Does she know you are setting her up?" Daniel asked, raising an eyebrow at her.

"Well, no, but don't worry about that. Here's her number! She was in Italy for a semester, but she'll be here tomorrow. What is your name?"

"Daniel Bak. I also like K-dramas," he said.

Hyun Tae stifled a groan. Daniel was not shy about being charming or cheesy.

"Oh!" she said, obviously pleased. She ripped a piece off the schedule she'd printed out for Hyun Tae, wrote her daughter's name and a local phone number on it and handed it to Daniel. "She's funny, nice and very talented. Don't wait too long!" she said.

"I won't," Daniel promised.

She handed the schedule to Hyun Tae, her eyes on Daniel. Hyun Tae noted that a good chunk of Monday and Tuesday was now missing from the top.

"Thank you," Hyun Tae said with a polite smile.

As they walked away, Hyun Tae sighed. "That poor woman has no idea who you are."

9

Daniel looked down at the number in his hand. "That's why I'm here. I'm nobody."

"Well, try to stay that way, at least until I figure out this professor."

"Of course," Daniel said in agreement, but there was a distracted look on his face. "You staying on campus? I've got a call to make at home."

"Yeah, I've still got a few things to do."

"See you later."

The girl in the photo *was* beautiful, Hyun Tae conceded to himself, but the last thing he needed was an irrelevant distraction.

Chapter Two

Chase stared in horror at her schedule. It was a mess. Standing in front of her mother's desk in the admissions department on the day before the start of term, Chase frowned at the badly spaced classes, a few of which weren't even relevant to her degree.

"Mom," she said, her voice a croak.

"Hmm?" Her mother looked up from her desk, blinking with innocent blue eyes, her dark brown hair swept into a bun that showed off her silver streak.

"What the heck . . . what is this? A *fitness class*?"

"You needed an extracurricular."

"So why not pottery or something?"

"You don't have to do anything but show up. It will be easy!" Her eyes flicked to the heart monitor on Chase's wrist where blue numbers blinked softly. "You don't have to do the weights."

"Then why be in it?" Chase dropped the schedule to her side, putting her monitor out of view. Although it almost looked like a fitness tracker, it had an entirely different purpose, and she detested it. "And a biology class? I'm in the art program!"

"You had to have a science class. And artists should be well-rounded."

Her mother picked up the phone as it rang, and a few more students lined up behind Chase. The registration office was crowded and busy, with hoards of students standing in front of counters and desks, some demanding changes and others confused or even panicked about their classes. Chase knew she couldn't loiter in the office forever, gawking at her poorly constructed schedule.

Her mother hung up, and Chase quickly asked, "Can I change it? Can I swap some classes?"

"Sorry, hon, I can't. We're really busy, and the classes are pretty much full. It's not so bad!"

"You're in registration," Chase hissed, leaning over the counter to lower her voice. "Can't you rig it or something?"

"That wouldn't be fair. And you know I've only had this job a few months. How would it look, my 'rigging' things for my daughter?"

Chase tapped her fingers on the counter. She loved her mom, but right now Chase was running out of patience. It wasn't just the schedule. Her mom was going through some kind of midlife crisis or something, and Chase seemed to be in her crosshairs.

Her mother gave her a pointed look. "Do you have a map? Go find your buildings and get some lunch from the cafeteria. Did you get your student card?"

"Not yet. Mom, I've got a three-hour gap between . . ."

"Get your card first," she ordered. With a smile that crinkled her eyes at the corners, her mom added, "Your hair looks nice today."

Chase absentmindedly ran a hand through her wavy blond hair, and then her mom motioned for another student to move forward, which shuffled Chase to the side and out of line. So much for nepotism.

With a sigh of resignation, Chase slung her yellow backpack over her shoulders and left the bustling office, pushing past a gaggle of excited freshmen having some kind of loud reunion in the doorway, and finally escaped into the wide, tall foyer. She held up the now slightly crumpled schedule. Early morning fitness class, a two-hour break, and then a biology class. With a lab.

Her phone buzzed, and Kiki's smiling face popped up on her screen. Chase answered, walking toward the cafeteria. "Hey Kiki!"

"You're back!" her friend cheered. "Four months is way too long. How was Italy? Are you an art master now? Wait, never mind, tell me that later. Where are you?"

"On campus. I haven't stopped by the apartment yet, though. How are you?"

"Great! I'm just getting unpacked, and then I'm going to head over to the bookstore. Want to meet there? Our room looks great by the way."

"Did you meet the other roommates?" Chase asked.

13

"Not yet. So bookstore?"

"Yeah, I can do that. I'll eat lunch first and meet you there."

"Sounds good. Can't wait to see you!"

"See ya." Chase smiled. She kept in contact with a few friends from high school, but Kiki was her best. They had both attended Riverside City College for two years, neither of them having any idea where they wanted to go with their lives. But when Chase's mom scored a job at Bates University, suddenly Chase had access to a shiny new arts program at reduced tuition. Kiki hadn't even questioned it and had followed her over.

Chase slipped her phone into her backpack and then set off for the cafeteria. Ever since Chase had come home from her summer abroad in Italy, her mother had been acting strangely. There was the weird fascination with Korean television dramas and then there was the blind date. It made her mad just thinking about it. If she could figure out how to get out of it, she would. She just didn't know how yet.

As she left the air-conditioned building, the sun hit her skin with blistering heat, and despite shorts and a thin cotton T-shirt, sweat gathered at Chase's hairline almost immediately. An older student passed her on the sidewalk, his eyes glued to his phone and earbuds around his neck. Another group of girls talked loudly on the path ahead of her.

She reached the cafeteria building, which had an enormous glass wall on the front where groups of round tables and bright purple chairs could be seen from the outside. She walked up the concrete steps and through the double glass doors where the air-conditioning washed over her with a blast of icy relief. The first thing she smelled was pizza. The cafeteria had been built on two levels, with tables and chairs in front and the food line at the back. Students buzzed with conversation, talking over giant textbooks and huddling together in tight groups as they discussed their classes.

Self-conscious all of a sudden that she didn't have anyone to sit with, Chase grabbed a dark green tray. *Awkward transfer student alert.*

She got in line behind a pretty redhead with a tall, statuesque build. She was talking politely to a boy in front of her in a way that revealed they had just met. *Flirting Level 9.2,* Chase decided, which was more than she could say for herself. She was about a 4, mostly because flirting just felt awkward. Real romance shouldn't take that much work, in her opinion. It should just happen.

"Can I help you?" a sweet, plump elderly lady asked from behind the glass partition. Steam from one of the containers of food kept fogging up her thick glasses.

Chase perused the options. "Can I have grilled cheese and a bowl of tomato soup?"

The lunch lady ladled the soup into a bowl and placed a Styrofoam plate with the grilled cheese next to the bowl on her tray. "Anything else?"

"That's it, thanks." Chase smiled.

The Asian kid behind her asked for a salad. She caught a glimpse of him out of the corner of her eye as he got his plate of food. He was wearing white skinny jeans, navy sneakers, and a sort of silky gray T-shirt that definitely looked designer. They shuffled along in line until finally it was her turn to pay. Chase handed the thin student cashier her card. He looked at the debit card briefly before handing it back to her. "You need your student card."

Chase took the card, suddenly nervous. "My what?"

The student had dark blond hair and kind features, but his look of exasperation told her he was thoroughly fed up with answering this question. "Your student ID card. You pay for lunch with it. You can't get lunch any other way."

"What, seriously?" Chase looked down at her tray. Her stomach gurgled. "So I have to get my card and then come back?"

"Sorry."

She swallowed. "My mom didn't say anything about a student ID card." The cashier gave her a blank look of disbelief, so she added, "She works in registration."

"Okay. Well, sorry, but you need a student ID."

Someone sighed behind her. She was holding up the line.

"Excuse me," a low voice said from behind her. Chase looked over her shoulder and found the guy with the designer shirt leaning toward her. He held out a student ID card, and reaching over her, handed it to the cashier. "Just pay for both."

Chase turned to face him, her eyes widening. "Oh . . . ah, wait . . ."

The cashier hesitated.

"No, don't do that," Chase insisted. *No, no, no! Don't do that! I don't like owing a complete stranger, thanks very much.*

The guy gave the cashier a nod so full of confidence, Chase was pretty sure anyone would have obeyed an order from him. The cashier swiped the card.

Chase realized she was staring. For one thing, this guy was otherworldly beautiful. He had high cheekbones and warm brown eyes that tilted up at an exotic angle. His chin sloped down to a square point from his razor-like jawline. She almost couldn't find words to respond to him. And besides that, he held himself like he owned the school.

His eyes flitted to her. "You can go now."

"Oh." Direct. And people thought *she* was made of stone. "Thanks. Sorry."

"It's fine." He had an accent, but it was barely detectable.

She scurried forward with her tray, her face hot and her calm ruffled.

"Miss," he said suddenly from behind her.

She whirled around to face him but miscalculated the motion by a mile. She collided with the generous stranger, her tray flying off to the side. Tomato soup splattered all over the floor, washing over both their shoes in a torrent of scalding liquid.

The guy jumped back and then looked up from his shoes to her face, his scowl a mixture of incredulity and shock.

The racket in the cafeteria quieted almost instantly. All eyes turned to them. Chase stood there like an idiot with tomato soup trickling down her leg and seeping between her toes. She couldn't seem to find her voice with the entire cafeteria staring at her.

Finally, he spoke. "Are you okay?"

Was she? She looked down. "My feet burn. I think it's okay, though." *Holy crap I'm so sorry! I'm such a klutz!* As usual, her inner voice couldn't get past her shy exterior.

He sighed and put his tray on a nearby table before bending down to pick up her things. Chase quickly knelt down next to him and helped put everything back on the tray. Around them the chatter slowly returned, until the echoes of the other students' voices filled the space once more. The cashier brought her a white towel. While she mopped up the soup, the gorgeous stranger rested a forearm on one bent knee and rubbed the corner of his mouth with his thumb.

She glanced up from the now-orange rag to his face. He was just watching her, his expression unreadable.

"I'm really sorry," she said, mumbling her words.

"I wanted to tell you that you forgot your card."

He held the blue debit card out to her. She took it sheepishly, pocketed it, and stood up with the tray piled with ruined food and the stained towel. She wasn't sure what to say. "Are your shoes ruined?"

He looked down at them. The laces had gone orange. "Yes."

"Sorry." They stared at one another, and then she said, blurting the words out, "Can I pay for dry cleaning?"

"It's fine." He took the tray from her, handed it to the cashier, and then ignoring his own tray, walked to the back of the line. She stood off to the side of the cashier, watching her would-be rescuer in confusion. Did she ruin his salad or something?

He reached the back of the line, and then, looking at her like she was the crazy one, motioned with his head for her to follow him.

Chase started. *He wants me to get back in line with him?* The least she could do was follow along. She went to stand next to him, and he took by her shoulders to maneuver her in front of him. The lunch lady with the foggy glasses asked what she wanted. The guy motioned with a silent hand for her to order.

Chase's eyes went wide. "Please don't."

"Cheese sandwich and tomato soup," he said to the lady. The lunch lady looked between them in amusement.

As they shuffled down the line with her new tray, Chase found herself saying, "I can pay you back."

"It's no problem, Chase," he responded. She started, and he explained, "I saw your name on the debit card. I'm Kim Hyun Tae."

"Kim?"

"Hyun Tae is my first name."

She nodded, even though she was pretty sure she still couldn't pronounce it correctly. "Hyundai."

A smile tugged at the corner of his lips. He checked his phone, typed something out, and then finally they had reached the end of the line. He handed the cashier his card again.

After the lanky kid swiped the card and returned it, Hyun Tae nodded his head in a way that almost seemed like a bow—obviously that was goodbye, and Chase took her tray in a firm hold. "Thanks again."

"My pleasure," he said, the response automatic. And then he left, taking his tray and walking to the far end of the cafeteria.

Chase looked down at her tomato soup. That could have gone better.

Chapter Three

The first thing Chase did when she met Kiki in the bookstore was relay her tale of woe. Kiki managed to keep her face straight, but Chase could tell she found the whole thing hilarious. Kiki's pixie-like face, accented by her spiky, platinum-blond hair, showed every emotion she felt. Especially if it was funny. Her hazel eyes had a way of twinkling when she found something amusing.

"What was in that soup? I think your toes are still orange," Kiki said, joking, as they hefted their full backpacks up the steps of their apartment building. It was a small unit with four apartments per building—two on the top and two on the bottom. The top floors had small outdoor decks, which they had thought would be fun. Four girls were living together in the two-bedroom apartment. Like most buildings in California, it was made of a light brown stucco with white trim and modern touches. Somehow the landscapers kept the little patches of grass green on the miniature lawns.

Chase shielded her eyes from the sun as she looked up at the apartment. "So, you haven't met our roomies yet?"

"I saw a car in one of our parking spots, so someone has to be here," Kiki said. Each of the apartments had only two spots, so they knew that parking would probably be interesting.

They opened the apartment door, and the sweat at the back of Chase's neck prickled as cold air conditioning washed over her. The apartment was cute. It was an open floor plan. In the living room, two comfy tan couches faced each other and with a glass coffee table between them. Behind it, the dining room had a simple, square dining table and suede chairs. That led right into the tiny kitchen that Chase was pretty sure would require some tricky maneuvering if more than one person needed to use it. Everything was clean, and the windows let in plenty of natural light.

Kiki dropped her backpack near the entrance and kicked off her sandals with heels. "What do you think?"

"It's really nice," Chase said with a nod of approval.

A girl popped her head out of one of the rooms down the hall. With a bright, white smile, she waved and entered the living room. "Hey."

Kiki waved back, a little too enthusiastically, like a prom queen from a parade float. "Hey. I'm Kiki."

"I'm Chase."

"Laura," the roommate said. Her black hair, highlighted with caramel, had been straightened and fell a little below her shoulders. "Nice to meet you. Janelle is out getting groceries."

As Chase slipped her backpack to the floor and removed her sandals, Kiki said, "Nice to meet you, too. What's your major?"

"Pre-med," Laura said. "You?"

"Art."

Laura looked toward Chase, and Chase quickly added, "Same."

Laura's dusky rose lips pressed against a smile. "Art? At Bates?"

Kiki sat on the couch, stretching her long legs out before her. "I know most people here are science gurus, but they just opened up the arts program. So it was easy to get in. Also Chase's mom works here, so her tuition is cheap."

Laura seemed to approve. "Cool. Once Janelle gets here, I guess we can go over cabinet space for food and stuff."

Janelle, it turned out, was very much Type A. In crisp tones, she relayed to her roommates the "system" for marking food, and sharing a cabinet for snacks, and whose pans were whose, and which ones could be shared. Chase wasn't surprised to hear that she was in bioengineering.

Chase had a feeling that she would spend most of her time with Kiki in their room. They had a desk on the wall between their twin beds and a TV on the opposite wall.

They spent most of their night unpacking and watching reality TV while Kiki caught Chase up on her summer. As she brushed her hair before bed, Chase knelt on Kiki's purple comforter to look out the only window in their room. She pointed to a house that neighbored their unit. "Is that a real house or a student house?"

Kiki leaned over her to get a good look. "Huh. I don't know. It looks like a real house. Ooh, it has a pool."

"I want a pool," Chase muttered.

Kiki gave her shoulder a shove. "Don't be greedy."

Chase made a lunge for her roommate, but Kiki danced out of the way and threw Chase's shorts in her face. "What time is your first class tomorrow?"

Chase pulled the shorts off her face and then dug the crumpled schedule from the back pocket. "Eight in the morning."

Kiki pulled a disgusted face.

With a sigh, Chase threw the paper on the desk, piled her long hair into a bun at the top of her head, and flopped facedown onto her bed. She set her alarm for seven.

*****

Chase drove her beat-up Ford Focus down a palm-tree lined street on campus, looking for a place to park. True, she could have walked but she wasn't in the mood. Besides she was about to burn a bunch of calories. The fitness building was easy to spot, a huge brick structure that sprawled out over a sizable portion of the campus. On her third time around the block, she spotted a car leaving a spot and mentally prepared herself to parallel park. It only took two tries, which she thought wasn't bad. She hadn't driven in four months. Also, the rearview mirror had a tendency to fall off, so she had to keep readjusting the duct tape.

She poked the rearview mirror back in place and checked her hair. She had put it up in a neat ponytail, a few strands from her long bangs smoothed to the side.

Her black yoga pants hugged her hips and a slim T-shirt gave her room to move without being too tight. There was a small Deadpool logo on the back of the neck that looked like a red and black oval, barely recognizable as the Merc with the Mouth unless you were a fan.

Slinging her backpack over one shoulder, she locked the car and headed into the building, hoping the first day wouldn't be as boring as she expected. She slipped her earphones in with a sigh and scrolled through her music for her favorite playlist. She smiled when she saw the one her sister, Jonni, had downloaded for her. She'd titled it "Try This." Jonni had found the Korean entertainment obsession first, but it had spread to her mom fairly quickly. Jonni had good taste, even if she was six years older than Chase, so the music was probably something she would like.

She hit the playlist and some unrecognizable pop song in Korean rang out with an epic, irresistible beat.

"Love me, love me *neomaneul saranghae.*"

She had no idea what they were saying when they stopped speaking English, but she liked it. Her song was interrupted by a text from a number she didn't recognize.

"Hi, Chase," it said. *"My name is Daniel Bak. You don't know me, but I met your mom, and she told me that you wouldn't mind going on a blind date."*

She stopped in her tracks. She'd avoided thinking about the blind date because she couldn't seem to come up with a good solution. Should she say she was busy? Or get it over with? She texted him as she entered the brick physical education building. *"Yes, she told me about you."*

She wasn't rejecting him, but she wasn't committing to a date either. She found her way to Room 108, and as she settled in a desk, his response binged back. *"From your picture I could tell you don't need blind dates, by the way. If you want to back out, that's okay. I've never done this either."*

It made her wonder why he agreed to the blind date. Blind dates were risky things, and the potential for disaster was high. Was he unattractive? Would her mom set her up with someone who couldn't get a date on his own? The answer was probably yes. He sounded nice, though, and pretty aware of the odds it would be a bad experience. Chase bit her lip and texted back. *"I've definitely never been on a blind date, and I'm a little crazy for not disowning my mom."*

Other students were filling up the classroom around her, but Chase found herself waiting for Daniel's reply instead of paying attention to her surroundings.

"She seemed really nice. Maybe you should keep her."

"Ha! I'll think about it." She hesitated, and before logic could kick in and save the day, she sent another text. *"I'm in for a blind date."*

"Oh, good, we're both impulsive. What could go wrong?"

"LOL."

"Where do you want to go?"

The teacher walked in, and Chase hurriedly texted, *"Anywhere is fine."* She put her phone on silent, dutifully resolving to pay attention.

"Good morning, class, " said a middle-aged man with a fairly lean build with an iPad in his hand and a stack of papers balanced in the crook of his arm. He had salt-and-pepper hair and a hawk-like nose. His eyes scanned them all, no doubt assessing which ones would pass out if asked to run a mile. "I'm Professor Greene. Today is going to be boring, but we'll get through it. I'm going to get started by going over the syllabus."

As the teacher passed out papers, her phone buzzed once. Then twice. She tried to ignore it, but it was hard to resist finding out if he had made plans for them already.

Chase caved, looking down.

"Cool. How do you feel about race cars?" The second message clarified: *"Driving them around a track, I mean."*

She typed back, *"Wow, really? That sounds amazing. I'm in a class, though. I'll text you in a bit."*

"Yeah, me too," he said. *"ttyl."*

Professor Greene went over the syllabus, which Chase only half listened to, opting instead to scribble doodles of Spiderman swinging from stacks of waffle skyscrapers into the margins. When they had gone over how dangerous weight lifting could be (or something, she assumed), they were led to the fitness area for a tour of the equipment.

Chase surreptitiously checked her phone, but Daniel hadn't gotten out of class either, it seemed.

She looked up from her phone just in time to realize that she was too close to the person in front of her. She gave him a "flat tire," stepping on the heel of his sneaker, which caused him to trip. She froze, face guilty.

He turned, brows raised beneath red-tinted black hair.

"Sorry," she started to say, but the word died on her lips. *Perfection.* That was all she could think. *Complete and utter perfection.* His skin was smooth and creamy, his eyes warm and kind, and he had the kind of kissable mouth that seemed to naturally smile, even at rest.

He stared back, and his features lifted into a smile. "Hi . . . no, it's all right. Don't worry about it."

Chase swallowed.

With a soft chuckle, he adjusted his shoe and turned to follow the group across the gym. *Hot,* she thought a little guiltily, *too bad he's not my blind date.*

Chapter Four

Daniel texted her as she got back to her car after the fitness class. *"Days you are free?"*

"Friday?" Belatedly she realized how fast she had sent that. She hoped that speed didn't reveal her lack of social life.

A paper flapped in the wind, taped onto her windshield. Chase put her phone away, peeling the paper off to find that she had a parking ticket. Looking around, she didn't see any meters. What had she done wrong? Below the citation, the building and room number were listed if she wanted to contest.

She crumpled the paper, slumping into her car with a huff. Of course she was going to contest it! She hadn't done anything wrong.

The parking and permit office was in an older building, the linoleum cracked in some places and a musty smell hanging in the warm air. A line of students stood in front of a large security window, where pamphlets about road safety and parking permits were piled on a table nearby.

While she waited, her text alert dinged. *"Friday works for me, too. You out of class now?"*

"Yeah. Just got a parking ticket."

"They love those. Sorry about that. I can pick you up on Friday at four, and you can drive fast cars without getting any tickets."

Chase smiled. *"Looking forward to it. Four it is."*

When she got to the officer at the window, she was torn between expressing her anger at the parking ticket thing and satisfying her curiosity about Daniel.

"How can I help you?" the man asked, not looking up from his desk.

"I got this," she said, holding out the offensive ticket for emphasis.

He looked up, adjusting his glasses. "Yes?"

"It's a parking ticket."

He frowned. "Yes. Do you have a permit?"

Finally, they were getting somewhere. "No, but my mom didn't tell me I needed one. If I had known, I would have come here first, but she didn't tell me."

"Your mom didn't tell you?" the officer repeated, still looking puzzled.

"Right. So I didn't know. "

He raised his gray eyebrows at her. "Fill out a permit application. They're on the counter. As soon as you finish that, come back here with a check for eighty dollars, and we'll give you a permit and a map of all the designated student parking areas."

This did not sound very sympathetic. "Do I still have to pay the ticket?"

"Yes, ma'am. You can pay it now if you like."

Realizing that she wasn't going to find any mercy here, she sighed and pulled a permit application from the stack and turned to go fill it out. It's not like they had signs to tell her! Did they? Maybe she really had been too distracted to notice…

She bumped into someone's chest. It bounced her back a full two steps, and then she looked up into a pair of dark, familiar eyes. What was his name? Hun Boon? Her cheeks burned as she took one more step back. No way she had bumped into this guy again.

He wore a white T-shirt, slim black jeans, and an expression of disbelief. So he'd heard her rant about not deserving a ticket because of her mom. Why did this keep happening to her?

"Oh, hi," she managed to say, the embarrassment from the day before coming back with brutal clarity. He stared at her. A normal person would have launched into a greeting. Would have apologized for bumping into her. Would have done something!

He continued to stare back, as if daring her to try and be the aloof one.

All of a sudden, she remembered that she had some cash in her pocket. She reached into her jeans and pulled out a crumpled ten-dollar bill and held it out to him. "For lunch yesterday."

A rush of air from the air conditioning washed over them, and the money fluttered limply in her hand.

"That," he said, glancing at the crumpled money, "is not necessary."

"You have to let me pay you back."

The officer at the window said, "Next."

A few students behind Hoon Bun shifted their feet, and his gaze slid over to them, clearly not interested in the ten dollars. She withdrew her hand and stuck the money in her pocket. "Well, I owe you a lunch," she said, trying to salvage the moment.

His whole body froze, and he slid his eyes down at her, as if he were terrified she might say something else, like offer to throw herself in front of a bullet to repay him for the life-changing soup purchase.

Painfully aware that she was blushing, she turned away and walked over to an old metal desk against the wall and sat down to fill out the permit. Was there a giant hole she could fall into and disappear? None appeared, so she bent her head down to fill out form, hoping he would leave soon.

She pulled her hairband out and let her hair fall around her face, hiding behind the waves. The faint scent of fruity shampoo was reassuring. At least she had that going for her. She hadn't worked out too hard and didn't smell like a hockey equipment bag.

She finished the form, still a little miffed at the unfair ticket and a little upset about trying to repay her lunch benefactor. Then she noticed someone pulling out the chair next to her. It was him, of course.

He put a permit form on the desk and began to fill it out. He was probably smart enough to get a permit before he tried to park on campus, and she was sure he didn't have to rely on his mommy to tell him how to do that. Peeking out from her hair she caught his name. Hyun Tae. H-Y-U-N T-A-E. She desperately hoped she hadn't called him anything else out loud.

She got up to pay for the permit, wanting nothing more than to get away from him before she did something else. Standing in line, she was acutely aware that he sat behind her. When it was her turn, she handed the officer the form and scrawled out a check for the fee. He gave her a tag to put on her rearview mirror and some information on where she was supposed to park.

She willed herself not to look back as she left the office, grateful her absurd schedule had allowed this annoying detour. Her next class was biology, and she headed there before she could do any more damage to her ego. She checked her phone again while she walked. Daniel had sent a close up of his elbow.

"I just realized you don't have a picture of me. I feel like this is my best asset."

Chase laughed, navigating the sunny campus toward her biology class. *"What's your second best?"*

A picture of his clean-shaven chin popped up on her screen as she entered the science building.

"I'm starting to think you have a third eye or something. You have my pic. Do I get one?"

She found the classroom, which was large because it was a core science class everyone had to take. The professor arrived late, but he didn't look like he was in a hurry. He was a lean man in his late thirties, with a handsome face and lazy green eyes that could not be described as anything but smoldering. Chase was amused; at least his class attendance would be good.

"Welcome to Biology 102. I'm Professor Kruljac." He had a Russian accent that gave him a little more unnecessary charm.

He took roll, and then he announced they would have a group project later in the semester. Chase could almost feel the silent groan of despair from the rest of the class. Why did teachers always think group projects were such a great idea? They were simply an extra stress factor.

A text buzzed, and Chase swiped open the picture Daniel had sent.

Her stomach dropped down to her toes. It was the handsome student from fitness class who she had stepped on. All of a sudden, the memory of his smile registered as impish. He had known the whole time.

Chase sent a mash of horrified letters. *"Ljasdofij28urjsalidjf;oiajf!!!!!!"*

"Lol," he responded. *"I'm sorry, I should have said something then."*

"YES"

"But this was more fun."

"OMG I can't believe you played me. How long did you know?"

"Just after you ripped my shoe off."

"You are the WORST."

He sent a chagrined looking emoji. *"We're still on for Friday, though, right?"*

Chase felt herself smiling. *"I'm ignoring you for my biology class now. Biology."*

"But?"

"But yeah, we're still on."

He sent a thumbs-up.

Chapter Five

Chase leaned close to the mirror and feathered her eyelashes with her mascara wand. She'd barely given herself enough time to change and refresh her makeup before her date with Daniel. She threw her heart monitor in her sock drawer. If she wore it, she might have to explain about her health condition, and she couldn't think of anything less sexy than pity.

She touched some gloss on her lips and gave herself one last look. She had put on a white shirt with a black stripe over the shoulders and a mesh overlay on the short sleeves. It was kind of sci-fi but in a nice way. Besides, almost everything else in her closet was a plaid button-down or had a graphic novel character on it. Her dark blue jeans fit snugly, and she'd chosen boots after Daniel had sent a text warning her not to wear flip-flops or sandals. She sort of looked like a race-car driver.

She went into her room, and Kiki looked up from her laptop. "Oh, yeah. That will work."

Chase raised her eyebrows and showed Kiki a selfie Daniel had sent after class.

"Whoa. Can your mom set me up with someone? He's really good-looking."

"I'm sure he doesn't need a blind date. I don't even know why he said yes in the first place."

"What are you guys doing? Dinner and a movie?" Kiki asked, laying on her belly and swinging her feet.

"Oh, no. That's too boring. He's taking me to a racetrack to drive a race car."

Kiki laughed. "What? Really?"

"Yes."

A knock came at their apartment door, and Chase stared at Kiki, suddenly nervous.

"Go get him!" Kiki growled, as if Chase were a bloodhound after a fox.

"Down girl," Chase said, laughing and snatching her purse from her bed. When she opened the door, Daniel was waiting. He was even more handsome than she remembered. He wore skinny jeans with a button-down shirt and a pair of Top-Siders. He looked as if he could be in an editorial shoot, calm and collected, his expression coolly disinterested. He smiled at her, his eyes warm and shy. "Hi, Chase."

"Hey," she responded, smiling back because she couldn't help it. He was really cute.

"Did I come too early?" he asked.

"Five minutes. But I'm ready."

"I should have texted you first; I'm sorry."

39

"You're fine," she said, and a small part of her brain laughed silently at the double meaning. She hoped he would take it at surface value.

"My car is parked out front."

For a moment, she had a post-traumatic flashback to her parking tickets, and she sighed.

"Should I have parked somewhere else?" he asked, concern in his voice.

"Oh no, I was just thinking about this stupid parking ticket class I have to take. I somehow managed to get three parking tickets this week. That has to be some kind of record. After the first ticket I got a permit, but apparently that only pertains to maybe ten percent of the available parking spots."

"Ha. My roommate has to take the same class."

"Oh, good. I won't be alone."

"Nah. It could happen to anyone."

She stifled a laugh. One blind date point for him.

They walked out of the small courtyard and down the sidewalk. The usual line of dull sedans was there, but some show-off had a bright blue BMW convertible, the top down. She was wondering what kind of college student had the money for that until Daniel stopped in front of it and opened the door for her.

She wanted to say something, but she didn't want to sound overly impressed or make him feel awkward. She got in the car and blurted out, "Nice car."

He touched his hair in an oddly nervous gesture and said, "Thank you. Um, do you mind if the top is down?"

She twisted her hair back and pulled it into a bun, securing it with a hairband she had in her jeans pocket. "Nope. I'm totally prepared."

The car smelled brand new, and she shifted her legs on the black leather seat, checking her boots to make sure they were clean.

Daniel pulled out of the parking space, and they drove down residential streets. She tried hard not to feel really cool hanging out in a nice car with a hot guy, and failed. She bit her lip to keep from smiling. She didn't want to start off the date being an idiot, at least, not right away. The day was perfect, not too hot, and the wind fluttered the tendrils of hair along the back of her neck, but the silence between them begged for someone to start a conversation. She was thankful he went first.

"So I don't know much about you. What are you going to school for?"

"Art—hopefully animation."

"Sounds like fun."

"Yeah, well, it's competitive. It's kind of a long shot that I'll get to work on movies, but that's what I'd like to do."

He glanced at her. "It's not that much of a long shot."

"Unless I'm not good at it."

He laughed. "Right. Then it would be."

She'd been curious about him, too, so she turned the conversation. "What are you going to school for?"

"International relations."

That sounded vague. "Like for business?"

"Sort of. I already travel a lot, so it makes sense."

"What do you travel for? Vacations or you have a job already?"

He touched his hair again, as if he were uncomfortable. "I mean, I have traveled a lot in the last few years."

That didn't explain anything, but he didn't seem to want to talk about it, so she let it go.

"Do you know other languages?" she asked, wondering if she would find out what country he was from. His English was very good, but she could tell it wasn't his native language.

"Korean and Chinese. Some Japanese. And you? Your mom mentioned you were in Italy. Do you speak Italian?"

"Very badly. *Più piano, per favore.* My favorite phrase. Slower, please."

He laughed. "So what did you think of Italy? I've always wanted to go there."

She already learned that trying to sum up four months was too hard, so she settled on her favorite things. "I loved it. I liked the ruins the most. No, wait, the food. That was amazing."

"So you like Italian food?"

"Oh, yes. So good."

"We could go to an Italian restaurant after the racetrack, if you like."

"Yes! Do you like Italian?"

"I like pizza, if that counts," he said, laughing.

"So, not Italian. What do you really like?" she asked, hoping he would finally clue her in to where he was from.

"My mom's cooking. She makes really good glass noodles, but my parents are in Korea. So I miss that."

"Hey, you're Korean!" She hadn't meant to sound surprised.

He laughed. "Yes."

"I mean, my mom and my sister are all obsessed with K-dramas and K-pop. Like, really obsessed."

"Oh yeah. I like K-dramas too."

"No, like *really* obsessed. You don't even know."

He grinned. "I have a general idea."

"My sister gave me some music," she said, pulling out her phone.

"Which ones do you like?" he asked.

"I don't know all their names yet. I really love them even if I can't understand anything when they don't sing English phrases. You don't want to hear me try Korean."

He glanced up in his rearview as he got off the exit. "How do you know? I might."

They connected her phone to the car's sound system and listened to the playlist Jonni had given her.

To her surprise, Daniel started singing, belting out the high parts, his voice strong and on key. When he gave her a cheesy wink, she laughed at him.

"C'mon," he said, coaxing her. "Give it a try."

"Absolutely not," she said.

"Why not?"

"Because you actually sound good."

He pretended to be looking at the road, but he was smiling.

They arrived at the racetrack, pulling into a deserted parking lot. The racetrack was old, but there were sections of shiny new stands and glass box seats rising up two stories. She'd been there once with her dad when he had gotten tickets for a race from work. She remembered it being very exciting and loud. They also had great hot dogs.

She stepped out into the summer heat, brushing back a strand of hair and looking around. "No one is here? Is it always this empty on a Friday afternoon?"

"No, I'm friends with the owner, so he let me have a few hours."

"You're kidding me." She stared at him. All the evidence pointed to him being wealthy, though he seemed to want to avoid the topic.

He ducked his head and avoided her eyes. "He's a really nice guy. So we're going to need to put on a tracksuit—for safety reasons. Is that okay?"

"Sure." Once again, he'd deflected her when he didn't want to talk about something. Like renting out the speed track at a national raceway for a few hours for a blind date.

He led her to an entrance that went under the massive bleachers surrounding the black asphalt track and over to a line of outdoor garage bays. They were all empty but one, which had a red Mustang GT with a big logo on the hood. Its aggressive lines and wide tires looked fast.

Daniel pointed to it. "So that's the car. You drive manual?"

Disappointed, she shook her head. She hadn't thought about race cars being manual. It looked like she wouldn't get to drive one after all. "No, but that's okay. You can drive."

He didn't hesitate. "Well, do you want to learn? I could teach you, if that's okay."

"Like, now? Today?"

He shrugged. "Sure. Why not?"

"I would love that," she said, wondering if it was possible to learn in an hour.

He walked over to a chair piled with clothes and two helmets. "Here's the racing suit. It will protect you from fire damage if we have an accident. Which we won't. But you should wear it anyway."

She walked into the bathroom next to the garages and changed into the tracksuit. The small cement bathroom was dim but clean, the square mirror over the sink too small to be of much help. The tracksuit was too big, and she had to roll up the sleeves and the cuffs on the pants. She also waddled in it. So much for being a cool girl version of Speed Racer.

When she stepped out, Daniel was waiting for her, having already changed. He looked good in the suit, confident and lean. She tugged at her sleeves, looking up at him. "It's a little big," she explained.

He grinned. "You look cute." He handed her a helmet. "And you'll need one of these."

She put it over her head and fumbled with the straps under her chin. He leaned down, examining the tangle. "Can I help?"

46

"Sure."

He straightened the straps, pulled them through the rings, and tightened them, holding her gaze for a moment, his fingers lingering on the sensitive skin beneath her jawline. Chase resisted the urge to swallow, and looked up from Daniel's hands to his eyes. Quickly, he stepped back and put his own helmet on. Unlike her, he made a great Speed Racer.

He explained that the helmets had speakers so they could talk to each other. They tested them, and she found that she liked the sound of his voice close to her ear.

"I'll drive first and explain how to shift," he said. "Also, you have to climb in the car through the window. It doesn't have doors."

Between the too-big suit and the limited vision from her helmet, it reminded her of an astronaut trying to land on the moon. As she wrangled her legs into the window, he hovered next to her, presumably in case she fell, but she was grateful that help wasn't necessary.

When he started the engine, it roared, the thunder echoing off the garage walls. "The clutch pedal is to your far left. Very important," his voice said in her earpiece.

"Far left. Important," she repeated, craning her neck to try and see his feet. Her helmet bumped against his, and he laughed, reaching over to give the straps of her helmet a playful tug. "Don't worry. We'll do a lot of practicing."

He explained how he used the clutch for each gear, and drove out to the track and sped up, going through all the gears. "Clutch, shift. Clutch, shift."

She repeated him, watching him as he shifted down and back up again.

"Put your hand on mine while I shift to get a feel for it," he said, and she put her gloved hand over his. After a while, he switched their hands, his on top of hers. "Okay, now you're going to shift when I tell you. Are you ready?"

"Ready."

"Listen how the engine revs up before I shift. Okay, when I say shift, shift."

She tightened her hand and she waited, listening until the engine whined louder, and she heard him say, "Shift."

She pulled back, but the stick shift didn't move. He gripped her hand and moved it into gear. "It's not going to break! We'll do it again."

This time she used more force, and it moved into the next gear. He took his hand away from hers, letting her shift as they drove around the track a few times until the motions were automatic enough that she had the confidence do it on her own.

He pulled the car off the track and parked it, the engine idling loudly as he undid his harness, and slid out of the car, climbing easily out the window. She had to take off her gloves to get out of the harness, and her climb out was not that graceful. Daniel waited by the driver's side to make sure she could get in, although he didn't try to hold her hand or help her. His attempts to avoid physical contact were obvious and kind of sweet.

When she got in the driver's seat, she fumbled everything. Her harness wouldn't cooperate, her helmet kept bumping into things, and when she tried to put on her gloves, it was as if she were using someone else's hands.

"We'll take it slowly," Daniel reassured her, his low voice calm and unhurried. "And it's okay to stall. I did that a lot when I first learned."

She pressed the clutch and turned the key. Nothing. The engine didn't come to life. She tried it again and once again nothing happened. Daniel tilted his head and watched her foot on the clutch as she attempted to start the car a third time.

When she looked over at him after failing again, a slow smile of understanding was spreading across his face. "Your seat isn't up far enough. You're shorter than I am."

"Oh, really?" she muttered, although she had noticed that her head only came to his shoulder. "I'm that much shorter?"

"Yeah," he said, sounding amused.

She felt around for the lever under her seat, but her helmet wouldn't let her look down, and the gloves weren't helping either.

"Um, I can find the lever for you, if that's okay."

"Sure," she said, trying not to sound frustrated and nervous.

He reached under her legs, his arm brushing against the inside of her knees as he felt for the lever. Even through the thick layer of material, the heat from his arm radiated up her leg. His hand found the lever, and he gave a hard tug, jerking her forward so her shoulder rested against his. He straightened, and Chase slowly let out a breath she didn't know she had been holding. It took her a few moments to gather her wits and remember what she was supposed to be doing. This time she was able to push the clutch to the floor, and the engine started.

She stalled the car several times trying to get it out of first gear, and sweat beaded on her forehead as she struggled to get it right. She sighed loudly in the microphone and tried again.

"It's okay to stall," he said. "Use more clutch this time and let it out slower."

Oh sure, I'll just focus on this car after you had your arm against my leg. She tried again, letting out the clutch so slowly her thigh began to ache, but this time she was able to move the car forward. The pitch of the engine rose, and she heard him quietly say, "Shift."

She pressed down on the clutch and successfully moved it to the next gear. After that it was almost easy, his guidance low-key but always right when she needed it. She drove around the track shifting up and down through the gears. She watched the speedometer climb, elated. Then she became aware of her heartbeat. It beat hard against her chest, the pace rising. She accelerated, trying to pay attention to the pitch of the engine, but fear crept in, and her lungs constricted. *No, not now.* She shifted into the next gear, but her foot was hesitant on the pedal, and the gears ground until she stomped down harder on the clutch. Her heart was fluttering. It had been months since her last blackout, but if it happened now, she could kill them both.

Keeping her voice calm, she said, "Could you take over?"

He lifted his brow, his eyes widening. "Sure, pull over anywhere."

She tried to do it slowly, but her heart was hammering harder and faster by the second. She brought the speed down and slowed the car to a stop, though her hands were shaking so much, she forgot to pull up the brake and the engine stalled out.

"Are you okay?" he asked, but everything was going black, and his voice sounded far away. If she could get her helmet off, she might not pass out. She pulled off her gloves with trembling fingers and pulled blindly at the harness, not bothering to hide her frantic breathing from the mic in her helmet.

His hands grasped her harness, and there was no apology this time as he quickly jerked her free. "My helmet…" she said.

His fingers were on the straps when she lost consciousness.

She woke to find Daniel kneeling beside her, panic in his eyes. She lay on the track, her helmet tossed a few feet away. "Chase, can you hear me?" he asked.

Her hand went to her heart. "I'm okay." Her voice was surprisingly strong and even.

With one hand he cradled her head to shield it from the asphalt, and in his other hand he held his phone. "You're not okay. You passed out. We should go to a hospital."

Her heartbeat was still fast, but it was getting closer to normal. At least, normal for her.

"No, don't do that." She sighed, closing her eyes, "I have a heart condition that makes my heart beat abnormally fast, and if I'm stressed sometimes I pass out. But I'm okay."

"Your heart is beating too fast?" he asked, not sounding at all reassured.

"No, I mean, yes, but I'm okay."

"Are you sure?"

"Yes," she said, sitting up, her hair falling over her face, her hand still protectively over her unpredictable heart. "Embarrassing," she muttered, avoiding his gaze.

He reached out as if he were going to brush her hair back, and then he stopped. "I'm not that kind of blind date."

"What kind is that?"

"The jerk kind who would make you feel embarrassed about something like that. You could have told me. I would have understood."

In a small voice, she said, "I almost killed us."

"No, you didn't. I was right there. I wouldn't let anything happen."

"I'm so sorry."

"Are you really okay?"

She nodded, moving to get to her feet. He held out his hand and she let him pull her up. He retrieved her helmet, slipping it over her head. "We'll have to drive back to the garage. Are you going to be all right?"

She waved a dismissive hand at him. "Of course."

He had to search for his gloves, and his helmet lay on the other side of the car.

"You threw stuff everywhere," she said, her eyes following him as he picked it all up.

He gave her a look. "I was scared."

Sighing, she said, "At least I'm memorable."

She let him help her over the window, but before she could attempt to put on the harness, he looked down at her. "Please, let me help you. Just this time."

She moved her hands out of the way without protesting. He quickly pulled the straps around her and buckled them into place. He drove them back to the garage and continued to do everything for her, helping her get out of the harness, pulling her out of the car, and even taking off her helmet. She was still shaky, and she realized she hadn't eaten since breakfast, so maybe food might help.

"Are we still going to dinner?" she asked as he took her helmet.

He stared back at her. "Shouldn't I take you home?"

"I think I need to eat," she confessed, hoping she didn't sound demanding. "A burger and fries. Nothing big."

The worried lines between his brows eased, and he said he'd wait for her to change and then they'd leave. She went into the small bathroom and pulled the tracksuit off, leaning down when she felt light-headed. She got her clothes on and checked the mirror, which showed smudged makeup and disheveled hair. She rubbed at her makeup and smoothed out her hair.

"A little food and you'll be fine," she said to herself. A small wave of fear came and went. She'd told him she was fine, but it wasn't quite that simple.

Daniel was buttoning up his shirt when she stepped out. She caught a glimpse of nicely toned abs before he muttered a quick, "Sorry," and hastily finished the last three buttons.

She thought maybe she should reassure him that she would recover from the accidental ab sighting, but she let the moment dangle. She still wasn't feeling like herself.

He tugged his shirt down and looked at her. "It's a long walk back to the car."

She put a tentative hand against her heart and after a moment when she realized what she was doing, dropped it, hoping he hadn't noticed.

He exhaled, avoiding her eyes for a moment before saying, "You look tired. If you pass out again, I'm going to feel terrible. Can I carry you across the parking lot? It's easy for me, I promise. You don't weigh much."

"I'm not going to pass out," she said, trying not to think about everything he'd already done for her.

He didn't look as if he believed her, but he didn't ask again. "If you feel like you are going to…"

"I'll leap into your arms."

He laughed, and she thought he turned a little red. "Okay."

The walk back to the car was uneventful. He opened the door for her and got in the driver's seat and paused. "I feel kind of bad. This wasn't exactly the best blind date. Now I'm taking you to a cheap fast food place for dinner."

"Well, it's not your fault. Besides, if you took me somewhere expensive, I probably wouldn't even enjoy it. I like fast-food."

He held her gaze and took out his phone. He spoke slowly and deliberately. "Make a note: Chase is a cheap date."

She laughed, surprised. "Is that for future reference?"

He looked away, a half-smile on his lips.

They found a drive-in burger place painted in retro reds and blues, with tables and awnings on a patio. They chose to sit in his car with the top up, rolling the windows down, enjoying a cool evening breeze and fading purple twilight as they ate burgers and fries. Her heartbeat had even calmed to an acceptable level.

"That was delicious," she said with a sigh, licking ketchup off her fingers.

"Are you feeling better?" he asked.

"Yes."

He gathered up the wrappers and stuffed them in the bags, looking away from her as he cleaned up. "I'm going to worry about you now."

"Nah. Don't do that. I'm okay."

"I can't believe I gave you a burger instead of taking you to the hospital. I must be crazy."

She wanted to reach over and pat his head, but his red-tinted hair was so perfect, she didn't want to mess it up. "Relax. You did the right thing."

"Hmm. Maybe the burger made up for the rest of the date."

"Absolutely."

He started the car, and they drove home, listening to more K-pop, although this time he didn't sing. She'd stressed him out. Sighing, she waved her hand in the wind as they drove, and then looked over at him, trying to think of something comforting to say. "It was an amazing blind date. Five star. "

He glanced over at her, his face betraying no emotion. He picked up his phone and held her gaze as he spoke into it. "Note: Chase makes me feel good."

Keeping her expression as deadpan as his, she took the phone from his fingers. "Note: Chase just tells the truth."

He cracked a smile and nodded at the phone. "Go ahead, and do it for real."

"The note?"

"Yes."

Amused, she poked around on the phone screen until she found a voice recorder and repeated it. "Note: Chase just tells the truth."

"Wait. Did it record?" he asked.

She replayed it, inwardly laughing at his pleased smile when he heard her voice. She handed it back to him. "All right. There you go. Forever on your phone. Now I can never lie."

When they got back to her apartment, he walked her to the front door, his hands in his pockets. "Anything else I can do?"

She hesitated and then said, "Can we keep that between us?"

Kiki was the only other person besides her family who knew about her heart problem. And now Daniel. Something told her he was a safe place for secrets.

"Of course. But be careful. If you get in trouble or need me, call."

"I will."

In the shadows, his eyes were so dark she couldn't read them. The silence between them drew out, and she wondered what he was thinking. A door slammed from another apartment, and voices and laughter echoed in the night. He gave her a polite smile. "Maybe we could go out again."

"Okay," she gave him a little smile. "I'd like that."

"I'll see you soon."

"You too," she said, and gave a wave as she opened the door. She wondered if he wanted to kiss her. Maybe he was afraid she would collapse in a heap of thrill. He was terribly good-looking. She just might.

Chapter Six

Chase winced as the nurse peeled an electrode off her skin with a little too much force. She always had sticky spots on her skin after an EKG. She sat up and pulled her yellow, gray, and navy plaid button-down back over her stomach. The nurse gave her a distracted smile, tossed the electrodes onto the cart, and wheeled the EKG machine out of the office. "Doctor Gehren will be in after he takes a look at this."

Chase nodded and pulled out her phone. She already knew what he would say. But every time she had an episode, she had to go in for the same tests, the same results, and the same sinking disappointment that no one really knew how to help her. Just in case. In case it got worse. At the moment the only flutters she felt were about her date with Daniel over the weekend. It had been so much fun, she found herself looking forward to seeing him again.

After about fifteen minutes of playing mindless games on her phone, Dr. Gehren finally walked into the small room for patients. He was a young doctor, and she knew from previous discussions with him that he had a family and had quickly become a nationally respected doctor in cardiology.

"Everything looks about the same, Chase," he said. "What happened to trigger an episode?"

"Race car driving," she admitted a little guiltily.

Dr. Gehren raised an eyebrow. "I am sure you know that your case is tricky. You need to take extra care that you don't put undue stress on your heart. Your resting heart rate is still at one hundred and fifty, which for you is par for the course. It hasn't gone up or down, and the EKG is unchanged. We'll count that as a good thing. Stay out of that red zone."

"I know. It didn't last for long."

"It's good you came in anyway. As long as nothing changes, keep doing what you are doing. Come in when you have an episode. Do you need a prescription refill?"

Chase shook her head. "No, I'm good for now. Thanks."

She left the office fighting her unease. The heart monitor on her wrist rarely beeped into a red zone, so it was easy to just ignore the undiagnosed threat. But every few months she got a dose of reality. Her resting heartbeat was between 150 and 160—the beats per minute most people reached during rigorous exercise. She was like a walking hummingbird.

She had gone through a slew of tests in her early adolescence, all ruling out A-fib or atrial flutter as the cause. Her heart seemed to be otherwise healthy. They couldn't quite figure out what caused her heart to receive incorrect electrical signals, but what they did know was she was at increased risk for stroke and heart failure. Her heart would eventually get tired. For the time being, she only felt the effects when her heart rate jumped to 200 or above. It was a high number to endure, but somehow her body had adapted to it. She took beta-blockers, and other than regular checkups, she could only keep an eye on her state of health.

Chase got into her car and adjusted her rearview mirror, her hand lingering on it. The heart monitor blinked back at her. "Oh, shut up," she muttered.

At least she was done with the checkup and could move on with her life. And then she realized that she was only going from one unpleasant task to another because she had her "parking class." With a sigh of disgust, she cranked up her A/C and threw the car into reverse. Only a school administration would come up with the idea of punishment disguised as education.

She made sure to park in the spot corresponding to her parking permit, and she walked across the campus to the administrative building where the class would be held. She had put her laptop in her backpack because she wasn't sure what the class would require. Actually, she was pretty sure it was just a time-sucking half-hour torture session in the form of lecture, but maybe she could look like she was taking notes while she scrolled through the internet.

She found the classroom on the second floor. It was a tiny, windowless room with white walls, gray carpets, and crowded rows of ancient desks the other classrooms probably refused to use. They were the kind of one-unit particleboard desks that were made for 12-year-old gangly youths, but administrators somehow expected adults to use them.

Chase had cut her timing a little close. With only two minutes to spare before the start of class, most of the seats had been filled. She found a vacant spot in the middle with one empty desk in front of her. She might actually be able to see the whiteboard instead of craning around someone taller.

But then a tall figure seated himself right in front of her, and Chase rolled her eyes in defeat.

A bored-looking, middle-aged professor entered the classroom and began a rehearsed spiel about why they were all in this class, and how they need to respect the rules. Et cetera. To Chase's relief, the lecture wasn't long, and the teacher turned out the lights and lowered the projection screen, so they could watch a film about parking rules.

As the campus-produced movie began with a bright, cheerful student chirping about the usefulness of parking regulations, Chase shifted to the side to see around the beanpole in front of her. Someone tapped on her shoulder. She looked back, and in the darkness a girl said in an apologetic tone, "I'm sorry. I can't see."

Chase righted herself. Half the projector screen was still blocked by tall, dark, and obtrusive. She didn't want to see the movie, but she didn't want to *not* see it, either. Everyone else could. She tapped his shoulder. When he turned around, she jumped back so quickly that her desk scraped loudly against the floor.

It was Hyun Tae.

Something inside her just seemed to give up. No matter what she did, it was going to be some kind of embarrassing blunder, so she might as well embrace it.

"Can I help you?" he whispered.

She leaned forward and whispered back, "It's just that you're blocking the screen."

He didn't seem at all surprised that they had bumped into each other again. He looked from the screen to her. His head dipped down noticeably, as

64

if gauging her height. "If you are short, you should sit in the front."

"I can sit wherever I want." A few students turned to look at her as her whisper rose a few decibels. She lowered her voice, "I'm here now, so just move."

He leaned closer, twisting in his desk so the side of his face hovered just beside hers. She held her breath, feeling a flip of her traitorous heart as the clean smell of his soap distracted her from her irritation. She must not have affected him the same way, because he smoothly replied, "Did your mother also forget to tell you that 'please' is the polite way to ask?"

Heat rose from her chest straight to her cheeks. She started to protest, but he was already turning back around to face the film, a ghost of a smile at the corners of his mouth. Chase gave an indiscernible huff of disbelief, staring at the broad back that still completely blocked her view.

She put her foot against the back of his chair and slowly pushed it forward, the metal feet scraping against the tile with a dull screech.

He twisted his head to glare at her.

Chase raised her brows and made a motion with her hand for him to move over.

With a scowl, Hyun Tae scooted his desk forward to distance himself, but he made no move to clear her view.

She would just have to move to the empty desk at the very back of the room. She didn't really care about the film, which was probably almost over. But she was afraid she might do something violent if she stayed behind the polite jerk.

She grabbed her laptop and stood with the intention of bending down to scoop up her backpack. But she stepped on the backpack instead, and her feet twisted into the straps. She slapped her hands down on her desk to catch her fall, but her laptop kept flying. She watched it soar through the air like a rectangular Frisbee before it crashed to the floor, skidding and scraping with the sound of plastic parts bouncing off its surface.

"Well, crap."

Hyun Tae shook his head.

*****

Chase flopped facedown onto her bed. "Why," she moaned into the bedspread. "Why?"

Kiki popped a bubble from her gum and noisily sucked it back into her mouth. "What? Did you spill soup on Hun Boon again?"

"It's Hyun Tae. And much worse."

"How could anything be worse than that?" Kiki asked, sitting up in her bed and crossing her legs.

Chase pointed to her backpack. "I broke my laptop."

"Oh, that sucks."

"Because I tripped. In front of the soup guy."

"Oh," Kiki said, her voice sympathetic.

Chase rolled over onto her side and kicked the backpack with one toe. "I tripped and basically chucked it across the room. He's in my parking class! Can you believe that?"

"He's stalking you," Kiki said, spiking her white-blonde hair as she chewed her gum.

"Right? Seriously this guy is everywhere." Her phone buzzed, so she pulled it out of the front pocket of her backpack. "Hello?"

"Buddy!" It was Jonni.

"Hey, Buddy," Chase said. "What's up?"

"Oh, you know. The usual." A kid screeched in the background, and Jonni could be heard chastising someone. When she came back, she sounded a little breathless. "Sorry. There was a problem with a chip clip. So how was your date?"

Talking to Jonni was kind of like talking to someone with multiple personality disorder. She had three kids and almost no sanity left because of it. "It went really well."

"Like how well? IVY! Do not clip his ear! Sorry. How well? Details."

Chase bit down a laugh. "I don't know. He's really cute. And nice. We went to a race car track, and it freaked me out, but he was really cool."

"And?" Jonni prompted.

"And I don't know. I guess we might do something else. If he calls."

"No kiss? Lachlan, stop th—Okay that's it! Give me the clip. Right here! In my hand."

Chase waited for Jonni to take care of the chip clip problem.

"Wow," Jonni blew out a sigh. "Okay. Kiss?"

Chase snorted. "Buddy, it was a first date. No kiss."

"Lame."

She shrugged. "I had a really fun time. If he calls, I'll definitely hang out with him again. He was really...chivalrous? Yeah. Like a gentleman." *Unlike the polite jerk who seems to witness all my moronic accidents.*

"That's awesome. Mom will be glad to hear that. How about your classes? Do you like them?"

"Mom gave me some weird classes, but actually they're good. Except the parking class I have to take because this school is psychotic about their parking rules."

"That sounds...horrible." Jonni sympathized.

"Oh! And I shattered my laptop today."

"Yikes." Chase heard Jonni say something away from the mouthpiece, and she thought she heard her mom's voice in the background. "Mom is here. She says she knows someone who can fix it for you."

"Are you guys watching K-dramas again?"

"Not until the kids are asleep. So yes. But anyway, do you want the number for the computer guy? She says he's really good, and he's a student, so he won't cost much."

"Okay," Chase said, puzzled. It wasn't like her mom to have a computer guy's information on retainer.

"Oh, Mom is calling him now." Jonni said. "He lives right next to you, so she's going to set up an appointment for you to visit him."

"Really?" After a few minutes, Jonni said, "Okay, you're set. He's home, so you can just bring it over and drop it off. He'll have it fixed by next week, and Mom says she can cover the cost."

Chase pulled on her lower lip. "Mom is up to something."

"What? Why?" The volume of Jonni's kids rose suddenly, and she growled. "Okay, I have to go. Good luck with your laptop! Call me if that guy asks you out again."

"Okay, Buddy. Talk to you later." Chase hung up, puzzled.

Kiki looked up from her textbook. "What is it?"

"I don't know. I have a weird feeling about my mom all of a sudden. Like she's setting me up with a computer nerd."

Kiki shrugged. "She might be. Doesn't mean you have to date him."

"True," Chase agreed slowly, her thoughts churning. "Whatever. I'll be back in a few minutes."

Kiki bounced her eyebrows to let Chase know she had heard, and she put on her headphones as she read through a textbook with a pink highlighter in hand.

Chase grabbed her backpack again, stuffed her feet into her black boots, and headed out the door.

She walked out of her apartment building, and, checking the address her mom had texted her, realized that it was the nice house next to their unit. What was a rich kid doing fixing computers for poor students? And, on closer inspection, the house was gigantic. She couldn't tell until she passed through the front gate and began walking up the long driveway. It was a modern build with an all-white exterior, lots of tall windows, and a kind of edgy, stacked boxes structure. The hike up the driveway was enough to discourage anyone from trying to get a closer peek.

As she finally reached the circular court in front of the house, she headed for the front door, which was, in fact, double glass doors with elaborate iron handles and framework. Potted palms lined the walkway. She found the doorbell and rang, looking without shame through the glass to the opulent interior.

She jumped when the door opened. For some reason, she hadn't seen the man come to the door from the side, and he stood in the doorway, blinking at her through stylish black-rimmed glasses. He was about her age, with one hand resting casually in his dark gray slacks. His slouchy, white shirt with thin, dark green horizontal stripes made his whole appearance seem relaxed. He had a very tall frame, which was graceful in a way, matching his delicate features and straight, honey-colored hair.

He was Asian. This was more than a coincidence. Her mom was definitely crazy.

"Are you Chase?" he asked. His voice was soft and melodic, tinged with an accent.

"Yeah. Sorry, my mom didn't tell me your name."

"Joon Suh," he said, not smiling but not particularly rude, either. He just looked bored. "Come in."

Chase took a few hesitant steps across the threshold and sucked in her breath. The foyer alone looked more expensive than her apartment building. White marble, sparkling chandelier, huge vases, and a shimmering mirror above a posh foyer table. Was this his family's house? He was a college kid?

71

"What happened to your computer?" Joon Suh asked as he led the way from the foyer to an open, pristinely white living room and then back to a wide, contemporary kitchen.

"It uh...fell. The screen cracked, and it won't turn on."

He looked over his shoulder, stopping to give her a once-over. "You dropped it?"

"Sort of. Actually, I tripped, and it flew across the room."

His light brown eyes widened slightly. She thought maybe he muttered something in his language, but it was too soft to hear. Joon Suh motioned for her to follow him. "I will look at it."

When she pulled it out and set it on the light gray granite countertop of his kitchen, the CD drive popped open and fell off the edge. She winced. "Yeah it's bad."

Joon Suh didn't touch it, but he bent to examine the cracked exterior. He was so beautiful and delicate looking, with perfectly smooth skin and a languid grace when he moved. "You should get a new one."

"What?" Chase fluttered a hand over the laptop. "But all my artwork is—"

His mouth twitched into a smile, and he adjusted his glasses. "It was a joke. Sorry."

"Oh," she breathed. Not funny.

"I can fix it," he said as he straightened. "Come back next Monday. I will need to order parts for it."

"Is it going to cost a lot?"

There was a hint of amusement in his eyes, but he didn't smile. "No. Don't worry."

She liked that he wasn't chattering and trying to sell her on anything. It made him seem trustworthy. "Okay. Thanks. Do you need my password?"

"I'll get paper for you to write it down." He pulled his hand out of his pocket and went to the other side of the magazine-ready kitchen to rifle through a drawer for paper and a pen.

"Joon Suh-ah." A voice in a lower tone called from the top of the stairs.

"*Eoh*?" Joon Suh responded as he bent over the drawer. It sounded like he was saying, "what" but with an unfamiliar "o."

"*Uyu-ga isseyo*?"

Joon Suh leaned over to the fridge, opened it, and peered around the door. "*Ani,*" he called back.

The oddly familiar male voice sighed loudly, and footsteps sounded on the stairs.

Chase took the paper from Joon Suh, her thoughts going to her mom. Ten dollars the helpful computer guy was Korean. She didn't know how her mom knew Joon Suh. Maybe he'd come to the admissions office.

Joon Suh's eyes went over her shoulder, and he gave a full, white-toothed grin.

Chase turned around.

Hyun Tae stood with his hands resting low on his hips. He looked past her to Joon Suh. He motioned to Chase with a hand. "*Igo mwoyeyo?*"

Lightheaded, Chase put a hand on the counter to steady herself. She turned back to Joon Suh. "How did my mom meet you again?"

"I met her at school. She asked me if I fixed computers for students."

"Do you?"

"No," he grinned again, this time a little mischievously. "But Hyun Tae told me about her. So I said yes. Don't worry. I am very good with computers."

Chase spun back around to Hyun Tae. His mouth turned down slightly; his dark hair was ruffled. She pointed to him. "You know my mom?"

"Yes. She is in admissions. She asked if I wanted to go on a blind date with you. I said no."

The embarrassment was so overpowering that she didn't know what else to do other than to acknowledge the horror with a simple, "Oh."

He looked back at Joon Suh. "*Na do?*"

"*Ne,*" Joon Suh said, a laugh still in his voice. "*Kyopta.*"

74

Hyun Tae sighed, but his expression softened. He gave Chase a nod. "He will fix your computer."

"Thank you," was all she could manage. Her mom had tried to set her up with Hyun Tae? And then another thought occurred to her. She asked Joon Suh, "Do you know Daniel Bak?"

The two Korean men exchanged looks. Joon Suh was smiling again.

"He lives here," Hyun Tae said as he grabbed a clean glass from the counter.

Chase stared.

Hyun Tae poured himself a glass of cold water from the fridge, apparently uninterested in her existence.

"You all...live together? Here?"

Joon Suh gave a nod of his head.

Chase looked around the cavernous house. "Is he here now?"

Hyun Tae turned and leaned his back against the fridge door to close it. He raised his eyebrows. "No. Why?"

Chase zipped up her backpack and slid it on her shoulders. "Thanks for helping. I have to go."

Joon Suh watched them both intently, his eyes following them like a spectator would. He held out a hand as if not entirely sure she would shake it.

She did, hastily, and then waved to Hyun Tae. "See you in parking class."

He raised his glass to her.

And then she booked it out of there. The house of Koreans.

She was going to kill her mom.

Chapter Seven

Chase's alarm went off at nine. She fumbled for it, her eyes still shut, fingers scrabbling around the desk next to her bed as she sought her phone. When she finally had it, she peeled her eyes open to shut the alarm off. She was pretty sure they made it just complicated enough that you would be forced to wake up while the thing blared. Her foggy brain stared at the screen in confusion. *Why did my alarm go off at nine? My class isn't until noon.*

Then she remembered. The parking class. She grumbled loudly into her pillow, smacking it with her fist. Had it already been a week since the last one? It wasn't enough time for her pride to recover and be ready to face the polite jerk again. Maybe she didn't have to face him. If she sat in the front of the room, she could pretend he wasn't there. *But then he would be able to see me the whole time.* That was definitely worse.

She rolled out of bed, landing on her butt first and then slowly creaking to her feet like a rusty cyborg. Tuesdays and Thursdays were supposed to be her sleeping in days, and even worse, she clashed schedules with Janelle at this hour. Janelle hogged the bathroom shamelessly and bustled through the tiny apartment like she was the sole rent payer. Neither Janelle nor Laura seemed to "get" Chase yet. Any conversations they all shared were short and direct. Not a lot of bonding happening in her apartment.

Chase stumbled to the bathroom, but as she suspected, Janelle was still in it. Breakfast, then. Or something resembling it, anyway. She had forgotten that she needed to wake up early and had stayed up late watching TV and texting friends.

She grabbed a granola bar from the cabinet, poured a glass of milk, and scrolled through her new texts as she stood at the counter. She smiled as she chewed; Daniel had texted her just after she had fallen asleep the night before.

"You fell asleep with your messenger open. I talked to myself for half an hour."

"Sorry!" she texted back. *"I will send a warning message before I pass out next time."*

Still grinning, she grabbed her medication from the medicine cabinet and opened the cap as she stared at the new message that popped up. *"How many hours of sleep is that? Four?"*

She laughed to herself, popping the two pills in her mouth and swigging them down with milk. She froze. The pills felt a lot bigger than usual.

Dread prickled down her spine as the giant pills went down her throat. She grabbed the pill bottle and turned it around to read the prescription sticker.

Eegan, Janelle. Take one tablet by mouth twice daily as needed for pain.

HYDROCO/ACET A 5-325 mg

Chase stared at the bottle. *What did I just take?!* She'd just taken two of something that was not meant to be taken two at a time. She ran to her room, pulled open Kiki's laptop, and searched for information about the drug.

Vicodin. She had just swallowed a double dose of Vicodin.

Her forehead fell to her palm. What the heck? What did that mean? A quick Google search told her that she would probably be super- groggy. It wasn't too dangerous that she had accidentally taken two; the internet said it was one of those vague "not advised" things. Not ER-worthy anyway.

She shut Kiki's laptop and trudged back out to the kitchen. She put the Vicodin back in the cabinet where it sat right next to her beta-blocker. Same bottles. Totally different medication. Great.

She briefly considered trying to make herself throw up, but she knew she wouldn't be able to trigger her gag reflex. She couldn't throw up at will. Plus the internet said she should be okay. Just sleepy. It was only a stupid parking class, so if she had to be tired and unfocused in a class, at least it was that one. And she would have to start over if she missed it.

Finally resolved, Chase finished her milk and granola bar, hoping the red-headed rule stickler wouldn't notice that two of her Vicodin were missing. Even Janelle wouldn't count pills from her wisdom tooth surgery months and months ago, right? She hurried to brush her hair and put some makeup on before she left.

As she walked across the campus, the cool morning air woke her up from her sleepy fog, and she found herself feeling optimistic about the day. By the time she reached the classroom, she was a little sleepier. She suddenly found herself a lot less concerned with where she sat and plopped herself down in the seat to the right of Hyun Tae. He looked over at her briefly. She gave him a close-lipped, squinty-eyed smile. He went back to scrolling through his messages.

Chase shrugged. That guy needed to loosen up or something. How could a twenty-something guy be so serious all the time? She looked over at him, and as he faced her again, she imagined Grumpy Cat's face in place of his handsome features. She snorted, leaning forward to laugh into her arm. And then she couldn't seem to stop laughing, her whole body shaking and eyes tearing with the effort to stop herself from making a spectacle of herself.

Hyun Tae narrowed his eyes at her.

As soon as the professor entered, Chase calmed herself and took a deep breath. Wait, what was she doing? That was crazy, what she just did. She willed the oxygen to reach her brain and relax her onslaught of giggles. It worked, and she slumped into her seat, her limbs like gelatin.

The professor announced that his instructions were to put the students in pairs and have them create three scenarios where a student was faced with a choice to act for or against the campus rules. "In creating these scenarios," he explained with all the enthusiasm of a public service announcement, "help your imaginary students understand the reasoning behind the rules."

Chase had a strong urge to make a loud raspberry, but she held it in.

With two fingers, the professor paired students up with the person sitting next to them. Chase bounced her head as she counted along the rows until she got to her own. Her head bounced over to Hyun Tae, who was already staring at her. His cheekbone rested on his closed fist, and he raised his brows. She gave him a little wave.

The classroom was filled with the sounds of several desks being shuffled over so the pairs could collaborate. Hyun Tae stood up from his desk, picked it up, and placed it flush against Chase's. She reached over and fumbled with her backpack and pulled out a notebook. Her fingers felt tingly and fat, like she was wearing Vienna sausages over them. When she settled herself with the notebook, she looked up to Hyun Tae.

He was very close. Chase blinked up into his warm, brown eyes, noting that for once he wasn't scowling or looking down on her. He was just staring at her, almost as if assessing her expression.

Her cheeks went hot. "Sssoooo," she said in a drawl.

"Are you okay?"

"You ask me that a lot," she said, pointing a finger. "Just saying."

His eyes trailed from the crown of her head to her chin. "You seem strange."

"That's not very nice."

He seemed to shrug it off. "We should complete the assignment then. Do you have ideas?"

Chase tapped her pen against her blank notebook paper. "The first one…is a girl."

"That's not really important."

"That's like…the first step to making a person," she said, her tone seriously. "It's a girl. What else?"

82

He sighed. "I think an obvious choice would be if the student had to choose between a handicapped parking spot and a spot much farther away."

Chase pulled on her lower lip, nodding. "Okay. Oh, but she has a dog in the car."

His brow furrowed then. "What?"

"Like she doesn't want to leave her dog so far away. Makes it a harder choice." Why was he looking at her like that? Didn't that make sense? She rubbed her forehead. "Or not. Okay no, fine. No dog. I was just saying."

His eyes flicked to her in confusion before he went back to writing down the scenario. "I'll write it down."

"Good idea." A quilt of sleepiness had settled over her, making her skin tingle and her vision swirl. This is what Vicodin did? She had to get ahold of herself. She was starting to sound like she was drunk. While Hyun Tae wrote the first scenario in neat script, she doodled a dragon on the corner of her paper. And then the picture sort of grew, and it was shooting hearts and swirls out of its mouth, and down below the dragon, the Grumpy Cat was getting showered in confetti and stuff.

"Is everyone finished?" the professor asked from the front of the classroom.

Chase's head popped up. She looked at Hyun Tae, and he tapped a long finger on his paper, which he had filled with words. "I finished for us."

Her eyes widened. "Oh you didn't have to! That's like…cheating."

"It's fine."

"I guess it's not exactly rocket science," she said, giggling. She put a hand over her mouth. That was a suspicious sounding giggle.

He leaned in close to her, almost like he was going to kiss her. Chase froze, and her eyes fluttered closed as a faint smell of some kind of manly soap wafted off of him. When she opened them again, he had moved away and was rubbing the corner of his mouth with his thumb. "You don't smell drunk."

Her back went rod straight. "I'm not!"

"Are you sick?"

"N-" she checked herself before her loud outburst came out. Lowering her voice to what she thought was a whisper, she hissed, "No."

He regarded her suspiciously.

Chase waved a hand. "It's good. I'm good. Oh look, those guys are presenting."

As the pairs of students presented their work, Chase found herself fighting sleep. Serious sleep. Like she hadn't rested in three days, and her body was going to shut down and force her to sleep whether she wanted to or not. She leaned her chin on the heel of her palm, and her eyes started to close. She sat up suddenly, her instincts telling her that if she let herself sleep, she might not be able to wake up easily.

Instead, she grabbed her pen and leaned over Hyun Tae to doodle on his paper. Something to cheer him up while he presented. He didn't protest, and she felt his eyes watching her as she leaned over his arm and scribbled kittens hanging off his words and batting at his neatly dotted "I"s. His arm was warm. As if her head was made of metal, and his shoulder was a magnet, she dipped down toward him until her head rested on his hard shoulder. She kept doodling. Maybe he didn't notice.

Finally, it was their turn to present, so Hyun Tae gently lifted her head off his shoulder and stood to present their scenarios. She didn't even really hear them. She was too focused on staying awake, and that would have definitely sent her into an instant coma. After he finished, he sat back down next to her. The teacher thanked the students for their work, and then they were dismissed. Finally.

Chase dropped her notebook before she was able to get it into the backpack. She started to stand up from her desk and fell over immediately as she collided with the desk that was still up against hers and blocking her exit.

Hyun Tae caught her arm, and he supported her as he moved his desk out of the way. He let her go, holding out his hand as if she might fall again. "Are you sure you're not sick?"

Chase guffawed at her own awkwardness and shook her head to clear away the sensation that the earth was tilting. "I mixed up my pills today. It's okay though. I Googled it."

He frowned slightly. "What pills?"

She snorted again, suddenly giggling and leaning against the desk for support. "I took Vicodin! It's like Tylenol on 'roids."

"I know what Vicodin is," he said. "It wasn't yours?"

"Nope!"

"That could be dangerous. We should take you to the hospital."

"Oh no." She held out two hands and backed up a few steps. "No, for real, I'm good. Google said I would just be kind of sleepy. Do I look sleepy?"

"You look high."

"How dare you?" she asked, her chin tilting up. "No, I just need to go home and nap." She gave him a wave. "Thanks, though. Bye."

He didn't say anything. Chase's hands really went numb then, and the heavy pull of sleep tugged at her the more she walked. She slammed against the double doors trying to exit the building. Those were the wrong doors. She shuffled to the right, slammed against the doors, and stumbled out into the morning sunshine.

A hand took hold of her wrist, pulling her to a halt. Chase twisted around to find Hyun Tae squinting against the sunlight and staring down at her. He let go of her wrist. "Let me walk with you."

She balked. "Why?"

"You took strong medication. It would be safer."

She studied his face. Those high cheekbones and his defined, sharp chin made him look severe almost all the time, but his eyes had softened. He looked concerned. And sexy. She couldn't help but think it, but really, everything about him was just confident and hot.

She shrugged. "You don't even know where I live though."

"True, I don't," he agreed.

They walked side by side for a little while, she with her arms swinging and he with his hands in the pockets of his black jeans. He had on a blue and green button-down shirt, open at the chest where a tight, white T-shirt showed through. The sleeves had been rolled up to his elbows, and she saw an expensive-looking watch on his wrist.

"You dress like a CEO," she said suddenly.

His mouth twitched up into a smile. "Oh yeah?"

As his smile deepened, she noticed that he had dimples. She giggled and doubled over, halting their progress.

He leaned over, putting a hand on her back. "Are you okay?"

"You have dimples?"

"Yes, I do."

She collapsed into another fit of giggles. "Cuuuuute!"

He straightened and shook his head. "Yes, unlike you, I dress well and have cute dimples. That's why I take pity on you."

She flipped upright, mustering all her dignity. "I have lots of things. I'm not just," she said, gesturing at herself, "this. Just saying."

His hands returned to his pockets, and he leaned back slightly. "Oh?"

"Watch. I can do this." She got a running start and then did a sloppy heel click. She missed the landing, of course, crumbling to the ground. She started to laugh again.

He helped her back to her feet, this time keeping his arm around her shoulders. She couldn't help noting that Daniel had almost never touched her, even on their date. This guy kept doing it. "You should keep your feet on the ground," he said, a touch of laughter in his voice.

She turned her head to look up at him, comforted by the feel of his shoulder cradling it. "I think you are less cranky now."

"Cranky?" He cocked his head to the side, as if considering the word. "I see."

"Do you know the Beatles?" she asked.

"I know them," he said, dimpling.

"We all live in a purple submarine!" she sang loudly.

He reared his head back in surprise. "You really are high."

She ignored him, continuing as they walked across campus, "We all live in a purple submarine! A purple submarine! A purple submarine!"

But that was the only line she knew, so finally Hyun Tae had to put a hand over her mouth to mute her off-key performance.

"Save your energy," he advised.

She nodded solemnly. "Sure. Yes."

They walked in silence then, and Chase's vision grew blurrier. It was getting hard to keep her eyes open. Her legs felt like mushy pasta.

Hyun Tae tightened his hold around her. "Chase?"

She yawned. "Uh?"

"Are we almost there?"

She nodded so hugely, her chin hit her chest. "Almost there." She stumbled over her feet, and it was then she realized that her muscles weren't cooperating anymore. She waved a hand. "Wait. Just a sec. I need to sit."

He helped her to sit on a low stone wall that surrounded a garden on the edge of campus. She knew her house was only a block away. She was almost there. "It's like…a river or something," she said, slurring her words.

"Chase?" he asked. His face swam into view as he crouched down in front of her. "Chase?"

She groaned and curled up into a ball on the wall. "Too tired."

"You can't sleep here," he said slowly, as if speaking to a child. "Where do you live?"

"The river," she said, yawning. It was too late. Her eyes had closed. The darkness was so warm and comfortable. Her body was floating. Was she really lying on stones? It felt so nice.

"Chase," Hyun Tae's voice said from far away. "Wake up, Chase."

She mumbled incoherently and sighed in contentment. The dreams welcomed her with open arms, and she floated straight into them.

Chapter Eight

Hyun Tae looked down at the girl from his parking ticket class. She lay curled up on the stone wall, one foot dangling over the edge, her eyes closed in probably the deepest sleep of her life.

For a few moments, he entertained the idea of just leaving her there, and then he sighed out loud. Daniel would kill him.

Hyun Tae leaned down and scooped her off the wall and into his arms. She was completely limp, her head falling back and one of her arms flopping out. He hoisted her up until her head fell against his chest. At least now it didn't look like he was carrying a dead body.

"Why?" he muttered under his breath, looking around self-consciously. He really didn't want to be seen carrying an unconscious girl back to his apartment. Right now, no one was around, but if anyone saw him, he was fully prepared to just call 911 and have an ambulance take care of her. He really didn't need this hassle. He'd been going to Dr. Kruljac's class since the start of school, but he hadn't learned anything of value about the professor. He had learned more than he wanted to about Chase, though.

She wasn't that heavy, but she was dead weight, and the two backpacks on his shoulders weren't light. He was only half a block from home. He'd take her back to the house and let Daniel figure out what to do with her.

Her hair smelled like tropical flowers, and her body was soft against his. The image of her singing that ridiculous song came to mind, and he almost laughed. He wondered if she would remember any of it, and he kind of hoped she would.

He'd made it to the front door when his phone buzzed. He shifted her weight and leaned back so she would lay against his chest while he pulled his phone from his pocket. With her cheek nestled against his neck, he got the phone out, and he put his arm back around her while he glanced down at the number.

Ahn Jung Ho. He really needed to take this call, but he had a drunk person gently snoring into his neck. It must be urgent if Ahn Jung Ho had bothered to stay up this late to call him.

He once again leaned back so Chase wouldn't fall off while he reached up to the security pad. He hit the numbers and then opened the door, grabbing Chase as she slid sideways. Her head lolled back as he caught her. He kicked off his shoes as he walked into the living room and nearly dropped her on the couch in his haste to catch Ahn Jung Ho's call.

"*Yobesayo?*" he said.

There was silence for a moment, and then Ahn Jung Ho's smooth voice answered.

"Hyun Tae." Ahn Jung Ho had been with Hyun Tae's father for years, and he had known Hyun Tae since he was born. He took care of all of the family's business, putting things in place and then stepping away into the background. He'd perfected the art of always being there without calling any attention to himself. He'd done it so well, Hyun Tae had never even put Ahn Jung Ho in any category, other than just knowing he was always there.

"Yes, Mr. Ahn."

"I was making travel arrangements for your return home in December. I believe your last day of classes is December sixteenth. I have a ticket for December eighteenth, leaving L.A. at nine-thirty in the morning. Will that work for you?"

Chase was a little too close to the edge of the couch, and she began sliding, her head rolling towards the edge. Hyun Tae put a foot on her ribs to hold her in place as he shrugged the heavy backpacks off his shoulders and answered.

"Yes. Yes, that would be fine. Can you text me the details a few days before my flight?"

"Of course." There was a pause. "How are your studies?"

"They are going well. School is not hard here."

"You will get good marks, then. Your father will be pleased to hear it," Ahn Jung Ho replied.

"Yes, please tell him for me," Hyun Tae said as Chase continued to roll off the couch. He leaned down and pushed her back on it, one hand on her shoulder and another on her hip, mindful of where he put his hands.

Mr. Ahn's voice was crisp. "I will do that. Enjoy the rest of your day, and I will see you in December."

"Thank you, Mr. Ahn."

Hyun Tae ended the call and sat down on the couch next to Chase, looking down at her. For someone who was so irrelevant, she continued to make herself a nuisance in his life. He'd had to throw away his favorite pair of shoes because of her.

A crackling sound came from behind him, and he turned.

Joon Suh stood there, a bag of chips in his hand, munching as he looked at Chase. "What did you do to her?"

Hyun Tae scowled. "I'm the victim here. She took two Vicodin, and it made her high, and then she passed out on the way home. I didn't know what else to do with her."

"She doesn't look comfortable."

Hyun Tae had to admit that Joon Suh was right. Her head was turned sideways and her body was crooked from where he'd shoved her back on the couch. He stood up and pushed her around until her body was straight and then put a pillow under her head.

Joon Suh nodded in approval. "Better."

"Do you know when Daniel is getting home?"

"Nope," Joon Suh said. Joon Suh wasn't taking any classes, and he didn't really care about their schedules.

"Not helpful," Hyun Tae said, absently pulling Chase's sandals off. She had really small feet. He wondered if she wore kid sizes.

Joon Suh started talking again, and Hyun Tae looked up, pulling thoughts away from Chase's shoe size. "...if you want to look at it."

"What?"

Joon Suh raised an eyebrow at him. "I'm done with the program. It's finished."

The full impact hit him, and he stood up. "So we're ready to load it up at the lab?"

"Yep."

He was thinking about when he would be able to find time to get to the lab when he noticed the monitor on her wrist. "What's that?" he asked, pointing to it, and Joon Suh walked over, squinting.

"It's a heart monitor. She's at 135 beats per minute. Kind of high for someone who is almost comatose."

"Why is it so high?"

Joon Suh shook his head. "She must have a problem, or she wouldn't be wearing a monitor at all."

Hyun Tae rubbed his hands through his hair. "Should I take her to the hospital? She didn't tell me she was sick."

"Maybe she isn't sick. If she told you she was okay, she's okay. She would know."

Hyun Tae sat down on the couch next to her. He couldn't just leave her if there was something wrong. "How long do you think she'll be out?" he wondered out loud.

Joon Suh shrugged. "Two Vicodin is enough to make you sleep for a little while, especially if you don't weigh much."

"I guess I'll have to stay here and make she sure she keeps breathing."

"Want something to drink?"

"Yeah."

Joon Suh shuffled out to the kitchen and came back with a bottle of water and a protein bar. "If you need me, I'll be upstairs."

"Thanks."

Chase hadn't moved since he'd put her on the couch. The only indication she was okay was the rise and fall of her chest and the blinking numbers on her wrist monitor. He stared at her for a moment, and then he got out of his chair to pick up the light blanket draped on the back of the couch. He shook it out and covered her. He settled next to her and tried to study, glancing up every now and then to make sure she was still breathing. When he realized he couldn't concentrate, he gave up.

"You really are something," he muttered to her.

She sighed in her sleep, and the corner of her mouth lifted in a sleepy smile.

Chapter Nine

Chase struggled to emerge from a deep sleep, but her consciousness was slow to catch up. She was under the weight of some kind of embarrassment, but what was it?

"*Jeohui appaneun ajigdo mollayo?*"

Chase groaned. Even in her dreams she was hearing Korean now?

"*Geurae. Sugohaseyo.*"

No, wait. That sounded real. Her head pounded, and she was impossibly tired, but she managed to pry one eye open. Lots of white. White marble floors, a white fluffy rug, and the edge of a glass coffee table swam in her vision. The monochromatic scheme seemed familiar.

She realized that her mouth was hanging open, and she closed it, only to find that it was painfully dry. She swirled her tongue around in her mouth, trying to wet it, and with another groan, pushed herself up onto her elbow.

Hyun Tae sat on the couch at her feet.

Chase jumped back, scrambling to sit up. "What?"

His elbows rested on his knees, and a phone dangled from one hand, where he absently turned it with his fingers. He brought the phone to his chin and tilted his head. His eyebrows rose a fraction.

Chase looked down at the soft, light green throw over her legs. She was sleeping on his couch. In his living room. In his house. And then it all came back to her in a wave of acute embarrassment.

We all live in a purple submarine!

She brought her hands to her mouth, eyes widening.

That seemed to satisfy him, and Hyun Tae stood. "You remember, don't you?"

She let her head fall back against the well-stuffed linen couch cushion. "No," she moaned.

"At least you know."

"Know what?" she asked, raising her head an inch to peer at him.

"What a pain you were."

She groaned again, smothering her face into the linen. "Why?"

"I don't know. I don't have those problems."

She forgot her embarrassment for a moment and sat up straight to glare at him. "You are so cranky."

He shrugged. Instead of the black Converse he had been wearing before, he had on a pair of toeless slippers.

He put his phone into his pocket and began to walk toward the kitchen. "Would you like water?"

"Yes. Please," she said.

He went into the kitchen and returned with a glass of water. He held it out, his face unreadable.

Chase took the glass and sipped at it, wondering how she was going to come back from this.

Watch. I can do this.

She flinched, forcing the water down her dry throat. Did she actually attempt a heel click while, essentially, high? She had to try and recover from this. If Daniel knew…

She froze mid-swallow. Her eyes found Hyun Tae's in panic.

"What?" he asked.

"Daniel lives here," she said in a croak.

Hyun Tae checked his watch. "He should be home in a few minutes."

She bolted to her feet, clanged the glass onto the table, and stumbled out of the blanket in her haste to escape. "Sorry about all this. And thanks."

He stopped her with two hands on her shoulders. "What's wrong?"

She put a hand to her hair and realized that it was a disaster, falling out of the bun she had piled on her head that morning. Limp strands fell around her neck and face. "Did you tell him about this?"

"Not yet."

"Don't!" she pleaded. "I think he likes me. So don't."

He stared back, deadpan.

She gave a tug against the grip he had on her upper arms. "Seriously, if he sees me like this—"

The front door opened and closed.

Chase gasped, and she hurriedly tugged the hairband out of her hair. It fell in waves down her back, and still between Hyun Tae's arms, she tried to gather it up back into a bun. But she dropped the hair tie. With a growl of frustration, she bent to retrieve it.

Her hair must have flipped Hyun Tae in the face, because he stumbled back with an angry, "Ah!"

She half stood up to apologize, and the top of her head collided with the bottom of his chin.

His hands grabbed her arms again, probably to keep her from doing any more damage to his face, but she had bent down to get the hair tie again, and they both lost their balance. She fell right on top of him. He grunted as she slammed her hands against his chest to catch her fall, and he prevented her from putting too much weight on him by grabbing her waist.

Chase looked up just as Daniel came from the foyer into the living room. He stopped, phone in his hand and eyes wide, mouth parted in surprise.

Her hair was down and disheveled, and Hyun Tae had his hands on her waist as she lay sprawled on top of him.

Hyun Tae broke into the first wide grin she had ever seen on him. And then he laughed.

Chase scrambled to her feet, running a hand through her hair and trying to get away from Hyun Tae. "Daniel!"

Daniel's lips twitched. He held a button on his phone, and into the mouthpiece he said, "Note: Chase is a player."

"I'm not!"

Daniel pursed his lips, and Chase stared at him helplessly.

Hyun Tae rolled over and jumped to his feet, surprisingly lithe. He took his time, fixing the cuffs of his shirt. "*Wasso?*" he asked in Korean, still smiling.

Daniel joined them in the living room, one hand low on his hip, and a smile on his lips. "*Nega gakjanghaeya dwae?*"

Hyun Tae shook his head. "*Anya geogjeong an haedo dwae.*" He stooped to the floor, hooked a finger through Chase's hair tie, and handed it to her.

She took it, swallowing hard to quell her nausea.

Daniel stood there, as if waiting for an explanation. Chase opened her mouth to give him one, but Hyun Tae beat her to it. "Your girlfriend is a drug addict."

Daniel raised an eyebrow.

Chase gave the polite jerk a tight-lipped expression that said, "I'm going to kill you."

"Can I walk you home?" Daniel asked. He seemed to be fighting a laugh.

"Yes," Chase said gratefully. She quickly twisted her hair back into a bun, smoothed the sides, and came to stand next to him.

Daniel looked down at her bare feet. "Where are your shoes and bag?"

She winced and reluctantly looked to Hyun Tae. He went to the couch and retrieved them from under the coffee table, letting the worn sandals dangle from his fingertips like they were radioactive and holding the backpack in the other hand.

She hurried to take her belongings. Then she jammed the shoes onto her feet, shouldered the backpack, and followed Daniel out to the foyer.

His eyes slid down to her, his expression an even mix between suspicious and amused.

Chase grimaced. "That looked weird."

"Yup," he agreed. "Let me take your bag."

She let him take it from her, and he slung it over his shoulder.

As they walked outside, Chase suddenly realized that it was almost dark out. She had slept nearly the entire day on that guy's couch? She cleared her throat. "Hyun Tae and I have a parking class."

"He told me," Daniel said, watching her with a bemused expression.

"This morning I accidentally took two Vicodin instead of my regular medication. It was an accident, I swear!" she said. "And Hyun Tae happened to be there when I…sort of…conked out. I'm not a drug addict," she added weakly.

"Are you okay?"

"Just sleepy."

"You were asleep on my couch all day?"

"I guess so," she mumbled. "It's so awkward." An image popped into her head of all the doodles she'd drawn in Hyun Tae's notebook.

"It's kind of funny though," he said, grinning.

"Really?" she asked, hopeful. Funny was better than disappointing. She really wanted him to like her.

"Are you sure you're okay?"

She nodded. "Yeah. I feel bad for Hyun Tae, though. He probably thinks I'm crazy."

"Probably," Daniel agreed.

Well you didn't have to agree. In the sunset, Daniel's burgundy red hair shimmered with highlights, and Chase wondered if it was as soft as it looked. His white teeth flashed in the deepening darkness as they stopped at the foot of the stairs to her apartment. "I'm teasing. He thinks everyone needs his help."

She squinted against the glare of the setting sun, wrinkling her nose. "Really?"

He stared back at her and then sucked the breath in between his teeth, as if he'd just discovered something. "You're cute when you're embarrassed."

She reached over and pulled her bag off his shoulder. "Seriously, though. That was so humiliating. I sang "Purple Submarine" and...did all kinds of stuff. It was so bad."

"You sang for him?" he asked, mock jealousy on his face.

"Unh. It was really amazing."

He laughed. "Don't worry. If he really didn't like you, he would have dropped you off at the student health center."

She put up a hand. "Yeah, yeah. Let's not talk about it anymore."

"Okay. But you're all right?"

"Yeah."

He stared at her for a beat, as if he might say or do something else. But then he touched his hair, and looked down. "You owe me a date, right?"

"Just tell me when, and we'll go."

"You got it. See you later," he said with a wave.

Chase climbed wearily up the steps to her apartment, turning at the door to watch Daniel walking down the path toward his house. She sighed and twisted the doorknob. At least Kiki would have a good laugh.

But the apartment was empty when she stepped inside. She flipped on the light and dropped her things in her bedroom and went out to the kitchen, opening the fridge. Nothing in there appealed to her. She should probably be really hungry, but even her appetite seemed groggy. She settled on a bowl of cereal. Stirring the cereal around, she picked out the marshmallows. The memory of falling on Hyun Tae flashed into her mind. She scrunched her eyes closed. Was there a pill that gave you amnesia? She needed that.

Her phone dinged, and she looked down at the text.

"Hey."

She smiled. Daniel. *"Hey."*

"I forgot to tell you something."

"What?"

"I'm going out of the country for a week. So can I take you out when we get back?"

"Sure."

"You won't forget about me?"

She turned the phone upside down, watching the messages flip to follow, and turned it back again, thinking. He hadn't told her where he was going, or why. She supposed it wasn't any of her business.

"Of course not. I'll be here. Embarrassing myself on a daily basis."

" Wish I could stay. I'll be in touch. Okay?"

"Okay. I won't go anywhere."

"Sleep tight."

"You, too."

She leaned back in her chair, trying to shove away a pang of disappointment. She was going to miss him.

Chapter Ten

Chase stared out her windshield as the heavy rain pelted the glass and dinged off the front of her car. It *would* rain right as she got home with a car full of groceries. It was one of those rare chilly days, where the wind was a little brisk, and the rain would slide down her neck in icy droplets that made her shiver. She wished she had worn a hoodie or something.

Chase bolted from her car, running around to the trunk and fumbling with her keys to open it. By the time she had it open, she had slowed down. She was already drenched. No use in fighting it.

She managed to grab everything in one trip-- even with a gallon of milk--and slogged through the puddles in the parking lot to waddle up the two flights of stairs to the deck in front of her apartment. Her wrist monitor beeped when she reached the top, completely out of breath and slightly light-headed. Okay, so the groceries were a little heavier than she thought.

Her wet, slippery hand fumbled with the doorknob, but she wasn't able to get it open while still holding all the bags. The wind whipped against her back, plastering her soaked shirt against her skin and causing a shiver to ripple through her. She banged her toe against the door. "Janelle! Lauren!"

No one came to her rescue.

Chase gritted her teeth and put her bags down. Her cereal boxes were soggy, and the produce had inadvertently gotten a good rinse. She wrenched open the front door and then scooped up her bags, only to have one of them catch on a nail from the deck and rip open, spilling cans of Spaghetti-Os and a bag of jasmine rice onto the wet patio.

Chase gave in to a growl of rage, tossed her other groceries into the foyer, and ran back out to scoop up the fallen groceries. By the time she stumbled back in, closing the door behind her, Janelle had wandered out from her room wearing a robe and holding her hand splayed out like she had just painted her nails.

"Hey Chase." Her big green eyes swiveled to Chase's muddy sneakers. She had stumbled through the door and onto the carpet while trying to save the food. "Careful with your shoes. It's white carpet."

Chase blinked at her roommate and pushed a limp strand of wet hair away from her face. She took a step to the side so she was on the foyer.

Janelle sighed loudly and turned away. "Just letting you know."

Chase kicked off her sneakers and brought her groceries into the kitchen. She dropped everything on the table and then hurried back to her bedroom to change into something drier. Kiki was still in class, and she sometimes stayed at the library to get her homework done so she could focus.

Chase put on a pair of sweatpants and her old PE shirt from high school. She toweled off her hair and then headed back to the kitchen to get her ice cream in the freezer before it melted.

As she put the food away, Chase wrote her name with a sharpie on each of her items. It was a system Janelle had come up with to separate their things from one another, except for staples like baking supplies, which they shared.

When she had finished, she went to the front room to peek out the window. It was still raining steadily, with powerful gusts of wind buffeting the rain around so it looked like the roll of the ocean. At least her classes were over for the day.

Chase grabbed her charcoal pencils and sketchbook from her desk and plopped down in the middle of the living room to work on a new piece. Inspired by the rain, she sketched another piece that she felt would fit perfectly with her portfolio for the career fair. Her protagonist moved in the picture, fluid like water, and shadowed by the storm around her. Chase had a good feeling about this one.

Her phone dinged from her bedroom, but she ignored it. She was mesmerized by her own pencil. The lines were so smooth. Everything seemed to be coming together just perfectly. A little thrill went through her as the picture, almost against her will, became an ethereal creation with soft curves and precise proportions.

Tearing herself away from her sketch, Chase decided to check her assignment book to make sure she had everything done for tomorrow. She scanned her notes for the day. No homework except a biology presentation due tomorrow morning. She wasn't thrilled about the prospect of presenting the PowerPoint on the difference between RNA and DNA, but at least it was already done.

Her phone buzzed, and she remembered someone had texted her hours ago. Chase fished her phone out of her purse and found she had two texts from Kiki and one from an unknown number. She was hit with a little pang of disappointment that she still hadn't gotten a text from Daniel since he had left the country, but she pushed it aside and clicked on the unknown number's message.

"Hi Chase, this is Hyun Tae. Joon Suh finished repairing your laptop. Can I bring it over?"

Chase looked at the time stamp. It was from just now. She looked out the window over Kiki's bed. It was dark out, but she thought she could still hear rain. She quickly texted him back.

"You don't have to if it's inconvenient. I can pick it up tomorrow."

"I'll be over in five."

"Crap." Chase tossed her phone onto her bed and rummaged through her clean laundry basket for a bra.

Kiki sauntered in with a bag of Doritos and a bowl of sour cream. "What are you doing?"

"Soup guy is coming over."

"I don't know if soup guy suits him anymore," Kiki mused, sitting cross-legged on her bed and dipping a Dorito in the sour cream. "Parking pal? Drug dude? Humiliating Hyun?"

"Hilarious," Chase said in a drone, shuffling inside her shirt to hook the bra into place.

Kiki giggled to herself as she bit into the chip.

Chase managed to get her hair into a presentable ponytail just as a knock sounded on the door. She looked down at herself.

Kiki nodded in appreciation. "Yes, that's a high school shirt that says 'Riverside Dolphins Win! We do it on porpoise.' It fits with your whole," she gestured with her hands, "thing."

Chase sighed in resignation and hurried to answer the door.

Hyun Tae stood under a black umbrella, a laptop case slung over his shoulder. For once, he was dressed casually, wearing a baseball-style graphic T-shirt, distressed black jeans, and Converses. He dipped his right shoulder to slide the strap off and handed her the bag.

"Joon Suh says he is sorry it took the whole week, but you needed parts ordered in."

"Thanks." She took the bag from him.

Water coursed over the sides of his umbrella as they stood staring at one another, and then the rain seemed to increase two-fold. A blast of wind smacked him with a wall of water. His eyes squeezed shut, but other than that he didn't move.

Chase opened the door a little wider. "Want to come in?"

Hyun Tae glanced up at his umbrella, as if he might be able to see the storm through the black fabric. "Maybe for just a moment."

He stepped through the door, closing his umbrella and taking care to keep the dripping water on the tile entranceway.

Chase gaped as he shook water from his black hair and then wiped his face where the droplets had gathered around his lips. He stilled, and lowered his hand.

113

Whoa, snap out of it, Chase. "Um, are you thirsty? I can make...tea." *Lauren has tea somewhere, right?"*

"Thank you," he said with a nod of his head.

Oh wait, seriously? Yes? Okay then. She took his umbrella from him, setting it against the doorframe and then motioned for him to follow her into the kitchen.

Hyun Tae's eyes surveyed the apartment, and since he seemed preoccupied with looking around him, Chase went to the cabinet to grab two mugs. She went to the spice cabinet to poke around for the tea without making it too obvious that she never drank it.

She found an almost empty box of "Sleepytime vanilla" herbal tea. She snorted. *Maybe he'll zonk out on my couch.*

"What?" Hyun Tae asked.

Chase looked up from the box and swallowed her grin. "Oh, nothing. Just...remembering something. Is this okay?"

"I'm sure it's fine," he said, a ghost of a smile on his lips. "Thank you."

As ever, he was the polite jerk. She put two cups of water into the microwave and set the timer.

As the microwave hummed in the silence, Hyun Tae continued looking around him, apparently unconcerned by the silence and obviously interested in where she lived. But Chase found herself squirming. Most people didn't let this happen. They would chatter to fill space. So now she had to do it.

"What's your major?" she asked him.

"Biological engineering," he responded. "And you," he guessed, "are an art major."

"Did Daniel tell you?"

"No. You have charcoal smudges on your hands, and I saw your drawings in class."

"Oh." She turned her hand over, and indeed, the whole outer edge of her right hand was black with charcoal. "Yup, you're right." She side-stepped to the sink and washed her hands. Preparing drinks with dirty hands? Why not add it to the Humiliating Hyun list.

The microwave dinged, and she reached in to grab the mugs. Even the handles were scorching hot, so she quickly withdrew, shaking out her burned fingers.

Wow, Chase, she thought, doing a mental facepalm. *You derp duck. Pull it together.* She grabbed a folded towel from a drawer and took the mugs out and put them on the counter. She plopped two tea bags into each cup of scalding water. They floated to the top. Was she supposed to leave them like that?

Hyun Tae opened a drawer, and having guessed correctly, took out two spoons and put them in the mugs to weigh the tea bags down. His arm brushed against hers

115

as he stood next to her, but he made no move to back away. "You could have offered soda."

"You seem like a tea guy." She looked up at him, and her stomach did a flip-flop. How could a grown man have such flawlessly smooth skin?

One side of his mouth quirked up. "That's very thoughtful."

"What else do you put in your tea?"

"Nothing."

She glanced at the tea, which was slowly turning an amber color. "What? No sugar? Or honey?"

"No."

"Oh."

They stood there watching the tea steep. Which, Chase realized, was unbelievably boring of her. She reached deep into her "hostess" self, which was buried under layers of awkward social situations, and took a step back so she could face him better. "So you like science?"

"It's a part of the family business," he said, leaning one hip against the counter and folding his arms. "My father owns a biotech company called KimBio."

The way he said "Kim" sounded like "keem." She tried to plug that into her memory so she could say his name correctly. "That's cool. So you'll probably end up working for your dad then?"

He looked like he was struggling to understand. "Work for him?"

Did he think she was stupid? If so, she wasn't sure why. "Yeah...or do you not want to? You said it was the family business, so I assumed."

"Ah, no I will not work for him. I will inherit it."

"Oh! You'll get to be CEO?"

"I have to be," he said, as if it were obvious.

"Right out of college?"

"Yes. I've been learning the business for years already."

"Sounds like the royal family," she said, joking.

He seemed entirely serious as he considered this. "It's pretty close. Shareholders have an understanding that regardless of who the son is or how capable he might be, he will likely be in charge of the company. Unless he shames the family name somehow."

Chase tilted her head to one side. "I didn't know that's how it worked. I've never heard of a son or daughter inheriting a company like that...not that I know much about the business world."

"It is more common in our country, I think," he said.

"And you want to take over KimBio?"

He didn't even hesitate. "Yes, I do."

He's pretty intense for a...twenty-year-old? He looks a little older than that though. "How long until you can graduate?"

His eyes kind of smiled, like he knew what she was really asking. "I am a junior. But I am twenty-three."

She reached over and stirred her tea. It looked amber-ey, so she put the hot mug to her lips.

"It's probably still ho-"

"Ah!" She buckled forward as the tea scalded her mouth and throat. Gingerly, she put it back onto the counter. *Great, now I won't be able to taste anything for a day.*

Hyun Tae rubbed the corner of his mouth. Without another word, he went to the fridge and pulled out a cold bottle of water. He stopped so close to her that she could smell his expensive soap and then took her hand in his. It was the hand she had burned earlier. He gently placed the water bottle in her palm and wrapped her fingers around it.

"You are not a tea person, Chase."

"Nope," she agreed, a little mesmerized by him.

"Thank you for the drink," he said, suddenly stepping back. "I should probably go, though. I have a lot of homework to finish before tomorrow."

"Okay. Sorry about the tea thing. I'll give you a soda next time."

He gave a small smile. "Good night, Chase."

"Good night."

He opened the door, turning back to look at her one last time, his dark eyes meeting hers for a second before he closed the door against the rain. She sighed and leaned back against the counter. She picked up the repaired laptop and opened it. It looked as good as new. She took it to her room, and Kiki looked up, taking her headphones out of her ears. Chase could hear the music coming from them.

"Wow. You are going to go deaf."

"It'll be worth it."

Chase opened her laptop, thinking about what Hyun Tae had said about taking over the company, as if he had no choice. More like, he wouldn't have it any other way. No angst about being forced to be in the family business or whining about other choices he might want to make. It wasn't hard to imagine him in a suit, drily surveying his corporate kingdom.

How big was his family's company anyway? She'd never heard of KimBio. She Googled it, wondering if it would come up at all. It did. The website was in a different language, but there was an English option. So far it looked really legit and sort of complicated with a lot of tabs and information. She clicked around, but it looked like it wasn't meant for the casual web surfer.

Even in English, it was very technical. Too bad she was an art major.

So was KimBio a big company? She typed in a search for the top twenty Korean companies. KimBio came in at six, behind a few names that looked familiar. So it wasn't some company operating out of his dad's basement. It was pretty big. Next question, of course, was if Hyun Tae was as wealthy as he seemed.

She poked around and found the name of the CEO—Kim Sang Sik—and looked him up. There was a nice big article about him and even a sentence about his family. She found Kim Hyun Tae. And another word she'd never seen before. Chaebol. Apparently it was the Korean equivalent of business royalty. Although the businesses were operated by experienced CEOs, the sons of those company owners were expected to inherit the entire empire.

Super-rich families who controlled a lot of wealth. So he didn't just smell like money; he was drowning in it.

No wonder he thought she was such a hot mess. He had bigger things to think about. She could barely manage to buy soup for lunch.

Pulling up the presentation she was supposed to be working on, she put on her headphones and got to down to it. She had a couple of ideas on how to present it and some decent graphics. After a few hours, she went through the whole thing, wondering if it would be long enough. Professor Kruljac had said two minutes and explained, in his thick Russian accent, that anyone not prepared at their designated time would receive a zero for the assignment, as if he relished the idea of dropping their grade for being unprepared. She saved the presentation on a thumb drive and closed her laptop.

Chapter Eleven

She woke up early the next morning, before her alarm, having second thoughts about her biology presentation. She played it again and tweaked it with a few extra facts and a few more pictures. It would be her first project in that class, and she wanted to start the semester off right.

Surveying the clothes in her closet, she wondered what to wear. The presentation wasn't that big of a deal, so she could probably wear anything. Red jeans and black T-shirt with a tiny little Spiderman face on one sleeve. Discreet geek.

She left the house, mentally rehearsing. The air still smelled like rain and the sunshine made the wet grass sparkle, which put her in a good mood.

The classroom was empty when she arrived, but it filled up five minutes early. She was second in line, which was better than being first.

Professor Kruljac sat at his desk, working on his laptop. The big screen filled up most of the wall, which seemed a little unnecessary to Chase. She wasn't presenting it to Carnegie Hall, just thirty acquaintances, all trying to pass a class.

The first girl to present walked confidently up to the desk, hooked up her computer and rolled through her presentation. Chase only dozed off once during the middle, so it must have been pretty good. The girl finished and disconnected her laptop.

Chase bounced up from her seat, scooping her laptop from her desk. Professor Kruljac connected her laptop to the projector and stood back to let her pull up her work. Her screen remained black. She tapped at a few keys, chewing on her bottom lip for inspiration. Her phone buzzed in her pocket. She ignored it, tapping again at her laptop as people began shifting in their seats. Why wasn't it working? What had happened to it? Maybe Joon Suh's fix hadn't worked.

Mr. Kruljac asked if she needed to use a classroom laptop. She dug in her pockets for her thumb drive, telling herself don't panic, everything would work out fine.

A knock came at the classroom door, and everyone turned to look, even though the window on the door was too small to see anything. Mr. Kruljac pointed to two computers sitting on his desk. "You can use my spare laptop there."

As he walked to the door, she took the computer that was already open, figuring he had to mean the one that

123

didn't require her to enter a password, and began to set it up, praying nothing else would go wrong. It came to life, and she inserted her thumb drive, holding her breath. The desktop on the screen was cluttered, filled with all kinds of files.

Where was the thumb drive file? She waited for the icon to appear, suddenly forgetting what it looked like. It was orange, right? She moved the mouse around the desktop, searching. The icon flashed over to the right, and she slid the mouse toward it. She blinked. Had she dragged something from the desktop to her thumb drive? She didn't have time to worry about it. She clicked on the icon and let out a breath when she found her presentation. It came up, and she started her report. As if to make up for all the technical glitches, it went smoothly.

She closed the presentation and pulled her thumb drive out, looking up at Mr. Kruljac. He was standing by the door, arms folded, assessing her presentation. She closed the computer she had used, and he frowned. He took the laptop and put it under the desk. "Next," he said. His reaction wasn't very encouraging.

When the next presentation started, Chase tried to pay attention, but her eyes were heavy. Why did these things make her so sleepy? She slid her phone out of her pocket and discreetly checked her texts.

She saw Daniel's name, and her heart jumped. Finally.

"Sorry I haven't been able to text. How are you?"

She really wanted to text him back, but there was no way to do that during class. As the presenters all took their turns, she waited impatiently. Would this class never end? How many times did she have to hear about double helixes? Helixi? Why had everyone opted for a safe, boring presentation?

"Class, those who have not presented yet will do so at our next class. For those of you going on the Bates field trip, don't forget that the bus leaves from parking lot B at eight thirty a.m. sharp. Do not be late. We will not wait for you. See you then."

Chase jerked her head up. Had the agony ended? And what time was she supposed to be at the parking lot again? Eight thirty or nine thirty?

She gathered up her things, typing on her phone.

"I'm good. Where are you?"

"Tokyo." He must have been waiting for her to answer.

"I don't believe you. Prove it with a selfie."

"Now?"

"haha! of course!" It wasn't like he had to worry about not looking good. Maybe it was midnight. What was the time difference between Japan and California? He might have adorable bedhead.

A picture popped up of a huge indoor dome that looked like it could seat thousands, the ceiling made from interlocking geometric shapes.

"That's amazing! But no pic of you?"

"I'll trade. You first."

Chase held up her phone and took a quick selfie. Ooh. Too quick. She retook it, changing the angle and adding a filter. Much better. She sent it and waited.

He responded with another text. *"Ah, you're so pretty! Thank you."*

She snorted and sent back three dots.

"..."

"Did I say something wrong?"

"Where. is. my. picture?"

"Of me?"

"AAAAAHHHH!! YES!"

"Sorry, I can't. I have to go. I'll send you one when I have more time."

"Did you just play me?"

"I don't understand your English. I just learning to talk it."

"haha. When are you coming back?"

"Two days. See you soon! Take care!"

"You too."

She put her phone away. What was he doing in Tokyo anyway?

Later that night, Chase sat on her bed, chewing on the end of a pencil and trying to ignore the lonely silence of her bedroom. Kiki was out with friends. Because she was cool. And Chase had nothing but sketches and homework to look forward to. Her phone buzzed, causing her to jump and drop the pencil. She pulled the phone out from under her pillow. It was a picture of Daniel, wearing a white button-down shirt that was open at the collar, and he was smiling. The sun was shining, so it must be daytime for him.

"You look good! What time is it there?" she asked.

"2:00 - in the afternoon. Tomorrow."

She tried to wrap her head around that and gave up. "So what is the future like?"

"A lot like the present. Did I wake you?"

"No. I was studying."

"Did your mom set you up with any more blind dates?"

"LOL. No. No more blind dates for me! You're it." Too late she realized that smacked of commitment. Before she could figure out how to fix it. he replied.

"Good."

She raised her eyebrows. Daniel was glad she wasn't dating anyone else. She wasn't sure how to respond. Unable to think of anything, she changed the subject.

"My laptop broke after Joon Suh fixed it. Do you think he would look at it again?"

"Sure."

"It died right before my biology presentation."

"Sorry. Bad timing!"

"So he wouldn't mind?" She didn't know Joon Suh at all, so maybe he would think she was a nuisance.

"I'll ask him for you."

"Really? Thank you!"

"You're welcome." A few minutes later, he texted back. *"Joon Suh says he can look at your laptop again. And he apologized".*

"For what??"

"Because it broke again so soon. He'll figure it out for you. He might come over tonight."

"It's not that urgent."

"Joon Suh isn't used to messing up."

"LOL. okay."

"I gotta go. See you soon."

"Ttyl"

Sighing, she pulled her laptop out of her backpack. Sad little laptop. Maybe it could be fixed, but maybe it was too damaged. She didn't have the money to buy a new one, and she didn't want to tell her parents. They'd already been stretched enough with her trip to Italy, even though she'd earned the plane tickets herself by saving up for a year. She'd been able to afford her apartment here because her mom was a university employee, so her tuition was paid for. But there wasn't any extra money lying around.

Someone knocked at the front door, and it opened. She sat still, listening as Janelle answered it. She could tell by Janelle's high-pitched, giggly "hello" that it was a guy, and he was probably really good-looking. A low voice answered, definitely male.

"Chase!" Janelle called. "Someone is here for you!"

She looked down at her clothes. She wore leggings, a big flannel shirt she'd stolen from her dad, and mismatched socks. By all indications, it would be Hyun Tae at the door. Stepping into the living room, she was pleasantly surprised to see Joon Suh. He looked past Janelle and right at her, his dark eyes impassive.

"Can I have your laptop, please?"

She turned, obeying the command without thinking. He hadn't even said hello. When she returned, he took it from her with long, elegant fingers, and handed her another one. "Use this one until I fix yours."

Blinking at him, she finally found her voice. "No, I can't take your laptop."

He let out an exasperated breath as he turned to leave. "I wasn't asking."

The door closed behind him, and Janelle stared at her. "Who. Was. That."

"The computer guy who fixed my laptop."

Janelle looked at the door, her eyes glazed. "Mmm," she murmured.

Chase went back to her room, throwing herself on her pillows and opening the laptop Joon Suh had given her.

She found her thumb drive and clicked it into the USB port. All her files were there, including the English paper she'd been working on. There was one she didn't recognize, though. *5274 Report 09.14.* What was that?

She clicked on it. It was all in Chinese or something, but there were a few English words scattered about in what looked like a business report. Bates University stood out, and then there was KimBio. Wasn't that Hyun Tae's family company? She scrolled through briefly, but none of it made sense.

This document wasn't hers; that was for sure. For a moment she thought it must be Joon Suh's, but then remembered she was looking at files from her own thumb drive. It had to have been that file from Professor Kruljac's laptop. Hopefully it was just a copy. Obviously KimBio and Bates worked together in some capacity—like maybe Bates did research for KimBio or something. She should probably tell Professor Kruljac in the morning, in case she had removed the file from his desktop.

Getting back to work, and feeling grateful to Joon Suh for his eccentric generosity, she finished her paper. She couldn't resist checking her phone for a text from Daniel. She smiled when she found one. *"Good night."*

Chapter Twelve

The yellow school bus in front of Chase roared to life, its guttural chugging bringing back memories of middle school and riding on a noisy bus before she had gotten her license. The smell of exhaust filled the air as the group of students she was among waited to board one of the two buses. Most of the students were excited about skipping biology class, but the group behind her seemed most interested at the prospect of getting a peek into Bates's research facility.

A laughing student backed up into her, smashing her face into his backpack. He turned around and quickly apologized. He was pretty cute in a jock-ish way, with buzzed red hair and a dusting of freckles across his pale skin. He must have thought Chase was cute, too, because he held out a hand. "I'm Josh."

Chase shook it. "Hi."

"Which biology class are you in?"

"Just 120." *How do so many boys on this campus have the confidence to talk to girls like they've already met?*

He nodded, lip jutted out. "Do you like it? I'm majoring in electrical engineering. Biology isn't my thing."

She got the impression that he wanted her to be twitterpated with his future job prospects, based on his major. She nodded, unsure what to say to that. She wasn't actually impressed.

He hunched his shoulders a bit, looking uncomfortable, but forged ahead anyway. "So, do you?"

"Do I what?"

"Like biology."

Oh yeah, he asked that. "Not really," she admitted, hoping her frankness would give them something in common.

But it seemed to put him off. "Yeah, it's a hard subject." He paused. "Sorry, what was your name?"

Come on. I didn't say it, and you know it. "Chase."

Josh's group suddenly erupted into a chorus of laughs, and he turned to see what the ruckus was about. One of his friends started to tell him the joke, and he was sucked back into his group's circle.

Chase pulled out her phone. Well, that was more like her usual encounters with men. Her random Korean friends were starting to distort her reality of success with the other sex. Incidentally, she didn't have any new texts from Daniel, either.

Although the bus was crowded, Chase was able to grab a seat to herself at the back. She stretched out her legs and listened to her K-pop list on her phone, hoping to know a few words and surprise Daniel on their next date. Maybe her ability to say some of the Korean words would impress him. She laughed to herself. Daniel would probably tell her it was "cute." Which was good with her.

It didn't take them long to arrive at the Bates Research and Engineering Center Gray and blocky, it blended into the other corporate buildings around it, with its thin rectangular windows and the concrete pillars at its entrance.

Chase filed into the building with the rest of the class, some of them holding notebooks and pens, and most of them just talking with their classmates or looking bored like Chase. Two professors Chase didn't recognize led the students up the stairs and through a set of doors that required security clearance badges. One of the professors explained that as heads of their departments, they worked closely with the research facility as biomedical engineers themselves.

They walked down a hallway, and the glass walls allowed Chase to see into the laboratories as

134

they passed. Most of it seemed to be pharmaceutical testing. She watched a doctor in a white lab coat, wearing white booties, a white shower cap, and purple latex gloves, insert a tube into a machine and press a button.

They moved on, going through corridors where the professors described the work each of the engineers and scientists were engaged in. Chase filtered to the back of the group and then stopped to rifle through her purse to rustle up a stray piece of gum.

The blip of a door made her turn around. An employee holding a brown leather laptop bag was going into one of the few rooms that wasn't a giant glass box. He had on a black baseball cap and glasses, but his profile seemed familiar.

Hyun Tae? That couldn't be him, could it? But it looked like him.

She looked at the group as it disappeared around a corner. Curiosity got the better of her because if it was Hyun Tae, then what was he doing in the Bates laboratory? She trotted over to the lab door, grabbing a fistful of her maxi dress to keep it from snagging around her ankles.

Chase peeked through the narrow window, but she couldn't see anything except tables of equipment and books. If that wasn't Hyun Tae, it would be a little embarrassing, but she had to know.

She cautiously opened the door and poked her head around the corner. If the *beep, beep, beep* of the door hadn't alerted him, the slamming noise it made when she let it crash closed would have.

Hyun Tae looked up at her from across the room. He was sitting in a computer chair in front of a desktop with one hand on the mouse. The baseball cap was pulled low over his forehead, and thick glasses swallowed his handsome face almost more than the blazer collar he had flipped up in an odd fashion statement.

"Hey," she said, waving and feeling dumb for even following. "Saw you in here."

His eyes flitted to the side, almost as if he were resisting the urge to look behind him. "Hi, Chase." He stared at her for the barest of seconds, and then went back to his computer, clicking away with the mouse. "You here with the field trip?" he asked, his eyes on the screen.

"Yeah. Are you on the same field trip, or do you work here?" she asked. "I know KimBio works with Bates on stuff, so you probably have some kind of in with them."

Hyun Tae looked up. "What was that?"

"That...you and Bates...I mean since your dad owns KimBio...isn't that why you're at this school? Because the companies work together? Professor

Kruljac let me use his laptop for something, and I saw a document that says KimBio and Bates work together. That's why you're allowed in here, right?"

Hyun Tae tapped a few more buttons, clicked with his mouse, and yanked a USB drive out of the computer and slipped it into his bag. He stood and pushed his chair in. "No, I'm on the university research team."

"Oh! I had no idea."

"Yeah, it's no big deal." He took a few strides toward her, stopping so close she had to tilt her head.

"Right, sorry. Just funny seeing you here."

To her surprise, he pulled her around and put his arm casually across her shoulders. She went stiff. This was not like him at all.

"It's not that strange," he said. "I'm the research team, and we both have the same professor."

"Oh yeah, sure," Chase said, entirely distracted by the fact that he had a firm hold on her shoulders and seemed to want her to walk with him that way.

Hyun Tae scooted them forward, and Chase tripped on the hem of her dress. Was this his way of hitting on her? It wasn't working.

He opened the door and led the way past two more laboratories. Chase was torn between relaxing into the warmth of his hand on her bare shoulder or squirming out of his grip. He slowed his stride and abruptly dropped his arm from her shoulders. "You going back with the group, or can I offer you a ride home?"

Chase tried to think of a reason why he would be so interested in how she was getting home. "I'm supposed to be on the field trip."

He gave her a crooked smile. "And?"

She couldn't explain all the charm he was throwing at her, but maybe this was Hyun Tae in his natural environment of lab equipment and technology. She stifled an inner laugh and continued their odd, friendly conversation. "And the bus ride here was good enough. I think I could live without another. If you don't mind."

"I don't mind. Joon Suh is picking me up. He's outside, waiting."

They walked down the long corridor in silence for a few moments, and then he asked, "You said you saw something with KimBio and Bates together?"

"Yeah, a document I accidentally grabbed off of Professor Kruljac's laptop. It was all in another language, but I made out the names. Looked like some kind of report. "

"Ah," he said. "So you were using your professor's laptop. How did the presentation go?"

Again, this was unexpectedly social of him. "Good. I survived."

He opened one of the double doors to the exit. "You don't get nervous?"

"No. I just want to get it over with. Do you have to do presentations as part of the research team?"

"Not really. It's mostly lab reports, data double-checking, and listening to lectures."

"And checking your email for literally ten seconds on a random computer."

He gave her a look that said *very funny*. "I was just checking on something that I couldn't access remotely."

A shiny black sedan sat at the curb, and Hyun Tae stepped forward and opened the back door for her. The movement was so smooth, it reminded her of a valet or chauffeur, though she was pretty sure he'd never had a job like that.

She slid into the black leather backseat and saw that Joon Suh was at the wheel. He turned and gave her a courteous nod, his features friendly, if not exactly smiling. She waved.

Hyun Tae slid into the seat next to Chase and leaned forward, one arm braced against the headrest. "*Geugeos.*"

Joon Suh twisted around to look at Chase, his eyebrows raised in faint surprise. "*Geurayo?*"

Hyun Tae took off his ball cap and glasses, tossed them into the front seat, and then sat back, responding with a lazy, "*Eoh.*"

Joon Suh turned to the front again, a faint smile on his lips.

She had no idea what that was all about, and she was faintly irritated that they didn't speak English in front of her. Ignoring them, she opened her purse and dug around for that gum she couldn't find earlier. She scooped her wallet and keys out of the purse, and shoved around some receipts while she looked for it. She found a piece under some loose change.

Hyun Tae was doing something on his phone, tapping and scrolling.

Chase unwrapped the piece of gum and folded it into her mouth. Ordinarily, a quiet car ride wouldn't bother her, but there was an odd tension in the air. After a few minutes, she asked, "Are you playing Sweet Smash?"

He turned the phone, so she could see. "I'm practicing Chinese."

"Of course you are." Just working on his third language.

Hyun Tae put the phone back in his pocket. "We're almost at your place."

Chase reached for the handle as Joon Suh pulled up in front of her apartment complex. "Thanks for the ride."

"Of course. And Chase," he said, ducking down to catch her gaze as she climbed out of the car.

Chase poked her head back through the doorframe. "Yeah?"

"Get rid of that document."

"Sure." He was really fixated on that file. Obviously, it all had something to do with his family's company and very little to do with getting an A in Biology. Either way, she would probably never know.

Chapter Thirteen

"Chase!"

Kiki's voice pierced through Chase's dream. Groggily, she forced herself to wake.

"Chase, it's nine-thirty!"

Her mind snapped awake. She started into an upright position, her bleary eyes trying to adjust. "What? What time?"

"Girl, you overslept!" Kiki's platinum blond hair looked white with the morning sun shining behind it. And then her words sunk in.

Chase gasped, flinging herself out of bed. *"What?!"*

Kiki handed her an outfit, looking sleep-drunk herself, and waved her friend off to the bathroom. "Go!"

Chase scrambled to get dressed. No time for a shower. Time to brush teeth? She made time for that one. No makeup though; she would be going for the earthy artist look, apparently. Kiki had given her a somewhat sheer, flirty pink chiffon top, dark jeans, and a lightweight scarf. California autumn, if there was such a thing. She stomped her feet into her brown knee-high boots and twisted her hair into a messy bun while Kiki handed her a plain bagel.

Chase held the bagel between her teeth as she gathered her purse, keys, and finally her portfolio bag. Before she could rush out the door, Kiki slammed a pair of sunglasses onto her head. Kiki's hazel eyes widened crazily. "You got this."

"I go' fis," Chase said, nodding with the bagel in her mouth.

Kiki gave a thumbs-up.

"Fank 'oo!" Chase called before leaving. What would she do without Kiki? She had almost slept through the art job fair.

As she gunned it through the small streets to the school auditorium, Chase's heart rate slowed down a little. She checked her wrist monitor. It was a little high but still blue. And she would make it there by ten.

She rushed through the auditorium doors two minutes before ten, paused to adjust her shirt and brush a few hairs from her face, and took a look around at the tables. Art programs, graphic designers, animation companies, gallery owners, fashion studios, book publishers, and art institutes–this was the biggest gathering of art-related professionals Chase had ever read about. Bates University had pulled out all the stops to encourage art students into their new program. And likely pulled all their strings to get these people here.

Chase took a deep breath and went to the first table. Video game design. Each table had a small line of students, but she had gotten there at the very start of the event, so it wasn't too crowded yet. This was her chance to speak with the professionals and have a conversation about what they were looking for and what she might offer them. The video game designer wasn't quite her style. They each knew it after a few lines of conversation.

She moved on, visiting the architecture firm, a gallery owner, and an art institute from New York. She showed some pieces from her portfolio to the institute director, and he gave her a form to fill out if she was interested in applying for their program. It was a thought, anyway. More importantly, he seemed to like her work.

When she came to the company Imagimation, her nerves went so taut, her whole body felt wound up. Animation. This is where she wanted to be, but she wasn't likely to get there right away. Still.

She approached the table, and an older woman with short, dark brown hair gave her a brisk smile and held out a hand. "Kara Winscot."

"Chase Bryant," she said, smiling back, shaking Kara's hand, and remembering to be firm and confident.

"Are you interested in animation?"

"Yes, it's my emphasis. I'd really like to find my way into this field at some point."

Kara's expression lit up after hearing that, and she held out a pamphlet to tell her about their company. They did a lot of animation support, contracted out by larger animation studios in need of extra hands. That meant there was a possibility of her digging into a bigger project at some point.

"So that's what we're about. Can I see your portfolio?" Kara asked.

Chase placed the folder on the table and laid out her charcoal drawings.

Kara's eyes flared as she looked at the first piece. "This is beautiful," she said frankly.

Chase tried to quell her happy grin.

"Really, this is amazing. The way you captured blurred city lights and buildings with charcoal...and then bent it around your subject here. It's like a domed lense. The proportions are perfect."

Chase grinned outright. "Thank you very much."

Kara tilted her head. "I feel like she's in the city, but not part of it. It's really intriguing."

Chase was pleased. That had been her goal.

145

As Kara flipped through the other pieces, all of them depicting her main subject with everything else out of focus around her, the animation professional started to nod her head. "We have waiting lists of interns who line up to come to our company. But I'll be honest with you Chase. I like this. I think you have potential."

Chase leaned against the table to steady her legs, fearing she might fall over. She could hardly think what to say. "Th-thank you. I really appreciate that."

"Can you bring a completed portfolio– including these works–to our building in L.A.? We'd like you to apply for an internship with our company."

She handed Chase an application. "Fill this out, and come to our office on November third." Kara scrolled through her phone. "There's a slot open at three p.m. for the intern applicants. Are you interested?"

"Absolutely," Chase said immediately. "I'll be there November third at three p.m."

"Our address is on the application." Kara gave her a smile that softened the harsh contours of her face. "I'm impressed, really. I look forward to your interview."

Chase shook her hand, in a daze. "Yes, me too. Thank you." As she gathered her pieces, putting them carefully back into her portfolio bag, Chase's ears went hot and her pulse accelerated rapidly. This couldn't be real, could it? An animation studio had actually offered her an interview to intern with them after she graduated. Unreal.

She met with people at the other tables, showing her work to schools and graphic artists, but her head was with Imagination, for the most part.

All she had to do was nail the portfolio.

Chapter Fourteen

Hyun Tae woke up late on purpose, something he rarely did back home. The sunlight warmed his bare back, just enough to make him lazy. Finally he sighed, rolling over and reaching for his phone on the nightstand to check the time. It was late, but that was okay. He didn't have any classes this early.

He sat on the edge of his bed and scrubbed his head, rubbing his eyes to wipe the sleep away. Reaching over, he grabbed the shirt he had thrown off the night before, when it had gotten too warm, and pulled it over his head. He padded downstairs into the kitchen. He grabbed a pitcher of cold water from the fridge and checked his phone. It was full, as usual.

He scrolled through his email accounts, all of them with various names and different purposes. The ones for school stood out from all the rest because they were in English, and he flicked over to his school file, so he could sort through them first before attending to the company. The first email was a reminder that he had passed his parking ticket class. He shook his head. What a waste of time that had been.

He was about to scroll past the next few subject lines when one of them caught his attention. His biochem class would be cancelled that day while they tried to get a substitute. What had happened to Professor Kruljac? A slow fear kindled in his chest as he clicked on it.

Professor Kruljac will be unable to teach the rest of the semester. A substitute professor will be assigned to your class by the next class time–all assignments and tests currently on the syllabus will remain due.

He stood up from his seat, the phone in his hand, staring down at the message. It could not be a coincidence that the professor was disappearing as soon as he and Joon Suh had installed that program.

He rubbed his forehead. What else could it be? He thought back to moment in the lab when Chase had walked in on him, the flash drive dangling from her keychain. She'd said she had Kruljac's files right in front of Bates's security cameras, when KimBio was still getting all the feeds. It was the reason he'd tried to shield her from them when she saw him in the lab, but it must not have worked. They had heard her and seen who she was. What if KimBio was doing damage control? What if they'd pulled the professor to try to cover their tracks? Would they try to get Chase's flash drive or her computer? Yesterday, when he had driven her home, he had hoped her innocent confession would come to nothing, but KimBio never let anything go.

Professor Kruljac had been carefully groomed for a year. They would never waste that kind of investment unless they were truly spooked about something. A young college student who had inadvertently taken sensitive information and then talked about it inside Bates might be enough. His only hope now was that all KimBio wanted from her was the file on her thumb drive. It was a slim hope.

He pulled on some jeans, a white T-shirt, and a simple black blazer, and grabbed his keys and wallet from his bedside table. By the time he hurried down the stairs, Joon Suh was in the kitchen, a cup of coffee in one hand, and his phone in the other. He looked up as Hyun Tae walked by.

"What's wrong?" he asked, his eyes cool, hiding any hint of curiosity.

"I might need you later. Don't go anywhere."

Joon Suh gave a slight nod of his head.

Hyun Tae didn't take a car. He just walked down the driveway and headed to the apartment next door. If he was lucky, she was still home. What happened after they retrieved the flash drive from her was another matter entirely. He should have been watching her. He should have known they would act. Maybe being away from his father had made him start to feel secure. He could never afford to do that.

He approached the stairs and then paused. He could hear voices on the other side, one of them yelling something, but it was friendly loud, not angry. He stepped away from the stairwell behind the privacy wall that led to the inner courtyard. Chase came out of the door, a bagel in her mouth and a large portfolio carrier on her shoulder, her sunglasses on her head. She ran down the sidewalk to her car. Wherever she was going, she was in a hurry.

The sunlight caught her hair, and he was suddenly reminded of the first time he'd seen her, on a phone screen held by her mother's trembling, nervous hand. Smiling at the camera, her blue eyes were stunningly clear. She had been pretty then. She was even prettier in person, fumbling over tea bags and trying to avoid conversation with him. He didn't blame Daniel for taking a chance with her. Hyun Tae just didn't have time for that sort of thing.

Hesitating for only a second, he slipped from his hiding place, waiting for her to drive away. He walked, watching as her car drove down the street for a few blocks and then took a turn down a university road. He couldn't be sure, but she looked as if she were going to the south side of campus. As he followed her route, he saw signs for the. art recruitment fair. Art students holding portfolios streamed down the sidewalk. She was an art major, so of course she would be at the recruitment fair.

He used the time as he walked to think. KimBio's thugs didn't waste time. They would probably go through her apartment looking for the flash drive. They wouldn't find it because she carried it with her. They would go after her. They might not even wait until the apartment was empty to go through it. Someone might even be there now. He had to keep Chase away from her apartment until he could be sure it wassafe. He was sure KimBio would be after her, not her roommates. Pulling his phone out of his pocket, he called Joon Suh.

Chapter Fifteen

Chase squinted against the glare of the noon sun as she exited the gymnasium. The light glinted off a giant metal column, and she slid her glasses off her head and onto the bridge of her nose. As she juggled her heavy portfolio bag and purse, digging around for her phone, a chirp that alerted her to a text. She found the phone in a random pocket of her purse and leaned to the side to adjust the straps of her bags and check the message.

"Joon Suh sent your laptop to a friend to fix. Do you want to pick it up?"

It was Hyun Tae. Chase tapped out a response. *"Sure. Should I meet you at your house?"*

"No, it's in one of the math labs–are you on campus?"

"Yep. Meet you there?"

"On my way. Meet me in front of the east wing."

"Okay, see you in a few. Thanks!"

Chase weighed the effort required to take her bag back to her car in the parking lot versus the effort of lugging it across campus. She'd have to carry a laptop back with her, so she rushed to the parking lot, unlocked her car, and threw her portfolio into the backseat. She tried not to get out of breath, but the high California sun beat down on her, and she didn't want to keep Hyun Tae waiting. Despite her best efforts, she got sweaty and winded.

She stopped in front of the double glass doors and checked her heart monitor. It was a little high. She took a deep breath through her nose.

"Everything okay?"

Chase jumped, and found Hyun Tae already leaning against the wall a few feet away. He had his hands in the pockets of his black blazer, which he wore over a white cotton V-neck shirt. A black laptop bag was slung over his shoulder.

She took a deep breath again. "Hey. Yeah, sorry I'm late."

"You're not." He stepped away from the wall and opened the door for her. "It's on the third floor."

"Thanks," she said, smiling and swiping a strand of hair away from her face. There had to be one time she could meet him face to face and actually be composed.

As she passed, his eyes flitted to her wristband. Chase averted her gaze and stepped into the building, expecting the usual wash of cool air to suck the heat off her blistering skin. But it was muggy inside.

Hyun Tae looked around the wide, tall space. "Looks like they're doing construction."

Chase noticed plastic tarp over some of the windows, and the floor was only half-tiled. "It's okay to go this way?"

"Looks like it," he said, shrugging. Hyun Tae led the way across the bright space to the elevator and punched the button.

The elevator dinged, and the doors opened.

They exchanged raised eyebrows. "Guess it's open," Chase said.

He gestured for her to go first, and then followed her, pressing the three once inside. The doors closed, and the elevator smoothly hummed into life, lifting them past the first floor.

Chase looked down, tapping the toe of her boot against her heel. Hyun Tae stood close to her, hands at his side and sharp features staring forward.

Suddenly Chase was jerked forward. She flung her hands out to catch herself, and an arm went around her shoulders to steady her. Hyun Tae stumbled, and they crashed against the wall as the elevator shuddered and jolted to a stop. The lights blinked out, leaving it almost completely dark.

Chase looked around, bewildered, and Hyun Tae supported her into a standing position. He punched the number three button. It didn't light up. He hit the button to open the doors, and nothing happened. There wasn't a phone on the elevator's panel, but there was an alarm button. He used his thumb to press the button. No sound, no light. Nothing.

Hyun Tae rubbed the back of his head.

"Um, what's going on?" Chase asked. The only light in the space came from the top of the elevator–some kind of phosphorescent glow sticks.

He craned his head around, up at the elevator ceiling, and then toward the closed doors. "I think we lost power."

Chase felt her heart start to hammer in her chest. "That sounds bad."

He must have heard something in her voice because he turned to look at her. Calmly, he responded, "It's not. We'll be fine. If they are doing work, it might be a temporary power outage. The power will come back soon."

Chase pulled out her phone. "We'll just call the school and let them know we're trapped."

"Good idea."

Chase pulled up her mom's number, but when she tried to call, she realized she had no service. Her phone wasn't picking up anything. "My phone is down," she said. "How about you?"

Hyun Tae pulled out his black phone, tapped the screen a few times, and then shook his head. "Mine too."

"Crap." Chase tapped her phone screen, pulling up numbers and browser windows. There had to be some kind of Wi-Fi she could pick up. Even if she couldn't get service...

"It's not working for me," he said. "You?"

"Nothing." Her pulse accelerated a little more.

"It's okay. Elevators are built with safety mechanisms."

She held up her phone. "How is this okay? It's really sketchy that I'm not even getting Wi-Fi."

He slid his bag to the floor. "Someone will see that this elevator got stuck. Try not to worry."

Chase couldn't bring herself to stop trying. Maybe her phone would suddenly pick up a signal. A droplet of sweat slid down the back of her neck. She uncoiled her thin scarf and stuffed it into her purse. It was getting hotter in the small box already.

As if thinking the same, Hyun Tae shrugged off his blazer, neatly laying it over the bar that ran along the back wall.

Chase tried not to look, but her eyes couldn't help themselves. They gravitated toward his arms, which were now perfectly emphasized by the tight sleeves of his white T-shirt. It was almost unfair that a man already blessed with those angular features had artistically sculpted arms.

She quickly looked back at her phone. Although she was starting to realize it was a waste of time. She stared at the doors.

"Don't," Hyun Tae said.

She dropped her phone into her purse and leaned against the adjacent wall, adopting Hyun Tae's relaxed pose with arms crossed. Her eyes flitted back to the doors.

Hyun Tae sighed loudly through his nose.

"If we could just get them op—"

"Just wait," he intoned, staring ahead.

"For what? No one knows we're here."

"Someone will come."

Rationally, she knew that they were in an elevator that was part of a large and busy math building. If the power had gone out, someone would fix it quickly. Or at the very least, a janitor would notice the elevator was stuck and call someone. But when?

"I think we took the wrong elevator," she said. "There's construction here. What if something is wrong with this elevator? Or no one comes here because it's sectioned off?"

His dark brown eyes met hers, and he straightened as well. Although his hands were at his side as if he did not care, his words were laced with genuine reassurance.

"Chase, we're going to be fine. It's annoying, but we're safe. Just try to relax."

"I'm relaxed," she lied.

His expression shifted slightly to indicate his doubt.

Chase slid down the wall until she was sitting, legs splayed out and head leaning back.

Hyun Tae sat down as well, so they were facing one another with the door to Chase's left. He bent one leg and balanced his wrist on it, letting his fingers dangle.

Chase sighed and rolled her head to stare at the door. *How do I always get stuck with this guy?*

He didn't seem bothered by the whole situation, and he closed his eyes with his head lean back against the elevator wall.

What, you're taking a nap right now? What if we suddenly plunge to our deaths? That probably counts as dying in your sleep, actually. I mean if I have to die in a nasty elevator accident, maybe it would be better to...

Chase's stomach growled loudly, practically echoing off the metal sheeting.

Hyun Tae cracked one eye open, the corner of his mouth twitching up.

Chase brought her knees to her chest. She should have eaten a better breakfast.

Hyun Tae sat forward, unbuckling the clasps of his shoulder bag and rifled through it for a moment. He pulled out a decent-sized cooler bag. As he unzipped it, the smell of fresh turkey sandwiches wafted through the air. He pulled one out and held it out to her. It was in a brown paper sleeve, and it looked kind of like a fancy cafe sandwich.

Chase held up her hands. "I don't want to eat your lunch."

"I have two."

"That's still eating half your lunch."

He bounced it in the air. "It's better than listening to your stomach. It's loud."

She winced. "Oh. Well, thanks." She took it, and she was pretty sure drool nearly fell from her mouth before she took a bite. It was the best turkey sandwich she had ever had.

He also tossed her a bag of chips and an apple. They finished their lunches in silence, and Chase decided to save her chips in case they were in the elevator for a long time. She pulled out her phone. Still no service. With her head leaning against the wall, and the muggy warmth combined with her full stomach, Chase suddenly felt exhausted. Her eyes grew heavy. She fell into a restless sleep, where she knew her mouth kept dropping open, and she would surface to consciousness just long enough to snap it closed. And her head kept dropping. At some point, she found a comfortable position, and she fell into her dreams.

When she woke, it was with a start. Like those dreams where she had stepped off a ledge and startled herself awake. She realized that she had been sleeping on Hyun Tae's shoulder. He leaned back to look down at her.

She straightened up, away from his shoulder. "Sorry."

His dark brown eyes stared into hers, but he didn't say anything reassuring.

She cleared her throat, looking around the elevator. The dim lighting gave no indication of what time of day it was.

"It's four," he said.

She stretched and sighed. "Phones?"

He shook his head. "They don't work yet."

Chase kneaded her forehead. "So we're still stuck."

Hyun Tae stretched out on the ground, putting his bag under his head. "Looks like it." He closed his eyes, his face visibly relaxing into slumber. Chase dug around in her purse for something to do. She found some receipts and a pen, so she scribbled on the back, sketching out a few ideas for the completion of her portfolio for Imagination. Blue pen wasn't exactly her most inspiring medium, though.

After a while, she looked up to find Hyun Tae lying very still, his breathing even and arms slack. He must have actually fallen asleep. She put her stuff back in her purse and stood in front of the door again. She couldn't stand not knowing if they were right in front of the floor and could easily just climb out of the oven-like box they were stuck in.

She wiggled her fingers into the gap between the doors, and then she angled her body, so she could give the door a good tug. It was difficult to get a good grip. She thought she felt a little give, but her strength alone wasn't opening them. She readjusted her grip so her fingers went deeper between the doors and heaved.

She lost her grip, and her fingers scraped against the door. She fell back against the wall with a bang.

Hyun Tae sat up as Chase grabbed her hand and hissed in pain.

Chase shook her hand out and then squeezed her middle finger, trying not to actually groan out loud. She had ripped back her fingernail. Red dripped onto her brown boot. She examined the throbbing finger to find it steadily dripping blood from under the nail.

Hyun Tae stood. "You tried to open the door."

"Yeah."

He reached out. "Let me see." Chase tentatively held out her hand, and he tugged her wrist, so she stepped closer. She recognized the scent of his deodorant or soap from that time he had come over for tea, and it was almost intoxicating. She subconsciously leaned into him. He peered at the nail. "It's not all the way off."

He lightly touched it, and she jerked. "Ah! Stop, ow!"

"Sorry." He kept his hold on her hand and looked around. "Do you have something to wrap it with?"

"No. Just some gum and receipts." She tried to wiggle her hand free. "It's okay; I'll just use my shirt or something."

The blood was starting to trickle down her hand and onto his. She must have really ripped it hard if it was bleeding that much. He released her hand and bent down to dig through his black bag. He came back with a napkin from the lunch box, and he gently straightened her finger so he could wrap it around the bleeding nail.

Chase held onto it, shuddering more at the thought that she had ripped her nail off than at the actual pain.

Hyun Tae gave her an exasperated look.

She huffed and looked down, rubbing the spot of blood on her boot on the back leg of her jeans. *Well this is turning out to be a spectacular afternoon.*

After Chase had eaten her bag of chips and resolutely ignored a very full bladder, she showed Hyun Tae how to play a four-letter-word game involving the strategy of changing one letter at a time to get from one word to another. He seemed to like it because his vocabulary was diverse, but English was still his second language. "It's good practice," he said, smiling. He didn't even seem to mind that Chase beat him soundly every time.

Eventually, even Hyun Tae started to check the time on his phone. "It's getting late," he muttered.

Chase paced the small elevator, which was beginning to feel more and more confining. She had to sit down when the urge to pee nearly became overwhelming. "I'm not going to make it."

Hyun Tae seemed to pity her because he suddenly looked agitated, his hands low on his hips. "*Jincharo, ge odiseo?*"

Someone banged on the elevator doors. "Hello? Is someone in there?"

"Yes!" Chase said, slamming her palm against the door. "Hello! We're in here! Can you call for help?"

There was some unintelligible mumbling, and then a loud male voice called, "Is anyone hurt?"

"No! We're fine!" Chase shouted back.

"Someone will restore power soon! Just hold on," the man responded.

Chase leaned against the doors, overwhelmed with relief. She looked over her shoulder to find Hyun Tae's shoulders drooping with relief as well.

A few minutes later, the lights blinked back on, the buttons once again glowed white, and the elevator hummed to life and finished its route up to the third floor. As soon as the doors rolled open, Chase hopped over the threshold to safety, clutching her bag to her chest. Hyun Tae followed without hesitation, apparently without any fear that the elevator would suddenly drop.

A middle-aged man greeted them, puffing out a loud breath of air as if he had been holding it. "Is everyone all right? Just the two of you in there?"

Chase nodded, looking around the dim, empty hallways of the math department. "We're okay. What happened?"

"This building is under maintenance," the janitor said, sweat beading on the bald crown of his head. "I'm so sorry. The power shouldn't have gone off, but those things happen in construction. This area was off-limits."

Chase couldn't help sliding a perturbed glance toward Hyun Tae. "Thank you for turning it back on."

The janitor nodded. "I'm just glad I was here."

Hyun Tae shook hands with him. "Thank you for helping. Can we grab her laptop before we go?"

"Sure, sure," the janitor said. "I'll help you get it and then lock up behind you."

"Thank you."

"Do we need to tell someone about the elevator?" Chase asked.

"I've contacted the project manager, and I'm the supervisor for the maintenance

technician staff, so we'll shut it down until we can call in a technician for the elevator. Again, I'm so sorry. We should have properly labeled it as a construction zone."

"It's fine," Hyun Tae said, looking around her as if he had lost interest in the conversation. "Let's get your laptop, Chase. Do you have cell service now?"

Chase checked her phone as they walked. Full bars again, thank goodness. "Yeah, but first I'm using a bathroom."

Hyun Tae led them down the halls, and after a quick stop at the restroom, they found the math lab. "Three twenty three, this is it."

The janitor unlocked the door for them and then flicked on the lights. Hyun Tae looked around the room, his black jacket still slung over one arm and his hair tousled after the long hours stuck in the elevator.

Poor guy. He did me a favor to help me get my laptop and got us stuck in an elevator all day. He'll probably never speak to me again.

Hyun Tae came to stop at a locker and then spun the dial on the lock deftly to open it. He held up her laptop. "Got it."

"Thanks," Chase said weakly.

The janitor led them down the stairs, and when they reached the front doors, he apologized again and asked if they were okay, and when Chase assured him they were, he locked the doors from the inside and pulled out his phone to call someone.

Chase and Hyun Tae walked down the steps, and the dark campus was more or less deserted, with random stragglers making their way from the few buildings that remained open late. The sun had already set, and the moon peeked out above the library building ahead of them. Chase took a deep breath of clear air, and a little shiver went down her arms.

She realized they were walking toward the parking lot. He didn't offer, but she guessed that he was seeing her to her car. "You probably have to be somewhere. I can get to my car okay."

"I don't mind."

She could almost see him digging around in his vast etiquette library, so he could do what he thought was the right thing—walk her to her car. "Do you know where your car is?" he asked.

It was a valid question. It had been all day since she'd seen it. "Actually, I do."

He stared at her for a moment, as if assessing her chances for success at reaching her vehicle without his help, and then gave her a polite smile. "Goodnight, Chase."

"Night."

He walked away from her without looking back. She turned on her phone to see her messages. She had a text from her mom and two from her sister with cute pictures of her kids covered in glitter. And then the text she had really been looking for.

"I'm back."

Chase smiled. *"Hey! Sorry I didn't respond until now. It's a long story. How are you?"*

Daniel answered almost immediately. *"Are you okay?"*

"Yeah, yeah. I'm fine. Just hungry, so I'm going to get something to eat."

"I'll meet you somewhere. Where are you?"

"Cool! I'm on campus, heading to the south side parking lot. I can drive."

" I'm very proud of you."

She rolled her eyes, still grinning. *"Har-har. Where do you want to eat?"*

"I'm in the mood for pizza. Japan doesn't make it like the US does."

"Sounds amazing. Call me when you get to the parking lot. Or should I pick you up?"

"Nope, I'm already on my way. I'll call you when I get there."

"See you then!"

Chase slipped her phone into her bag, and as she neared the parking lot, searched around for her keys. Her pace slowed as she came around the side of the auditorium and down a double set of stairs shrouded by fluffy shrubs and squat, healthy trees. She paused in the middle of the stairs to zip her bag pocket.

Footsteps came quickly down the stairs behind her, and in the next moment, her arms were wrenched painfully behind her back. Someone gave her a rough shove, and she stumbled to the side, into the dark copse of greenery hidden from the yellow lights on the other side.

Another hard push slammed her against the trunk of a tree, the rough surface of it scraping through her thin shirt and stinging her cheek. Her keys were wrenched from her grasp while a leather-gloved hand clamped down on her mouth just as she tried to scream. A man pressed his body against her back, trapping her between him and the tree. She tried to struggle, to kick, but it was no use.

There was another man because he yanked her bag off her shoulder while the first held her in place. He rifled through the contents. Chase tried to bite the first man's hand, but he slammed her head against the tree, growling something she couldn't make out. Her vision swam, and her heart rate jumped as she gasped for air through her nose.

Her temple throbbed, but she knew that wasn't what was making her head go fuzzy. The alarmed beeping of her heart monitor sounded through the quiet night, echoing the chaos within in her. The second man scrabbled at her wrist, trying to get it off. The beeping became more insistent. It became harder to breathe. She feared she might throw up, and her body buckled.

The second attacker succeeded in ripping off her heart monitor. And then it was deathly quiet.

Chapter Sixteen

Walking away from Chase had been hard. She had looked tired, the flimsy napkin bandage on her finger dark with dried blood. Her heart monitor had stayed blue the entire time. Although he hadn't expected to be trapped for that long, she had handled the stress remarkably well. Joon Suh had taken the job of keeping her out of her apartment today seriously. It couldn't have been easy to hack into the building's elevator system but his long-time friend had pulled off more difficult feats than that.

Joon Suh answered right away.

"What did you find in her apartment?" Hyun Tae asked.

"A couple of bugs. I think I got them all," Joon Suh said with bored confidence.

"You think?"

"It's not easy. I'm ninety-nine point nine percent sure I got them all. If anything is left, it's audio, not a camera."

Hyun Tae switched the phone to his other ear, as if he would be able to hear better news that way. "There were cameras?"

"Well, yeah."

"Do I want to know where?"

Joon Suh sighed. "It's a girl's apartment. What do you think? It's clean now."

"How did you get past the roommates?"

"They all had classes, and I only needed twenty minutes to sweep for cameras. As long as Chase wasn't there, they're okay. KimBio only wants Chase and the file."

"What kind of footage did KimBio get?" A cold rush of fear washed over him at the thought of what might have been recorded. Lives were ruined this way.

The smirk sounded so clearly, Joon Suh could have been right next to him. "Nothing that would go viral."

"So easy to predict. Almost sucks all the fun out of it." He paused. "Joon Suh."

"Yes."

"I can only hold my piss for seven hours, not eight."

Joon Suh laughed and hung up.

He was almost to his car when he heard a strange sound, a beeping that was rapidly

172

accelerating, the pace frantic and dangerously high. Chase.

He ran back, tuned in to the beeping, his eyes searching in the dark for her. He saw two figures in black, one of them shoving Chase against a tree. The beeping stopped, and he had to temper a burst of panic. One of the thugs had just removed the monitor. Controlling his anger, he focused on coming up behind the one who was holding it. Keeping the guy holding Chase against the tree in his peripheral vision, he snatched the black baseball cap off the first one and slipped it on his own head and then swept his heel down on the back of the assailant's knee. As the man folded to the ground, Hyun Tae kicked him on the side of the head. The guy finished falling to the ground and didn't get back up.

Hyun Tae had already turned to the guy holding Chase, ducking his head to hide his face. The thug turned to confront Hyun Tae, and he snatched the man's wrist, breaking his hold on Chase with a twist of the assailant's arm. The man stepped away from her, his other arm flailing out. Pivoting on his heel until he was behind the man, Hyun Tae brought the captured arm up painfully high. The man jerked his head back, trying to head butt Hyun Tae in the face. Using the man's backward momentum, Hyun Tae grabbed his throat and bent him down to the ground on his back. Sparing a glance at

Chase, who was leaning against the tree and staring at the men, he made a quick decision. He didn't know how much she could see, but he didn't want to waste any more time with this guy. He brought his elbow down on the man's nose, feeling the cartilage give. The man cried out and rolled over, clutching his broken nose.

The man he'd kicked in the head was getting up, although not doing it very well, swaying on his feet and feeling around for something to hold on to. Striding over to the man, Hyun Tae reached into his jacket and found the gun he knew would be there. He released the clip and let it fall into his hand. He put the empty gun in his jacket.

Leaning close, Hyun Tae said in Korean, "Take your friend and get out of here. Now."

The man with the broken nose had managed to crawl over to them, still holding his face.

Moving carefully, the man with the disarmed gun reached down and pulled his accomplice up. Hyun Tae kept his face averted, his head down. They stepped away from him, staggering off into the dark.

Hyun Tae turned to Chase, stuffing the clip in his back pocket. She had crumpled to the ground, one hand clutching her chest as she sucked in air. Her hair had tumbled out of the bun she had it in

174

earlier, and it fell around her face in strands that stuck to the perspiration on her cheeks and neck. Her heart monitor lay on the ground, the numbers glowing a faint blue. He picked it up and walked over to her. She didn't say anything; her eyes on the mulch under her pale fingers.

He crouched down next to her, and after a moment's hesitation, shifted his body so he could lean her shoulders against his chest to take her weight. He took her right hand, trembling so hard it shook her fingers, and slipped the monitor on her wrist, closing the clasp. He waited, watching the monitor catch up to her heartbeat, the numbers plateauing out at 215. "You okay?" he asked.

"Just a minute," she said, her voice low. "Just a minute."

The monitor beeped loudly, as if affronted that its user had suffered distress. The numbers blinked down to 208.

200.

175, and suddenly blue.

After a few seconds, her pulse stayed steady at 165. From what he'd heard from Daniel, this was a fairly safe rate for her. "Okay?" he asked again.

Her body sagged, and she kept a hand on her heart. "Yeah."

The ringing of her phone echoed through the silence, and Hyun Tae turned to find it had been thrown a few feet away when the attackers had looted through her belongings. He shifted her again, and she leaned against the tree without complaint. He reached for the phone, and to his relief, found it was Daniel. He swiped the screen to answer. "Daniel."

Daniel answered. "Hyun Tae?"

Hyun Tae spoke in Korean. "I need you to meet me at the stairwell to the south lot. They attacked Chase. She's okay, but I want to go after them, and she shouldn't be alone."

"You said you were going to watch out for her."

Hyun Tae switched the phone to his other ear. "She's okay."

"What else has happened to her?"

"Are you coming?"

"Try to keep her out of your sick family problems for thirty seconds until I get there."

"Don't be so dramatic," Hyun Tae muttered before hanging up.

"Shouldn't we call the police?" Chase asked from behind him.

He turned around and came to crouch before her again. He shrugged his jacket off and put it around

176

her shoulders. She let him, staring up at his face, her blue eyes dark in the moonlit shadow of the tree.

He wanted to talk her out of calling the police, but he didn't know how. He rubbed his forehead and realized he was still wearing the baseball cap. He kept it on. "I think I know who those guys are, and the police aren't going to be able to catch them."

"I really think we should call," she said.

He calculated how much time it would take for the police to respond versus Daniel arriving. It might work out.

"You're probably right," he said, handing the phone to her.

She looked down at her phone and then hit 9-1-1.

He stayed next to her on the ground as they waited, though what he really wanted to do was pace. Chase was curled up, her knees tucked in and her arms wrapped around her body.

The Z4 pulled up to the parking lot, and Hyun Tae stood up, relieved. Daniel ran over to them, and Chase stood up to meet him. Daniel reached out to steady her, his eyes concerned. "Are you hurt?"

"No, I'm okay," she said and gave him a small smile.

An odd stab of irritation needled at Hyun Tae. What was she smiling at Daniel for? He hadn't done anything to help.

"The police will be here soon," he told Daniel, hoping he understood that he had to go find out who they were.

"Got it."

Hyun Tae turned and ran across the parking lot toward the main street, where he'd seen the two men take off. Letting his pent-up anxiety loose, he ran, measuring how long he'd had to wait and how far they might have gone, his eyes scanning the cars that passed. It was crazy to think they would still be around somewhere, but he had to try. He needed to know for sure who had sent them.

They would have parked close if they were still here. A car door slammed, and a bunch of students got out of an SUV, laughing loudly. He slowed down, not wanting to attract attention. A small breeze rustled through the palm trees overhead as he approached the crowd, keeping his head down. They flowed past him as if he weren't there.

Still looking at all the cars, his hopes sank. Then, in a split second, his brain registered the black, nondescript sedan several cars behind the SUV, and the two men sitting inside of it, one of them with a cell phone up to his ear. Hyun Tae had one moment to avert his face and change direction. He'd found them.

He circled back around to the car, pulling his shirt up over his nose. He had a moment of deja vu. He had never been the victim then, nor the attacker, yet it was all familiar, as he if he was the understudy finally stepping into a role he had hoped never to play. Dark memories from his childhood surfaced.

Hyun Tae turned a corner, coming up behind the man on his cell phone—a beefy-looking thug he hadn't seen earlier. He must have heard Hyun Tae because he spun around, and with no hesitation, dropped his phone to heave a punch at Hyun Tae's face.

Hyun Tae dodged, blocked with his forearm, and, in one swift motion, hooked his right arm around the man's, twisted around behind him, and braced his right hand on the man's shoulder, effectively locking his punching arm up behind him. With his left arm, Hyun Tae strangled the man's neck, causing him to gurgle in anger. Two kicks to the backs of his knees brought the thug face down on the ground, struggling, but useless.

The car doors slammed, and without looking up, Hyun Tae released his chokehold on the prone assailant, so he could draw the gun from the back of his waistband and point it at the men who now froze just in front of the car. Granted, the gun wasn't loaded, but they didn't know that.

"Who sent you?" Hyun Tae asked in Korean.

The man spit blood onto the ground.

Hyun Tae put the cold muzzle against the back of his head. "Just thought I'd ask first. Don't move." Hyun Tae used his right hand to snatch the guy's wallet from his back pocket. He flipped it open to find a wad of cash and only one card inside. With his thumb, he slid the card out of its sleeve. Unmarked, white key card with three numbers on the bottom right corner.

A KimBio access card. He had seen them dozens of times on security guards and contractors. Hyun Tae tossed the wallet away from them, standing slowly with the gun still drawn. "Get out of my sight before I unload your clip on you."

They scrambled to obey, their shoes crunching on gravel as they rushed back to their car, slammed the doors, and screeched away from the curb.

With a sigh of disgust, Hyun Tae dropped the gun and lowered his shirt from his face. They were definitely sent by his father. Taking his phone out of his pocket, he dialed Joon Suh.

He heard the sound of someone's ringtone around the corner. It was a popular Korean boy band, crooning some cheesy love song.

Joon Suh stepped out of the shadows, his phone in one hand and a bottle of water in the other. He took a sip and stared at Hyun Tae. "*Gwaenchanh-a?*"

180

"How long have you been following me?"

"I'm always following you." Joon Suh shrugged a shoulder and his backpack slid off. He unzipped it and knelt down, picked up the gun and put it in the backpack. He offered Hyun Tae the water.

After a long drink, Hyun Tae gave it back, asking, "How is Chase? Did she give a police report?"

"Yes, but the police want to talk to you."

Weariness setting in, he nodded.

"So were they who you thought they were?" Joon Suh asked as they walked.

Hyun Tae went to rub his hair and found the ball cap still on his head. He took it off and threw it on the ground. "Yes, they had a keycard. KimBio."

"Messy."

"Yeah."

"Did they recognize you?"

Thinking back, Hyun Tae didn't think they had. "No."

Joon Suh kept quiet while they walked back to get Chase, and Hyun Tae let his mind flood with unpleasant memories: things done in the dark, secrets he wasn't supposed to know, and the desire to change it all. It was going to take a long time, but he'd learned to be patient.

They walked back to the mostly empty parking lot, where two police cars were parked next to a big tree.

Daniel stood next to Chase, who fiddled with her heart monitor as a police officer talked to her.

When he and Joon Suh approached them, Chase looked up, and for a brief moment, he thought he saw relief in her eyes.

The officers asked him about the attack, and he answered as methodically as possible, leaving out the part where he'd taken the gun, trying not to be distracted by the thought that Joon Suh was wearing a backpack with a handgun stuffed inside. Joon Suh didn't seem to be bothered by it, standing calmly and chatting with the other officers as if he didn't have anything more dangerous than a laptop and some notebooks strapped to his back. He was a brilliant poker player.

The officers said Hyun Tae was lucky none of them had guns and that he should have avoided a confrontation. He didn't argue, but he didn't agree with them either.

The officers offered to take them home, but Daniel said he could get Chase to her apartment, and Hyun Tae decided to walk home with Joon Suh.

When Daniel opened his car door, Chase got in and slumped in the front seat, drawing her knees up.

Hyun Tae leaned down to her window. "You okay?"

"Yes. Just tired."

Hyun Tae and Joon Suh walked back to the house, though Hyun Tae had to exercise all his self-control not to call his father and demand answers. Hopefully Chase wouldn't mind hanging out with them for a while. Her apartment wasn't an option. He had no idea who else his father would send. He also wondered how long he could keep protecting her without telling her anything.

They walked up to the front door, and Hyun Tae was pleased to find it locked. Daniel wasn't taking any chances. Before Hyun Tae hit the security pad, Joon Suh put a hand on his arm. "I haven't checked on Chase's roommates in a while."

Hyun Tae realized he hadn't even thought about them. "Good idea. I'll see you when you get back."

Joon Suh slipped away into the shadows.

When Hyun Tae walked in, Daniel was sitting on the coffee table facing Chase, who sat on the couch. A pile of gauze and bandages from a medical kit lay next to him. He was working on Chase's hand, stopping for a moment to acknowledge them with a nod. Chase had been staring down at the torn nail with a frown of concentration. She also looked up at them and gave a small smile. She still looked pale, but she seemed calm.

"How is your finger?" Hyun Tae asked her.

She gave a small shrug. "It's just a nail."

Daniel tilted his head and said in a low voice, "It looks like it hurts." He picked up a roll of medical tape

183

and pulled off a length of it and then ripped it with his teeth. He taped the finger and turned it to inspect his work. "That should stay."

Chase wiggled the bandaged finger. "You should go to med school. You have mad tape skills."

Daniel tried not to show it, but Hyun Tae saw the corners of his mouth turn in a pleased smile before he could slip into nonchalant mode. He really liked this girl.

He had to admit Daniel had a way of putting her at ease, which was probably a good thing. He went to the kitchen and started the coffee pot, watching it while his mind turned over the day's events. He'd managed to keep Chase out of her apartment and harm's way, but only by trapping her in an elevator. How was he supposed to keep an eye on her? He couldn't count on Daniel; as much as Daniel wanted to be around for her, he couldn't. His life was way too complicated for that.

He didn't think the gun-toting thugs had meant to hurt Chase. It looked as if they were searching for her thumb drive and the file she wasn't supposed to have. Although that was a little desperate. Didn't his father realize that once information had been lifted, it could go anywhere? His father was a brutal man, and shrewd, but he was getting old. He was still doing things the old way.

His father had made the professor disappear—carted him off somewhere to get him away from Bates before he could do any more damage. Trying to get the file from a clueless college student was just pointless. He had to show his father that Chase was not a threat somehow. Or at least give a reason for his dad to leave her alone. And would it help if they told her what was going on and why?

The coffee finished dribbling into the pot, and he began pouring it into one of the cups. Daniel came in the kitchen. "Chase asked if we had chamomile tea."

Hyun Tae stared at him for a moment, trying to pull his thoughts away from his father's machinations. "Do we have that?"

Daniel reached up to the cabinet next to him and pulled open the door. Boxes of tea were stacked in neat rows with various labels, some in Korean and some in English. He picked through them until he found it and slid it across the counter.

Hyun Tae opened a cabinet and took out the teapot, filling it with water. He fired up the gas stove and set the teapot down on the burner a little harder than necessary. She didn't even like tea. She drank soda.

"Your angry tea is going to give her indigestion," Daniel said in Korean.

Hyun Tae scowled at him and went to the fridge to grab a Coke, handing it to Daniel. "She probably won't mind this."

Daniel found a glass, threw in a few ice cubes, and poured the soda. He thrust the glass back at Hyun Tae. "You give it to her. I'll make the tea. With warm kindness. I don't want her stomach to get upset."

Hyun Tae took the soda and shuffled into the living room, experiencing an emotion that he hadn't in a long time. Guilt. He didn't want to tell her that his family was to blame for what had happened to her.

Chase sat on the couch, cradling her phone on her stomach, looking at her bandage. He offered the soda stiffly, like a robotic vending machine.

She took it, with a small "Thank you."

She sipped the soda, looking up at him through her thick lashes. She actually looked kind of dainty, until she began drinking it in earnest, gulping it down like she'd been in an arid desert on the edge of survival for days. She wiped her mouth with the back of her hand when it was empty, avoiding his gaze. Then her eyes widened, and she gave a small hiccup.

He frowned at her. "Your stomach is going to explode if you do that. Just let it out."

186

Her cheeks turned pink.

He clapped her on the back and she burped loudly. She put her hand back over her mouth, looking up at him in surprise.

Daniel came in with a cup of tea and a cup of coffee, and he gave Hyun Tae an annoyed glance. "What did you do to her?"

"Me? Nothing. She burped."

"Soda," she explained, her cheeks still pink.

Daniel sat next to her on the couch and offered her the steaming cup of tea. "Here. This will calm your nerves."

She took a sip and set the cup down on the plate, biting her lip and avoiding Hyun Tae's gaze. "Thank you both for helping me. You've been very kind."

"About that..." Daniel began, and hesitated.

She stood up abruptly, looking chagrined. "I'm not staying. I didn't mean to impose."

He put a hand out to stop her. "No, I'm trying to ask if you'll stay over. I think we'll both feel better if we know you are in a safe place."

"Oh! Well, I don't know. I mean, I should get back to my apartment. And I don't want to impose on you."

Hyun Tae didn't want her going back to her apartment, not yet. "If we are asking you to stay, it isn't an imposition. Right?"

"Sure. I mean, no. Actually, I don't really mind."

At that moment, the front door opened, and Joon Suh stepped into the living room. "I went to the apartment."

Hyun Tae quirked on eyebrow. Joon Suh used his words so sparingly he sometimes neglected to give any useful information at all. "Is everything okay?"

"Yes. I'm tired of watching them. Chase should stay here tonight."

Chase glanced at Daniel, and they both shared a smile, which looked sappy, in Hyun Tae's opinion.

Daniel picked up the teacup and offered to her. "Great."

Chase slid down the couch and sat next to Daniel.

"I'll get some blankets," Hyun Tae said, before she could change her mind.

Upstairs, he pulled the down comforter off his bed and grabbed a couple of pillows. His phone buzzed, and he swiped Joon Suh's message open.

She can use my shower. I'm using the library right now.

Hyun Tae considered Joon Suh's offer. If they were going to have her stay overnight, they could at least make her comfortable. He dragged the comforter down to the living room and laid the pillows out on the floor.

Daniel was re-examining her bandage as if he'd just casted her for a broken femur. "It looks like it will stay."

Hyun Tae cleared his throat, and they looked up at him. "Joon Suh says you can use his shower. He's in the library, so he's not in his room."

Chase shook her head. "I don't have anything to wear. I'll be fine."

Hyun Tae knew she probably wanted one. They'd both been stuck in an elevator for eight hours, and it had been a long day. "You can borrow our clothes."

Daniel stood up and offered her his hand. "Come on, I'll let you choose something from my room. I have a bunch of sweats and T-shirts.

She took his hand and followed him up the stairs, walking on the balls of her small bare feet, like a dancer. He'd never noticed the way she walked before.

A while later, while Hyun Tae was pretending to watch a documentary on alien mummies, Daniel came back down and grabbed the remote, turning on the TV. "She looks tired," he said.

"She'll probably crash after her shower. It's been a tough day," Hyun Tae said.

Daniel scratched his chin and then said in Korean, without looking at Hyun Tae, "What are you going to do about keeping her safe?"

"I will find a way to let my father know she's not a threat. Or give him a reason to leave her alone."

189

"Like what?"

"I don't know yet. I'm thinking."

"She could have been hurt tonight. Well, she was."

"The fingernail thing happened in the elevator because she tried to open it herself. That wasn't my fault."

Daniel shook his head, obviously displeased. "Joon Suh said he found cameras in her apartment. How long is that kind of stuff going to be happening to her?"

"Not anymore. I'm going to take care of it." Hyun Tae said in a low voice, even though he was speaking Korean, looking over at the stairs in case she came down.

"What a mess," Daniel said, though there wasn't as much blame in his voice as there could have been. He knew what Hyun Tae's father was like.

They sat in silence, watching the channels slide by on the menu. They landed on a sports channel and sat there watching a soccer game neither of them cared about. They didn't hear Chase come down the stairs, her bare feet too soft to hear until she was in the living room.

She'd tucked Daniel's T-shirt into the too-big pajama pants, reminding Hyun Tae of the old ladies

190

who walked circuits around the city park near his home in Seoul. Her face was clean, and she looked very young without makeup. Her long blond hair was wet and combed straight down her back, and she smelled like Joon Suh, his soap wafting off her skin. She sat on the floor next to the couch, touching her wet hair self-consciously as she watched the game with them.

Daniel slid off the couch to sit next to her and bumped her knee with his. "You okay?"

She covered a yawn with her hand and bumped his knee back. "Yep."

She slumped back against the couch, relaxed. She was quiet, her eyes a little glazed as she watched the game. Hyun Tae could have started a countdown as her eyes grew heavier. She blinked long and slow, and then her eyes closed, her head falling. She jerked her chin back up.

Daniel nodded toward the pillows. "Tired?"

She gave a sleepy smile and sighed. "Yeah."

She crawled over to the comforter and snuggled under it, nudging her face into the pillow. "Sorry," she said, slurring the words, her eyes closing and staying that way

After a while Daniel looked over at him. "Out."

Hyun Tae smirked tiredly and stood up, stretching. "I'm taking a shower. You staying down here for a while?"

"Yep."

Chase sighed in her sleep, and they both looked over at her and then at each other. "We can sleep down here and keep an eye on her," Daniel said.

Hyun Tae slid his phone out of his pocket and checked the security system. "*Gureo.*" He liked to think he would stay awake like some guardian sentinel, but he knew he was too tired. He would probably pass out soon. This girl was exhausting.

Chapter Seventeen

Chase thought she might be hallucinating. She had that confusing sensation of waking in a place she didn't recognize.

Everything was bright and white, and she had somehow ended up on a floor, her shoulders sore and body aching like she had spent the entire night at the gym. But at least she was warm, cocooned in soft blankets and fluffy pillows. And Hyun Tae slept beside her, his dark lashes fanned out over his creamy skin, lips parted slightly as he breathed steadily in and out.

It came back to her suddenly. She was in the Korean house. She shifted slightly, not sure if she wanted to snuggle deeper into her blankets, or if she should crawl away from Hyun Tae. Memories of the night before assailed her, and she opted for burying her face in the down pillow beneath her. It was too much to take on mentally all at once. She was grateful Hyun Tae had been there the moment those men had chosen to mug her, but it all was too surreal.

When she lifted her head from the pillow, two brown eyes blinked groggily back at her. Hyun Tae raised his head a fraction, his thick black hair disheveled and brow furrowed in confusion.

Chase froze, not sure how to react.

He kind of grimaced, as if he too realized they had all fallen asleep on the floor together the night before.

His eyes met hers, a definite twinkle in their depths. With a cat-like stretch, he arched his back and reached his elbows above his ears. Then he winced and turned his arm over to peer at a dark bruise that had formed on the outside edge of his forearm.

"Hey, are you two awake?" Daniel asked from the kitchen.

Chase turned to find Daniel shuffling from the kitchen area into the spacious living room. He had morning hair like Hyun Tae's, the redness of it glinting in the bright sunlight that streamed through the many windows. He wore flannel pajama pants slung low on his hips, and a red T-shirt that was only partially tucked into the front of the pants.

He absently twirled a spatula between his fingers. "I didn't want to wake you," he said to Chase. "Hungry?"

Her heart skipped a beat, and it had nothing to do with her medical issue. "Yeah, I could eat."

"Great."

194

As he walked back into the kitchen, Chase did a quick appearance check in a mirror hanging on the wall. Yikes. Crumpled, oversized white T-shirt tucked into Daniel's pajama pants, which were cinched up around her waist to keep them from falling down. She honestly didn't want to know what had happened to her hair.

She reached down to pull up the long socks she had borrowed from Hyun Tae, hopping as she did, and then she hurried to join Daniel in the kitchen.

Daniel stood in front of the stove, working a few frying pans with pancakes, eggs, and bacon. He looked over and smiled, completely scattering her thoughts. He was just too perfect.

Hyun Tae walked in and peered over Daniel's shoulder for a moment and then mumbled something in Korean.

Daniel rolled his eyes. "Mrs. Hwan came, but I told her we could handle it."

Hyun Tae paused in the act of retrieving a glass from the cabinet. "She came here?"

"Yeah, but I told her...oh." Daniel and Hyun Tae both turned their gazes to Chase, who stood in front of the island.

Chase looked at each of them. "What?"

"Just..." Daniel started.

"Never mind," Hyun Tae said, as if brushing off an insignificant matter. He finished taking down three glasses and brought them to the table.

Was it a problem that she spent the night? She couldn't be the first girl. Not wanting to speculate any further, Chase took a seat at the glass, rectangular table. The smell of bacon made her stomach growl with anticipation. It was the thick, juicy kind with some kind of sweet glaze over it. Daniel set the butter dish next to the fluffy pancakes and then finally took a seat next to her.

Hyun Tae took the seat at the end of the table and piled food on his plate.

Daniel cleared his throat. "So about what happened last night."

Hyun Tae looked up from cutting pancakes, his eyes meeting Daniel's. "*Jigeum?*" he asked.

Daniel nodded. "She has a right to know."

With a sigh, Hyun Tae put his utensils back down and angled his body toward Chase.

She looked between the two of them. "What is it?"

"Your muggers last night," Hyun Tae said, seeming to choose his words carefully. "They were not random attackers."

Chase blinked. "Okay."

Daniel spoke up. "Hyun Tae filled me in on what happened during your field trip this week."

"Uh huh," Chase said, not exactly sure what he meant.

"When you saw me in the computer lab at the research facility, I was downloading a program to the Bates network."

"Right," she said slowly.

"And then you mentioned that you had seen a document proving that Bates and KimBio work together. You said it in front of a lot of cameras."

Chase's eyes went to her purse, where her keys dangled, the thumb drive innocently hidden beneath them.

"KimBio and Bates do not work together," Daniel said. "They are competing to finish the same research."

Chase let that sink in. "So what I saw...that wasn't a collaboration."

"It was research theft," Hyun Tae said. He gave her a steady stare, as if assessing her reaction. "Professor Kruljac, our biology teacher, has been funneling research data from Bates to KimBio through a program."

Chase went rigid.

"Not Hyun Tae," Daniel quickly assured her. "That's why you saw him at the lab that day. He was installing a program to stop the one Professor Kruljac had created."

"Why?" Chase asked. "Isn't it your company?"

"My father and I have...differing views on success. Even for him, all of this has been too bold. Even rash, I would say. I came here to stop a scandal from happening before he could get caught."

"And I walked in on it."

"Yeah," Daniel agreed. "When you revealed that you knew about Bates and KimBio, Hyun Tae's father undoubtedly heard it. Those men last night were sent to retrieve your flash drive, and Professor Kruljac has disappeared because he's been compromised."

Chase stared at her food, now gone cold. "He can have the flash drive. I can't even understand the document."

"I know," Hyun Tae said. "And I'm going to make this right. You are caught in my family's drama, and I never wanted that to happen. If you give me the flash drive, I'll find a way to convince my father your involvement was a mistake."

Chase nodded and stood up from her chair to cross the room to where her keys were. She grabbed the flash drive, fumbling with the keychain, and then put it in Hyun Tae's hand a little too roughly. "They attacked me last night for this?"

He didn't say anything, but he swallowed and looked down.

Daniel watched her, his gaze guilty, as if he was somehow responsible for this. He wasn't. And she knew Hyun Tae wasn't either, really, but she was suffering the aftershock of her fear the night before. And it made her angry. At him, at the whole situation. In an overly polite, clipped tone she said, "I guess I should go, then."

"Your things are in the guest room," Daniel said, standing. "I'll take you there."

Hyun Tae was still staring at his hand, clasped around the thumb drive.

Daniel led her to a hallway on the first floor, his hands in the back pockets of his jeans. "Hyun Tae protects the people around him. I promise. He's going to fix this."

She hoped so. Thinking back over yesterday's events and the attack, she realized Hyun Tae had made sure she was safe, and that's exactly how she felt when she was near him. She wasn't even sure why.

The guest room was surprisingly cozy, with soft creams, dark wood furnishings, and pictures of forests displayed on the walls. On the soft blue coverlet of the queen-sized bed, Chase found her clothing. It had been dry cleaned and carefully laid out flat, along with a mesh bag filled with all kinds of useful toiletries.

"Feel free to take your time. We'll be ready when you are," Daniel said.

"Thanks."

Chase heaved a sigh when he was gone, alone at last and suddenly burdened with the weight of everything. Determined to retreat back into her apartment as soon as possible, Chase did the bare minimum. Clothes on, hair combed and in a ponytail, and teeth brushed.

When she made her way back to the living room, she found both Hyun Tae and Daniel already dressed and waiting for her, as if they knew she wouldn't find any reason to stall or prolong her stay.

Hyun Tae held out a hand. "May I put a few numbers into your phone?"

"Sure," Chase said, unlocking the screen and handing it to him.

He tapped away for a few moments while he explained, "You'll find my number, the number of our driver in case you need a pick up at any time, anywhere, and Joon Suh's number and email. Don't hesitate to call any of us."

"Of course," she said, like an intern at orientation.

"In the meantime," Hyun Tae continued, walking toward the front door, "I will think of some way to clear your name of any involvement. I am sure with me directly involved, my father will see reason."

"Appreciate that," Chase said.

He didn't miss her derision, and he handed the phone back to her without a smile.

Should I shake his hand, or…? She half-expected to be handed a company ID card, complete with a lanyard.

As they stepped into the warm sunshine, Hyun Tae led the way down the front path toward the driveway, and Daniel fell into step behind her. Even though Hyun Tae had assured her that she would be safe now, being out in the open made her skittish. She didn't like being exposed.

As they made their way down the long driveway, Daniel suddenly stepped in front of her, next to Hyun Tae. "*Jeogi.*"

Hyun Tae gave a short nod, answering in English. "I see it."

"What?" she asked.

They had reached the end of the driveway, and both men looked to the left, focused on a patch of bushes clustered around the front gate. Chase peered into the leaves, and then the sun reflected off something. A small camera lens. Was someone hiding there and taking pictures?

Chase's heartbeat accelerated. She was still being watched.

Hyun Tae made a slow turn, body relaxed, but eyes focused intently on Chase as he proceeded to close the gap between them. He came so close to her, she could see the gold flecks in his dark brown eyes. He slid an arm around her waist, pulling her up against his body, and with his other hand, he cradled the back of her head.

"Don't slap me," he murmured, so low it was almost a whisper.

And then he lowered his lips to hers, catching them in a firm, but gentle kiss. Chase's eyes flew wide open, and her hands went to his chest, as if to push him away. But he gave the barest shake of his head before pulling her closer and deepening the kiss. Chase couldn't help it. Her eyes fluttered closed, and she found her hands clutching his shirt instead of pushing him away. He tasted minty and clean, and his lips were so marshmallow soft she wanted to melt like the chocolate on a s'more. Whatever this was, it was really, really nice.

When Hyun Tae broke the kiss, he ducked his head and whispered, "Hug me, and then walk back to your apartment. I will call you soon."

Dazed, Chase obeyed, twining her arms around his neck, and he gave her a tight hug that made her feel small and protected. He stepped away and gave a little wave. "I'll call you," he repeated, this time at a normal volume.

Chase blinked at him, waving, and then briefly caught a glimpse of Daniel. His lips were tight, his eyes glaring, but that was his only reaction. Guilt hit her, even though she suspected that what Hyun Tae had done was for a good reason. She waved to Daniel, and then on shaky legs turned to walk back to her apartment on her own.

When she had turned the corner, she released a pent up breath, and realized that her monitor had been beeping a warning to calm her heart rate. It was as if the world and all its sights and sounds came rushing back to her, as though her senses had momentarily been stunned along with her brain. "What the…"

She quickened her pace, suddenly desperate to be back in her apartment, back where she could breathe normally. She hurried through the short maze of sidewalks to her building, jogged up the stairs, and flung open the door, slamming it closed behind her. She stood with her back to the door, staring at the familiar living space.

Kiki looked up from the dining room table, a spoonful of Lucky Charms halfway to her mouth. "There you are! Where have you been? Are you blushing?"

Chase pushed the heels of her hands against her eyes. She opened her mouth to speak, but nothing came out.

Chapter Eighteen

When Chase went around the corner, Hyun Tae turned away and walked to the house. The back of his neck prickled, and he could feel Daniel's eyes boring into him. He'd never wondered how solid their friendship was or if it had any limits, but what he'd just done would test those fairly quickly. Never mind that Daniel could have a thousand beautiful girls back in Korea if he wanted; he seemed to have settled on a short, blond trouble magnet.

Daniel also had a sixth sense about cameras and being watched, and no one handled being the object of intense scrutiny like he did. It was second nature to him. His face hadn't shown much expression after the kiss.

Neither of them said anything until they were in the house, and even then, Daniel did little more than to give a casual look toward the windows before moving away from them and retreating to the kitchen. Joon Suh had disappeared, cat-like in his ability to slink off to his own space.

Away from the windows, Daniel leaned back against the kitchen counter and folded his arms, staring at Hyun Tae.

Hyun Tae stared back at him and slipped into Korean. "You angry?"

Daniel narrowed his eyes, which just made him look like a model smoldering for a cologne advertisement.

Hyun Tae didn't blame him, but he hadn't known what else to do. "My father won't hurt someone I care about."

In reply, Daniel turned and walked away.

Hyun Tae had expected an argument or an angry outburst, but not this. Alarmed, he called out, "*Hyung!*"

Daniel stopped and turned around. "You didn't think about how she would feel, did you?"

Hyun Tae could have told him that Chase did, in fact, seem to enjoy it, at least according to her heart monitor. He thought of her body relaxing in his arms. Annoyed, he tried to focus. She was distracting even when she wasn't around.

More importantly, he couldn't do this alone. Chase had to cooperate, for her own safety, and Daniel had to trust that Hyun Tae wouldn't steal his girlfriend. "You know I'm not like that, right?" Hyun Tae said.

Daniel glared back at him, and for a moment, Hyun Tae worried that Daniel wasn't going to forgive him for this.

"Do you like her?" Daniel asked.

"Is that what you think? That I would do that to my friend?"

Daniel's angry expression faded, and there was doubt in his eyes. "I don't know. Maybe."

"I didn't know what else to do. You know how crazy my father is."

A few more moments of silent staring, and then Daniel walked over to the fridge and took out a bottle of water. He unscrewed the top and sighed, looking down at the water.

"They took a picture of you and Chase. That was good, right? Your dad will believe it?"

Hyun Tae shrugged. "I hope so. I don't think he knows you went out with her, so that's good."

"We barely went out once anyway. We haven't had time. So I guess it's believable. I can't be seen with her from now on, though."

"Right. I'm sorry."

Taking a long drink, Daniel wiped his mouth. "I'll live with it."

"If she can tolerate fake dating me until we can get the thumb drive to him, then she'll be fine."

Daniel took out his phone. "We need to talk to her about this. We'll have to come up with an excuse for her to come over right now because she just left. I'll say she left a book here."

206

"Sounds good." Hyun Tae decided to go upstairs and work on some homework while they waited to hear back from her.

He sat down on the couch next to the window in his room, his laptop open, though he wasn't really looking at it. His mind was starting to work on the problem of how to fake a believable relationship. He was used to his parents spying on him. They had always provided him with everything—expensive cars, clothes and any kind of technical device he wanted, including phones.

The price was that they expected to know everything about his life. He'd even gone on a few "blind" dates, which in Korean terms meant meeting a potential wife. Although the girls were always pretty, for which he was thankful, he'd never been truly tempted, much to his parents' disappointment. Part of the reason was his lack of privacy. For once, this was going to be to his advantage. He'd have to make this relationship get deep fairly quickly. His father would wonder why there were no texts between them before this.

His phone hummed, and when he looked down at it, his heart froze. It was his father. That was a good thing. He could get this over with in a simple conversation. He took a breath, cleared his throat, and picked up the phone. He answered in Korean. "Hello."

"We have not talked since you left Korea. You should have called." His father's voice was relaxed and neutral.

Hyun Tae took the reproach without arguing. He never tried to call his father because his father never took his calls. When Kim Sang Sik wanted to hear from his son, he called him, not the other way around.

"I'm sorry I didn't call sooner. How are you? Are you well?" Hyun Tae asked.

"Yes. And you? Are you eating well?"

"I am eating well here, yes."

There was a brief pause, and Hyun Tae waited, his body still. Now that the polite conversation was over, his father would probably talk about what was really on his mind.

"Do you miss home?"

Surprised, Hyun Tae tried to follow his father's line of thought, but he couldn't. Should he say yes? He didn't miss home, but perhaps that was what his father wanted to hear. "Only a little. My friends here take good care of me."

"Do you have American friends?"

"Yes, a few." That wasn't really true. He'd met a few in his classes, but he'd been so intent on installing the program at Bates that he hadn't really put much of an effort into his social life. His father

208

would know that he hadn't gone out with anyone but his Korean friends, so he had to be careful.

"Such as?" his father asked.

"I met a few friends in my classes. I have been too busy to go out with them, though. I'm putting all my efforts into my studies."

"Ah, I see. You should meet more American friends. These connections can be important later in your life."

Hyun Tae agreed with his father on that point. This was also a good time to bring up his "relationship" with Chase. "I am dating someone here." He paused. "She is an American."

"An American girl?" his father managed to make the surprise sound genuine. Maybe he was just surprised that Hyun Tae was admitting it. "I don't know if your mother will approve. What do you know of the girl's family?"

Nothing. The answer was nothing because he wasn't interested in Chase. "We have just begun dating. It's hard to find out about the family of a girl when you just meet her."

"You are not serious about this girl then?"

This was important. Even though he had supposedly just met her, he must convey to his father that his interest in Chase was very strong, but not foolishly so. "I know that I've only begun dating her, but she is very special to me."

"Ah. You realize that sincere feelings take time, of course."

"Yes, of course. I simply feel that we have good potential."

"Even so, I have not met her. Your mother's wishes also need to be taken into account."

"Of course." Hyun Tae had come to the conclusion that his mother would probably never approve anyone that she hadn't personally chosen.

"Do not disappoint us, Hyun Tae."

"I won't, Father."

"Your mother is sending you something healthy to eat. Don't eat too much American food."

"Tell her I said thank you. I will be careful."

They said good-bye, and Hyun Tae hung up. If all went well, he would date Chase for a few weeks—long enough to straighten out the misunderstanding with Chase and the document—and then they could both move on from this. He stood up and paced by the window for a few minutes. She hadn't even agreed to do it. He hoped she would go along with it because he had no Plan B.

His phone hummed, and he got a text from Daniel.

"Chase forgot one of her books; she's coming over to get it."

He wondered if she was mad at him. She didn't seem that angry when she went back to her apartment.

He heard the knock at the front door, but he didn't go down right away. He told himself it was to give her some time with Daniel, but he was also procrastinating.

When he finally went downstairs, Chase was sitting in the living room. She wore jeans and a black T-shirt with a small, barely visible logo on the bottom hem, near her hip. He recognized the *Legend of Zelda* insignia. She'd put on makeup, which made her eyes exceptionally blue, and she wore some kind of pink lip gloss that looked like it was bubblegum flavored. Or cotton candy. She'd tasted like bacon when they kissed out on the front lawn less than an hour ago, which made sense because they'd just had breakfast and...

Shoving the oddly irrelevant details out of his mind, he went into the living room. Daniel sat next to her, but not too close, probably because they were in front of large windows and could be seen.

Hyun Tae stuffed his hands in his pockets, but he didn't move to sit down.

Daniel spoke first. "I talked to her about fake dating you for a while. Obviously, it's kind of strange."

"Yes, it is," he said. The thought crossed his mind that he'd never had to beg a girl to date him, but he ignored it. He owed her an apology, at least. "I'm sorry

211

about kissing you without asking, but I felt like it was necessary."

He expected her to tell him off, but she didn't. She avoided looking at him or Daniel, as if she didn't want to talk about it. "Yeah, I know."

She wasn't mad, but she wasn't exactly enthusiastic about the plan, which was fine. He did need to know that she was committed to it, though. "So you think you can do this?"

She shrugged. "Sure. But…" she halted, her gaze going to Daniel's. "You have to promise that we'll end the pretend dating the second your father stops thinking I'm a corporate spy or whatever."

"Promise," Hyun Tae said in unison with Daniel.

"Right." She stood up, looking over at Daniel. "So I'm dating your best friend."

"Don't say it like that," Daniel said as he led her back to the front door.

Chase hesitated as she went to open it. "I suppose we should at least hug," she said, looking over at Hyun Tae.

He concealed his surprise. He thought she would want to avoid touching him if she could. Maybe she wanted to know that she was in control, which he understood. "Okay."

She opened the door and stood up on her toes to reach around his neck, though he still had to lean forward. He hugged her back, and she stepped away, smiling. It wasn't the most sincere smile he'd ever seen, but Chase wasn't an actress or a liar. This wasn't going to be easy.

When she had walked away, Daniel kicked the door shut. "Just remember, she doesn't mean any of it."

Hyun Tae turned his back on his friend. "Neither do I."

Chapter Nineteen

Chase wiped her forehead with a bent wrist, careful not to smear paint from her brush on her skin or clothes. Her project was nearly finished, and she knew if she didn't complete the thing tonight, she wouldn't have the heart to give up her weekend to come in to the studio and get it done.

She bent forward, peering closely at the purple gourd in the last of the nine squares sectioned off on her canvas. She lightly stroked the brush over a thick line, deepening the violet-hued shadow cast by the lilac gourd over roughly textured straw. An exercise in color. Her professor in her watercolor class wanted them to master colors before moving on to anything more complex. They were instructed to make a grid of nine boxes on the canvas, and then to paint the same small still life in each box, but with different colors. It went unsaid that the flow of the piece from color to color should be harmonious in some way. And they would also be graded on the accuracy of each still life, and how well they matched from box to box.

She just needed to put the finishing touches on her purple box, and then she could go home and snarf something delicious. Something cheesy maybe...

"Why a pumpkin?"

Chase nearly jumped, almost smearing her painting, but some inner reflex prevented it, and she closed her eyes in annoyance. "Hyun Tae."

He stood in front of her with the canvas between them. "Sorry, did I disturb you?"

"Yes, you did."

"I would apologize, but since I had to come find you after you were two hours late for our date, I don't feel very bad."

Chase gave him a blank look. And then it came back to her. "Ah, our date."

He just stared at her, hands lightly hanging on to the strap of his over-the-shoulder bag.

Chase would have scratched her head, but then she remembered the paintbrush. "Right. I forgot."

"Yes, you did."

She gave him a slow, annoyed blink.

Hyun Tae nodded down at the artwork. "How much longer do you have?"

Chase considered the project. "No more than an hour maybe."

"It'll have to wait, then."

"You'll have to wait," she said, correcting him. "I have to finish this before the weekend."

Hyun Tae checked his watch. "It's already five."

Chase gave a shrug. "You can't rush art."

The look he gave her said he very well could, but he seemed to resign himself to it and pulled a chair up behind her.

Chase looked over her shoulder. "You're just going to watch me?"

He motioned silently with his hand for her to continue.

She turned back to the purple square. But she found that focusing was hard. Every time she looked behind her, he was in the same position. One ankle crossed over his knee, arms folded, and eyes right on her. He didn't even have the decency to play a game on his phone or something.

She settled, and she knew it, finishing in a record time of fifteen minutes just to have it be over with. It still looked good. She knew the teacher would find no fault with it. But if she'd had a little more time, the hue would have been just a smidge deeper…

"Looks great. Time to go." Hyun Tae stood beside her suddenly, holding out a white rag for her.

216

Chase whipped it out of his hands, wiped her fingers, and gathered her things in silence. He had rushed the art, darn him.

She kept her annoyed silence until they reached the outer doors of the art building, and then Hyun Tae took her hand in his, threading their fingers together.

"You love me," he reminded her.

Chase exhaled her pent up irritation, looking up at him as he brought their twined fingers up between them. He transformed his face, dimpling with a small smile and giving her an encouraging nod.

She pushed the tempest inside of her back into a bottle and gave a forced smile. "Right."

They walked out of the building hand in hand, and whether or not there were actually cameras clicking away at them, Hyun Tae had repeatedly warned her over the last few days that they must assume there were.

Hyun Tae opened the door of his black Tesla, and Chase slid in, breathing in the leathery new car smell of the interior. As Hyun Tae took his seat behind the wheel and started the engine, Chase asked, "So where is this date going to be?"

"I gave you the whole schedule on Monday. It's in your phone."

"Yeah, but we're two hours late. I figured that you would have reworked the horseback riding on the beach thing."

He stretched his arm out behind her headrest as he turned to back out of the parking spot. "Yes, I canceled the horses."

There is a God.

"I had dinner reserved at an Italian restaurant in Newport Beach. It's too far to go now, so I made a new reservation at Rossa's." He checked his watch again. "We might make it on time."

Chase looked down at her paint-splattered tennis shoes. "That's fancy isn't it?"

"I did mention it was a decent restaurant."

"I forgot."

He slanted a look her way. "There's a bag in the back."

She turned around and saw a brown shopping bag with embossed, decorative letters splashed across its side. Some upscale place she had never heard of, most likely. Chase hooked a finger on the edge of the bag and peered inside to find a lightweight, peach blouse and brown high-heeled sandals. "Do you have a secret girlfriend I don't know about?"

Hyun Tae shrugged. "I asked the store associate what was popular."

"She has good taste."

"Hurry and get dressed. Ahn Jung Ho, my father's assistant, made the reservation change. Which means my father knows."

Chase scrambled to the back, shucked off her tennis shoes, and slid her feet into the strappy, real leather sandals. She turned one foot, then the other. They looked awesome. Her eyes found his in the rearview mirror. "I'm taking off my shirt. Don't look."

He just shook his head, not even bothering to respond.

She narrowed her eyes at him, but he kept his gaze focused on the road ahead of him. At least she could count on the cyborg not to be a pervert. If he even had actual physical reactions to anything. It was almost offensive.

When she had the shirt on and her old clothes thrown into the shopping bag, she hopped back into the front seat and fastened her seatbelt. "Well? Better?"

He glanced down at her. "Better."

They arrived at 5:43, just two minutes before the reservation time. With the valet parking, they made it to the hostess table with the minute hand firmly on the 9 of the giant, ornate clock against the left wall.

"Table for two, Kim," Hyun Tae told the hostess.

The round-faced, blond hostess gave them a bright, practiced smile, and she quickly led them to a small table in the middle of the restaurant. It was packed, and Chase wondered how Hyun Tae got a reservation for such a popular place on a Friday night with only an hour's notice. Then again, after some more research into what a chaebol was, maybe it would have been stranger if he hadn't been able to.

After the menus were placed in front of them, Chase scanned the room for anyone with a paparazzi camera.

"Don't bother looking," Hyun Tae said, opening his menu.

"It's been a week. Are they still suspicious?"

"Knowing my father, yes. Either he remains suspicious until we break all contact, or he remains suspicious until we marry. Even then, he would probably watch."

"That's creepy."

Hyun Tae's eyes met hers over the rim of the black menu. "Yes."

Chase cleared her throat and looked over the choices. Everything was in Italian. A smile tugged at her lips, but she quickly suppressed it. "I'm thinking about trying the cappellini con gamberi al portofino, but since having it piccante in paraggi, I'm not sure it will have the same gusto. What do you think?"

He looked amused. "I think the absence of red pepper flakes will not detract from your meal too much. But if you really want spice in your meal, I hear their cozze al pomodoro piccante is very good. The recipe was brought back from Naples. Although I'm sure the cappellini in paraggi was good."

Chase didn't try to hide her annoyance. "Is there anything you aren't smug about?"

He leaned forward a little. "Nothing you would know any better."

"I'll bet I could run circles around your English grammar."

He seemed to consider that. "Maybe."

"It's a gourd, not a pumpkin."

He tilted his head as if he didn't hear her correctly.

She gave him a grin. "See? English. My great equalizer. I was painting a gourd. Not a pumpkin."

"What's the difference?"

"A pumpkin is a kind of gourd."

He looked like he was cataloguing the word. "Gourd. Got it."

The waitress came to get their order, and Chase ended up getting the shrimp and angel hair dish after all, and Hyun Tae ordered some kind of seafood medley. They ate mostly in silence, although Hyun Tae politely asked about her artwork, and she told him about the internship interview she had next month, and what kind of pieces she was working on.

He let her in on the fact that he had had a group project that week with a classmate he didn't particularly care for. And that he did the project entirely on his own, and wrote the classmate's name on it.

Chase slurped down the last of her soda. "What did your classmate think?"

"He said thank you," Hyun Tae said with a shrug. "He knows he will get a perfect score."

She shook her head. "Arrogant."

A dimple peeked out from his right cheek.

The waiter came to clear their plates and leave the bill, which Hyun Tae took care

of by slipping his card into the envelope. "I will let you know what next week's date will be. I think if you came over to our house once or twice next week as well, it would reflect well on our relationship."

"Yes, that's true," she agreed, part of her amused at how they'd turned something like romance into a strategic goal.

He seemed to notice it too because he cleared his throat and said, "I don't usually date, so if my instructions seem to be lacking in real warmth, you should let me know. "

"Yeah, you might want to mix it up a little. Look at this text." Chase pulled out her phone and opened the Kakao Talk app, which was a Korean texting app that Hyun Tae had insisted they use. "Look at the time stamp on all your love notes."

Hyun Tae didn't bother to look. "I know what time I sent them. It makes sense that I would think of you just before bed, don't you think?"

"Not at nine thirty every night, on the dot! It's weird."

He frowned. "I see."

The waiter came to their table then, and handing Hyun Tae the bill envelope, she bent down to whisper, "I'm sorry, sir, but this card was denied."

Hyun Tae's brow puckered in confusion. He took the card, replaced it in his wallet, and handed her a different one. With a murmur of thanks, the waiter took it away, and Hyun Tae pulled out his phone to text someone.

"Problem?" Chase asked.

He finished his text. "Don't know."

The waiter returned. Card denied. Hyun Tae jammed the card back in his wallet, slapped it closed, and looked at his phone again. The waiter stood at the chair patiently, trying not to hover, it seemed.

Chase leaned over the table toward him. "What's wrong?"

"My account has been frozen, I think."

"Who?"

His eyes locked with hers. "My mother. It's her way of letting me know she isn't pleased."

"Oh."

Hyun Tae's phone buzzed, and he swiped the screen, putting it up to his ear. *"Ne."* He listened for a few moments. *"Eoh, Joon Sooh-yah, eonjejjeum nae sin-yongkadeu gochyeojul su iss-eo?"* Another pause, and then he nodded his head. *"Araso."* When he hung up, his expression was grim. "It's frozen. It's not legal because it's mine and not connected to my parents, so I can have it fixed. But not right now."

Chase didn't hesitate. "Got it. Let me get my wallet."

"I'm sorry," he said, with a touch of embarrassment.

"No problem." She pulled out her debit card and handed it to the waitress. And then began to do mental calculations. "Wait, how much was the bill?"

"One hundred and fifty six dollars and twelve cents."

Chase's eyes widened. "Um, what?"

He gave her a sideways glance. "You don't have one hundred and fifty dollars in your bank account? How do you pay for food?"

"I eat ramen! And cereal."

She didn't know if the look in his eyes was incredulity or pity.

"Crap," she said.

Predictably, her card was denied, and Chase's armpits started to sweat. "Okay. Well, this is really embarrassing."

Hyun Tae lowered his voice as he spoke to the waitress. "I apologize. Something is wrong with my accounts. If you would give us a moment to figure it out?"

"Of course," the waitress said, hurrying away to give them some space. A few patrons were giving them more frequent looks. Some of the chatter had died, and it went up in volume again when the waitress left.

Chase leaned into Hyun Tae again. "What now?"

Hyun Tae's gaze was distracted, and he shook his head. "Joon Suh is in L.A. for the weekend."

"Maybe Daniel could–"

"No." His dark eyes met hers, and a muscle ticked in his jaw.

"Right, that would be super embarrassing. But the only other person is like...my mom or something. That's way worse."

They were out of options. It had to be her mom.

"It will be okay. Don't worry," she said, pulling up her mom's number and dialing it. As her mom's coo of delight about their predicament chirped over the phone,

225

Chase gritted her teeth. Her mom's fondest dreams had come true; she was dating a Korean guy.

Hyun Tae avoided looking at her, and he rubbed the back of his neck.

It came as no shock to Chase that her mother was more than happy to drive right over and bail them out. Especially considering that her date's name was Kim Hyun Tae. As she hung up, Chase grimaced.

Hyun Tae didn't look terribly happy, either, and he stood up slowly with a sigh, holding out a hand to her. She took it, and he led her away from their table. Chase saw many curious glances cast their way.

Hyun Tae put a hand to the small of her back, guiding her around a corner and blocking her from the stares. Chase looked up at the hardened line of his jaw. "It doesn't bother me," she said, reassuring him.

"It bothers me."

She almost smiled at the chivalrous gesture. Such a polite jerk, this fake boyfriend of hers.

When they reached the front, Hyun Tae stopped to speak with the hostess. "There has been a technical error with my bank account. We have a friend coming to help with the bill in just a few minutes."

The hostess blinked rapidly. "Oh, a…a technical error?"

"Something is wrong with my account," he reiterated.

She appeared to be confused by that, and Hyun Tae rubbed his neck again. *He has a nervous gesture.* Chase was able to pick up that up despite her own discomfort. Hyun Tae in distress. An interesting development.

The hostess picked up the phone at her desk to call her manager. "I'll just check, but I'm sure it's fine."

Chase and Hyun Tae took a seat on a padded bench in front of the entrance, and Hyun Tae pulled out his phone again and checked it. After a while, they just stared out at the parking lot.

Finally, her mom's car pulled up. Her mom's, not her dad's. The decade-old silver Lancer, dented in the front and missing all its hubcaps, came to a squeaky stop outside the restaurant. The valet went to get her keys, and her mom waved him away with a smile, like she was passing up a free mint. Her curly, gray-streaked hair escaped from a clip in a wild array of coils and frays, and she had on Capri leggings and a summer camp T-shirt from when Chase was fifteen, and mismatched socks poked out of her worn, lime green sneakers. She must have been out for a jog when she got the call. All love and support, she hadn't paused a second before rushing to their aid. Not a single second.

"Hi honey!" she said, smiling, her blue eyes locking on her daughter for only a moment before lighting up with pure rapture upon seeing Hyun Tae. "And hi again, Hyun Tae!"

He held out a hand. "Thank you so much for coming, Mrs. Bryant."

"Oh, please," she said, waving a hand and still smiling brightly. And then she looked around at the restaurant. "Look at you two, exploring the town."

Hyun Tae cleared his throat. "Yes, sorry again. It wouldn't have been a problem but–"

"No, no!" Chase's mother said, quickly reassuring him. "Really it's no trouble." She pulled her bright orange purse around and zipped it open. "How much was the bill then? Oh, never mind; here, just take my card," she said, giving him a little wink.

A groan of despair rose in Chase's throat, but she clenched her teeth in a smile.

Hyun Tae gingerly took the card from her mom's fingers and then handed it to the hostess, who hurried to the back to take care of the bill. Chase's mother just stood there, beaming, between the two of them.

The silence grew heavy, so Chase attempted to fill it. "First date," she said to her mom.

Her mother's grin became comically exaggerated. "How wonderful!"

"Yeah," Chase said, completely out of words.

Hyun Tae smiled politely. "I've wanted to ask her out ever since you showed me her picture, but I wasn't sure she'd say yes."

"Well, that's why you should always take a chance," her mom said with a knowing gleam in her eye.

Chase's phone binged with a text, and she pulled it out. Daniel had sent her a message. *"Hey, still on the date?"*

She clicked her phone off with a sting of regret that she had to ignore him. All week she had done her best to keep in touch with him, to assure him that he was still on her mind.

The hostess returned, holding out the receipt for Hyun Tae to sign. He took the slip of paper and then, after an awkward moment of hesitation, handed it back to Chase's mom.

She balanced the receipt on her knee as she signed it. Then she paused, looking up. "Oh, the tip. Let's see, fifteen percent...or eighteen?"

She started to juggle the pen, receipt, and her purse as she looked for her phone, but Hyun Tae said quickly, "Ah, it would be about thirty dollars."

Her mom clicked her tongue against her teeth. "Nice. Impressive. Okay, thirty dollars..." When she finished filling out the receipt, she handed it back to Hyun Tae, who then gave it to the hostess.

"I can pay you back as soon as I get home," Hyun Tae said, reassuring her.

Her mom swiped a dismissive hand again. "Take your time; no rush. Stop by my office anytime; I'm there Monday through Friday."

"Eight to five," Chase muttered under her breath. *Mom, he knows what school office hours are.*

He gave a slight bow of his head. "Thank you."

"See you soon, honey!" her mom said, waving at Chase as she walked away.

Chase gave her a smile and a wave, "Thanks again, Mom."

When she had puttered out of the parking lot, Chase looked over at Hyun Tae. He was staring at the place where her mom's car had been, a curious expression on his face.

"Sooo...that's my mom," she said.

He looked back at her for a moment, and then he said, "It's a good thing this isn't a real date. I'd feel really stupid."

For the first time since she'd met him, she was at ease. Maybe because he'd been the one tripping over himself. Sort of. The credit card thing wasn't really his fault, but still, at least it wasn't her this time. "Well, obviously you needed some practice. When your next real date goes well, you can thank me."

He laughed out loud. "You're not going into psychology I hope. You'd be a terrible therapist."

"You're laughing aren't you?" she asked.

"Yeah, I am."

A valet drove the Tesla up to the curb, and Hyun Tae opened the door for her. "Be sure to tell Daniel how bad it was. He'll want all the horrible details."

Funny, and true. Maybe this fake dating thing wouldn't be a big deal. That was a relief.

Chapter Twenty

Midterms made the days all fly past. Amid the flurry of studying and projects, she had a fake Korean boyfriend in the background, texting her animated love emojis and taking her on amusing, if still a trifle awkward, dates. A baseball game where she ate too many hotdogs, a new action movie that made him jump so hard he spilled their popcorn, and a quick meal at a Mexican restaurant when neither of them had time to spare before tests descended on them.

When she came to their house to study, Daniel kept her company, letting her lean against his legs while she sketched on her laptop or highlighted her art history books. Hyun Tae gave them space at the house, pausing only to remind her of upcoming dates or to text him back if she had forgotten. But she found her eyes looking for him when he left the room. And then missing Daniel when she couldn't hang out with him in public.

She probably would have worried more about it if she didn't have so many deadlines looming. As it was, she pushed the boyfriends aside and focused on her demanding art projects and the fact that some high profile scouts would be reviewing her portfolio two weeks after midterms. She had finished the portfolio, digitized it, and compiled the work perfectly some time before, but she couldn't resist tweaking pieces here andthere. It consumed her more and more, the closer the date came.

Chase forced herself to concentrate on her grades. Biology in particular kept her on her toes. She did okay on the midterm, but when she got past that hurdle, she found that their next unit of study on exponential growth models was a little too much math for her liking.

Needing a quiet place to study, she hit the library. She was looking for a good spot to settle in when her phone chirped, *kataoh*. It was the notification for Kakao Talk, meaning Hyun Tae had texted her. She had become pretty fond of the app, which had goofy Smileys and an easy interface that just seemed more fun than regular texting. She swiped Kakao Talkit open, and found a little animated bunny rabbit making a dizzy face along with Hyun Tae's message.

"Finished my last midterm. Want to go somewhere to celebrate?"

She sent back the same bunny character, but rolling on the floor with an empty bowl of rice beside it, its stomach a round ball. *"Does that mean food? If food, then yes."*

"Always food with you. Yes, I meant we should eat something. I'll pick you up at six."

Chase sent him a character making a thumbs up sign and then pocketed her phone. She smiled a little. Lately their texts were becoming less for show and more like something between real friends. Boyfriend and girlfriend or not, they were spending a lot of time together. And Hyun Tae was a lot like her–he thawed over time. There were still the cheesy declarations of love in between the actual conversations, but it didn't hurt anything to be honest with herself. Even fake, outrageous compliments felt nice.

She sensed someone looking over her shoulder. She turned her head and came eye-to-eye with Daniel.

Happiness bubbled up inside her, and she looked around to make sure they were alone. "What are you doing here?"

He held up a physics book. "Homework. Still having a hard time with biology? I thought we nailed that study guide."

"We totally did, and I aced the midterm. It's just that we started this exponential population growth thing, and the teacher won't let us rely on a program."

He crinkled his nose. "Math. I got you."

Her eyes roved over his flawless skin and the darker shade of red he had recently dyed his long, perfectly chaotic hair. She could soak in that twinkly look of his for days. "How did your midterms go?"

"As far as I can tell? Not bad." He looked around as well, careful to make sure no passing students saw them standing too closely together. Daniel angled his body, so her shoulder brushed against his chest. "It's nice to have more free time for a while."

"Yeah," Chase agreed, smiling up at him.

"Speaking of which," he lowered his already soft voice, ducking his head down closer to her. She could smell the coconut shampoo in his hair, and her stomach did a somersault at his nearness. "Want to get out sometime? Mr. Kim seems to have chilled out."

An emphatic "yes" almost leaped out of her mouth. She stared at his Adam's apple, all too aware of the heat from his chest against the skin of her arm. "I really wish we could."

"Maybe we could just get a coffee while we do our homework tonight."

She briefly met his gaze before looking straight ahead at his neck again. "I would, but Hyun Tae planned a date."

"On a Wednesday? Isn't that usually a Friday thing?"

It hadn't occurred to her that it was unusual for him to schedule an impromptu date. "I guess so. Maybe he has other plans for Friday."

"Huh. Well, that's Halloween. We could go to a party together. Lots of people," he coaxed. "Perfectly 'safe,' if you know what I mean."

She gave him a half smile, looking up at his eyes again. "I forgot about Halloween. That could be fun."

"No one would be suspicious of friends showing up at a big party together. With costumes, they might not even recognize us."

"I mean, yeah, probably…" she said, trying to go over all the possibilities. She would have to double-check with Hyun Tae, just to make sure it really wouldn't ruin any of their careful planning. He said he had a definite timeline to ease her away from the "relationship" without causing any fuss or raising any suspicions. She just had to follow the plan.

Daniel lifted a hand, studying her face. "You have an eyelash. Can I…?"

"Oh, yeah," Chase swiped at her skin. "Where is it?"

He leaned in close, eyes focused on her left cheek just under her eye. "I'll get it; hold on." As he brushed a delicate touch across her skin, he suddenly froze. His body stiffened, and he tried to casually take a step back, but she could tell it was hurried. He turned his face away from her. "Hey, I'll text you about the party."

"Right, sure. Everything okay?"

"Yup, fine. Text you later," he said again, and then with a wave stalked out of the aisle.

Chase stood for a second in utter confusion and then turned back to the biology books. A text came in not three seconds later, a message from Daniel.

"Kid with the phone behind you might be taking pics. I'll see you later."

Chase surreptitiously glanced to her right, but she couldn't see anyone. A shelf was in her way. She moved down the aisle as if to look at books, and as she did, a man sitting at a table just around the corner came into view. He looked like he was scrolling his phone, headphones in. But Daniel was right; he was not a student, and he was definitely Korean. And when his eyes locked with hers, he mouthed something and then got up to leave.

Well, crap. She wasn't sure if he was there to take pictures of her, but she wondered if she had stood a little too close to Daniel. They had looked pretty normal when they were talking...right?

Distracted, she sat down and tried to concentrate. It bothered her for a while, but after a good hour of figuring out how to accurately determine the growth rates of wolves and rabbits, she let it pass out of her mind. Her experience in the parking lot that one night still gave her the jitters, so she wondered if that was making her a bit paranoid.

She studied longer than she expected, and when she looked down and saw 4:33 blinking back at her, she hurried to pack up her things and get back to the apartment. Hyun Tae might be more relaxed, but he still hated it when she was running late.

Kiki sidled next to her at the bathroom counter in the apartment, her hazel eyes squinty. "You know this is fake dating, right?"

She frowned. "Like that even needs to be said."

"Okay," Kiki said, shrugging. "But if I were to tell you that my brother has a karate tournament, and I'm inviting you, what's the first thing that comes to mind?"

It popped into her consciousness immediately. *Hyun Tae has done Jui Jitsu since he was five.* Chase knew what she was getting at, so she endeavored to look nonchalant as she picked up her lip gloss. "I don't know, I guess that I'd totally come because you're my best friend, and Xander is adorable."

"Right." Kiki dug around in Chase's makeup bag, found some eyeliner, and touched up her cat eyes. "So your first thought wasn't something that had to do with Hyun Tae. Because pretty much everything we talk about gets pulled back to your fake boyfriend. Just thought you should know."

Kiki was right, of course, and Chase had sort of noticed it, but it seemed hard to stop herself from doing it. "If you say so," she said.

Kiki rolled her eyes, finished up her eyeliner, and swatted Chase on the butt. "If you actually end up liking him, it's not bad. Just be honest about it. I'll see you later tonight."

"See ya," Chase mumbled, and then she rolled her lips together to spread the lip gloss. Kiki might be on to something. Maybe she should be more careful about how close she really got to Hyun Tae.

He texted her at 5:30, asking her to meet him on campus at the entrance to the gardens. Chase had never really been to that part of campus. Because it was situated between the horticultural and agricultural buildings, she had no need to visit. She looked down at her white lacy dress and hoped that they weren't planning on sitting in the grass or something.

At 6:05, she made it to the arched trellis that marked the entrance to the gardens, a little out of breath from having to walk across the campus when she couldn't find any parking. And she quickly discovered why. There was some kind of event going on, and as she approached the walkway, music and crowd chatter came from within.

She spotted Hyun Tae waiting off to the side, one hand in the pocket of his khaki cargo shorts, Creamsicle orange button-down rolled up to his elbows, and aviator sunglasses reflecting in the evening sunlight. He even had on brown leather flip-flops, which surprised her. He had his phone up to his ear, but as soon as he saw her walking toward him, he said a few short words and hung up.

"Hey," she said, waving.

"You look great," he responded, and he put a hand to the small of her back, pulling her close to him and giving her a kiss on her hairline.

Chase's body react instantly with giddy excitement. *It's fake*, she told herself firmly. *Chill, Chase. Chill.* "Thanks. So what is all this?"

"You didn't see the signs all over campus?" He pointed to a little sign staked into the dirt not far from them. It read, "Ag fair! Food, booths, and fun for everyone! Barley Gardens, October 28, 4:30-9:30."

"Ah. Right, the ag fair."

He rubbed the corner of his mouth with his thumb.

"Stop that; I know that look. Yes, okay, I'm oblivious."

He gave a little shrug, as if he had no idea what she was talking about. "I promised you food. Thought this would be more interesting than another restaurant."

"Well, we might as well have fun, right?" she asked.

They walked up the brick path, passed on all sides by students and families talking excitedly as they went to and from the fair. It didn't take long for Chase to catch a whiff of the food, and when they reached the open, grassy area where the fair had been set up, she honed in on a sausage stand.

One of the departments had set up a "make your own sausage" booth, where patrons could choose to make their own sausages and have them cooked, or simply buy one of the sausages made ahead of time. Chase watched as a line of students struggled with the sausage maker, breaking the skin as they tried to fill it with the ground meat of their choice. Right next to the stand, students at a fry-making station cut potatoes with a grid press and then watched as their wedges were fried and salted for them.

Chase kept walking, forgetting momentarily about her hunger. She was more interested in observing.

She watched Hyun Tae's expression for any hint that he might be interested or disgusted by the things they were looking at, she thought he maybe looked less leery

241

of a German lamb dish called doner kebab, which consisted of spit-roasted lamb in flatbread with goat yogurt, tomatoes, onions, pickled cucumber, and red cabbage. They each took their flatbreads in little paper sleeves and ate their way through them as they strolled through the informational stands, games, and events.

Chase wiped a bit of goat yogurt off the side of her mouth, looking up at Hyun Tae, who had a faraway expression after they had passed a petting zoo. He hadn't said much, which wasn't abnormal, but she could tell his mind was somewhere else. Even in silence, his eyes usually danced from object to object. She wondered if she should just let him be; sometimes a person just needed to be in their own head for a while.

But then she heard a shout ahead of them, and the crowd parted rapidly. She saw the goat just a second before it would have run right into them, and she grabbed Hyun Tae's arm, yanking him back so hard they almost fell into the stand to her right. The panicked animal thundered past them. A group of men ran after it with lassos in hand.

Hyun Tae had put his hands on her upper arms to steady both of them, and he looked down at her in surprise. "Thank you," he said.

"We almost got run over by a goat."

He gave a soft laugh. "America." His eyes traveled over her face, finally broken out of his daze. "Sorry. I wasn't paying attention."

"It's cool. Stuff on your mind." She had barely managed to keep her flatbread from squishing up against his chest, and she pulled it away from him, making a loud crackling sound.

He set her away from him. "Yes, I do have a lot on my mind." He paused, as if he wanted to say something more.

Chase waited, hoping he would elaborate. Hyun Tae started to walk again. "My program to block KimBio was too late. They got the research."

"All of it?"

"All of it."

"Dang."

"Yeah. It was disappointing." They stopped under a tree just behind a line of booths, and he raised his glasses onto his head as they both took a seat in the grass. In the shade, the weather was almost cool, prickling her skin pleasantly.

Chase took a bite of what remained of her dinner, watching him again as he looked down at his hands in thought. Finally, she asked, "Is there anything we can do?"

He lifted his hands in a defeated gesture. "Not likely. Once they have it, not even I can undo it."

"I could tell Bates what happened. It might alert them in the right way or something."

"You can't do anything," he said with a pointed look at her. "Don't even go near the administrative offices. I mean it."

She gave a half shrug. "Yeah. And you'd be caught if you did that, right?"

"Yes, it would expose me immediately."

"Doesn't your dad know how much you dislike what he does?" Chase asked.

"He hardly knows me. I went to boarding schools in Korea and here in the U.S. He loves me as his progeny and takes pride in my accomplishments. But he doesn't know me."

It sounded awful, having parents who admired from afar but didn't take an active role in what kind of person he had become. She wanted to give him a hug. And invite him over for dinner where her sister Jonni would ask him all kinds of uncomfortable, probing questions, and her mom would fawn over him with her cooking, and her nieces and nephew would dance around him to get his attention.

She wondered, not for the first time, when he had decided to actively fight his father at the risk of his position and the company.

Hyun Tae put his sunglasses back in place and stood, holding out a hand to her. "What's important now is getting you untangled from all this, right?"

She smiled. "At least I get free food out of the deal."

He gave her a smirk, took her hand in his, and led her back to the crowd. She convinced him to grab a mason jar full of cream and shake it with her until they could turn it into butter. It took forever, and she couldn't stop laughing at the look on his face as he furiously shook it, willing it to just turn into butter already. And when he didn't stop until it was the perfect butter consistency. They opened the jar, and she dipped a finger in to taste it. "It's good!"

He took a taste, and then shrugged. "Yeah, I like it."

Jar of butter in hand, they made their way through the last of the fair, ending near the back entrance to the garden where a student band had set up and played covers of hit songs.

Hyun Tae checked his watch again. "I'm sorry, but I have a meeting to catch in Seoul. Can I walk you to your car?"

"Yeah, yeah, sounds good," Chase said. She tried not to sound disappointed.

The sun had already begun to set, and they walked quietly side-by-side in the deepening darkness. Chase cradled the mason jar against her chest.

The temperature was so perfect, she didn't even notice it, as if there was an absence of heat or cold in the air. Warm sunlight glowed between the trees of the campus walkways, and she took a deep breath of clear air and reveled in outdoor bliss. When she looked up at Hyun Tae, he was watching her.

She raised questioning eyebrows.

"You look happy," he commented.

"Yeah, I guess. Why?"

"No reason." He turned his eyes to the front again.

When he dropped her off at her car, opening her door for her and keeping a watchful eye on their surroundings, Chase wanted to take his face in her hands and turn it toward the orange and pink sunset. She wanted to tell him to just look at it and let go for a few seconds, to appreciate the moments when they came. Maybe he needed someone to tell him it was okay to have those.

Chapter Twenty-One

She came home one day from class to find a black box with a white ribbon sitting on the kitchen table. Kiki was sitting next to it, licking peanut butter off a spoon, her platinum hair particularly spiky today. Dark eyeliner outlined her hazel eyes, which were leaning toward gold in the afternoon light.

"Hurry up and open it already. You know I have impulse control problems."

"Is anyone else home? How do you know it's mine?"

Kiki said, "No one else is home," and pointed to the tag that read "To Chase."

"It's for me?"

Kiki nodded, the spoon in her mouth.

"From?"

Kiki gave her a wicked smile. "I'm not telling. You got yourself into this love triangle; you figure it out."

"It's not a love triangle," she said under her breath, dropping her backpack to the floor and picking up the small tag attached to the bow.

Enjoy –Star-Lord

She knew Kiki was watching her, but she couldn't help the smile that tugged on her lips. She reached over and pulled on the ribbon slowly. It wasn't Hyun Tae. She would have received a text or some kind of schedule. Gift on Tuesday. This had to be Daniel, so maybe it had to do with the Halloween party on Friday.

The bow slid off the shiny black box, slithering into a pool of silk at the sides. She got her fingers under the lid and pulled it off. The top fit so snugly to the bottom of the box that it made a sucking sound as she pulled it up. Kiki was standing now, peering into the box.

It looked like a lot of black leather, and Kiki raised her eyebrows as Chase lifted the first piece of clothing out. Black leather pants unfolded, and she laughed. "What the heck?"

The next piece was a black leather top, with a bright green top that looked like it should go under it. Underneath those was a pair of black leather boots and a belt with a holster on it. She could tell there was more, so she dug under the tissue paper and found a futuristic-looking laser gun. Open mouthed, she realized what it was. "Oh. My. Word. It's Gamora. From *Guardians of the Galaxy*."

Kiki examined the belt and the holster. "Chase, this is real leather. This isn't just bad cosplay. This is top of the line."

"If this all fits, this could be the most amazing costume I've ever had," she answered, still stunned. It was all beautiful, the box, the costume and the laser gun. She put them in the box and walked reverently with it back to her room. "I'll be right back. Pray for a miracle."

Kiki narrowed her eyes. "I don't know if a perfect fit would be a miracle or creepy."

Chase closed the door to her room and put the box on her bed. Then she did a happy dance. With a saucy hip wiggle at the end. She stripped down in record time and pulled on the leather pants. They slid on easily at first, but she had to work to get them over her hips, which had her a little worried and a little surprised.

She jumped around, getting into the pants all the way. The button snapped easily, though, the waist a perfect fit. The black leather was shiny and kind of sexy. There were seams that curved up on her thighs in a geometric pattern, which she guessed was probably exactly like the movie version. She pulled on the green shirt and then the black top, which fit perfectly, surprising her again. He didn't have any illusions about how buxom she was...or wasn't. How did he know?

She pulled on the boots. He'd gotten those a little big, but not too bad. She put the belt on and dropped the

249

cool laser gun in the holster, turning around to examine the results in the full-length mirror on her door. She'd been transformed into a space mercenary, and it looked good. Hot, even. She bit her lip. Too sexy? She turned around, checking out her booty. Well, she couldn't help it if she looked good in black leather.

Taking a deep breath, she opened the door. Kiki's mouth dropped open.

"Holy black leather hotness, Batman. You look amazing! He's a total perv! He got it perfect!"

Chase whipped the laser gun out of her holster. "Fear me. I'm wanted in seven galaxies."

"Ha. Well, somebody really wants you in this one, that's for sure."

Chase stomped around the living room, pretending to shoot at various objects. The laser gun lit up and made a fairly convincing laser sound. "I want to wear it everywhere."

"You should. It would be a waste not to. In fact, don't wear anything else. There's no reason to."

"I know. This is so cool, I can't stand it." She holstered the laser gun and then sighed. "Daniel. He melts me, I swear."

Kiki eyed her. "You say that like it's a bad thing."

"Uh, no, I just...feel guilty because we have to sneak around. Like we're the fake couple, you know? It's so unfair to him."

"And you," Kiki said, staring at her pointedly.

"Yeah, and me."

She slid her hand down the leather, wondering how much it cost. He had really gone to a lot of effort for her, and a pang of guilt gnawed at her.

She wanted to send him a picture, but she couldn't. Her phone had to belong to Hyun Tae's father right now. Irritation welled up in her. When would they be done with this?

Kiki already had her phone out, however. "You look great. I'll send it to you."

She almost protested, but decided not to. She had told Kiki that she was fake dating Hyun Tae, but she hadn't told her about the possible phone surveillance. Kiki would have gone to the police.

"Thanks." Maybe having it on her camera wouldn't matter as long as it wasn't a text.

"Pose," Kiki commanded.

Chase took the gun out and tried to stand like someone who shot aliens, her right hip a little to the side as she smoldered at the camera.

"Grrr," Kiki growled and said in a bad French accent, "Like a leetle cat, so fierce."

Chase burst out laughing.

251

Kiki stared down at the picture and then showed it to her. She did look fierce, though the effect was a little diminished by the kitchen sink in the background. "Nice," she said, and Kiki sent it to her.

Her phone buzzed, and she checked it. Hyun Tae.

Miss you. Trick or treating Friday night?

Disappointment hit her hard, making her stomach drop. Why? They were supposed to have Friday off. Maybe he had realized that as a couple they should be together on Halloween. She should have thought of that as well, but she was thinking about Daniel. How could he do this? He knew how much Daniel wanted to see her. What if she texted him that she was taking her nieces trick or treating? But she might be followed to the party and get caught lying to Hyun Tae. She was suddenly aware that Kiki was watching her. She knew disappointment showed on her face. "Hmm. Potential bad news," she said, and went into her room, trying to think.

It wasn't that she hated being with Hyun Tae. If anything, she was finding it easier to be with him, but Daniel was sweet and giving, and deserved better. She wanted to be there for him, but she couldn't. She didn't even know if she would be able to tell him how sorry she was if she couldn't go. She

252

began pulling off the leather costume, and every piece she took off made her disappointment even sharper. She wouldn't get to wear it. That was going to be hard on him, maybe more so for him than it was for her. The longing on his face when they were at the library was burned into her memory.

Dressing in her jeans and T-shirt, she fought back her frustration. She looked down at Hyun Tae's text. He'd said they would be able to break up at some point. Why not now? Hadn't they gone out enough? What if she broke it off for him? Remembering the night when the men had pushed her against the tree, she sat on the bed and put her head in her hands. The truth was that she was afraid. She didn't want that to happen again, and the only person who knew if she was free from Hyun Tae's father was Hyun Tae. She had to trust him. Maybe she should ask him if they were getting close to breaking up. She didn't want Daniel to give up on her.

She sighed, and texted back. *"Miss you too. Are you home?"*

He texted back immediately. *"Yes."*

"Are you studying?"

His next reply took a little longer, as if he were trying to guess what she wanted. *"Yes, but I can take a break. You coming over?"*

He'd guessed correctly. *"Yes."*

"See you soon :)"

Hmm. He was getting good at this. She folded the costume up and put it carefully back in the box, her fingers lingering over it.

She opened the door and found Kiki still sitting in the kitchen. She looked over at Chase. "Need to talk?"

Chase shook her head. "No, I'm okay. It's just hard. This fake dating is starting to be a problem."

Kiki pushed out her lower lip in a sympathetic pout. "I'm sorry."

"Thanks."

Kiki stood up and gave her a hug, which sort of made her feel better. She broke away and went out the door, a heavy weight on her chest. It was nice outside, a light wind in the air and the sun warm on her skin. She hoped Daniel would be there, so she could tell him in person. She didn't want to think about how he would feel if she told him she couldn't go through a note.

She knocked at the front door, and it opened immediately. Hyun Tae drew her in, his arm going around her before he closed the door. He wore a plain white T-shirt and dark jeans, and he smelled as if he had just showered. As soon as the door clicked shut, he let her go and stepped back to a polite distance. "Something wrong?" he asked.

She wrapped her arms around herself and nodded, kicking off her flip-flops and setting them next to everyone else's shoes. There was a pair of slippers there for her, and she put them on. Hyun Tae had put the slippers there shortly after they'd begun their charade. He was all about the details.

"Is Daniel here?" she asked.

He shook his head. "No, sorry."

She drew in a breath and paced. "We were supposed to go a party on Friday. I need to talk to him. Do you know when he'll be back?"

"He told me, but I think you are taking a chance going someplace to meet him without me. It's just too risky. And no, he's not here. As in...not in the States. He went back to Korea for a few days. He's coming in tonight."

"I wouldn't know," she groused, looking away from him. "We can't text. We can't email. We can't do anything."

When he didn't say anything, she looked up. He was regarding her with a speculative look in his dark eyes. "That's what he said."

Surprised, she blinked at him. "When? You talked to him?"

"Sort of. He told Joon Suh. Who told me."

"Oh." She went back to pacing. What could she do? Complain? Hyun Tae didn't seem to care. She stopped pacing and put her hands on her hips. "Well, do you know if we're almost done? I mean, is your dad satisfied yet?"

He let out a quick breath, and his smile was decidedly cynical. "That is not a word I would ever use to describe my father. Satisfied."

"I'm serious. This is getting really hard on Daniel."

"Getting? As in you just noticed that this is killing him?"

Taken aback, she stumbled for a reply. "Well, no, I meant that it's getting worse. He's having a really hard time. Isn't there anything we can do?"

"If he actually cares about you, then he'll survive. He knows how important it is to stay away. He'll be fine."

She thought of the pretty black box sitting on her bed. "I need some kind of time frame."

He rubbed the back of his neck. "I don't have one. We could...I don't know. Maybe when I go home over the break, I can get a better idea of where his mind is at."

"I can't do this for much longer. I don't think Daniel is going to..." she trailed off. She was afraid to say it. "Wait for me."

He looked down at her, his eyes dark and unreadable. "You really have no idea how much he wants to be with you, do you? Is it possible that you are that oblivious?"

Annoyance made the blood rush to her cheeks. "Why do you think I'm here? I'm worried about him."

"I told you. He will survive. He knows how important this is."

"Okay, fine," she said. There was no point in discussing it any further. There was nothing either of them could do right now. She kicked off the slippers with a little more force than she needed, and stuck her feet back in her flip-flops. She reached for the door, but Hyun Tae grabbed her wrist, stopping her. She stared back at him in surprise.

"You can't go yet. If you came over here to make out, then you wouldn't leave after two minutes."

"I wouldn't come over to make out with you!" she said and then rolled her eyes. "You know what I mean. I would just be visiting."

"And?"

And he was right. She slid her feet out of her flip-flops and retrieved the slippers. "And are we staying in the living room or going in the kitchen?"

"Living room. I'll be right back."

She settled in the big, cream-colored recliner and got a book out of her backpack. He came back and took the longer couch. He unwound some earphones and then paused. "Do you mind if I listen to music?"

"No, of course not. Go ahead," she said. "I was going to do the same."

They both sat, earphones in and staring at their respective homework for a while. Every now and then, she would glance up at him. He didn't have any expression as he worked, his eyes fixed on the screen, his black, silky hair falling just above his brow. She wanted to ask him what he was working on, but she didn't want to be intrusive. A few times he almost caught her looking at him, but she quickly glanced back at her book. It's a good thing he had lousy peripheral vision. Or at least she hoped he couldn't see her.

Chase made it to exactly thirty minutes and took her earphones out. She was about to announce that she was ready to go home, but he asked, "Hungry?"

She was always hungry. "No, thank you."

His mouth twitched and he got up. "I'm having a sandwich. We have peanut butter if you'd like a peanut butter and jelly sandwich."

"You like peanut butter and jelly?"

"None of us likes that stuff."

"Then why do you have it?"

He gave her a sideways look. "Why do you think?"

"Oh. Oh! That's very nice of you."

Bribed by the peanut butter and jelly, she lingered for another hour and then rolled up her earphones. "Is this long enough, you think?" she asked.

He put his laptop aside. "Yep."

At the door, she put her flip-flops back on and went for the door handle. He reached out and held it shut. "Wait."

"What now?" she asked, trying to figure out what she had missed.

He ran his fingers through her hair, messing it up a little with a detached professionalism. "If I'm kissing you, then you'd walk out like this."

"Good thinking." Without asking, she stood up on her tiptoes and ran her hands through his hair and gave it a good scrub. It was soft under her hands, and she resisted the urge to muss it longer than necessary. Then she tugged at his shirt, pulling it askew.

"There. You aren't the only one with a reputation to uphold."

He raised an eyebrow. "Thank you."

On her way home, she realized the visit hadn't accomplished anything. She still had to break the news to Daniel somehow that Hyun Tae wasn't going to try to break it off with her yet. Total fail. At least she knew Daniel would be home tomorrow.

The next day, after her classes, she texted Hyun Tae again. *"I'd like another sandwich."*

"LOL. Come and get it".

She rolled her eyes. Flirt.

She knocked at the door, feeling a bit of deja vu. *Please be home, Daniel,* Her heart beat faster.

The door opened, and he stood there, his hair darker than the last time she seen him, his warm eyes smiling down at her, though he didn't move to touch her. He wore a button-down shirt and jeans that looked good on his slim body.

"Hi," he said, his voice low.

"Hey," she said, unable to hide the smile that spread across her face.

"Would you like to come in?"

"Yes, thank you," she answered politely.

She stepped in, and he slowly closed the door behind them, his eyes on hers. As soon as it clicked shut, she threw her arms around him. "Hi," she said again.

He hugged her back, lifting her off her feet and laughing. "I missed you."

"Did you? I heard you went back to Korea. You were probably too busy to think about me."

He set her down, his fingers sliding off her arms. "It's true. I almost forgot what you looked like."

"Did you?" she echoed him, teasing. She took out her phone and found the picture Kiki had taken of her in the Gamora outfit. "Does this help?"

He looked down at her phone and his face froze for a moment and then he looked back at her, admiration in his eyes, and something a little more intense. "Wow."

She smiled back at him and then took a deep breath. "Hey, so did Hyun Tae tell you?"

He lost his smile. "No. What is it?"

"We can't go on Friday. He doesn't think it's a good idea. He thinks someone might see us together."

For the first time, she saw real anger in his soft eyes. His lips tightened, and he shook his head. "No. That's ridiculous. We're going."

Her heart jumped, and she was about to chime in and agree with him when a quiet voice behind them said, "I'm just trying to be careful."

Hyun Tae leaned against the wall, his hands in his pockets. He had on sweats and a black T-shirt, his hair damp, sweat on his forehead, as if he had just been working out.

Daniel stared back at him and said something in Korean, his voice hard.

Hyun Tae answered him back, calmly.

Annoyed because she couldn't understand them and because she knew Hyun Tae wasn't bending, she said, "English, please."

Daniel turned to her. "It's up to you. What do you think? We'd be careful."

"It's not up to her," Hyun Tae said. "She's not going."

Torn between her fear of his father and her fear of losing Daniel, she didn't know what to do. She certainly didn't like Hyun Tae's lack of interest in her opinion. "Daniel, it's okay. Don't worry about it."

He ran his fingers through his hair, his expression pained.

She grabbed his shirt and tugged him toward the kitchen. "It'll be okay."

She had a plan.

*****

"So, are you cheating on your not-boyfriend?" Kiki asked, touching her lips with the black lipstick. She was going to the party as a Goth. As an accomplice to the forbidden date with Daniel, she was going to drive with Chase to the party. Chase had told Hyun Tae she was sick. Lame, but it worked.

Chase flipped her hair, posing in front of the mirror in the tight leather outfit. They'd found some green face paint at a costume shop, and she'd covered her face, neck and hands. She looked alien and mysterious. And very green. Her raspberry pink lipstick made her teeth look white. For once her heart monitor, seemed to blend with what she was wearing. It was like some space age wristband.

"Actually, I'm cheating *with* my boyfriend."

She wasn't sure boyfriend was the right word for Daniel. They hadn't even kissed. Yet. Daniel obviously cared about her, but he was taking his time showing it that way. Everything she'd learned about him so far told her that he was quiet about his feelings, but they were real. She liked that.

Also, there was something exciting about breaking out of the restraints of the fake relationship. She hadn't done anything to anyone, yet she was being forced to pretend to like someone. It was crazy. Well, being forced to pretend to like someone who was easy to look at. Either way, it hadn't been her choice. Tonight was her choice, and she was going to take it.

Kiki jumped up and down, like a fighter getting into the ring. "Let's do this!"

Chase laughed, her voice tinged with manic anticipation. They ran out to Kiki's little blue Fiat, stifling their laughter. It was dark out already, which only made them move more like stealthy thief ninjas. Or something. All the secrecy was scary and exciting at the same time.

They put on their favorite road trip playlist, blasting it as loud as they could stand it, screaming out the songs and laughing. The party was at an address unfamiliar to both of them. The GPS told them to take a road that went far out of town, then off the highway and up a steep road that wound up the mountain that had always sat on the horizon. Everyone had seen the huge houses on the mountain, the lights sparkling down from their lofty perches. They turned onto a small road, and Kiki lowered the volume on their music. Floodlights lit up manicured trees and gardens as they drove, taking them around turns until the house they were looking for came into view.

"Whoa," Kiki said.

A huge white concrete and glass house stood on the edge of a cliff, framed by softly swaying palm trees. It was on a series of different levels, all of them stacked on the mountainside, more lights gleaming from inside the glass walls. A huge grassy area was filled with shiny cars, most of them expensive looking.

"Wow. I hope this is the right party," Chase said, suddenly self-conscious about her costume. It was one thing to think she looked hot in her dorm room; it was another to face a crowd of strangers who might not be in costume.

"Me, too," Kiki said, and parked the car and turned off the engine.

They sat for a moment in silence, looking up at the house. Then at the same time they both pulled down their visors and checked their makeup in the mirrors.

"I'm so green," Chase said under her breath.

"Okay. Let's go," Kiki said, staring at her own reflection.

Chase stepped out of the car and bravely adjusted her belt. This had better be the right address, and Daniel had better be here. A low thud boomed from the house, and there was music and was that...splashing? Was there a pool?

She quickly texted him. *"I'm here."*

"I'll come and get you."

Kiki joined her, bouncing nervously on her toes. "Is he here?"

"Yeah. He said he's coming to get us."

She looked toward the house, and in the lights on the lawn she saw a slim shadow coming toward her. Her heart beat faster. He walked up to her, wearing a deep red leather jacket and matching pants, the leather snug on his hips and thighs. Star-Lord. He'd left his hair dark but swept it to the side, and it made him look smooth, confident.

"Hey," she said, smiling.

He smiled back, then his eyes left hers to greet Kiki. "Hey, Kiki. Good to see you. Thanks for bringing her."

Chase had forgotten that Kiki was there.

"Hey, Daniel. This house is amazing! Do you know the owners?"

"Yes. Come on in. I'll show you around."

He offered his hand to Chase, and she slipped her fingers around his, hoping she didn't look too starstruck. He was beautiful, his dark eyes intense. He leaned down and whispered in her ear, "You look amazing."

She almost giggled because her ears were ticklish and the big house made her a little nervous. "Thanks. You too," she whispered back.

They went up a walkway to a series of stairs, all lit by ground lights. The front doors were glass, and he opened them for her and Kiki. They stepped inside to music and lights and a crowd of people, all wearing colorful costumes. It was as if she'd stepped into a commercial. The girls were all gorgeous, and the guys all could have been models. The Korean girls all seemed to favor shorts, their legs long and shapely. Her hands went clammy.

He squeezed her hand, as if he could sense what she was feeling. Or maybe her clammy hands gave her away.

"Daniel!"

Chase scanned the crowd for the girl who had called his name. A beautiful Asian girl with round brown eyes and long, wavy hair came toward them. She had on a short, gold sequined skirt that skimmed her upper thighs, showing her long legs. She wore a black sleeveless top that clung to her slim body, and the way she moved her hips when she walked made Chase stare. She couldn't imagine what Daniel was thinking. Well, she could, but she didn't. She sucked in her stomach, and one of her feet snuck behind the other self-consciously.

The girl in had creamy, perfect skin and no discernible makeup, except for maybe mascara on her thick lashes. She smiled with dazzling white teeth.

"*Oppa*! Where have you been?" she asked, somehow managing to look demure, even though she'd just sauntered across the room like a Victoria's Secret model.

Chase remembered that *oppa* was some kind of nickname for boys. Was it all boys, or was that Daniel's name? If she called him *oppa,* would he know she was talking to him?

He smiled at the newcomer. "Si Seong, good to see you. You know where I've been. How are you?"

She shrugged so coyly Chase almost winced. Whoa. The cutesy factor here was pretty high.

"Lonely. When are you coming back?"

He kept his smile, but Chase detected a hint of impatience in it. "I'm in school, so it will be a while. I'd like you to meet my friends. This is Chase," he said, nodding in Chase's direction. The girl zoned in on Chase, her eyes going cool, doing the head to toe judgy thing and then smiling.

Chase gave a limp wave with a green hand. "Hi."

"Nice to meet you," Si Seong said.

"And this is Kiki," he said.

Kiki was having none of the subtle games. She stuck her hand out, like a car salesman going in for the kill. "How are you?"

Si Seong blinked and then gave Kiki her hand. "Fine, thank you. It's nice to meet one of Daniel's American friends."

"Likewise," Kiki said and pressed her lips together, spreading her black lipstick around her lips and licking them.

Chase arched an eyebrow at Kiki. Likewise? What the heck did that mean?

Following that display, Si Seong smiled uncertainly.

A young guy in a baseball cap waved urgently at Daniel from across the room and Daniel sighed. "Hey, I'll be right back. Is that okay?" he asked, looking at Chase.

268

"Sure," she said, ignoring the nervous desperation that made her want to beg him to stay with her.

He walked away, and the three girls looked at each other for a few beats, and then Kiki exhaled and smiled.

"So you know Daniel really well?" Chase asked.

Si Seong brightened. "Yes. I've known him since we were little. He's always watched over me."

Kiki frowned. "He's never mentioned you."

Chase winced.

"He probably doesn't talk a lot about home," Si Seong said smoothly, looking unfazed.

"Yeah, he's pretty shy," Chase said.

This earned her an incredulous look from Si Seong. "How did you meet him?"

"Blind date. My mom thought he was cute and set us up. Kind of...awkward. But he was really nice about it."

"A blind date?" Si Seong repeated as if Chase had just told her Batman wore Crocs.

"Yeah. Crazy, huh?"

"So he hasn't talked about Korea? At all?"

"Oh sure," Chase said breezily. "He has a younger brother, and he travels a lot."

Si Seong kept staring at her as if her act was crazier than Kiki's. Daniel was making his way back through the crowd. Si Seong flicked her eyes over to him and then stepped very close to Chase and said in a low voice, "You should Google your boyfriend sometime."

Kiki narrowed her eyes at Si Seong as she walked away. "Now that was one weird chick."

Daniel returned and apologized. He put his hand on the small of her back, saying in a voice loud enough for her to hear over the music, "Come on, I'll show you the backyard."

They followed him through the house, dazzled by the lights. The main room had a high ceiling that went up two stories, a wall of windows looking out over a massive deck, and a pool. The furniture was placed in small seating arrangements, where people converged, laughing and talking, some of them looking over at them. Maybe it was her imagination, but the girls all seemed to take a keen interest in her, their eyes going from her boots to her hair, and she could almost hear them assessing her. The guys did the same; they were just more casual about it. They all seemed to know Daniel. As in, all of them, not just a few.

He took them outside to the deck, where the music was more muffled and a cool breeze blew through the trees and the pool sparkled in the lights.

"Hey!" a voice said, calling across deck. A tall, muscular Asian guy wearing a grass hula skirt over swimming shorts ambled toward them. There was a

270

flower lei around his neck, and he held a coconut in one hand with a straw poking out of it.

Daniel grinned. "Hey, Ki Suk. These are my friends. This is Chase, and this is Kiki."

Ki Suk swept Kiki into a hug. Kiki stumbled against him and looked over at Chase, her cheek pressed against his bare chest. She made an exaggerated happy face, rolling her eyes in mock ecstasy, and Chase couldn't help laughing.

"Welcome," he said.

Kiki smiled up at him. "Hi."

He stared at her, a speculative look in his eyes, and then held up the coconut drink. "I know where to get these."

She raised her eyebrows. "Fabulous."

He offered her his arm, and Kiki turned back to Chase. "You don't mind?"

"Have fun."

"Thought she'd like him," Daniel said as they walked away.

"Who wouldn't?" Chase asked.

He gave her a look, and she laughed.

"It's okay. I'm not insecure," Daniel said. "Come with me." He took her hand and led her across the deck and around the pool, toward a set of stairs that were hidden from the deck.

"Where are we going?" she asked. Her laser gun bumped against her thigh as she walked, and she was afraid she'd fall down the stairs in her too big boots. Her stomach was all butterflies and flip-flops.

"I want to show you something," he said, smiling back at her as he led her down the stairs.

Small lights lit the wood platforms that wound down the cliff wall. The stairs ended at the beach, where a candlelit table sat under a billowing tent strung with paper lanterns. The surf washed up on the sand, a hundred feet from the tent, and she realized that except for the water, she could barely hear anything else. Moonlight shone down on the waves, and torches flickered in the breeze. The table was set with white linens, and the silverware gleamed next to silver gilded plates.

"Daniel," she said. "This is beautiful. How did you do all this?"

He smiled at her. "You like it?"

"Yes! You did this for me?"

Instead of answering, he pulled out a chair for her. She started to sit down, but the gun hit the chair. She stood up, her cheeks going warm as she took the belt off. He reached out and took it from her, then pushed the chair in. She gripped the sides of her chair. It was all so beautiful, and she was covered in green paint and wearing black leather. She wished she could have worn something more romantic, like a dress. Suddenly shy, she looked down at the table.

"Is anything wrong?" he asked, sitting down across from her.

She glanced up at him and gave him a quick smile. "No, it's really nice."

The concern in his eyes did not fade. "What is it? Have I done something wrong?"

"It's just that this is all so beautiful, and I'm...green."

His face cleared, and he put his hand over his heart. "Oh man, you scared me. I thought you didn't like it."

"No, I love it. I just...you know," she said, gesturing to herself.

He reached across the table and took her green painted hands in his. "You're the most beautiful girl in the world. I love you in green, I love you in purple, in anything. You make me feel..." he stopped and hesitated. "No one has made me feel like this. Ever."

Her heart skipped a beat when he said, "I love you," even though she knew he probably didn't mean it that way. She bit her lip and smiled. "Thank you."

He released her hands and opened one of the silver tray covers. "I hope you're hungry."

The tent and the table were beautiful, but the food almost made her forget her surroundings. The kale salad was crisp with a tart dressing, and the soup had a smoky flavor. The steak was perfect, grilled and juicy, the marinade tangy. Chase tried not to eat too much, but her taste buds wanted more. She finally sat back and sighed. "You are trying to kill me with outrageously good food."

He laughed at her. "I wasn't sure if you would like it."

She shook her head at him. "I would have to be crazy not to like this. Seriously. Just out of my mind."

A breeze blew a lock of her hair across her cheek, and she brushed it away. He was looking at her, and her eyes went to his lips and then back up to his eyes.

"Do you want to go for a walk?" he asked, his voice husky.

She nodded, and he offered her his hand. They walked out almost to the water, and she looked down at her boots. "I guess I can't go in," she said ruefully.

He gestured for her to sit down. "I've got this," he said.

"Oh no, that's okay," she said. He moved toward her until his body was against hers. She looked up in surprise and then he hit the back of her knee with his foot and she crumpled to the sand, though his arms went around her so she didn't fall hard. He grinned down at her and bent down, taking the heel of a boot and pulling on it. It slipped off easily, and he frowned. He took the next boot and felt the toe of it. "These were too big. You didn't tell me."

"No one noticed. And you got everything else just right."

He even peeled off her socks, ignoring her protests. He rolled up her pants legs and then pulled her up from the sand. He kicked off his own boots, and they went out to the water, letting it wash up on their feet. It was cold and she laughed, although all she could think about was whether or not he was going to kiss her. She really wanted him to.

They kept looking at each other, and he kept...holding her hand. Was he afraid someone was watching them? It was impossible. They were on a secluded, private beach. Was it because she was green?

A wave rushed up out of the darkness, and before she could scramble back, the water hit her, turning her into him, and she grabbed his shirt. His arms held her, and he stood firm against the water. When it receded, she was still pinned against him. She looked up and was caught in his gaze. His heart pounded against her hands. Then he bent his head and kissed her, his mouth hesitant at first, and then more confident, the kiss deepening. One hand cupped her face, the other pulling her against him. He let her go, his eyes going to hers. She wished he hadn't looked at her then. His kiss was full of yearning, but she couldn't respond in kind. She felt nothing.

He kissed her again, lightly, and she didn't know what to do. She kissed him back, her mouth soft and yielding. Her heart was breaking...for him. She put her hand up and brushed a lock of hair from his face, and he closed his eyes, leaning into her hand. She didn't want to hurt him, but she was going to.

A flash caught her eye, and at first she thought it was the moonlight on the water, then she realized it wasn't. Cold terror flooded through her and she drew in a quick breath. "Daniel!"

He looked up, and the flash came again. His eyes widened, and at first he tried to shield her, turning his back to the place where they'd seen the light, cradling her head against his chest. They both stood there, frozen. Then they heard footsteps going up the wooden stairs. He let her go and sprinted after the unknown photographer. She stood in the water, her hands clenched into fists, staring after him in shock. Daniel ran for the stairs, and when he reached them, he jumped up two at a time. A shadowy figure clambered up to the top and disappeared.

She realized she was shaking. There was no mistaking Daniel's arms around her and his head bent to hers, no matter how dark it was. Fear made her mind race. Hyun Tae's father was going to see those pictures. He was going to think...she didn't know. What would he think?

She ran to the stairs, and as she climbed, she heard a loud noise. Her brain was slow to identify it. Her heart monitor. It was going crazy, the warning beeps so fast they were turning into one loud scream. She couldn't breathe. She stopped halfway up the stairs, a hand uselessly clutching at her too-fast beating heart.

"Daniel," she tried to call out, but it came out as a weak cry.

She concentrated on breathing, her heart monitor still beeping madly. She had to calm down, to not think about the pictures. There was nothing she could do about it now. Hyun Tae's father would never believe that they were in love now. Or maybe he would think she had betrayed his son and couldn't be trusted. And if she would cheat on someone she said she loved, maybe she was keeping other secrets as well. Maybe she was capable of stealing information. *Stop, please. Calm down. Just breathe.*

Her heart continued to thump, banging so hard against her chest that it hurt. She drew in a painful breath and sat down, willing her heart to slow its pace

Chapter Twenty-Two

Hyun Tae looked down at the text and didn't move for a good ten seconds. Anger, fear, disappointment, and betrayal all warred for first place. Betrayal won.

"Did she pass out?" he texted.

"No, but she is really sleepy from her medication."

Betrayal gave way to anger. Daniel had known what they were up against, and he'd crushed any hope for her safety in one single, stupid act. Hyun Tae swiped his keys off the counter, pocketed his phone, and walked out of the house, the night air cool. Light footsteps followed him, but he didn't turn around. He hit the fob, unlocking the car and then jerked the door open.

He got in, and the passenger door opened. Joon Suh slid in, looking over at him.

Hyun Tae started the car. "He couldn't help himself. He had to kiss her. And he got caught, because he's always being watched. All the time. And I told him."

Joon Suh closed the door. "Did he catch whoever took the pictures?"

"No. And her heart rate went ballistic."

Joon Suh frowned. "Is she okay?""

Hyun Tae pulled away from the curb. "She's going to be."

They drove in silence, Hyun Tae completely lost in his own thoughts. He knew Daniel was going to beat himself up over this, but for once he didn't have any pity for his friend. He'd trusted him, and Daniel had let him down. Hyun Tae had thought Daniel would care more about Chase's safety than his own need to see her, but that had been a huge miscalculation.

The house in the mountains belonged to Daniel's agent, and although Hyun Tae had only been there once or twice, it was easy to find.

He wound up the road to the big contemporary home on the cliff and parked his car. People were leaving, getting into their cars and talking in low voices. He didn't know if they'd been asked to leave or if they'd sensed Daniel wanted to be alone. Most of his friends in the business were sensitive to Daniel's situation and would have no problem giving him some space.

He kept himself from running up the stairs, but he still set a quick pace. Joon Suh kept up somehow, a silent shadow behind him.

When he got the to the front door, Ki Suk opened the door for him, his brow furrowed

The party lights were out and there were only softly lit lamps. He'd seen it in full party mode before, and it was pretty distracting. A young girl with green paint on her skin lay on one of the couches. He realized with a start that it was Chase. She lay with one arm over her eyes, her knees curled up, her chest rising and falling a little too rapidly, her heart monitor beeping at a rapid clip.

Kiki was standing with her arms crossed. Daniel paced next to Chase, his hands in his pockets, his face pinched with worry.

Hyun Tae ignored him and sat on the couch. He pulled Chase's arm away from her face. Her blue eyes opened, looking at him. Her raspberry pink lipstick was smeared. He reached over absently and wiped at it. His thumb turned green. "Hey," he said.

She swallowed, and her heart monitor sped up. "Someone saw us kissing," she said in a shaky voice.

He picked up the wrist with the heart monitor band on it and turned it over, undoing the clasp and sliding the band off, keeping his fingers on her pulse. It was going to be impossible for her to calm down with the thing beeping like that, even with medication to help her wind down. The noise was making his own heart rate rise.

"I know. It's okay."

"How is it okay?"

"Because I'm going to see my father."

"You're going to see him? In Korea?" Her eyes were a pale blue against her green skin, almost fluorescent.

"Yes. It's what I should have done in the first place."

"But I thought you didn't want to confront him. That you weren't ready."

He just sat there, feeling her rapid pulse under his fingers and trying not to be afraid for her. He finally answered in a low, calm voice. "I just didn't want to leave in the middle of the semester," he said. "But that isn't important now. I can deal with missing some class time to fix this. And I will. I might not be back for a while, but you'll be okay. I promise."

"You think he'll listen to you?"

"Of course he will. He only has one son. I'm a big deal."

She stared at him for a moment, and he was worried that she'd gone catatonic, then the corner of her lips lifted in a small smile. "You're a big deal?"

"Yes."

She sighed, and her pulse gradually slowed, sinking from desperate to slightly faster than normal, which was good, for her. There was a thin film of perspiration on her forehead. He rubbed his forearm over her brow. He looked at the green smear on his arm and then down at her outfit. "That leather looks very comfortable."

Her eyes closed, and she laughed, softly. "Oh, it is."

"Hmm. What do you say you spend some time at home? It's been a rough night."

She frowned. "At home?"

"Yeah. With your parents."

She shook her head. "Nah. They get worried. I'm okay to go home."

He didn't try to hide his skepticism. "Really? Can you walk?"

Pushing herself up, she got to her feet, swaying. "Ta da."

Kiki tilted her head. "C minus."

"B+," Chase disagreed, blinking.

"You win," Hyun Tae said.

"As usual," she said, looking pleased with herself.

Hyun Tae had a flashback to the last time he'd seen her on medication. She had a penchant for going loopy. Before she could move, he scooped her up in his arms, saying, "Don't do that dumb girl thing where you protest and tell me how much you weigh."

"I was going to warn you about the green paint I'm getting on your shirt."

"I never wear the same clothes twice. I donate them to charity."

"Really?"

"No," he said, and she made a face at him.

He met Daniel's eyes. Neither of them saying anything. The anguish was plain on Daniel's face. Hyun Tae spoke in Korean. "We're still hyungs, but you are making me do something I am not ready to do."

Daniel didn't flinch. "I am sorry."

Sadness passed between them. Hyun Tae could never trust Daniel the way he had before, and they both knew it.

He walked out of the house, Kiki and Joon Suh following him. The night breeze was tinged with the smell of the ocean, and the stars sparkled in the deep, black sky. Chase was looking up at them, blinking sleepily. How could his father think anyone this small was a threat? When they got to the car, Chase let go of him, and he let her down. Joon Suh opened the door and leaned the front seat back. She got in and attempted to put her seat belt on. He waited patiently, sitting on his haunches next to her, as she missed the buckle about a million times until it clicked.

"Is she okay?" Joon Suh asked in Korean.

Hyun Tae stood. "I suppose. If it were up to me, I'd take her to a hospital, but she says she doesn't need to do that. She just keeps taking that medication."

"She's lived with it most of her life. She should know."

"She also let me talk her into pretending to be my girlfriend. How is that working out for her?"

Joon Suh leaned back in his seat and didn't reply, his silence speaking his disapproval.

Hyun Tae waited for Kiki to get in the backseat and then got in the driver's seat and closed the door. He handed Chase's monitor to Kiki and started the car. He spoke again in Korean, muttering under his breath. "It's my fault, not hers."

Joon Suh answered him. "*Ne.*"

283

Hyun Tae drove down the long mountain driveway, glancing back at the lights in the big house. He knew Daniel would be watching them leave. He looked down at Chase, who was looking out the window like it was some fascinating light show. He could see why Daniel was so into her, and a small pang of pity for his friend hit him.

But it wasn't enough to squash the anxiety that churned in his stomach at the thought of confronting his father so soon. He had to be smart about it. He would watch the press, watch his father's movements, and try to formulate a plan that would not jeopardize his chances of taking over KimBio before his father retired due to old age. It couldn't wait that long, but neither could he sit back and wait for his own influence at KimBio to grow over time. He would have to find another way. Taking one last look at Chase, he had to wonder if all of this was better. Maybe she was fated to speed up the course of events in his life.

Chapter Twenty-Three

Chase carefully laid her portfolio flat on the back seat of her car. After a moment's hesitation, she shifted it so it sat upright between the front seat and back seat on the floor.

"You might as well just buckle it in," Kiki said, leaning against the car and watching her.

Chase straightened and then patted her hair, which Kiki had fashioned into a low, braided bun. "Very funny."

"Are you sure you don't want me to come with? I have no problem skipping all my classes. None at all."

"I'm touched," Chase said as she closed the back door. As she pulled her keys from her purse, Kiki threw her arms around Chase's neck. "Go get 'em, girl. Thundercats…"

"GO!" they both shouted, raising fists.

Chase started the ignition and pulled out of her parking spot. She turned on the radio, hoping to calm her nerves. She was more than just a little jittery but somehow still unbearably exhausted.

In a sudden burst of inspiration, fueled by the tension and regret from Friday, she had spent all Saturday and Sunday modifying her key pieces. She scratched away at it with her chalk pastels, shifting lines and changing the entire feel of the thing. She had stayed up most of Sunday night and all of the night before to get it done, but when she stepped back, she knew it was the right move. It made her a little nervous to show up without a digital backup of the crucial artwork, but it was a risk she was willing to take. It took the portfolio from a lot of separate pieces to a cohesive whole.

And, if she was honest, she hadn't had even one moment to think about Daniel. Or Hyun Tae. Or anything Korean at all.

As she paused at the stop sign leading out of her apartment complex, the passenger door suddenly jerked open.

Chase jumped, her heart thumping into her throat as she looked over.

Hyun Tae slid into the seat, slamming the door quickly.

"What the heck?" she demanded, anger rising as her panic subsided. "You can't just scare people like that."

"Sorry." He turned to give her a little smile. "I just had the sudden urge to go with you."

"Well, you could have called!"

"It was kind of last minute."

She realized then that his breathing was a little labored. Had he run from his house to catch up to her car?

He motioned to the road. "You have right of way."

"I almost died," she muttered. She pulled out onto the road, turning the radio down. "Soooo, this isn't exactly a couple thing we need to do."

"I'm not doing it for that."

She glanced away from the road to his face briefly. He looked straight ahead, completely serious. Puzzled, she dropped her barrage of questions and turned the radio back up to fill the silence she knew would ensue. He had his reasons, but he wasn't willing to discuss them.

She took a right into a residential neighborhood, settling in for the hour or so drive to L.A. She had the address of the building in her phone, and she hoped her GPS could get her there once they entered the city.

"Why did you turn here?" Hyun Tae asked.

"What?"

"Why aren't you taking the highway?"

"I like this route. It goes through a forest, and it's more interesting."

"You should take the highway."

Chase clicked her tongue. "If you're going to backseat drive, you can get out."

"I'm in the front seat."

She gripped the steering wheel instead of reaching for his neck.

Chase concentrated on the road, drinking in the bright sunshine and the green trees that whizzed past. She loved the mix of scruffy shrubs and pines, dotted with tall leafy trees that towered over the road. She opened her window, sticking out her hand to let it glide over the air as they cruised alone on the back roads.

As they went around a bend, the dusty ground flattening and stretching out like a desert before them, Chase noticed Hyun Tae glancing in the passenger's side mirror. She looked in her rearview mirror and saw a shiny black sedan following at a moderate distance.

The black car revved its engine, and, with a screech, sped up to make an illegal pass around her. It slid into place in front of them and then tapped its brakes, forcing her to slow down.

Chase scoffed. "What a jerk."

Hyun Tae kept looking at the passenger's side mirror. "Just watch the road."

Chase looked in the mirror. She had the unsettling sensation of seeing the same car at the same distance behind her. "What the…?"

Hyun Tae took out his phone and quickly tapped out a message. As he typed, he said, "Just keep driving. Keep a safe distance from the car in front of you. And roll up your window."

The black car in front slowed down further. The one behind inched closer.

"What is going on?" she asked, closing the windows.

"My father."

"Obviously, but what does he want this time? Didn't you explain the thing with Daniel?"

"I did." He kept typing on his phone, looking up and checking the road and the mirror every few seconds.

The front car tapped its brakes again. They were down to thirty-five miles per hour.

"Can I go around him? Are they trying to make me stop?"

"They don't know I'm in the car, so yes, they're trying to pull you over. Don't stop."

"Do I go around?"

"No, just keep driving."

Brake tap. Down to a crawl. "Well what do you want me to do? He's stopping me. You want me to just keep going while he stops —"

"Keep going until I tell you otherwise." Hyun Tae finished his message, put his phone in his pocket, and turned his full attention to her driving. "You're doing fine. Just wait."

"Wait for what?"

He focused his gaze on her. "Here's the plan. The best thing you can do right now is go along with them, so we don't get hurt. When he comes to a full stop, I want you to pull over as if to stop as well, and then hit the gas. Hit it hard, and get around him. You need to time it before the car behind us tries to box us in from the side."

"I can't."

"Don't panic."

Her heart monitor started to ding over the pop song still going on the radio.

Hyun Tae reached over to turn off the music. "We're not in any danger from these people, but I don't want you to be detained when you have an appointment to keep. Okay?"

"Okay." Even to her own ears, she didn't sound convinced.

The car in front slowed to a halt, and Chase kept a safe distance, allowing her car to roll almost to a stop. The car behind shifted to the left.

"Now," he said.

Chase slammed her foot on the gas, jerking into the opposite lane, and gunning it past the black sedan. She managed to pass, but the car behind them kept pace with her. "Now what?" Chase asked, her heart monitor increasing in tempo as she pushed her junker to sixty miles per hour.

"Just keep going," Hyun Tae said, phone out again and fingers tapping.

"Who are they?" she asked, her eyes going from the rearview mirror to the road.

"I don't know," he said, frustration in his voice.

She focused on a bend in the road, wishing that she had taken the highway after all. These desert back roads were the worst place for them to be.

The car behind suddenly roared and sped up so fast, it was on her left before she could react. They were parallel now, and he was going to pass her.

Chase's monitor went crazy. Her chest became tight; she tried to calm herself down, but the car veered close to them, forcing her to slow down and giving him the advantage. Her thoughts were getting clouded as her heart rate rose.

"Don't," Hyun Tae said. "Chase, you have to calm down. We can stop, and I'll deal with him. Don't race him and lose control."

"You said don't stop."

"That was before it got dangerous. Slow down."

"I am!" she said. Her heart banged furiously in her rib cage. *Calm, Chase. Be calm.* The other car sped up right behind her, and they were so close she wondered if they were going to push her off the road.

Up ahead, a bridge came into view, and the lanes narrowed. "Not good," she said.

"Calm. Steady," Hyun Tae said calmly, but then both cars got so close, one on her left and one behind, she could see the drivers. They weren't going to move.

"We're going to crash," she said, voice strained and high.

"Stop before we hit that bridge."

She pressed on the brake, and they jolted forward as the car behind tapped her bumper.

Adrenaline spiked through Chase's veins, her heart rate leaping to an out of control pace as she pressed down hard on the gas again. "I can't stop," she gasped. Her vision started to spot. "I can't stop."

"Stop the car, Chase!" Hyun Tae urged.

"I ca-I can't..."

Suddenly they were on the bridge, and the car on her left bumped her mirror to mirror, shattering the glass and rocking the car.

"Chase, no!" Hyun Tae shouted a warning, but the haze and the fear suffocated her, and she reacted without thinking, jerking the wheel to the right to avoid a collision.

The crash as they slammed into the concrete barrier jerked her body to the right, and then she whipped to the left, arms flailing out of her control, her limbs tossed like a rag. The engine revved, and she wondered if the car was still going forward. Her body went weightless for one frozen moment.

And then another impact, this one from the front that wrenched her forward so violently, it tore tendons in her shoulder as the seat belt jammed against her. She recognized the splash of water before her eyes adjusted. And then she saw the river. In her windshield. Nose down, the car began to slowly sink into the thin, brown ribbon of water that should have been under the bridge and not surrounding her car. Cold water seeped into her shoes and up her ankles.

"Chase."

The water bubbled up around her windshield, and someone unbuckled her seat belt. Two hands jerked her face around until she focused on a pair of angry brown eyes. "Chase wake up!"

She blinked. The sound of her beeping heart monitor pierced through the sound of rushing water and the hissing engine. Hyun Tae stared at her, his cheek bleeding from a shattered window. But his eyes were sharp and focused.

His hands cradled her face, and his thumbs brushed anxiously against her cheeks. "Chase, you can't pass out, okay? Do you hear me?"

She nodded.

"We're going to be okay."

She nodded again, her wits returning.

Hyun Tae took her wrist, ripped off the heart monitor, and threw it into the back. Silence. Blissful silence. He took her face in his hands again. "We're going to wait until the car sinks. Just a little. Then we can open the doors and swim out. Okay?"

The water had reached her hips now, and it lapped up against the windows.

"Chase, look at me."

She did, focusing on the rich brown of his eyes. "You're okay. Take a deep breath. Breathe with me."

It was helping. She almost always needed her medication to calm her down, but she knew she couldn't do that now. So she breathed, and she watched his eyes, his confidence seeping into her. Her heart slowed. Her head became clearer.

"Hey," he gave her head a little shake. "You with me?"

"Yeah," she croaked.

The water was up to her armpits. She looked around, positioning her body to float in the space with her head up high.

"Take off your shoes and get ready to open the door and swim out, okay?"

"I saw this on *MythBusters*," she said. Her voice sounded almost normal. The water splashed up to her chin. "But this is really, really scary."

"I know, but we're going to be fine." He turned to examine the door. "Any second now. Get ready."

Chase kicked off her high heels, awkwardly sitting and floating at the same time. She knew her heart was still in overdrive, but she forced her mind to stay alert.

"Come here." Hyun Tae pulled her over to his side, wrapping his arm around her waist so she practically sat on his lap. "We'll go out together."

The smell of lake water clogged her nose. Their heads were floating up near the top of the car, arms treading water.

"Deep breath," he said.

She filled her lungs, sucking in as much air as she could, and then Hyun Tae pulled her under. Murky water clouded her vision. In an instant, up became down, and all direction was lost to her, but his hands on her arm helped her remain grounded. He guided her hands to the door, and then through the muddy depths, she barely made out his hands pulling on the handle and pushing the car door. She pushed. He pounded against the metal door. A surge of panic hit her when nothing gave.

Suddenly, Hyun Tae jerked away from her, sliding to the left and grabbing her wrist. Her knee bumped hard against something as they swam to the other side of the car. It was so tight. The space was too small. Water was everywhere, and she swam up in a desperate search for air. No air. Just water.

Her heart hammered so hard she feared she was going to lose the breath she had stored in her lungs. A hand grasped her wrist again, and an arm went around her waist to yank her down against Hyun Tae. She saw the driver's side door then, and collecting her wits, she helped him push against the door. It gave.

Another shove, and it opened, letting in a current of swirling water as they both pushed. Her feet braced against something–the steering wheel?–and as the door widened, she frantically kicked her legs and swam through it into open water. Hyun Tae gave her rear end a shove, and she saw the glimmering surface just above her. Finally, her head broke the surface, and she gasped for air, swallowing a good mouthful of water as she gulped in oxygen.

The rocky shore was only a few feet away. She sliced through the water, swimming for dry land, and then her bare feet hit the muddy river floor. She stumbled out of the water, falling into a heap against the hot, dusty stones that jutted out from the bank.

Hyun Tae lay down beside her. Water streamed from his dark clothing, creating little rivulets in the dry earth that snaked down back into the river. Both of them lay there for a few moments, breathing heavily. The sun beat down on her chilled skin, and she rested her forehead against a jagged rock. In the distance, screeching wheels pealed off.

Finally, Hyun Tae crawled closer to her, taking her wrist and silently counting her heart rate. She knew it was still out of control. It was robbing her of strength and clarity of mind.

Her eyes snapped open when his arms wrapped around her. He tugged her across the uneven ground, rolling onto his back and pulling her half on top of him and pressed against his side. He squeezed her tight. "*Michikesoh*," he said under his breath.

She clutched the soaked cotton of his dark gray shirt, and let her head rest against the cradle of his shoulder. She didn't know what the word meant, but she got the impression that she agreed with the sentiment. Her heart began to slow down.

Behind them, the river rushed on in a soothing gurgle of white noise, not quite drowning out the ominous bubbling of the car that finished sinking to the riverbed. There were rectangles floating on the surface, and it took her a moment to realize what they were. She let go of Hyun Tae and pushed herself away, standing up, ignoring her shaky legs.

Her artwork swirled on the water, colors bleeding out into the water. She stumbled toward the river's edge. Hyun Tae scrambled up from the ground and spoke, but she could only see the ruin of her portfolio. She had no other copies. She'd been in too much of a hurry, and now all of her work was gone. She sloshed back into the river to try to save them, but Hyun Tae grabbed her and pulled her back. She couldn't stop her tears. If only she'd taken a few minutes to scan them or even take some pictures with her cell phone, but she hadn't.

"What is it?" he asked.

She shook her head, her throat choked and her vision blurry. It was all gone. "It was all I had. I don't have anything to show them. I have to start over."

Chapter Twenty-Four

Waiting for the water to fill up the car had been excruciating. Hyun Tae had been torn between hope and terror, his heart pounding while his mind kept track of the beat of hers, knowing it was fluttering like a hummingbird's, as dangerous as the water closing over their heads. He'd held her face in his hands, drowning in those perfectly clear blue eyes. He'd never seen that kind of trust before. She believed him when he said she was going to be okay.

He'd wanted to protect her, but things had turned out badly. Chase had no idea who Daniel was. The picture of Daniel kissing her on the beach had been plastered all over Korean celebrity sites. In America, that was not a scandal. In Korea, it was. Daniel was holed up at his agent's house, probably reading through all the hate mail, wondering if his career was going to survive.

But Hyun Tae hadn't cared about Daniel's career when his phone had blown up with the news about the star singer of boy band called Hipstar kissing a mysterious girl. Everyone in Korea had seen it, including his father. All their fake dates weren't going to mean a thing now. There was no reason for his father to leave Chase alone, especially if it looked as if she were cheating. His attempt to shield her by professing some kind of important relationship with her was flimsy when he'd first thought of it, but with the photo of her and Daniel, it just didn't matter at all.

He hadn't had a plan when he'd stopped her car this morning and got in. He just knew that his attempt to protect her had failed.

When the cars had begun following them, Hyun Tae had hoped they would just observe, but they hadn't. While being forced over the bridge, he'd managed to control his fear enough to get them out alive.

Now she stared out at the water, tears running down her face, her body shaking. He held her against him, wondering how he could stop this. The pieces of paper were beginning to float down the river. Her face was pale, and she looked shattered. He wanted to help her, but what was he supposed to do? Jump back into the river he'd just escaped? She kept shaking.

Finally, he snapped. He had to do something. He let go of her and stepped into the water, chasing after the pieces of paper. The water was cool, and the current hard as he walked in deeper. He gathered up the soaked artwork with as much care as he could, struggling against the river for what seemed like a long time, trying to capture every piece. He finally caught the last one he could see, and he fought his way back to shore, bone-weary. He separated the papers and laid them out in the grass by the river, not daring to look at them. She walked over, looking down at what he'd saved.

Her blouse was untucked, water still dripping from her skirt and down her legs, her feet bare. There were cuts on her forehead, and a bump on the side of her head was beginning to swell.

He didn't say anything, sitting on the grass and trying to catch his breath, watching her eyes, hanging on to the dim hope that he had saved something.

She walked from piece to piece, but her breath didn't slow and her eyes filled with tears again. A sick feeling plunged down from his throat to his gut.

Neither of them spoke as she crouched down on her knees and cried. He didn't dare try to comfort her. There was nothing he could do to help.

Voices called out above them, and Hyun Tae looked up. Two police cars and an ambulance were parked and people on the bridge were pointing down at the river. The texts to Joon Suh giving their location had worked.

It wasn't long before they were surrounded by people. Medics put Chase on an emergency stretcher, and she answered their questions in a numb, flat voice, a blood pressure cuff on her arm.

Hyun Tae gathered up her artwork, holding the wet papers carefully. Medics asked him about his injuries,

300

and he answered a little impatiently, trying to hear what they were saying about Chase. His chest was probably bruised from the seatbelt at impact and like Chase, he'd hit his head when he'd slammed against the window. Everyone told them they were lucky.

They said they were going to take her to a hospital because her heart rate was so high and she had a head injury. She didn't seem to care, her eyes going to the river when she wasn't answering questions.

Police wanted a description of the cars, which he gave to the best of his ability, knowing it wouldn't help. He knew where to find the men if he wanted to.

The morning sun glinted on the river. There was no sign of her car, and one of the police officers said something about pulling it out of the water. The medics carried Chase up the hill, and Hyun Tae followed them. Right before they lifted her into the ambulance, she looked over at him.

"You okay?" she asked.

He nodded. "You?"

"Yeah. Thank you for finding my artwork. Thanks for trying. And for saving my life."

He looked back at her, her wet hair plastered to her face, and her eyes a little swollen from crying. She gave him a small smile.

"I'll see you soon," he promised.

They closed the doors.

He watched the ambulance drive away, and a strong emotion hit him. A little dazed, he wasn't sure at first what it was. He was worried, but he understood that. He didn't know what his father had meant to happen, but he hoped it wasn't murder. He hoped it was an accident. This emotion wasn't about his father. It was about something else. It was so powerful he couldn't move.

A breeze moved the papers in his hand. He looked down at them, and the strange emotion grew stronger, flooding through him. He recognized the face she'd drawn, though the colors had run. The shape of the face was familiar, the eyes looking back at him with a wary expression. He imagined her small, quick hands tracing the lines and wondered what she'd been thinking when she'd begun to sketch. His chest tightened with anxiety. She'd drawn him.

All this time he'd been playing at being her boyfriend, calculating ways to appear as if he cared, and somehow she had seen through the ice to who he was. She cared about someone else, but she'd made room in her head for him, the real him.

He finally understood. The feeling that had taken him over him was fear. For the first time, he really cared about someone more than himself, and it was terrifying. He could control what happened to him, but he had no idea what to do when someone else's well-being affected his own that deeply. Watching her grieve over her lost artwork had hurt him too. He didn't want to have to listen to her cry like that and be helpless to fix it.

She might think she loved Daniel, but Daniel could never be right for her. He couldn't love her the way Hyun Tae could. Even as he thought it, Hyun Tae knew it was true. He loved Chase. It would be stupid to deny it.

Joon Suh walked down the road, past the police cars and curious onlookers. He wore linen slacks and a button-down shirt that rippled in the morning breeze. He scuffed his sandals in the gravelly dirt on the roadside, kicking up a cloud of dust. Stopping in front of Hyun Tae, he exhaled and stared at his wet clothes for a moment before asking, "You okay?"

His mind still on Chase, he answered absently, "Yeah."

"Where is Chase?"

"She's on her way to the hospital. I need a ride there."

Joon Suh furrowed his brow. "You need to see a doctor? Why didn't you just go with the ambulance?"

"Not for me. To see her."

"Why?"

"Because she is important to me."

Joon Suh processed this for a moment, then nodded. "Okay. Let's go."

They got in the Tesla and drove in silence, passing through the parched desert and toward the city limits. Hyun Tae couldn't stop thinking about how close he'd come to dying and how lucky he had been to save Chase. He finally said, "I'm going back to Korea."

Joon Suh frowned. "That may not be wise."

"Something is wrong with my father. His people almost killed us. He is out of control."

"What are you going to do about it?"

"I just want to see him."

Joon Suh gave a dark laugh. "You want to know what will happen? You will go to Korea. You will confront your father. No, you will *try* to confront your father, but you probably won't even get to see him. "

"He'll see me," Hyun Tae said, only half-listening because he could almost see himself standing in front of his father in the massive office, the high glass windows looking out over Seoul, the leather chair behind the black desk.

"He will tell you that if you are seen in public with her in Korea you will embarrass the family. And he's right. You think she is persecuted now? Wait until you date her in Korea."

Unfortunately, it was true. Except that no one knew who the girl in the picture with Daniel was. "You couldn't see who the girl was in that picture. All you could see was a girl with blond hair."

Drawing in a breath between his teeth, Joon Suh said, "Perhaps you should stay away from Chase."

"No. I'm not going to do that," Hyun Tae said. "Can you get me a plane ticket for tonight or not?"

"No."

Hyun Tae just stared at him.

Joon Suh breathed out in exasperation, which meant he was going to help.

Staring out at the horizon beyond the city limits, Hyun Tae went over his options. He could continue to stalk Chase, playing defense, or he could go on the offense and confront his father. He was ready for some offense.

The trouble was, Joon Suh was right about not being able to just attack his father head-on. Kim Sang Si was a mogul— the king of his economic empire, and the lengths he had gone to in order to achieve it had blackened his heart. South Korea had been a very different place in the 70s. Treacherous, uncertain, and cutthroat. His father had used claws to pull his company above his adversaries.

But despite the fact that times had changed, that there was no need to use a heavy hand in order to be the best, Sang Si held to the only method he knew worked. And now Hyun Tae had no choice but to find a way to pull his father down from his seat of power. He could have done it in ten years. Maybe five, if he worked hard. But now he needed to do it in the space of days.

"There is more at stake here than your girlfriend," Joon Suh reminded him.

Hyun Tae stared at his friend, knowing the reason his long fingers gripped the steering wheel. There was just as much on the line for Joon Suh. "I won't fail you," Hyun Tae said, reassuring him.

"Normally, I would believe you."

"I will come up with something."

Joon Suh didn't say anything more.

Without a definite plan, Hyun Tae wasn't sure there was much else to be said.

Chapter Twenty-Five

They wanted to keep her overnight. During the ambulance ride, her heart rate would slow down and then speed back up again, to the consternation of the EMTs. She kept remembering the water creeping up over her mouth and Hyun Tae pushing against the door. When they finally arrived at the hospital, the comfortingly familiar scent of antiseptic, the people in scrubs, and the dozens of questions were soothing enough to bring her fear back down. She stopped thinking about the water, and let the hospital distract her.

They had been close enough to L.A. to go to one of the nicer city hospitals, outfitted with enough rooms that patients didn't need to share. In her room, her TV was a flat-screen, and they fed her a decent meal almost right away. Even if she had to sit against a lump of crispy, flat hospital pillows, listening to her own heartbeat blipping away like the beat of a German techno dance song, she was grateful she was not sitting in a sinking car.

She hadn't been there long before someone knocked on the door. It was her mom, and she opened it slowly with a cautious smile, a neon blue bag over her shoulder. "Hi, sweetie."

"Hey, Mom."

The blue bag was the "Chase kit" her mom kept by the door for ER visits. It had her favorite snacks, a change of clothing, a comfortable pillow, flip-flops for the shower, travel-size toiletries, and a sketch pad and pencils.

"Looks like they got you set up already," she said. Setting the bag down by the stiff visitors armchair, her mom took a seat on the edge of the hospital bed. She was wearing white slacks and a loose, aqua-colored blouse, her feet in strappy heels, her gray-streaked hair a little windblown. Her eyes flicked from Chase's face to the rest of her, and then she reached over and pulled Chase into a hug, holding her tight.

Chase hugged her back, sighing.

Her mom sighed as well, touching Chase's wet hair, saying, "When you said you went off a bridge, I thought this was a totally different hospital visit."

"I guess I'm kind of invincible," she replied, letting go.

Her mom's gaze went to the heart monitor briefly. "Did you need any stitches? You don't look too bad. Just some bruises."

"Nope." Chase self-consciously touched the bruise on her cheekbone. She hadn't even felt the impact, whenever it had happened. The few scratches from the glass would heal in no time, the on-call physician in the ER had assured her.

"So what happened?"

The version she and Hyun Tae had repeated to the police and to anyone who asked was fairly tame, and it made no mention of mysterious cars trying to run them off the road. They both knew that there was no use in starting a manhunt for people who wouldn't be found.

"Some jerk tried to pass me on the bridge. I got too close to the rails and overreacted. I never thought I'd be in a car that went over a bridge. But I'm okay."

Fear passed over her mom's face, but only for a moment. Chase knew her mom kept things low-key on purpose, hiding her own fear for her family's sake when things went bad.

Her mom gave a brittle smile. "I'm glad you weren't alone when it happened."

"Hyun Tae knew exactly what to do. It was all okay. The car is toast, though."

Her mom laughed, the worry fading in an instant. "Oh, good. I was so worried about that. The car is so important to us."

"Poor car."

"So what about the other person who ran you off the road? Are they being charged or something?"

"I don't know. I think they drove away. We gave a description." A useless description of a black sedan with some guy in a baseball cap that wouldn't help anyone.

"The police will find him," her mom said with quiet confidence. "What comes around goes around."

"I don't really care. I'm just glad I get to be here, enjoying that beeping sound. So relaxing," Chase said, nodding over at the heart monitor.

Her mom glanced over at it. "Well, you're down to 145. Sounds good."

"Yeah. I'm okay. No worries."

"Dad wanted to come, but he couldn't get a flight back home until tonight. He was in Dallas for a business meeting."

"Oh Mom, that isn't necessary! Tell him I'm fine!"

Her mom's eyes filled with tears for the first time. "You could have drowned, Chase."

"But I'm okay."

Her mom shook her head, her lips pressed together and her eyes getting more watery by the second. She didn't say anything, her emotions getting the best of her.

"Mom, stop," Chase said, a lump in her own throat.

Waving her hand to try and dry the tears, her mom reached out and awkwardly patted Chase's hand. "Okay."

Sighing, Chase settled back on the bed.

"Dad and I will be back later. I'm going to let you sleep. Will you be okay?"

"Yes. Really. Thanks for bringing my stuff."

Her mom gave her another hug. "We'll be back."

After she left, Chase unzipped the backpack, her fingers brushing against the jagged edge of her sketch pad as she went for her laptop. She paused, staring at it. Her ruined artwork was suddenly dredged up from the morning's events as she recalled the papers all in a line on the bank, drying into nothing more than blotchy colors. At first she had panicked, but that had died into a sort of helplessness. In any other situation she would have hurried to fix the situation. Now, her fingers curled over the notebook, listless.

Chase shook herself to rid herself of the memory, flicked the book aside with a little too much force, and yanked her laptop out of the bag. She would try to call Imagimation later, and explain her absence. First, she needed to talk to Hyun Tae, but a large part of her hoped that maybe he would do something behind the scenes, and his father would suddenly become a non-issue. Not likely.

She opened her laptop and sent Kiki a message, checked some of her mail, and then found her thoughts wandering to Daniel. Her self-imposed art seclusion had been in part to avoid him, but she couldn't help but wonder about where he was. Her fingers tapped on her keyboard lightly as she thought.

You should Google your boyfriend, that one girl had said.

Chase opened a search page. She hesitated, wondering if she maybe shouldn't. Maybe she wouldn't like what she found.

Daniel Bak. She typed it quickly and hit enter. His face popped up immediately on a Wikipedia article. *He had a Wikipedia article?*

Daniel Bak (Hangul, born August 23rd, 1992) is a South Korean pop star, and leader of the South Korean band Hipstar. Born in Seoul, South Korea. At fourteen he became the first member of Hipstar to enter the entertainment management company NY Entertainment, and second member of Hipstar, created in 2011.

Chase stopped reading, putting a hand over her eyes. That couldn't be real. She put her hand down and started reading again, suddenly unable to stop. It detailed his career in the music industry–his leadership of the pop band, his solo records, appearances on variety shows and in music videos, and a small acting role in a K-drama. It couldn't be real. She had to keep scrolling up and checking the picture to make sure it was actually him.

And then she Googled obsessively. Article after article filled her browser with his most recent scandal–her.

American entertainment bloggers wondered at the mysterious girl in the fuzzy pictures, speculating that she was so-and-so the Hollywood actress, or Miss Pageant whoever. Chase's face warmed as she looked first at the photos, which depicted her lip-to-lip with Daniel, their mouths slightly open and outlined by a light behind them. It was so clear that they were kissing, and a warm rush of embarrassment hit her.

The comments under the pictures were worse. Much worse.

Um what does he see in her? She looks like every other skinny in Cali.

#GoldDigger

Okay seriously, Daniel just hooks up with random strippers in bad costumes now?

#Lamestar

OMG his agents are piiissssed...

every Korean fangirl suddenly dies

It kept going, and it only got worse. Apparently American fans were more chill about the situation, but over in Korea there were protests. Chase found pictures of girls gathered outside the entertainment group's building, shouting, crying, and demanding emotional compensation for Daniel's behavior. "We feel betrayed," one of the fans apparently said. "We expected better of him."

It all made so much sense now; he had traveled all the time and refused to show her pictures when he was away performing. It became clear why Hyun Tae was so adamant that she and Daniel not be seen together, why he had been so upset that she had gone behind his back. Daniel was always a magnet for public attention back home in Korea. Somehow the attention had followed him here. If she had known...

Would she have done anything different? She didn't know.

There was a knock on her door, and Chase looked up, startled out of her reverie. "Yes?"

The heavy hospital door clicked open, and Hyun Tae entered, wearing a fresh outfit of dark jeans and a red plaid button-down rolled up to his elbows, and holding a vase with flowers. He held the vase out with a shrug, "From Ahn Jung Ho."

She almost smiled, but the tension in her chest wouldn't ease enough to let it through. "Sorry, who?"

"I mentioned him before. Just an assistant at the company." Hyun Tae's eyes went to the monitor behind her for a moment. "Why are you worked up?"

The sound of the beeping suddenly came into focus, and she closed her laptop. She was inexplicably irritated that she had just discovered something Hyun Tae had known all along and uncertain as to how she could bring it up. "It's not important."

She had never known Hyun Tae to be hesitant in his actions, but he paused in the middle of the floor, vase of sunflowers and bluebells poised in midair like he wasn't sure what to do with it. Finally, he walked forward, set the vase down, and pulled a chair up to the side of her bed.

Chase waited, watching his lean hands as they first adjusted his watch and then rubbed the back of his neck.

He sat up straight, eyes focused on her. "I want to apologize."

That caught her off-guard. "For what?"

"I have been stubborn. My relationship with my father and our company is complicated, and I had plans I didn't want to change. But you came, and I was not willing to let go of my plans. That put you in danger."

None of that made sense, but she waited, the pace of the monitor's beeping slowing with her heartbeat.

He shifted his gaze to the side, looking away from her. "When I was eight, I was sent to a boarding school in England for the first time. I didn't do well there. Academically I did fine, and my English improved, but my mother knew I was unhappy. She brought me home in the middle of the school semester, and my father did not know.

"When the driver brought me home, it was the first time I had seen business guests in our home. Father always took care of his business away from mother and me. This day he did not."

Hyun Tae had not met her eyes as he told the story, and Chase could not make herself look away.

"There was a man kneeling on the floor in the living room. An employee had a golf club. Another one held a gun to the man's head. If he tried to defend himself, father said he would shoot him. I watched it. All of it. Father didn't know I was there, and mother did not know I was home," he paused, swallowing visibly. "The employee just kept hitting him until the man fell down. I wanted it to stop, but I was too scared to say anything."

Cold chills ran through her. He'd only been a little boy.

Hyun Tae finally met her gaze. "The man survived, but he was crippled after that. I kept my secret for a long time. But it wasn't the last time I came across his 'business practices.' People were afraid of him. A few years later, a man named Seo Joon Young committed suicide. Joon Suh's older brother."

Her stomach dropped like an anchor.

"He was the one with the golf club. Joon Suh said that his brother did very well in my father's company. But what he did to get there was too high of a price. Even if he rose high enough that he no longer needed to carry out my father's orders, he could not forget the ruthless things he had done to get there."

Chase pictured Joon Suh's quiet demeanor, the way he worked with Hyun Tae, his reserved dedication. And she suddenly saw the remnants of grief, of a young man who watched his older brother suffer until he ended his own life.

"We decided at some point that we could not watch these things happen and do nothing. My father," Hyun Tae made an empty gesture with his hands. "He grew his business in a different time. To get ahead, you had to be a hard person. But even after using his claws to climb to the top, he never put them away. I don't think he knows how."

"So you want to stop him."

"I have wanted to for a long time," Hyun Tae said, seeming to relax as he moved away from his memories. "But it takes planning. What we were doing here to protect Bates and their technology was just a small act of defiance. My whole plan was to prove to the board of directors that I am a better fit for head of the company before my father retires. But I needed time to expose my father as inept and to prove my own capabilities."

"But you don't think you have more time," Chase said. She barely managed to keep a tremor from her voice.

The room was dark and heavy, like his story.

He shook his head. "This is extreme, even for him. To do these things against men in his circle is one thing. To go after a college girl...I don't understand it."

"So how do we fix it?"

"I haven't completely decided yet. But the reason I told you these things is because I want you to trust me."

"Well, I do trust you," Chase said, unblinking. "I've been at your beck and call for the past month. I wouldn't do that for just anyone, I promise."

"Then if you trust me, would you come to Korea with me?"

That stunned her. "When?"

"Whenever you can manage to pack a bag and come with me. We need to go to my home if I am going to change anything."

Chase looked down at her hands, with the scratches and the IV, and how they had taken tight hold of the stiff hospital blanket. "I don't know."

"We won't be gone long."

"Am I going to meet him or something?" A moment of panic gripped her.

"You don't have to," he said. "But you would be safest with me. And maybe if I show my father how serious my feelings are, it will buy me time."

"Are you that good at acting?"

His expression went blank, as if he had closed a door. "You don't have to worry about that."

"Well," she said, hesitating. "It feels like kind of a dramatic move."

"You just went over a bridge."

True. "If I went, it would only be for a few days?"

"Yes."

She glanced at him again.

Hyun Tae stared back, expectant and a little hopeful.

On the one hand, it was risky for her to trust Hyun Tae so completely. Any involvement with him had led them both into danger. But she couldn't ignore the gut instinct that he was trustworthy. "Okay."

"Good. I have tickets for midnight tonight. I will pick you up at eight."

Chase looked at the clock on the wall. "It's already three."

"Eight o'clock," he repeated.

"Eight," she said.

"I'll give you some time to get ready." Hyun Tae rose to leave, but he paused before going out the door. "Chase."

"Hm?"

"I will make it right."

She smiled, and it lingered even after he had left. After all the mayhem that had followed her since the start of term, there was one constant that did not waver. Hyun Tae had a thing for making it right.

Chapter Twenty-Six

Chase squirted a dollop of ketchup on the steaming breakfast burrito in her hand. Hyun Tae had not given her much time to get ready. After dropping her off at five, she had just enough time to shoot off emails to her professors, pack her bags, and shower. True to his word, he was at her door at eight, and he handed her a brand new phone to replace the one at the bottom of the river.

Hyun Tae had not complained when she had demanded that they grab something to eat before getting their tickets or going through security. He must have been fake dating her long enough to understand that food was high on her priority list. He left her at a breakfast kiosk near the escalators to the security checkout and went to get their tickets and check their bags.

As Chase took a satisfying chomp out of the soft burrito, sucking in air through her lips to counter the stinging heat against her tongue, she looked around the vast, open airport. White floors that had gone gray over the years, towering windows overhead, and the buzz of travelers as they moved from ticket counters to baggage check to security lines reminded her of vacations with her family and the thrill of spending the summer abroad in Italy.

She took a seat on a nearby bench and tried to eat without opening her jaw too wide. The bruise on her cheekbone still throbbed.

With eyes glazed over as she stared out the dark windows at the lights of L.A., Chase barely noticed the man until he was right in front of her. Her eyes slid up his lean legs, clad in black, over his black leather jacket, and to the face that was shielded with black sunglasses and a white and black baseball cap. She had a mouthful of the giant burrito stuffed in the inside of her cheek, and her chewing came to a sudden halt.

"Hey," Daniel said. Even in that conspicuously "incognito" getup, Chase knew him in an instant.

She stood, shocked. "Daniel?" she managed to say as she swallowed quickly.

He had his hands in the pockets of the leather jacket, and he looked from side to side. "Hey. Can we talk? I heard you were leaving with Hyun Tae."

Worried that he might be caught by a paparazzi or something, she motioned for him to follow her. She wondered why he had taken such a big risk to see her, especially in a very public place like this.

She found a "family restroom" not far away, and she knocked briskly before sliding in. Daniel joined her after a few seconds.

Daniel slowly removed his cap and glasses. "Hey."

321

She looked him up and down. "You look like you're going to bomb the airport."

He gave her a sheepish smile, "Yeah, I'm bad at staying out of sight. Read the tabloids. I'm always getting caught."

"Yeah, I noticed."

She saw him flinch a little at that. "I had to talk to you."

Chase knew it wasn't his fault, but she had a hard time putting all the internet hate out of her mind. He was a perfect guy. But this, what she felt between them, was far from perfect. She had no idea what to do with all the garbage she'd read.

"I just...I wanted to apologize." The look of sincerity on his face tugged at her sympathy. "You mean a lot to me, Chase. I got reckless. But when I felt I might lose my chance to be with you, I made a bad decision. And it harmed you." His eyes went to the scratches on her cheek and neck. "I'm so sorry."

He liked her. A lot. And he didn't want to lose her. She softened immediately. "You should be allowed to kiss someone you're dating."

A spark of hope lit his expression. "Yeah?"

But she couldn't fan it. She knew in her heart that whatever she had started with Daniel couldn't continue, and it had nothing to do with his fame. It had everything to do with what she hadn't felt when they'd kissed.

322

"Yeah. But Daniel I...when I had my chance. On the beach. When we were together—"

The door suddenly burst open, sending Chase's heart into frightened rabbit mode. Hyun Tae slid in, slamming the door closed with his heel. He glared at Daniel.

Chase stifled the urge to laugh. That's what happens when you don't the lock the door to the bathroom.

Daniel's look hardened a fraction. "*Hyung.*"

"I saw you from across the terminal." He gave Chase a what-are-you-doing look.

Chase bristled. She thought she had done pretty well acting like a fugitive, considering the circumstances.

Daniel had to back up a step to allow Hyun Tae into the small bathroom, and Chase found her leg pressed up against the side of the toilet. Daniel crossed his arms. "We were having a conversation."

"Conversation is over," Hyun Tae said.

"No one knows I'm here," Daniel ground out.

Hyun Tae actually rolled his eyes. "*Jincha.*"

Chase wasn't sure what to do. She needed to talk to Daniel, but she didn't want to do so in front of Hyun Tae. And she and Hyun Tae had a plane to catch. And no room for error. She couldn't get caught with Daniel again, or Hyun Tae's job of persuading his father she was harmless would become downright impossible. It was already improbable.

"I'll call you when we land," she promised Daniel. She was torn between wanting to tell him how she felt and leaving with Hyun Tae before any paparazzi could find them.

Hyun Tae made the decision for her. He grabbed her wrist and opened the bathroom door. "We'll talk later."

Daniel shoved his cap back on his head, for once letting his anger show. That was the last glimpse Chase had of him before she allowed Hyun Tae to drag her out of the bathroom and back into the busy terminal. He let go after a few steps, but he didn't stop walking.

She hiked her purse back onto her shoulder, trying to keep pace. "I do need to talk to him."

Hyun Tae checked his watch and held out her plane ticket without looking at her.

Chase checked her temper. Maybe part of her hadn't wanted to tell Daniel how she felt and didn't really mind having that postponed.

She followed him through the gate, showing her ID and passport. He sat down in a big first class seat, and she slid around him and sat down. The flight attendants were all beautiful young women, dressed in pale pastel blouses with ivory skirts, their dark hair pulled back. They were young with creamy skin and beautiful dark, tilted eyes. She knew they'd probably been chosen because they were pretty, but with all the K-dramas her sister had shown her, it was hard to believe that all

Koreans weren't like celebrities. She pulled her white T-shirt down over her jeans and tried not to feel shabby. She stole a look over at Hyun Tae, hoping he wouldn't notice.

Too late, his eyes caught hers, and she couldn't look away. She tried to think of something to say or any reason at all why she'd been staring at him, but came up with zilch.

His mouth twitched in a smile as he looked away.

When she had finally looked at her tickets, she was a little dismayed at how long the flight would be. Twelve hours was a long time. The low sound as the plane taxied off the runway lulled her until the pitch changed into a loud roar, and she was pushed back into her seat as it lifted off.

She had way too much time to think about how crazy it was that she was on a plane going to a place she was totally unprepared for. Never mind the language barrier, she knew no one but Hyun Tae. And she was missing a few days of classes to do this. At least, she assumed they wouldn't need to be there very long, and she had filled Kiki in on the lite version of the events.

Kiki had demanded a souvenir.

She knew she should sleep, but she couldn't seem to stop thinking. Hyun Tae hadn't taken long to relax. She looked over at him sleeping, his face calm. His hands were in his lap, limply holding his phone, the wire from his earphones wrapped around one finger. After a while, she got bored and fell asleep to the muted sounds of a few voices and hum of the plane engine.

When she woke, her forehead was against the window, and Hyun Tae was getting into his seat. She rubbed her eyes and looked out the window in a sleepy haze for a few moments, but then realized that she was just staring at her own reflection, lit against the black of night. Chase turned to Hyun Tae.

"So where will we be staying? At your parents' house? Will you talk to your father there?" she asked.

"Yes."

He looked down at his phone for a moment and then said, "Is that a problem? If you would like to stay in a hotel, I can arrange that."

"No, no. That's fine. We're only staying for a few days."

He rubbed the back of his neck. "Right."

She'd learned that he did that when he was uncomfortable, and she wondered if he thought they might need to stay longer. Before she could ask about that, a flight attendant announced that they would begin to prepare for landing.

Outside the window, the sky was still dark, but when she pulled out her phone, it said that it was 5:42 a.m., a day later than when they had left.

From the moment they got off the plane, Hyun Tae kept them moving. The Incheon airport was bright and clean, even in the predawn darkness. A pleasant woman's voice gave announcements about flights throughout the airport in English and in other languages, mostly Korean, which Chase had learned to recognize. She followed Hyun Tae to the baggage claim, and they collected their luggage. When he led her away from the crowd surrounding the baggage area, he said, "You should put on a coat. It's cold here."

She'd been too busy to notice, but now she saw almost everyone was wearing a jacket or a coat, and outside the terminal, puffs of white swirled as people spoke to one another. She opened her suitcase and got out her hoodie. Hyun Tae frowned. "Is that all you brought?"

"Well, I didn't have much time to think what I should bring," she mumbled, embarrassed, shrugging into the hoodie.

He slipped his coat off and put it around her shoulders.

"Oh no, I'll be fine," she said, in protest.

"Our car is almost here," he said, ignoring her. He put on another jacket, but it was lighter than the one he'd given her.

She had to be quick to keep up with him as he strode out of the terminal. He checked his phone, something he'd done a few times since they'd left the plane. The headlights of buses and taxis flashed by as they waited.

A black Lexus pulled up to the curb, and Hyun Tae held out his hand for her luggage. She handed it to him, and he pulled it around the back of the car. A smartly dressed older man was already stepping out of the car and rushing to get the suitcases. He bowed his head in a quick bob to Hyun Tae and to Chase. His eyes wrinkled at the corners, and his thin lips pulled back in a friendly smile.

"Good morning," she said, wishing she could have said it in Korean. All she knew was *annyeonghaseo*, which was hello, and probably informal.

He bobbed his head at her again as he picked up a suitcase and put it in the back. Hyun Tae opened the door of the car, and Chase stepped in, putting her backpack on her lap.

After Hyun Tae got in next to her, the driver asked a question in Korean, and Hyun Tae gave a short answer.

She allowed herself to gawk at the city lights as they drove. Round streetlights lined the boulevard, and blue street signs in Hangul were followed by green signs in English. She relaxed a little. She could probably get around here on her own if she had to. She looked at her phone. She couldn't call anyone, but she could text.

Suddenly, realizing she was preparing for a worst-case scenario where Hyun Tae turned into some kind of monster and she was trapped in Seoul, she almost laughed. *Calm down.* She was only here to meet his parents and go home. He could deal with everything after that. It wasn't really her problem. Maybe it was the jet lag and the fact that it was night, but it all felt surreal.

"You tired?" Hyun Tae asked.

"I shouldn't be because I slept, but yeah, I am."

"It's a long flight, but the house isn't too far from Incheon."

The sky lightened as they entered Seoul, and the traffic got heavier. Tall glass buildings reflected the delicate colors of the pink sunrise Most of the cars on the road were brands she recognized, although some of them were boxy and foreign-looking. People waited at bus stops bundled in coats and scarves, and the trees were all bare.

They continued driving until they left the tall buildings behind and entered a residential area. The homes varied from very modern to traditional, and the streets were pristine and wide. Most of the large homes hid behind walls, with only the peaks of their ceramic-tiled roofs visible. They came to a corner home behind a large, decorative brick wall, and the Lexus stopped. Evergreen trees with crooked trunks like bonsai trees climbed up from behind the wall, and the lines of a traditional rooftop rose over it, promising a place of rare beauty. She was so busy staring she didn't notice the driver had left the car until he opened the door for her. She stepped out, and Hyun Tae joined her with their suitcases.

"Is this your house?" she asked quietly, as if the entire neighborhood were listening in.

"It's the house I grew up in. I live in a guest house on my parents' property."

She quelled a small shiver of anxiety. She knew the whole point was to meet his father, but she wasn't quite ready. *No time like the present.*

329

Hyun Tae approached the thick wooden doors and pushed aside a small panel in the wall, which revealed a number pad. He punched in a five-digit code, and the doors opened.

They entered a garden in a stone courtyard that led to a framed wooden doorway at the top of a set of stairs. The house had white outer walls and windows framed by honey-colored beams, giving it a pleasing mix of both traditional and contemporary. In her mind she was sketching the clean lines and the way the light came in through the windows. She had never seen anything like this before, and for once, she hadn't brought her art supplies.

Hyun Tae picked up their suitcases and walked down a path that went around the side of the large house, away from the main entrance. Meticulously pruned evergreen trees sheltered the stone walkway, and from inside the walls, the city might not even exist.

A smaller house with a similar courtyard appeared around the corner, and Hyun Tae went up the stairs to the door and took out a key from his pocket and opened it. She followed him inside and waited while he shut the door. The floors were the same honey-colored wood as the doors and frames around the windows, and they shone bright with polish. The windows were all a frosted white glass, and the walls a soft white. Hyun Tae pushed open a sliding door and showed her into a living room with bigger windows. A light carpet softened the stark modern lines of the furniture, and she let the peace of it sink into her, despite the long flight and the impending anxiety of meeting his parents.

"We aren't waking your parents are we?" she asked in a whisper.

"Oh, no," he said, turning to her in surprise. "This is my part of the house. We won't meet them until later."

A huge weight lifted from her shoulders, and she almost sighed out loud.

"Come on back; I'll show you to your room."

He slid the door open and revealed another room with hardwood floors and white walls. It was more like a bedroom with a reading alcove, the alcove slightly raised. All the furniture was low, including the bed, drawing her eyes downward and making the ceiling seem higher. A large, intricately paper-paned window let in softly filtered natural light. The layout was tranquil and cozy at the same time.

"Wow. You didn't give me your room, did you?" she asked.

"Uh, no. Do you like it?" He seemed taken aback, as if the idea of giving up his room was a good one, and he wished he would have thought of it.

"Of course. It's really nice."

"There's a bathroom down the hall, here," he said, pointing to a door down the hallway. "My room is on the other side of the living room, if you need me."

She let his coat slide off her shoulders and gave it to him. "Thanks."

He took it, hesitating. "I know it's a big sacrifice for you to come here. I will get you home again soon."

She probably should have reassured him that it was no big deal, but her brain wouldn't come up with the appropriate response. She settled on a shrug. "Sure."

"Take your time, and rest if you need to."

He left her to unpack, but that wasn't much of an activity. She had a stack of clean clothes, which she put in the closet, and one pair of boots. She owned mostly sandals and flip-flops, but it was too cold here for those. And one pair of heels and a dress that she brought just in case.

She picked out some clothes and took her bag of shampoo and other stuff with her to walk out to the bathroom. It looked like she had it to herself, which was a relief. Maybe he had his own bathroom.

She took a quick shower and then dressed. She dried her hair and put on some makeup, wondering if Hyun Tae was waiting for her or if he was doing something else. When she opened the door from her room to the hallway, the house was still silent. She was definitely not used to that. Her thin white sweater didn't feel quite warm enough, but she didn't have very many winter clothes—mostly just hoodies. Her dark jeans were probably warm enough, and she'd put on some thick white socks to keep her feet warm.

Padding out into the hallway, she found the kitchenette. It was small with black countertops and pine paneling on the walls, making it feel warmer than the rest of the house. Hyun Tae was sitting at the table in front of his laptop, drinking coffee in a Starbucks paper cup. Another one was still in the cup carrier. She sat down across from him, wondering if he'd gone out to get it. He offered her the second cup, but she shook her head. "I don't drink coffee, thank you.

"It's herbal tea."

"Oh. Thanks." She took it. "Is there a Starbucks near here?"

"No. Joon Suh brought it."

She paused, her lips touching the edge of the cup. "Joon Suh?"

"Hi," a voice said behind her.

She turned to find Joon Suh walking in from the sunken living room. He wore a dark-colored cable-knit sweater and gray slacks. He was beautiful, as usual. She couldn't help smiling at him. He winked at her and spoke to Hyun Tae. "Are we meeting your mother this afternoon?"

Hyun Tae leaned back in his chair and examined his phone. "I told her we arrived, but it's early. She said we would talk later."

"How nice," Joon Suh said flatly.

Hyun Tae slid his eyes over to Chase, but neither of them said anything. It occurred to her he was dreading this as much as she was.

Chapter Twenty-Seven

He knew Chase was nervous. The calculated indifference in her eyes, and the way her chin tilted a little higher gave her away. If she looked bored, then she was scared.

Her damp hair was twisted over one shoulder, giving off a pleasant floral scent as she sat on his couch and picked at a roll he had snagged for her from the kitchen table.

His mother and father knew he had brought the American girl, and he wondered at the wisdom of just throwing her at them first thing in the morning. He imagined how his mother would chew her bean sprouts with firm, angry crunches as she silently despaired over his recent unpredictable choices. He didn't dare consider what his father would say. Neither of them spoke English, but he knew that wouldn't stop them from very clearly communicating their feelings to Chase.

Chase shifted her gaze to him, where he was standing on the other side of the coffee table. Her look said, "So now what?"

He rubbed the back of his neck, easing a muscle tic. "I thought maybe I would call my parents and arrange for dinner tonight."

Chase seemed to consider that. "Are you worried I'm tired?"

"You said you were tired."

"Yeah, but I'm not going to sleep."

They both stared at each other. Hyun Tae glanced at his watch. Seven am. His parents would likely be sitting down to eat breakfast in fifteen minutes. And breakfast was the only meal they usually shared. His father worked late. His mother had social engagements. Tying them down to meet Chase together would be difficult unless he had surprise on his side.

Chase pulled a piece of bread off the roll, popped it in her mouth, and chewed, watching him with raised brows. She was waiting for him to make the call. Finally, Hyun Tae gave a short nod. "Let's go down to breakfast."

The thin white sweater she wore was cute, but his parents lived in a traditional home with very little in the way of heating. "Do you have a sweatshirt?"

"That would look horrible."

It was true. He gave a shrug. "We'll go shopping later. Come on. My mother and father don't speak English, so I will translate the best I can."

He led her out of the room and down a long hallway. His rooms were attached to the main house, but with two separate outdoor entrances, he always had the privacy he

336

needed. However, as an unmarried student, it was expected he remain at the family home.

As they made their way into the main living areas, which had been built much more recently than the traditional structure, called a hanok, Chase smoothed her hair down around her shoulders. "So they pretty much hate me."

Hyun Tae glanced down at her. Tension and nerves radiated from her body, and a sudden, unfamiliar stab hit his heart. She was walking into the dining room of a man who had put her life in danger. Never mind that it had been an intelligent decision on her part to present herself to his parents; this was also the most difficult course of action to have chosen. He hadn't wanted to tell her that he had a plan all along. That he wasn't just going to throw her in front of his parents and hope they liked her.

But if he told her, she would stop him.

He swiveled around and faced her, halting in the middle of the modern, lush sitting room that adjoined the dining room. He liked that she didn't step away, but stayed close enough that he could still feel the heat from her body. She looked up, blue eyes vast and searching. Almost of its own volition, his hand briefly touched her chin. "Just act like you like me. I'll handle them."

He didn't know why he'd asked her to act as if she liked him. He winced inwardly because it sounded like wishful thinking.

She reached up and touched his chin, the same way he had touched hers, and to his surprise there was a hint of humor in her eyes, and maybe something else.

"It's not that hard."

His heart jumped and his brain derailed from his anxious train of thoughts for a moment. There was a connection between them, like two soldiers going to war. He didn't feel as if he were protecting her so much as they were both protecting each other.

They stepped down from the sitting room to a long, open dining room with a narrow table in the center and several doorways just off the central area. The kitchen was open to the dining room, and their family employee, Park Min Joon, was cleaning up after having just served breakfast.

His mother and father looked up as they entered. They both sat at the left end of the table, his father at the head and mother at his left elbow, so she was facing them when they stepped down. Several brightly polished, silver dishes steamed with side dishes and rice for their usual elaborate breakfast. His mother slowly lowered her silver chopsticks from her lips, her wide brown eyes staring in unmuted outrage at the horror of being presented with this girl first thing in the morning. His father did not change expression. He rarely did.

Hyun Tae bowed slightly at the waist, speaking in Korean. "Good morning."

His father took on a look of curious interest. His mother glared.

"I came back for our fall break a little early. I wanted you to meet Chase." He angled his body so he could motion toward her. "This is my girlfriend, Chase Bryant."

His mother set her chopsticks down on the table a little too forcefully.

Chase gave an awkward bob of a bow. "Hello, it's nice to meet you," she said in English.

His father sighed loudly, billowing the air from the back of his throat and out his nostrils like a dragon. He cleared his throat, "You're skipping class?"

Hyun Tae didn't have to feign a look of detached boredom when he shuffled forward in his slippers to take a seat at the table. He said, "My grades are fine."

His father grunted. He was a hard man with the looks of a soft sixty-something *ahjussi,* like any other male of his generation. A little rounded from age, but black hair still full and silky, brushed to the side with never a stray hair out of line. Hyun Tae had inherited his long face from his father, but the sharp angles were his mother's. She watched him pull out a chair for Chase across from them, her high cheekbones nearly as razor sharp as the glint in her surgically widened eyes. His mother had, at what cost he wasn't really sure, retained a flawlessly svelte body for as long as he could remember, but her age was slowly beginning to catch up with her in the softness of her thin neck and the crinkles around her eyes.

After Chase had been seated, and he pulled in his own chair, Park Min Joon quickly came up behind them, setting places for them with the same fine china already in front of the parents. He murmured a heartfelt greeting to Hyun Tae, genuine love in the aging man's eyes as he smiled at both him and Chase. Hyun Tae had real affection for Park Min Joon, as he had been the man who drove him to school and picked him up, provided him with food and clothing, and listened quietly as Hyun Tae told him about his day while he ate seaweed snacks at the kitchen counter as Min Joon prepared food for the next day.

Hyun Tae stole a glance at Chase. She sat straight in her chair, a neutral but pleasant expression on her face, and her hands in her lap. He scooped some rice into her bowl for her and then filled his to the top.

He had forgotten to explain how Korean side dishes are different from American meals, but she didn't seem to have a problem figuring it out.

Kim Sang Sik cleared his throat in a gruff way again, wiping his mouth with a napkin. Hyun Tae looked over at him, and for the first time noticed the change. There were more wrinkles on his face, the skin slightly sallow and eyes tinged yellow. A dark, mottled bruise marred the back and side of one of his hands, barely starting to turn yellow.

"How long are you visiting?" his father asked.

Hyun Tae stared at his father. They both knew he had noticed. "Not long."

He nodded. "Meet with me for dinner this evening."

"Yes, father," Hyun Tae said, suspicion beginning to grow.

Kim Sang Sik looked tired. And old. Hyun Tae couldn't have believed his father might have any kind of weakness, but he looked frail. It was disconcerting.

With his mind distracted, Hyun Tae barely registered his mother's next question. "Where did you meet this girl?"

Hyun Tae turned to Chase and translated, "She wants to know how we met."

Chase gave him a fake but appropriately pleased smile. "Well, I dropped tomato soup on your feet."

Hyun Tae turned to his mother, and in Korean answered, "We had a class together."

His mother's eyes moved from Hyun Tae to Chase and then back again, her expression hard but masked with a thin veneer of civility. "Her parents?"

"She wants to know about your family," Hyun Tae relayed.

Chase looked honestly happy to answer that question. "My Dad is an accountant, and my mom works in the admissions office for our school. I have one sister, Jonni, and she's married with three kids."

Hyun Tae translated that as accurately as possible.

His mother was unimpressed. Almost appalled at the normalcy of it, he had to assume. With no small amount of venom, she asked, "Will you live in America and stay with these people? Perhaps the mother could find you a job as a secretary."

"I have no idea what you mean by that," he replied, speaking in Korean, his tone bland.

His father cleared his throat again, giving them both an angry look of warning. He didn't like squabbling over his breakfast.

Hyun Tae saw Chase following this exchange, and he noticed the steely look of pride flash through her bright eyes. Just as he feared, Chase knew very well when she was being insulted. But she was taking it all pretty well.

Kim Sang Sik stood from his chair, throwing his napkin onto the table and finally acknowledging Chase with a nod. To his wife and son he growled, "Resolve it. Today." And then he was gone.

Hyun Tae watched his father leave, his confusion growing. Those were not the actions of a man who had been thwarted by a plucky American girl who threatened to overturn his entire empire with a thumb drive. He acted as if he couldn't be bothered with her.

He slanted a look down at Chase, who looked surprised herself. That wasn't what either of them had expected.

"I have an appointment," Hyun Tae's mother said, standing just as abruptly. She sent Hyun Tae a sharp look. "We will talk later."

Without a backward glance, she turned on her heel and clicked out of the dining room, the beading on her pink dress suit sparkling under the bright overhead lights as she exited. Hyun Tae looked down at Chase.

She squinted up at him. "I'm pretty sure that went better than we expected."

Hyun ate an egg roll, chewing thoughtfully for a moment. Finally he gave her a little nod. "It was less explosive. But it's still a problem."

"Why's that?"

"Have you finished eating?"

"Yes. Are we going somewhere?"

"I just want to check on something."

He led her through the modern house back to his rooms. After making sure the front door was closed, Hyun Tae went right to Joon Suh's room just off the living area.

He knocked once and opened the door. Joon Suh sat at his desk, upright in his chair with eyes closed, glasses held limply in his hand. He cracked open an eye as Hyun Tae crossed his modest bedroom.

Hyun Tae tapped his forefinger on the desk. "I need to see invoice records for our three largest warehouses."

343

With a sleepy intake of breath, Joon Suh sat up a little straighter, replaced his glasses, and flipped open his laptop. "This month?" he asked in English.

Hyun Tae bobbed his head. "I don't know what I'm looking for, but I have a suspicion."

Chase came to stand next to Hyun Tae, and he caught the scent of hibiscus again. He was momentarily distracted by the image of what it might be like to slide her hair over one shoulder, baring the back of her neck, all the while surrounded by that heady mixed scent of hibiscus and Chase's skin...

"Here's the Gwanak-gu warehouse."

Hyun Tae gave himself a mental shake and leaned forward to scan through the purchasing records, invoices, quality control checks, and thousands of other documents that filtered through their beauty products plant in the Gwanak-gu district of Seoul. His suspicion turned to dread. "Okay, I got it."

Joon Suh rubbed his eyes under his glasses. "You need to visit him, then."

"Yeah," Hyun Tae said, straightening but still staring at the screen. "I think I do."

As he turned to leave Joon Suh's room, Chase followed. "What is it?"

"My father seemed unlike himself," Hyun Tae explained, stopping outside the room to face her. The urge to gather her hair over her shoulder returned as he noticed she had pulled some of it haphazardly over her left shoulder and left the rest of it mussed and hanging down her back. He forced himself to focus. "I will know more after visiting the warehouse, but there is definitely something not right."

"Because of the documents you looked at?"

"Normally, everything must be approved and signed by my father on a once-weekly basis."

"Right," Chase nodded.

"None of the signatures were his."

Her eyes rounded. "Oh."

"He seemed..." Hyun Tae paused, searching for the right word.

"Sick?" Chase offered.

"Not well."

Chase nodded.

"And he did not react to your visit."

"I noticed the same thing," she said in agreement.

"So I am suspicious. Something may be happening in the company, and I need to speak with some of the employees."

"Was there one name on all the papers? Someone had to sign them."

Hyun Tae leaned against the wall, folding his arms. "There was."

He was glad Chase didn't have a hard time keeping up with the problem. She had a sharp mind that had always intrigued him.

"Who was it?"

Hyun Tae unlocked his phone to call the chauffeur around. "Ahn Jung Ho."

"Who?" Chase asked, bemused.

Hyun Tae smiled. "Let's call him the advisor."

"Sounds fishy."

He met her gaze, her anxious expression mirroring the sudden unease within him. "Exactly."

Chapter Twenty-Eight

Chase was prepared for a hectic shopping excursion on the street with vendors heckling them from brightly colored stalls. Instead, they drove through a street lined by sleek corporate skyscrapers to a building with glass facades and huge screens glittering in the morning sun. Apparently she was confusing James Bond movies about Asia with real life.

She had seen a lot of beautiful buildings, not only in Italy, but in L.A. as well. She was, however, taken aback when they stepped into the D-Cube City mall. The center was open to a sky-high ceiling, and there were multiple levels and stores with translucent walls. It was all much more opulent than she had imagined, and anything here would be out of her meager budget. Maybe they could find a clearance section somewhere.

Hyun Tae led her to a store where uniformed girls greeted them. They were both young and beautiful, with their hair tied back in silky ponytails. They wore no makeup, but their lips were glossed in a light pink, accenting their smooth skin. This did not look like a place with discounts.

In the women's section, an older woman in a crisp dark suit greeted them. Her hair was cut in a stylish bob, her creamy skin was free of wrinkles, but there was something about the softness around her chin that gave her age away.

"Good morning. How can I help you today?"

Hyun Tae looked down at Chase, waiting.

"I just need a coat. Something warm," she said.

"And maybe some sweaters," Hyun Tae added.

"A sweater," Chase amended, hoping she didn't sound cheap.

The woman smiled at them and gestured with a slim hand toward a sitting area with mirrors. Hyun Tae sat down on a sculpted white couch and patted a place next to him. Chase sat down, bewildered. "Shouldn't I be looking for a coat?"

"She'll bring them to us."

"She doesn't know my size."

Hyun Tae raised an eyebrow at her. "She knows what she's doing."

In just a few moments, the elegant woman returned, one arm filled with sweaters and the other holding two jackets. She smiled at Chase and opened a dressing room door. After hanging the clothes inside, she stepped out and held the door open for Chase.

Chase smiled back uncertainly and entered the dressing room. It was small, with dark red brocade wallpaper and a padded velvet bench. It had no shortage of mirrors, should she care to see herself from every

348

possible angle, and at the moment, the angle from the back was not very flattering. Her hair was a mess, and she ran her fingers through it and touched up her mascara. Then she remembered what she was supposed to be doing. Trying on clothes before they went to visit the manufacturing warehouse.

She slipped on a cream-colored sweater that felt like silk and warmed her instantly. She loved it, but she was sure it was out of her price range. She twisted around and caught the tag. The numbers didn't make very much sense. It was either 148,000 dollars or that was an item number.

"Do you like it?" Hyun Tae asked from outside the room.

She stepped out and struck a pose. "What do you think?"

He shrugged. "What else did she give you?"

She went back in and tried on a pink one in a delicate hue, and like the last one, very warm. She modeled this one and got the same tepid response from Hyun Tae, his eyes showing no traces of approval.

The third sweater was snug fitting, and she had to admit it flattered her. If he didn't like this one, then there was no pleasing him.

She even gave a twirl as he watched, his eyes expressionless. "It's nice," he said in a tone that indicated he was waiting for something more interesting to happen. She couldn't blame him. Shopping must be torture. He said something in Korean in a quiet tone to the woman, and she disappeared while Chase tried on the jackets.

They fit beautifully, as if the woman had found Chase's size and then had it tailored.

The woman swooped back to the dressing room, giving a discreet knock, but this time she was carrying dresses, pants, and tops that Chase hadn't even wanted to look at. Not wanting to offend her, Chase smiled and went back into the dressing room with the pile. She dutifully tried on everything, falling in love with every piece, her heart breaking. She was pretty sure she wouldn't be able to afford anything but a scarf.

After trying on the last item of clothing, she put her own clothes back on and picked up one of the jackets, eyeing the price tag. She walked out of the dressing room with the jacket and showed it to Hyun Tae. "I have no idea what this is supposed to cost."

He looked at the tag, frowning. "You need to learn how to figure out won."

"How much is it?"

"₩664,000 won," he said.

"That doesn't sound like something I can afford."

The woman had called over some assistants, and they began cleaning out the dressing room.

"Wait!" Chase called to them, and found the other coat. She showed it to Hyun Tae. "What about this one?"

He took her elbow and moved toward the cash register. "That is ₩775,000 won."

"Hyun Tae!" she hissed, her cheeks flushing. "What is that in American money?"

The woman and her entourage were following them to the register and laying the entire pile down on the wide granite counter. To Chase's horror, they began ringing up all the clothes.

"No, wait! I only want the coat!" she said.

The woman smiled sweetly and said something in Korean. The assistants began wrapping up the clothes.

Chase chewed on a nail, doing mental calculations of her bank account.

Hyun Tae cocked his head. "What?"

She grabbed his jacket, pulling him down until he was eye-to-eye with her. She whispered, "I can't afford any of this!"

Without taking his eyes off hers, he reached into his pocket and handed his card to the woman at the register.

"I know," he whispered back. "I'm paying. To thank you for coming here."

Shocked, she blinked at him. She wanted to argue, but she needed warmer clothes. "I can pay you back."

His eyes darkened dangerously. "It's a gift. Also, we arrived just in time for the thirtieth anniversary of the company. There will be a party, and I want you to feel comfortable. Okay?"

The girls at the cashier were staring at them as they put the clothes in the bags, and Chase's cheeks grew warm. "Okay."

The woman returned his card with a bow, and one of the assistants held out a gift to Chase, a small box wrapped in gold paper and a white bow. Chase took the box and bobbed her head. "Thank you," she said.

Hyun Tae took all the bags and made long strides out of the opulent store, tissue paper rustling as he walked, sounding like money. Chase struggled with her guilt and with the longing to open the beautiful little gold box. Outside the mall, their car was waiting for them, and the driver jumped out and took the bags from Hyun Tae as if he were ashamed that Hyun Tae had to carry them at all.

Chase settled herself in the car, the gold box in her lap. Hyun Tae arrived a few moments later, one of the jackets in his hands, which he gave to her. She gratefully shrugged into it, the silk lining brushing against her bare arms.

The driver started the car, and he looked down at the gift box. "You should open that."

She pulled the ribbon off and opened the box. A pair of matching leather gloves lay in the tissue paper. She pulled out the gloves and put them on, pleased. "Did you pick these out too? Or did they just give them to me because you just spent a million dollars on clothes?"

"The hostess picked them out. And it wasn't quite a million."

"Well, thank you for what you did. I wish you'd let me pay you back."

"I would be insulted. Please just accept the gift."

She looked out the window, tugging at her hair. No one had ever spent that much money on her before, and she wasn't sure she liked it, but it didn't seem to bother him.

Too conflicted to figure it out, she changed the subject. "So how do I figure out won?"

"One dollar is about 1000 won. Just take off three zeros, and you'll be close."

So both of the coats she'd picked out were far more than fifty dollars. "So being a millionaire doesn't mean much here," she said, amused.

He laughed. "Not in won."

When he laughed, it transformed his whole face, like an inspired painting. Just one shadow there, one little line as he laughed, and suddenly her chest hammered with the same excitement that followed a surge of creativity. She thought back to the car accident on the bridge, and how he'd held her. She suddenly wanted to matter to him. That was crazy. He was rich, ridiculously good-looking, and completely focused on other things. She probably wasn't even on his radar. By all accounts, she had done nothing but mess up his plans.

But yet, he was so extraordinarily kind to her. Could he really have been faking all that kindness on their dates? Seoul blurred by in the window. She was pretty sure now that she wasn't faking.

Chapter Twenty-Nine

Hyun Tae sat back as the driver took them away from the heart of Seoul to the Guro district, where the buildings became farther apart, revealing railroads and trains that brought vital commerce from Seoul to Busan, Incheon, and international transportation routes. His father's company had grown from hand lotions to biomedical engineering, a reflection of their country as a whole. South Korea was constantly shifting its economy to all the right places.

He tried not to look over at Chase too many times. He would never admit to her how much he enjoyed watching her nervous patience as the saleswoman kept handing her clothes. He could tell Chase didn't want to, but she was too polite to tell the saleswoman she could only afford a coat. The language barrier turned out to be useful. He had told the saleswoman to find enough clothes for the next week, for any occasion, and she hadn't disappointed. The hardest part was not showing how pretty he thought Chase was when she came out of the dressing room. He hoped he looked bored.

And he kept wanting to hold her hand. He missed the excuse to reach out for her. He liked how her small hand fit in his.

The car bumped over a set of railroad tracks, and he turned his attention to the manufacturing plant up ahead. It was vaguely familiar, but most of his time within the company had been at corporate headquarters.

If he had stayed in Korea, then the man he suspected of subverting his father's authority would have been his superior. Maybe Ahn Jung Ho would have been more careful if the boss's son were around, or maybe he would have tried to recruit Hyun Tae. Though his father could be difficult, Hyun Tae would never betray him.

They arrived at the gate, and a guard stepped out, looked at the driver, and then waved them through. The driver stopped the car in front of the main entrance. "Should I wait for you, sir?" the driver asked.

Hyun Tae replied in the affirmative. This wouldn't take long. He might not learn anything new.

A large concrete roof jutted out over the glass entrance doors, where his family's company logo was painted.

They went inside to a boring utilitarian interior, the concrete walls painted gray and white and the linoleum floor clean and polished. There was a clean, septic feel to the place, almost like a hospital. A man in a security guard uniform sat at a desk, eyeing them. He bowed his head and greeted them, using formal, polite language.

Hyun Tae nodded back and stepped toward the doors to the manufacturing floor. At that moment the doors swung open, and Ahn Jung Ho stepped through. He wore a white suit with a red silk shirt and a matching silk handkerchief in the breast pocket of his jacket. Alligator skin boots with silver tips clicked against the tiles as he walked, and his hair was cut so that the side part sloped over one eye. Beyond the outrageous style, his build was so slim that he bordered on the skeletal, his cheekbones high and sharp. His skin was so smooth it looked like plastic, without pores and slightly shiny. Two men stood beside him, though they were dressed more conservatively in dark suits.

"*Annyeong hasimnikka*," Hyun Tae said, using formal language on pure instinct. He kept his anger to himself, for now.

"I see you are return from school," Ahn Jung Ho said in English. Amused at the language switch, Hyun Tae played along, even though Ahn Jung Ho's English was fairly basic.

"I thought I would visit the plant. This is Chase, a friend who is visiting our family."

Ahn Jung Ho bowed slightly at the waist, holding out a soft, pale hand to Chase. "A pleasure to meet you. I am Ahn Jung Ho."

Chase took his hand. "Nice to meet you Mr. Ahn."

Hyun Tae was pleased that she remembered the family name came first.

Ahn Jung Ho looked toward Hyun Tae, continuing on in English. "You come here to look at our factory for the first time. You are curious?"

357

"It's not my first time, and I am always interested in KimBio. It's my family's business."

Ahn Jung Ho's face froze for a moment, then his lips stretched back from his teeth in an unattractive attempt at a smile. He ran slim fingers across the hair on his forehead, though he didn't actually reveal the hidden eye. "You should call me, so I can prepare for a proper tour."

"I didn't want to bother you," Hyun Tae answered and then nodded toward the doors. "I'd like to see the office."

Ahn Jung Ho didn't move, his eyes hard in his smooth face. One corner of his mouth lifted, a polite little smile that barely moved his cheek. He gestured at his men, and they opened the doors.

Hyun Tae walked past him, looking straight ahead. He didn't miss Ahn Jung Ho's fading smile as he passed, the man's face becoming as still as a wax figure.

The doors led them through a painted concrete block corridor that led to another set of doors, which opened up to the manufacturing floor. Workers in white lab coats and masks stood at machines that poured liquids and creams into jars and bottles. Large metal canisters, conveyor belts, and packaging machines filled the cavernous warehouse. Bright, cold fluorescent lights lit the space from overhead. A set of metal stairs led up to a top level, and Hyun Tae moved in that direction.

Footsteps followed him, and he glanced back to see Ahn Jung Ho and his men behind them. "I should not have brought you here," he said to Chase.

"They work for your father, don't they?" she asked.

"That doesn't mean they are good men."

They went up the metal stairs to a catwalk that took them over the production floor. Her small boots clicked rapidly on the metal to keep up with him, and he slowed his pace. At the end of the catwalk, they turned on to a balcony and went to the main office at the end of it.

When he opened the door, natural light flooded into the room from large glass windows onto a honey-colored natural wood floor. A wide monitor sat on a bamboo and stainless-steel desk. Hyun Tae walked over and sat in the leather chair, clicking the mouse. A login screen appeared. He would have to ask for the password to get on the computer.

Footsteps sounded at the door, and Hyun Tae looked up.

Ahn Jung Ho stood, his hands in his pockets, in a deliberately casual pose. "What are you looking for? Perhaps I can help."

Hyun Tae leaned back in the chair. "I want to know how the company is doing. Shouldn't a son know how his father's company works?"

Ahn Jung Ho's eyes sparked with anger, but he did not raise his voice. "You have not been here in many years. Suddenly, you are curious."

"So you won't give me the password?" Hyun Tae asked in the same friendly tone.

"Does your father know you are here?" Ahn Jung Ho asked instead, and Hyun Tae's heart sank. Ahn Jung Ho's face changed from defiant to surprised, and then a faint gleam of triumph lit his eyes. "You did not tell your father you are here."

Hyun Tae stood up. "I'm seeing him this evening. I'll tell him then."

Abandoning English, Ahn Jung Ho spoke in a soft, low voice as he stepped into the office, walking over to them. "Another poor choice you have made. One of many since you went to America. Should we list them?"

"Not as incriminating as yours," Hyun Tae shot back, watching Ahn Jung Ho carefully. "You almost killed us when you ran us off the bridge."

Ahn Jung Ho's jaw tightened, and then he answered, "That was an accident. Your girlfriend drives like a drunk grandmother. I am not a murderer."

Hyun Tae looked over at the two men standing outside the room. "I don't know if you are a killer or not, but I know you are a fraud and a thief, and you are going to ruin KimBio."

"You don't know who I am, do you?" Ahn Jung Ho said with a chuckle. "While your father has declined in health every day, I have saved this company. I have increased revenues. We now hold crucial research the board has been salivating over for years. You are the son of an aged man. You are no one. And you have someone precious to lose."

They eyed each other as Ahn Jung Ho walked across the floor to Chase, offering his hand to her with a smile.

She took it, confusion in her eyes. Hyun Tae fought the rush of anger. She didn't know she was being threatened.

To Hyun Tae's fury, Ahn Jung Ho raised Chase's hand to his lips and kissed it. "I hope you enjoy your visit to Korea," Ahn Jung Ho said in English.

Hyun Tae couldn't control his shaking as he stepped around the desk and took Chase's hand from Ahn Jung Ho. "Don't touch her again," he said in Korean, keeping his voice even.

He walked out of the office, keeping a firm grip on Chase, down the catwalk and across the plant floor. He'd been trying to save the company from reckless acts like corporate espionage, and he even thought he was protecting Chase, but this was not a far-off enemy. Ahn Jung Ho had been watching them, probably from the moment Chase crossed Hyun Tae's path. They had never been out of his sight. It wasn't his father who wanted to hurt Chase; it was Ahn Jung Ho.

Chase stumbled, and Hyun Tae immediately turned and caught her in his arms, silently reprimanding himself. He'd been so angry, he hadn't been paying attention. "I'm sorry," he said as she regained her footing, though he didn't let go of her as quickly as he should have.

"What's wrong?" she asked as they walked out of the plant and toward the waiting car.

"I'll tell you later," he said.

They got in the car and Hyun Tae told the driver to take them home. He sat back in the seat, staring out the window in silence. It was a few moments before he was aware that he'd spoken in Korean to the driver and hadn't explained anything to Chase.

"We're going back to my parents' house," he said to Chase.

She squeezed his hand, and he realized that he'd reached out for her, and she'd responded. He must really be losing it. He shouldn't have done that. He released her hand without apologizing and turned his head and watched the last of the Guro district slip away. Decades ago, there were businesses in Korea that had been very cutthroat, sometimes literally. Ahn Jung Ho was not that old, but he had learned from Hyun Tae's father, and the old ways were sometimes passed down.

How could he tell his father that the man he trusted was going to destroy the company? His father might not believe him. If his father trusted Ahn Jung Ho more than he trusted Hyun Tae, the company was going to sink into a tangled web of corporate theft and public disgrace. His father's life's work and his fortune would be ruined. But

362

if Hyun Tae wanted to keep Chase safe, he had to send her back to the United States and forget about trying to stop Ahn Jung Ho. He had no idea what to do.

Back at his parents' house, Hyun Tae carried all her shopping bags into his living room and set them down. Joon Suh was standing at the large window that looked out to the gardens, his back to them. He turned, looking over at Hyun Tae, and spoke in English.

"Did you go to the plant?"

Hyun Tae answered. "Yes. I didn't find out anything new. I couldn't get on the computer. I don't know exactly how to prove it, but Ahn Jung Ho has been behind everything. And what's worse, he's gotten everything he wanted so far. "

Joon Suh raised his eyebrows. "You can't prove it?"

"No. And he threatened Chase if I pursued it."

Chase looked surprised. "He did?"

Hyun Tae sighed. "Yes. I suppose you thought the kiss on your hand was charming."

"Oh, absolutely. Wet, fishy lips from some strange guy. So charming."

Her sarcasm was reassuring. She wasn't impressed or intimidated by Ahn Jung Ho. "Well, he told me to back off or he's going to...he just hinted that you might be in trouble."

"He really is a bastard," Joon Suh muttered.

"I'm not scared," Chase said, her eyes trusting.

Joon Suh said, "We need to know for sure that your father did not do these things."

Hyun Tae had no illusions about his father being an innocent man, though he had mellowed considerably over the years. Maybe even gone soft. "We need to find someone who has worked with Ahn Jung Ho. Someone who has been a part of the Bates spying."

"Professor Kruljac," Chase said.

It was so obvious, Hyun Tae didn't know why he hadn't thought of it before. Professor Kruljac's sudden departure from the school had been no accident; he knew that for certain. The professor had been a loose end in the Bates spying enterprise. It was possible he had been killed, but if he was still alive, then he'd probably have a lot to say about Ahn Jung Ho.

"Too bad we don't know where he is," he said, looking over at Joon Suh.

Joon Suh smirked. "I'm not magic."

"Without the professor, Ahn Jung Ho is going to get away with everything." Hyun Tae said. He didn't say it to pressure Joon Suh; he was just stating a fact.

Joon Suh put his hands behind his head and stretched. "Ah. I guess it's up to me."

Chase waved a dismissive hand. "You can do it, *oppa*."

Hyun Tae caught Joon Suh's eye, and they both sputtered into laughter. *Oppa* could mean an older brother, but it was used by girls to signify that they looked up to a guy they liked. When he was younger, it

364

made Hyun Tae feel like a man, but now that he was older, it was just funny.

Joon Suh messed up her hair as he walked away, still laughing.

Hyun Tae leaned back against the counter. "So Joon Suh is *oppa* now?"

Chase laughed, climbing up on the chair next to him, putting her elbows on the counter. "No. But it's cute. The idea of someone who takes care of you like that. It's very sweet."

He tried to think of something clever to say, but nothing came to him, His mind was locked up over her soft mouth and the way her hair fell over her shoulders. He could lean down and kiss her right now, and this time it would be for real.

She looked away and twisted her feet around the rungs on the chair. To his surprise, her cheeks were a little pink. Was that for him?

He stood up from the counter, his heart beating fast. "I better get going. See you tonight. Text me if you need anything."

She glanced at him, but only for a moment, and this time he knew he wasn't imagining the color in her cheeks. "Sure."

Back in his room, he slid the door shut and stood there for a moment, thinking about the look on her face. Then he smiled. She felt something for him; she just didn't know what to do about it. He put his hand on the door and leaned against it, so tempted to walk back out there and confess to her that he cared about her. He wouldn't say he loved her because she wouldn't be ready for that.

Pulling off his shirt, he focused on his dinner with his father. He had to figure out how to keep Chase safe. Maybe he wouldn't need the professor if his father believed him. Maybe if he just told his father what Ahn Jung Ho was doing, it would be enough.

He took his shower and picked out his clothes, opting for a cream-colored linen jacket and dark slacks with a button-down shirt. No tie. He looked at his reflection in the mirror, and he wondered what his father saw when he looked at him. His father had never said that he was proud of him, no matter how many awards Hyun Tae got at school or what he achieved. Pride would have been too much to hope for, he supposed.

Choosing to drive rather than use the family driver, Hyun Tae went to the garage and took his keys to the Mercedes 750i from the wall. As he opened the car door, the image of Chase sitting in the kitchen, her feet wrapped around the chair, her fingers twirling her hair as she waited for him came to his mind. His pulse jumped when he thought of being able to come home to her, not just tonight, but every night. She was tearing him apart, and she didn't even know it.

The road into the city was filled with traffic, the fading light of the afternoon changing the skyline from clean edges to dream-like shapes and colors. He found parking at the Lotte Hotel, and took the elevator up to the thirty-fifth floor to the Pierre Gagnaire à Séoul. When he arrived, the host led him to a table by the window. The sky by now looked like misty blue water, as if he were looking at an aquarium, the Bugaksan mountain barely visible in the deepening twilight. The precise opulence of the restaurant had the desired effect of making him feel like he belonged there, as if it were another home.

He sat at the table, looking out the window and resisting the impulse to check his phone or entertain himself. His father had an old-fashioned sense of etiquette. He would see it as an insult if Hyun Tae acted bored while he waited.

"Here you are, sir," a waiter said, and Hyun Tae looked up to see his father sitting down in the chair across the table. He wore a dark blue business suit with a white shirt and a gray tie with black stripes. His father paid attention to clothes, all of his suits custom-tailored. No one needed to explain who he was when he walked in a room.

Hyun Tae stood up and made a short bow, and his father motioned for him to sit down.

"So you are here," his father said in Korean. If translated into English it wouldn't make sense, of course. The greeting was a way of acknowledging someone.

"Yes, Father. You are well?"

"It was a long day." His hands shook as he reached for the glass of water.

"I'm sorry to hear that," Hyun Tae said, looking more closely at his father. Something was definitely wrong with him, but Hyun Tae didn't know what it was, and he didn't know how to ask.

They sat in silence as his father examined the menu and ordered a drink. The waiter swept the menus away and promised to return with the drinks. After a few moments his father looked up at him.

"Why did you bring the girl to our home?"

It was a fair question. If Hyun Tae were serious about a girl, as in wanting to marry her, it would have been a long process, mentioning her in phone calls, briefing his parents about her background, and cautiously waiting for their approval during each step. Then again, if Chase were just some short-term hookup, he would never have bothered to introduce her to his parents. Suddenly introducing her out of the blue was probably confusing. He'd done it because he thought his father was watching him, but the entire time, it had been Ahn Jung Ho. His father had no idea he was dating anyone.

"I'm sorry, Father. I realize this is very unexpected. Chase has become important to me very quickly, and I wanted you to know."

"You are going to marry her?"

There was no getting away from this question. Hyun Tae had known it would be asked, and he was relieved

368

Chase wasn't present. He was going to have to go all the way.

"Yes."

"She agrees?"

Hyun Tae realized he wasn't lying when he'd said he was going to marry Chase. He wanted to marry her, someday. However, now he was in different territory. What if he were completely honest about the fake dating? He knew immediately his father would think he was an idiot if he said he wanted to marry someone who wasn't even dating him.

"We haven't formally talked about when we want to get married. I hope you will be patient with us." It was the closest to the truth he dared to go.

He couldn't read his father's expression. "She does not come from a good family."

Hyun Tae knew exactly what his father meant, and it was true. A good family meant a prominent one with connections. Whether that prominence was in the U.S. or Korea didn't really matter, but a family that was distinguished by well-known success in either country would have been acceptable. His parents had been counting on a handsome, eligible son who would strengthen their social and economic position with a well-connected marriage. They had worked hard to build up their fortune, and it hadn't been easy.

He answered, "No, father. She is not. But I want to marry someone I love. I will work hard to bring you success in the business another way."

His father stared back at him, his jaw clenched and his gaze angry. Gripping the edge of the table, his father leaned forward, keeping his voice low. "You think this is acceptable? You will marry a girl who is nothing? Are we stupid parents who have failed?"

His father's words cut deep, but he understood why his father was so angry. A girl who didn't even have an education yet smacked of a decision made with body parts other than his brain, the ultimate embarrassment to any parent. He couldn't tell them why Chase was different, why he needed her, why she was so much more than a choice.

"I will make you proud. I will have my degree in June from a good school. I have never caused you shame." He couldn't promise his father would grow to like Chase, but he hoped that would happen. Part of him realized this should all be hypothetical, that Chase hadn't even so much as said she liked him. He couldn't predict what she would do, and he was fighting for her like he had a chance.

The anger remained in his father's eyes. "I must pass the company on to my heir. You must be worthy, but you are not. You are selfish."

"Father, please. Give me time to show you—"

His father stood and pushed his chair away from the table, standing up straight. "If you want to earn my trust, remove the girl from my home and beg my forgiveness."

Hyun Tae went to speak again, but his father turned and walked away. Hyun Tae was paralyzed by shock. He had no chance at all of talking about Ahn Jung Ho now or of warning his father. He realized that if he had never involved Chase, he would have had a better chance of talking to his father, but the game he'd played trying to make things right had backfired. He'd read everything wrong.The waiter came by with the drinks, and Hyun Tae apologized and tried to pay, but his father had already paid for everything. That made him feel worse, as if his father had everything under control and he didn't.

Hyun Tae drove home in a daze, his mind turning over all the possibilities, but there were only two things he knew for certain. He loved Chase and couldn't stop fighting for her, and he had to find that professor.

Chapter Thirty

Chase ducked her head closer to her mug of tea, letting the steam warm her frozen nose and cheeks. How Hyun Tae's family lived with the temperature hovering just above "I think I have hypothermia" was a mystery to her. Would it be rude to put on her new coat?

Curled up on the sofa with her laptop, Chase took a sip of scalding hot chrysanthemum tea, which wasn't as bad as she thought it might be, and closed out of a chat with Jonni. She had given her sister a quick update, assuring her that her boyfriend was being nothing but gallant and that she was enjoying Korea. It wasn't a complete lie. She pulled her soft cashmere sweater closer around her, warmed by it and the sight of the new clothing that sat by the door, still in crisp bags and sparkly tissue paper.

Joon Suh came out of his room, and Chase looked up, giving him a little wave.

He raised a languid hand in greeting, refilled his mug with coffee from the kitchenette, and then shuffled back into his room. He had been in there for hours looking for the professor and likely gathering evidence to counter Mr. Ahn's actions.

Her phone vibrated and she checked it.

"Hi." From Daniel.

She hesitated. She realized she hadn't thought about Daniel since she'd boarded the plane to Korea. She put the phone down on the counter and spun it around, as if it were an arrow that would point her in the right direction. It stopped at the refrigerator. She couldn't avoid answering him; he deserved better than that. She picked it up and texted him back.

"Hi, how are you?"

"You wanted to talk to me before you left."

Yes, she did. But she couldn't tell him in a text that she didn't feel the same way about him that he felt about her. *"I don't want to tell you in a text."*

"Is it good or bad?"

Her heart sank. He was pushing her into a corner. She didn't want to do this, at least not this way.

Then he texted her back, not giving her a chance to respond. *"You can tell me when you're ready. I'll wait. Just know that I'll always be there for you, wherever and whenever."*

"Thank you."

He must know that she wanted to break up, but he was letting her do it her own way. Somehow, all she could think of was Hyun Tae. She looked at the clock. It was 8:13, and

Hyun Tae wasn't back yet. Nothing had gone the way she thought it would—Hyun Tae's father didn't seem to even know she existed. And for some reason, Mr. Ahn had been behind the sketchy events back in California. But why?

The front door adjoining the main house to Hyun Tae's suite opened, and Chase stood up from the couch, expecting to greet Hyun Tae. Instead, she found herself standing before Mrs. Kim, his mother. At Mrs. Kim's elbow, a slim male employee stood mutely with a stack of towels in his arms. Mrs. Kim wore a lavender dress suit, complete with shiny gold brooch, matching jewelry, and sheer stockings. The only thing that gave away the fact that she was in her own home and not off to a board meeting somewhere were the fluffy white slippers on her feet. She had to be freezing.

Chase self-consciously pulled her sweater down over her fleece pajama pants.

Mrs. Kim gave her a slow blink, her grave eyes taking on a hard glint. She looked up at her employee, asking something in clipped tones.

He bowed his head, and he then addressed Chase. "Good evening." His English wasn't great, but she understood that at least.

Chase waved a hand. "Hi."

The employee, a man in his late forties, looked mildly uncomfortable. "Ma'am would ask, you are stay here?"

Heat flooded Chase's face. Hyun Tae didn't tell them she was staying the night? She tugged on the ends of her sleeves. "Oh, yeah. I'm just...visiting. For a little. I don't mean to impose if it's an inconvenience."

The man said something to Hyun Tae's mother, and the woman stared back at Chase and then walked right past her into Hyun Tae's suite.

So it wasn't okay. Embarrassed, Chase stayed in the living room, wondering what she should do. Maybe she could get a hotel, not an expensive one, of course. Her parents might pay for it. She was trying to figure out how to pay for a room when Hyun Tae's mother returned to the living room, sparing Chase another caustic glance, and then she suddenly stopped by the front door. She put a hand to her mouth, "Omo."

Chase followed the direction of her gaze. She was looking at the shopping bags.

Mrs. Kim bent over and pulled out the gorgeous, navy blue lace cocktail dress Hyun Tae had insisted Chase wear to the party tomorrow night. Mrs. Kim smiled, laughing and trailing her hand down the fabric of the dress. She spoke softly to her employee, her taut skin crinkling around her eyes and a pleased smile softening her face.

Chase didn't know what to think. Was Hyun Tae's mother admiring her son's taste in clothing?

Mrs. Kim put the dress back, grabbed the handles of all the bags, and still speaking in a low, happy voice to the employee, picked up the bags and opened the door.

She was leaving with the clothes, Chase realized, dumbfounded. She stood, unable to move, watching as Hyun Tae's mother swept past, catching her eye. Mrs. Kim's sweet expression fell for just a moment, replaced with a coy smile, triumph in her eyes. And then she was gone, leaving expensive perfume in her wake.

Chase went to the tan couch, sinking onto it. What had just happened? Had Mrs. Kim really taken all the clothes, or did she mean to put them away somewhere else? No, she had definitely just taken them.

So Chase wasn't welcome in the Kim family home, and everything Hyun Tae had purchased belonged to his parents, apparently. She was slightly embarrassed for him. He was trying to do something nice, and his mother had reversed it.

The back door opened, and Chase sat up again, holding her breath.

Hyun Tae backed through the door, his arms laden with brown paper bags giving off the most tantalizing, fried food scent. He hooked a foot around the door, closing it behind him as he teetered to the counter and deposited the grease-stained bags onto the black granite countertops. He looked over his shoulder with a slight smile. "I didn't eat much at dinner. Are you hungry?"

"Starving," Chase said, deciding not to say anything about the clothes or his mother's icy disapproval of her. "What did you bring?"

"Fried chicken." Hyun Tae began digging around in the bags, bringing out cardboard cartons of food. "No offense, but Korean fried chicken has KFC beat."

"None taken. If it's fried, I will probably love it."

They took everything to the coffee table in the living room, and Hyun Tae found a goofy looking game show Chase didn't understand, but it hardly mattered. It was background noise. And the chicken was mind-blowing.

Hyun Tae was mostly silent, his mind elsewhere as they both stuffed themselves on fried chicken, french fries, and something spicy but delicious called dokbokki. Chase blew air out of her mouth as the spice burned her tongue and nose.

Hyun Tae looked down with a smirk. "Too spicy?"

"What? Never." *Yes.*

He chuckled, wiping spicy sauce off his fingers with a napkin, and then his mood changed, became more somber. "I never even got to order at the restaurant with my father."

"What happened?"

He shrugged. "My dad is disappointed with my choices. It didn't go well."

Chase ran that through her Hyun Tae translator. "He's mad I'm your girlfriend."

He nodded, chewing a bite of chicken.

Chase sighed, bringing her knees up and leaning against the couch. She watched the TV mindlessly as she mulled over the situation. Hyun Tae had begun this dating ruse to protect her from his father. Only now they knew it was Mr. Ahn she needed protection from, and he probably didn't care about Hyun Tae's love life. He wouldn't back off just because she was dating the heir to the company. Actually, it might improve his situation if Hyun Tae's father was angry with his son.

She turned to Hyun Tae. "Why does Mr. Ahn want to hurt me? I didn't steal anything. Does he still think I'll expose the stuff he was doing at Bates?"

"I think I'm the target now. He is using you against me."

"Because I'm your girlfriend. I mean, everyone thinks I am."

Hyun Tae sat back, stretching his legs in front of him. "Eoh."

"Yeah," she agreed. It was on the tip of her tongue to tell him they should abandon the dating scheme and send her to America where she couldn't cause him any more trouble. She couldn't seem to make herself say it. Why couldn't she say it?

He didn't either. He just stared at his black socks.

She decided to change the subject before he thought of it. "Joon Suh has been working on finding that professor, I think. Or he fell asleep. But he's been in his room this whole time."

"If we can find him, then he can testify to the board and to my father. He needs to know what's going on, but he doesn't want to listen to me right now."

"If we can't find him, what will you do?"

Hyun Tae shrugged. "I don't know. Just hope Joon Suh can find something."

She turned back to the TV, wondering how much more time they would need. Hyun Tae's mom might find a way to send her back to the States very shortly, which wouldn't necessarily be a bad thing, she supposed. Except she really wanted to stay. She drew her knees up for warmth and resisted the desire to cuddle up next to Hyun Tae on the floor.

*****

"Chase?" Hyun Tae rapped softly on her door.

"Hi! Coming!" Chase called. She chewed on her thumbnail, staring at her reflection in the mirror. She looked pretty cute, but definitely not as formal as she could have looked if she'd been able to keep the dress Hyun Tae bought her yesterday. As it was, she wore a knee-length white cotton dress with a black belt and boring black pumps she got for a job interview once. She had curled her hair and let it flow down her back in blond ringlets and waves. No jewelry. But she didn't look bad...right?

Chase opened the door to find Hyun Tae and Joon Suh waiting for her, both dressed in black tuxes. Hyun Tae's jacket fit his slim build to perfection, tailored from broad shoulders to long legs with soft, silky material. His hair was combed to the side, and his smooth face registered surprise.

Chase looked down at her dress. "I know it's not the one you bought me. There was kind of a misunderstanding last night." She clutched her puffy coat tightly in front of her. She'd had that in her room when Mrs. Kim came by, at least.

Hyun Tae frowned. "What misunderstanding?"

"I think your mom thought the shopping bags were...hers..." Chase faltered as his features went from smoldering to anger. "I'm sorry. I didn't know what to say."'

Hyun Tae exchanged looks with Joon Suh. Hyun Tae said, "You should have told me."

She lifted one shoulder in a small shrug, remembering how helpless she'd felt when Hyun Tae's mother had walked past her with all the clothes.

He rubbed the back of his neck and lifted his eyes to the ceiling. "Chase."

"Sorry," she repeated. "But this dress is okay, right?"

He turned to Joon Suh. "What do you think?"

"It's Chase. She's always okay."

"Thanks," she said, giving him two thumbs up.

Hyun Tae took the puffy jacket from her hands and held it up for her to put on. "We'll have to go shopping again."

As she slid her arms into the sleeves, he held onto the lapels, his arms over her shoulders, and his mouth close enough that she could feel his breath tickling the back of her neck. "But you look perfect."

Chase shivered, trying to contain the bubble of excitement his words elicited. *He's just being nice,* she reminded herself.

A Mercedes was waiting for them in the driveway near the front gates, and they all bundled into its warmth, Joon Suh sitting in front, and Hyun Tae opening the back door for her. Chase decided to ditch the coat in the car and just deal with the momentary coldness from warm car to warm building. She clasped her hands in her lap and shivered.

The car turned left on a wooded road, going up a long driveway lit by hanging paper lanterns on either side. They pulled up to a circular driveway, where a line of cars deposited guests at the entrance of a glass building, its walls entirely transparent to illuminate the lush scene within. She saw at least two hundred elite guests milling around inside, their finery glinting in the warm glow of crystal chandeliers that dangled above their heads. Ladies minced gracefully in low-back gowns, Swarovski crystal trains, and satin folds of lush skirts. The men held flutes of champagne and moved smartly in their crisp jackets and polished dress shoes.

Chase stared down at her cotton dress and knew she wouldn't fit in.

When it was their turn, Hyun Tae came around to her side, opened the door, and offered his arm. He must have seen her panic because he placed her hand firmly on his arm, steering her toward the entrance. "Don't worry."

It was impossible not to. The blast of chilly night air raised goosebumps on her arms, and then they were inside, surrounded by warmth and the aroma of fine cuisine. A doorman took Hyun Tae's coat and scarf, and then Hyun Tae led them into the throng, getting stopped almost immediately by a portly, middle-aged man with a mole on one cheek. They shook hands, and in Korean, Hyun Tae introduced himself and then Chase. The man shook Chase's hand vigorously. "Hello, nice to meet you," he said in careful English.

Chase bobbed her head in greeting. "Hello, nice to meet you, too."

Joon Suh had taught her a few Korean phrases, but she figured if someone said hi in English, she might as well return the favor.

Hyun Tae and the man talked for a few moments, and Chase let her eyes wander. Everything was so grand; she could hardly believe it. A pianist in a white satin gown played a sweet, high melody that rang up to the high ceiling. Several waiters were weaving through the crowd with platters of hors d'oeuvres. The low hum of conversation ebbed and flowed, punctuated with a pleasant laugh here and there.

She began to relax, enjoying the beauty of the room and the people. Everyone seemed to know Hyun Tae, and there was always someone coming up to greet him. Keeping her hand on Hyun Tae's arm made her feel more secure. As long as she was next to him, she felt shielded from curious looks. He seemed to know this, and if he moved too quickly and her hand slipped, he would pause and wait until she was next to him again, putting his hand over hers.

As they worked their way through the crowd, Chase recognized Mrs. Kim standing with a small group of ladies, all of a similar age and all bedecked in jewels. Hyun Tae steered her in a different direction, and they headed toward a table where drinks and food were being served by chefs in white coats.

"Are you hungry?" Hyun Tae asked.

"Definitely," Chase said.

He handed her a plate. "I'll be back in a minute. I have to talk to my father while he's here."

Chase nodded, although her heart fell into her stomach. She wasn't social at the best of times, let alone here with a room full of strangers. "Go ahead; I'll find a seat somewhere."

"Thank you," he touched her arm briefly and then disappeared into the throng.

Chase looked at the food, pleased to see that most of it was pretty recognizable. She got meatballs, asparagus, and some kind of buttered pasta, and headed toward the far glass wall where she had spotted some bistro tables and chairs. On her way, she accidentally bumped shoulders with someone, and quickly turned to apologize. "Sorry! Excuse me."

The woman, small and thin with a flat nose and beady eyes, bobbed her head and mumbled something in Korean. And then paused. "*Suk Hee-ah, i yoja arah?*"

Chase stopped to face the woman, "Oh...sorry?"

She looked over her shoulder, and Chase saw Mrs. Kim standing with champagne in one hand, long fingernails tapping the glass as she fixed her gaze on Chase. Mrs. Kim gave her a shallow smile. "*Eoh, i yoja-ga akah nega malhaessdan yoja-yah.*"

Mrs. Kim's friend drew out an "*eoh*" sound, her eyes sparkling with interest. She gave a slight bow of her head. "Hello."

Chase bobbed her head in greeting. "Hi."

"*I Chase-ieyo,*" Mrs. Kim said. To Chase she said, "This is Mrs. Lee."

"Nice to meet you Mrs. Lee," Chase said. She wasn't sure if she should shake the woman's hand. With both hands supporting a heavy plate laden with meatballs, she figured she shouldn't go out of her way to make it happen.

Mrs. Lee, whose hair was similar to Mrs. Kim's, patted her curls and murmured something in Korean to Mrs. Kim and the other ladies. They all tittered, and a wider-set lady next to Mrs. Kim fanned her face.

Chase cleared her throat softly, wondering if she should go or if they wanted her to stay.

A thin, slightly taller lady with silky black hair pulled into a French twist bowed her head. "I am Chung Min Hee. I speak little English."

"Nice to meet you," Chase said, not trusting herself to repeat the name correctly.

Min Hee looked her up and down. "You live California?"

"Yes," Chase nodded.

Min Hee said something in Korean, and another round of laughter echoed from the ring of ladies.

Chase's face got hot.

"How long will you visit?" Min Hee asked.

"Uh, not long," Chase said, smiling tightly. "Hyun Tae just wanted to show me Korea."

Min Hee's eyes seemed very calculating. Her English wasn't great, but Chase could sense her circling like a hungry shark. She was going to bite any second. "A surprise visit?"

"Kind of," Chase hedged.

"*Eoh*," she said, nodding, a mask of forced sympathy falling over her porcelain features. "He should have told about the party." Empty look of concerned surprised. "He didn't take to shopping?"

Mrs. Kim looked positively gleeful. A cat with a belly full of warm milk.

Chase swallowed against a dry mouth. *Yeah, my dress is plain, I get it. Haha. You're all terribly clever.* "Ah, yeah, no time for shopping." She gave a weak laugh.

Min Hee crinkled her nose with a smile that was a little closer to a sneer. "I am happy he found distraction for school."

Your mom is a distraction. Chase nodded, smiling, and took a huge bite of her meatball.

Suddenly, an arm circled her waist, and Hyun Tae was there, his cool gaze throwing a bucket of cold water on the moment. The women instantly changed their expressions, fawning over him with phrases of endearment. He looked down at her, amused. "Why are you always eating?"

"I'm hungry," she said around the meatball.

He smiled, dimpling one cheek. "*Kyopta.*"

"I know what that means now," she said, smiling and pointing with her fork. It was like the gaggle of disdainful women had faded into the background.

Hyun Tae bowed his head, excusing them politely, and then he led her over to a small bistro table away from the crowd.

Chase put down the food, her appetite gone. "Nice party."

He looked around, putting one hand in the pocket of his dress pants. "Stealing research someone else has discovered and intimidating your competition. Definitely something to celebrate."

"Don't you want to run the company?"

"I do," he said. "But the right way."

Seeing him standing there, surrounded by wealth and prestige, and knowing the goodness within him that yearned to make a difference, Chase knew she had been acting selfishly. Somehow, somewhere along the way, she had fallen for him. She didn't want the fake relationship to end. But if Hyun Tae were to have any chance at achieving his dreams, she needed to let him go.

If it was so clear, then why was it so hard to tell him? *Because he likes you too.*

Hyun Tae took her hand, and Chase looked up at him, wide eyed in surprise. He had an expectant look on his face, like he knew she would get fluttery over the move. "Dance with me?"

The soft strains of a waltz floated through the air. "Sure," she said.

He led her over to the small dance floor where four other couples danced tranquilly to a classical tune Chase didn't recognize. Hyun Tae put a warm hand on the small of her back, cradled her hand in his, and then moved into the motions of a waltz.

She had done this before, sort of. Usually in a mocking kind of way, but she got the general idea of a waltz. With Hyun Tae leading, it was a no-brainer. She looked up from his bowtie to his face. And then she regretted it. Any stirrings of emotion she might have felt moments before were suddenly magnified ten-fold. His kindness and intelligence seemed to radiate from his soft brown eyes, and underneath that, something deeper. . Like she was privy to a great secret few were allowed access to—the subtle enigma that was Hyun Tae. He had let her in, and now there was no getting out.

Hyun Tae pulled her a little closer and leaned down to whisper, "Dancing makes your heart beat faster?"

"What?" Her question come out barely audible, a wisp of breathless tension.

He fought a smile.

Chase became aware that her monitor was beeping obnoxiously.

"Oh uh." She stopped, intending to remove it, but Hyun Tae deftly unlatched it with one hand, slipped it into his pocket, and continued their waltz. She had never seen him look at her like that. His gaze had darkened, and a current buzzed between them, stronger with every turn and pivot on the dance floor.

The song ended with a delirious rapidity that reminded Chase of those rare moments she had fallen asleep for what felt like a minute and woken hours later. Hyun Tae didn't immediately release her.

The ding of a spoon on champagne glass rang through the ballroom, startling Chase out of her stupor. She and Hyun Tae looked toward the small stage the performers were filing down from. Standing at the microphone, resplendent in a sequin-speckled, mauve suit, was Mr. Ahn. He flashed a blindingly white, toothy smile at the crowd, and murmured something into the microphone.

The crowd began to clap softly, and then Chase realized Joon Suh had materialized at her elbow. "Where did you come from?" she asked.

"I thought you would like a translator," he said.

Chase replied in a low voice, "*Gomawoh, oppa.*"

Still looking at Mr. Ahn, Joon Suh let a ghost of a smile cross his face.

"You're not allowed to call him *oppa*," Hyun Tae said.

Chase snorted, "Right, sorry."

He looked down at her, his expression completely serious.

"Oh…" Chase blinked.

Mr. Ahn said something loudly into the microphone, and Joon Suh leaned down to translate. "He says welcome to the company's fiftieth celebration. He's thanking members of the board and business partners. He made a joke, but it's corny. Ignore it."

Chase couldn't help laughing softly into her hand.

"He's going over the history of the company now and telling the story of how Kim Sang Sik built the company from nothing, fighting the economic...difficulties...in the seventies. It's kind of boring for Ahn Jung Ho, actually."

"Boring?" Chase asked.

Joon Suh narrowed his eyes. "He likes to be...I don't know the word. Drama."

"Sensational?"

"Yeah."

Chase had a sense of foreboding.

"He is praising Kim Sang Sik, Hyun Tae's father. He's thanking everyone for the opportunities he had. He began as nothing more than an intern, and was given opportunities to grow. He has been happy to serve the Kim family all these years. And..." Joon Suh, faltered, his skeptical expression deepening.

"What?" Chase asked.

Suddenly all the people at the party turned, and their eyes found Hyun Tae. Most of the onlookers smiled at him, giving a smattering of applause.

Joon Suh leaned down to hurriedly whisper, "He is praising the son and future Managing Director of KimBio, Hyun Tae."

Hyun Tae raised a hand, acknowledging the applause.

"Isn't that good?" she asked.

"I don't know," Joon Suh said.

Chase got the feeling that he didn't say that often. She looked up at Ahn Jung Ho, grinning down at Hyun Tae from the slick, white plastic stage.

Mr. Ahn made a joke, and the audience laughed. Hyun Tae's jaw ticked.

Joon Suh murmured, "He made a joke about the business not being cool for a young kid to take interest in. Stupid."

A few of the photographers took pictures of Hyun Tae, and Chase sidled away to stay out of the limelight.

Mr. Ahn continued, his tone sort of pandering, and she could tell he was making another joke. He gave a weak laugh, and the audience joined him.

"Wait," Joon Suh straightened, looking alert.

Hyun Tae jerked his head around, searching for her. His eyes locked with hers, wide with shock.

Mr. Ahn leaned into the mic, a smirk on his face, as if he were conspiratorially sharing a secret with the entire room. His next words rang through the room with the smug tone of a gloating victor.

Joon Suh grabbed her arm. "Let's go."

"Why?" Chase asked.

He didn't have time to answer. The flash of cameras suddenly exploded around them. They were focused on her.

"Chase!" A reporter called out, his English surprisingly good. "Can you comment on your relationship with Kim Hyun Tae?"

Joon Suh pulled on her arm, but they were surrounded by reporters and cameras. "He outed you," Joon Suh said in her ear. "He made a joke about you being Daniel's girlfriend first."

"Oh God," Chase put her head down, letting her hair fall around her face. Questions flew as reporters all clamored for her statement in a bunch of languages that jumbled together to make a wall of noise.

A swarm of people around her closed in with microphones, cameras, and questions she didn't understand. Chase's heart plummeted clear through her stomach. She backed out of the crowd, keeping her head down, smashing herself between hard shoulders and elbows as she tried to escape the nightmare. The noise was drowned by the rushing in her ears, and she knew her heart rate had jumped. Hyun Tae still had her monitor.

She was dimly aware that Joon Suh still had her wrist in a firm grip, and she followed him through the raucous crowd to the nearest set of double doors that led to a quiet, dark hallway. As the doors shut behind them, two security personnel stood in front of the doors, keeping the flashing bulbs and questions at bay. In the quiet space, Chase's labored breaths sounded too loud. She tried to quiet them.

"Just wait here," Joon Suh said. "Hyun Tae took another set of doors. I'll go get him."

Chase nodded, leaning against the wall and staring at nothing in particular. Most of the noise on the other side of the doors died down after a while. She wasn't sure how long she waited. She rubbed her arms. Picked at her nails. Had it been a long time, or was she just imagining that?

And then two arms were around her. She knew it was Hyun Tae before she looked up at him. He gave her a tight squeeze before setting her away from him and pulling her heart monitor out of his pocket. "Are you okay?"

"Yeah," she breathed. "That was crazy."

He didn't say anything. Clicking her monitor into place on her wrist, he watched the numbers.

Chase smoothed a hand over her bunched up dress. "So...he outed you."

He looked up finally, giving her a smile that didn't quite reach his eyes. "Come with me."

He took her hand and led her away from the double doors. They took another long hallway, and then they exited by a pair of metal doors. A blast of cold hit her as they walked out to the back parking lot. A single yellow light above illuminated the stark space. There was a Dumpster to her left and some empty wooden pallets to her right. Hyun Tae stood near the doors, under the sickly light that made the contours of his face look strange with unfamiliar shadows.

"What happened?" Chase asked.

Hyun Tae shrugged, "He made a scandal. I thought he might do something like that, but it was so public." He rubbed the back of his neck, not meeting her eyes. "You'll be all over the news. So will I."

"Can't you just fire this guy?"

Hyun Tae shook his head. "The board knows he is the most viable alternative if my father's health declines any further. I might be able to build a case against Ahn Jung Ho, but it will take some time. I need to do some digging."

Chase nodded. Something felt wrong here. "Just let me know how I can help."

Hyun Tae sighed, looking up at the stars.

"What is it?" She shivered, wishing she had been able to grab her puffy coat.

He unbuttoned his coat, and shrugging it off, placed its warmth around her shoulders. She let him, examining his face. He still wouldn't look at her. "Chase, this...all this...it might cost me the business."

She watched him, everything inside of her going still. She knew what he was about to do. Somehow she knew he had to, but she wanted to rebel. Only she couldn't. That stillness inside of her was stifling.

"I have to choose." He finally looked at her, eyes sharp. "And I have to choose KimBio. I can't have you near me."

Even expecting the blow, it hit her with a force that nearly knocked the breath from her. They hadn't said anything to each other that would define how they felt.

She hadn't told him how desperately she had begun to want him as the days went on. And he hadn't said out loud that he might care for her. Maybe she had imagined it. She swallowed hard.

Looking away, he continued, "I wanted to keep you safe, but now we know what the danger was. You're absolved of involvement in the research theft. At this point, you'd just be another hurdle for me to jump over. I think it's better if you—"

"I get it," Chase blurted out. Her throat felt swollen, and she swallowed again against it. "You don't have to say any more. I get it."

He nodded, looking at his shoes.

She crossed her arms, hugging herself to keep from losing it while she was still in front of him.

A car rolled up to them, some black sedan Chase didn't know or care to identify. Hyun Tae had his arms folded. "I made a call before I came to find you. I can help you with your plane ti—"

"It's fine." She cut him off, staring at the car. "Don't worry about it."

He didn't say anything, although from the corner of her eye, she saw his jaw clench. Why was *he* mad?

The back door of the car opened, and then a familiar flash of red hair gleamed in the darkness before she saw his face.

"Daniel."

Chapter Thirty-One

Hyun Tae watched helplessly as she got in Daniel's car. He deserved that, he supposed. She needed someone after he had dumped her like a cold, unfeeling jerk. *The company was more important than Chase.* Somehow she had bought that without much of a fight. Like she had already thought it herself.

It took a few moments for the cold wind to cut through his hazy thoughts.

He shouldn't have underestimated Ahn Jung Ho's desperation. Once he realized Ahn Jung Ho was the one following him around and stalking Chase, he should have sent her home for her own safety. Bringing Chase to Korea had been like dangling a steak in front of a starving lion. Ahn Jung Ho had pounced. The reporters had gone predictably crazy. They'd been trying to find out who Daniel's mysterious girl was, and Ahn Jung Ho had given them the scoop of the year. Even better, they'd found another scandal. The girl had not only dated a pop star, but she'd somehow snared the KimBio heir. They were going to love to hate her.

His phone buzzed in his pocket. He ignored it. Whoever it was, he didn't know what to say to them. Chase would surely think he was a coward-—deserting her like that. He only hoped that if she was thousands of miles away, she would at least be safe from all of this madness. His father was likely furious. It would have been unlikely enough that a twenty-three-year-old senior in college would be given any kind of say in a company as huge as KimBio. Now he looked reckless and irresponsible, unworthy of his father's company.

He could turn away and leave it. That occurred to him in a moment of terrifying clarity—he could give up. All these years he had watched his father hurt those below him to build his empire from stone and dirt to glittering towers of glass and steel. All those years he had dreamed of taking the power freely offered on the silver spoon of his birthright and turning it into a force for good. He could not undo the terrors his father had inflicted on the people around him for almost forty years, but he could make them worth something, maybe.

But now it seemed like a bleak future. The only way to fight men like Ahn Jung Ho would be the same way his father had. Ruthlessly. Hyun Tae didn't know if he had that fight in him. And with Chase now alone wherever she was, hurt, confused, and publicly humiliated, he didn't even have a right to pursue that happiness. He couldn't be that selfish. To let her stay would mean pain and hardship for her for as long as she was there. He couldn't bear to see her attacked again. In any way. No, all he had left now was this company. And even that he wasn't sure he could salvage.

His phone buzzed in his pocket again, and he silenced it.

Hyun Tae's hands and face were getting stiff with cold as he stared at the dark parking lot before him.

The door behind him opened, and Hyun Tae turned his head.

"Hyun Tae?" It was his father's driver.

Hyun Tae ignored him.

"I apologize for interrupting, but it is urgent. Your father has collapsed."

Hyun Tae spun around. "What did you say?"

"He is on his way to the hospital, sir."

He started forward, taking his phone out of his pocket. "Why, what happened?"

"I don't know, sir. If you'll come with me—"

"Yes, I know, take me there." He pressed a name on his phone and held it up to his ear. "Joon Suh, where are you?"

Joon Suh answered in his usual way. "Out front."

"Did you know about my father?"

"Who else would have called you? Yes."

Hyun Tae frowned, going back into the building and heading down the hallway toward the front entrance. "Wait for me. We can go to the hospital together." When he hung up, he pocketed his phone again, and hurried through the softly carpeted hallways to a side door that would take him to the car. Joon Suh was waiting for him in a silver sedan, and Hyun Tae slid into the seat next to him.

"You lost your coat," Joon Suh said, looking down at Hyun Tae's bare hands.

"It's fine."

"*Hyung…*" Joon Suh hesitated.

"Don't worry about it," Hyun Tae said, cutting his friend off before he could bring up the emotions that would surely fog his thoughts if he gave into them. "What do you know about father?"

"Nothing, but I think after what Ahn Jung Ho said, he might have had a shock."

Hyun Tae nodded. That didn't surprise him, especially given his father's age. They were quiet for the rest of the drive until they pulled into the garage of Seoul National University Hospital. Hyun Tae's mother called as they were exiting the car. "Oma," Hyun Tae said, his voice subdued.

"Your father had a heart attack," she said. No preamble. The blame was clear in her voice.

"Is he—" Hyun Tae couldn't ask what he wanted to. "Is he all right?"

"He isn't dead," she said, biting anger in her voice. "Not yet."

"I'll be right there."

She hung up on him, and Hyun Tae tamped down a growl of anger. He knew some of this was his fault, but most of it

399

was Ahn Jung Ho. Whatever else Hyun Tae decided about his life, he knew he would not allow Jung Ho to get away with anymore treachery against his family's company.

"This way," Joon Suh said, looking down at his phone. "I got a text for which floor to wait on. He's still in the emergency room, but they're taking him to surgery soon."

Hyun Tae crossed the darkened parking garage, the echo of his footsteps breaking up the empty silence around them. They took an elevator up two floors and emerged into a brightly lit, white hallway where a male nurse with a clipboard was waiting to board after them. Hyun Tae knew his way around the hospital vaguely, and he and Joon Suh hooked a left toward the emergency waiting room.

Everything was white. The walls, the desk, and the squeaky tile floors. Several tan, pleather couches and chairs were lined neatly in the sparse room where a few people sat either looking at their phones or the TV. Hyun Tae's mother stood stiffly in a corner, still wearing her dark purple gown. She stared at him as he walked in.

"Mother," he said in greeting.

"He is in surgery already," she said. Her thin face nearly trembled with anger. "Is it true?"

He knew what she was asking. He contemplated playing dumb, but he thought better of it. "No, it isn't true."

"She isn't that girl?" She pulled out her phone, struggling with it for a moment until she pulled up the tabloid picture of Chase and Daniel on the beach. "This is not her?"

"That's her, but she and Daniel did not actually date. She has been my girlfriend all along."

"You would date her?" she demanded. "This girl? This tramp? She kissed another man while dating you."

Hyun Tae wasn't sure how he could explain them both out of this. "I need you to trust me. Chase isn't like that."

His mother scoffed, throwing her phone back into her white clutch. "Enough. I see what this is. No need to explain further."

There was so much more to say. So much that his mother would love about Chase if she really knew her. But Chase had no connections, no money, and now no reputation to speak of. It would be a futile effort to convince his mother with words. Not that it mattered now.

Hyun Tae stood beside his mother, and they waited.

After two hours, a nurse came through the double doors and called, "Park Suk Hee?"

His mother raised a hand, and they made their way across the waiting room to the nurse. She held a clipboard and lifted a sheet. "Are you the family of Kim Sang Sik?"

"Yes," his mother said.

"If you will come this way, the doctor would like to speak with you."

They followed the nurse through the doors and down the hallway to another elevator. They went up to the third floor and finally to a high dependency unit with several rooms surrounding a shiny white nurse's desk.

An aging doctor with balding, wispy hair and large glasses waited for them at the desk while writing on several stacks of papers. He looked up, his eyes sharp, despite his distracted appearance. "Family of Kim Sang Sik?"

"Yes, I am his wife," Hyun Tae's mother answered.

The doctor bowed his head. "He is recovering well from surgery. We performed an angioplasty after it appeared that he had a coronary blockage. We also placed a stent in the blocked artery to prevent future cardiac distress."

"How is he?" Hyun Tae asked.

"Really, quite well, all things considered," the doctor replied, adjusting his glasses. "If you would like to see him, he is awake now."

They followed him to a spacious room, well decorated and built with a beautiful view overlooking the city of Seoul. Two humidifiers puffed gently near the large hospital bed, where Sang Sik rested with his eyes closed.

402

Hyun Tae hung by the door, waiting for his mother to go first. She sat daintily in a chair beside his bed, and Sang Sik turned his head, speaking to her softly. She responded, and with a nod of her head, stood up. She came to the doorway, and with pinched lips said to Hyun Tae, "He wants to see you immediately."

Hyun Tae went to sit in the chair by his father's bed.

He had never seen him look so gaunt. Dark purple circles ringed his yellowing eyes, and the cannula in his nose was held in place by strips of clear tape that seemed to cut into his soft, wrinkled flesh. "Son," he said.

"Hello, Father." Hyun Tae kept his shock at his father's haggard appearance to himself, but a tremor of fear went through him.

With a grunt, Sang Sik fixed his eyes on Hyun Tae. "I have been sick for many months now."

"You never told me."

"No. It was not your place to know."

Hyun Tae nodded.

"I want...your word." Weak though his voice was, Hyun Tae could hear the conviction in it. He waited, allowing his father to finish without interruption. "I want your word that you will protect my company."

Hyun Tae was stunned. That wasn't what he had expected his father to say.

His father narrowed his eyes. "I know about Ahn Jung Ho. I know his abuses in the company—that he targeted you and the girl."

Anger that his father had known that but done nothing hit Hyun Tae like a wave. But then, he realized, there was likely very little his father could have done about it if he had been sick.

"But I see now, that you are my future. Son. I must have your word."

Hyun Tae bowed his head. "I will protect your legacy, father."

Closing his eyes, Sang Sik nodded in satisfaction. "I will summon the board immediately. You are my named successor."

"Father, about Chase——"

"No." Sang Sik's eyes snapped open again. "Do not speak her name. Do not be distracted. The board will not allow it."

Hyun Tae's shoulders sagged. "I am sorry, Father."

"Protect my company. Then you may repay me."

Hyun Tae stood from the chair, bowed, and left the room with his heart heavy. It did very little to comfort him that his father was reluctantly handing over the reins to him. Even with his shares and Sang Sik signing his over to Hyun Tae, the board of directors still had a legal right to any decisions about the managing director of the company. If the board did not agree on him, it would never happen.

He had promised his father he would protect the company, but Hyun Tae feared it was already a lost cause. This board meeting was going to be a massacre if he didn't find a way to combat the tabloids and somehow prove that Ahn Jung Ho was abusing the company. There were signatures on several purchase orders, but even if he spent all of the next day poring over those papers and compiling, it would only prove that his father had been ill, and Ahn Jung Ho had dutifully stepped in to fill the role.

Joon Suh stood by the nurses' desk, one arm bent and resting on its surface.

Hyun Tae leaned his back against it, hands in his pockets. "He's giving me the shares."

"That's good."

Hyun Tae looked up at his friend derisively.

"I think I might have found some unaccounted for cash flow," Joon Suh said. "We could try that. When will the board meeting be?"

"Tomorrow or the day after. The board is probably eager to know what's happening with the company. My father is ill; they will be nervous."

Joon Suh nodded and then put his phone to his ear when it buzzed. "Hello?" He spoke in English. He listened for a few moments, nodding his head. "Okay. I'll be right there."

"What is it?" Hyun Tae asked.

"I'll email you the cash flow spreadsheet," Joon Suh said, buttoning up his coat. "I have to go."

"Go where?" Hyun Tae asked, demanding to know.

Joon Suh just raised a hand in goodbye and disappeared.

Hyun Tae frowned after him. Was his friend deserting him now, too? He stood alone at the desk, staring down the empty hallway for a long time, hollow and uneasy inside.

Chapter Thirty-Two

Chase huddled under the long dark coat. Daniel had put a comforting arm around her as she shuffled into the car. She had betrayed herself by looking back at Hyun Tae one last time. He just stood under that yellow light, arms crossed. And then the car pulled away, and she was left staring at her own cold fingers.

After a few moments, Daniel put a blanket over her legs and looked at her. She looked away, too embarrassed to tell him what had happened. The look in Hyun Tae's eyes when he'd held her as they danced seemed so real, but maybe it had all been in her head. She obviously didn't understand him at all.

The loneliness and the embarrassment created a big dark hole that swallowed all her pride. She wanted so much to let Daniel comfort her, to just stay in his arms and feel protected and cherished, but she couldn't. Hyun Tae didn't care about her, but that didn't mean she had feelings for Daniel. He deserved to know.

Gathering her courage, she looked up at him. He met her gaze, waiting.

Tears welled up as she said, "He really was faking. I was too, and then it felt real, and I believed it. I'm such an idiot."

The smile he gave her was sad. "It hurts a lot. I know."

Oh, great. She was crying. "I'm so sorry. You're so sweet...but I just don't feel the same way, Daniel. I'm so sorry." Sweet? That was so condescending.

Daniel put his arms around her, patting her back. "It's better to just cry. It's not healthy to keep it in."

So she didn't. She cried and let all the humiliation and confusion wash over her. She loved Hyun Tae. She loved how good he was, how safe she felt with him, and all the little ways they seem to fit together. But he had let her go. The embarrassment of realizing she had misread him wouldn't go away. When she was done crying, she felt completely drained, empty of pain or anything else. She was also exhausted.

Her voice was thick when she finally spoke. "Where are we going?"

They'd been driving for at least an hour or more.

"In a big circle. We drove around Seoul twice."

"What?" she asked, looking up at him in surprise.

"You kept crying."

She was too tired to laugh. "I'm so sorry."

"I'm your friend, right? I don't want you to feel alone."

She winced.

"Don't feel sorry for me. If you just want me as a friend, then I will love you like a friend. I am here if you need me."

She wished that she loved him, but she didn't. "Well, I don't deserve that. Everyone else thinks I'm some sleazy chick stealing all the hot rich guys and their favorite celebrity."

Daniel raised an eyebrow. "I'm hot?"

"Yes, a million screaming girls say you are hot. I'd be an idiot not to notice. They all want me dead, you know."

"It makes me feel bad that I did that to you. It's my fault that people hate you."

Her stomach growled, and she put her hand over it, self-consciously. "I don't care about a bunch of crazy netizens."

"You're hungry."

"I don't really want food right now."

"You always want food," Daniel said. "We could stop somewhere and eat."

"I can't go out like this. I don't even know what I look like. I'm sure I look terrible."

Daniel brushed a strand of her hair out of her face and gazed solemnly into her eyes. "Don't take this the wrong way, but right now I'm the good-looking one."

She laughed. "That's fair."

"I have an apartment," he said, his voice tinged with a teasing note. "There is also food in it. If you would like, I can take you there."

There was nowhere else for her to go. Certainly not Hyun Tae's parents' home where she wasn't welcome. Without Daniel, she didn't know what she would have done. She'd seen some English signs in the city, but it was a very big place, and she only had an American debit card with a few hundred dollars on it. She didn't know if anyone would accept her money. "Thank you."

Daniel leaned down and bumped his forehead against hers. "It will be okay."

The driver stopped after a few minutes and turned into a parking garage. Daniel said something in Korean to the driver, and he answered, "*Aniyo.*"

Daniel settled back in his seat with a sigh. "We weren't followed. My driver is very good at losing paparazzi."

Nevertheless, his driver waited for a few moments, looking around the garage before he opened the doors for them. As Chase got out, she pulled Hyun Tae's coat around her. Daniel guided her to an elevator, and they stepped into it.

The long coat went almost to her ankles. She slipped her hands in the pockets, huddling in it. It smelled like Hyun Tae, and her heart jumped. She wished she hadn't fallen for him. Somehow, she would have to move on. It was unhealthy to waste time on someone who didn't feel the same way, and she just wouldn't do that. She would go back to school and forget about him. She'd get a new apartment that wasn't so close to the Korean house and try to find new friends. Or at least bury herself in artwork until she forgot everything about him.

Her right hand found something in the pocket, and she closed her fingers around it. It felt like a lock. She pulled it out and looked at it. It was a little gold lock with some initials, and there was a small key in it. She looked at the initials. KHT and CEB. Kim Hyun Tae and Chase Elizabeth Bryant. Why would he carve their initials in a lock? It was very beautiful, like something from a jeweler not a hardware store.

Daniel sucked the air between his teeth, and she looked up at him. His hand hit the stop button on the elevator, and she rocked as it came to a halt. He took her hand in his and picked up the lock. He stared at it for a moment, then gently put it back in her hand and closed her fingers around it. His mouth twitched in a bitter smile.

"What is it?" she asked.

He started the elevator again. "There is something I want to show you."

When it reached the top floor, he closed the doors and hit the garage floor button.

"Are we going somewhere?" she asked.

He answered, his eyes on his phone as he texted. "Yes."

When they reached the garage, the driver was waiting with the car door open. Chase got in, and Daniel sat next to her, but this time he didn't reach for her. They drove in silence, and she had a strange feeling that Daniel had just learned something. She turned the lock over in her hands, opening it and closing it again, wondering what it was meant to lock. Was it a gift that Hyun Tae had meant to give her? Seemed like a strange gift for, *Hey thanks for fake dating me. Sorry I ruined your life.*

They drove through the city, the lights on the buildings bright, but not as bright as a green tower that spiked up to the sky. They stopped on the street in front of the tall tower.

"Do you know what this place is?" Daniel asked her after he had stepped out of the car and held the door open for her.

"No. It looks like the space needle in Seattle," she said, stepping out into the night, still drowning in Hyun Tae's coat, the lock clasped in her hand.

"It's called Namsan Tower. Come with me."

She followed him. The place was filled with couples, all holding hands and smiling at each other. Everyone who was there seemed to have someone.

They came to seven trees that looked like Christmas evergreens. She looked closer and realized the trees were actually made of locks. Thousands of them, all locked together made these trees. The fences were also filled with the locks that had hearts and names on them.

She looked down at the lock. "What are they?"

"Couples come here to put their locks on the fences and trees. It means they will love each other forever. They close the lock and throw away the key."

Chase could not move, staring at the sight. Hyun Tae had made a lock for them. He had never told her anything, but he had a lock made with their initials.

She was afraid to ask the question on her mind. "Did he do this as part of the fake dating? To prove something to his parents?"

Daniel slowly shook his head.

She had thought she was done crying, but she wasn't. "Do you think he loves me?"

He stared back at her, pain in his eyes, his voice low. "Yes."

Her fist closed around the lock, and she felt a sudden surge of triumph. She hadn't been wrong, then. She hadn't misread him. He had sent her away to protect her from the problems around him. He was still underestimating her, and she'd have words for him about that later, but right now Hyun Tae needed her.

And then she really looked at Daniel. At his expression. And she realized he needed her, too. Putting the lock back in her pocket, she wrapped her arms around his torso, hugging him close as his arms came around her.

He chuckled, although there was an edge to it. "Is this the part where you tell me how important I am to you?"

"You are," she said, her voice dry and scratchy.

413

Daniel sighed. "I know."

Chase didn't know what else to say. What had seemed so right in the beginning now felt all wrong with Daniel. She had no reason to feel that way. And in the process she had hurt him deeply.

He clasped her upper arms and pulled her away, putting her at a distance so she could see his face. "I'm okay, Chase. You don't get to choose who you love. I know that. I love you," he admitted, the words seeming to catch as they left him in a whoosh. "I do. And I think I always will. But he needs you right now."

She nodded, tears pricking the corners of her eyes.

Daniel seemed to steady himself. "So let's go save his stupid self. What do we need to do?"

Chase willed herself to close out the tumultuous emotions that were vying for attention. "I think I have a plan."

"Great."

"Can I borrow your phone?"

Daniel handed it to her, and then she realized everything was written in Hangul. With a sheepish smile, she handed it back. "On second thought, maybe I could ask you to make the calls for me."

He gave a little smile. "Who are we calling?"

"First?" Chase's resolve hardened. She could do this. Hyun Tae needed her to pull this off. "Call Joon Suh."

414

Chapter Thirty-Three

Rain pattered against the slick black leather of Hyun Tae's Burberry dress shoes. The droplets plopped one by one at first, sliding down the toe of the shoe, until suddenly there was a downpour, and it started to seep through the collar of his white dress shirt. Reluctantly, he left the concrete courtyard of the towering KimBio building and found shelter in its expansive foyer.

*****

An attendant in a crisp, black dress suit uniform came around the sleek semicircle desk to bow at the waist. "Mr. Kim, we are so glad to see you. Will you follow me this way, please?"

He nodded, feeling a strange sense of numb ambivalence. He knew what he was walking into here. Joon Suh had forwarded the financial discrepancies to him a day ago, but after his best record digging (which was nothing compared to anything Joon Suh could accomplish), he had nothing more than an accusation of sloppy accounting. With the tabloids still featuring a kiss with an unknown girl, it would be nothing. A candle flame in a great monsoon.

They had gathered in the boardroom at the top floor. The custom designed, light maple desk was shaped like a long V and dominated the galley style room. Everything but the warm table had been decorated in a monochrome scheme, which gave a stark appearance to the scene that awaited Hyun Tae. A small army of black and white business suits sat at attention for his arrival.

The only flash of color came from Ahn Jung Ho, standing at the head of the room in a cerulean blue suit, mustard shirt, and burgundy bowtie that matched his dark tinted sunglasses.

Hyun Tae took his customary seat at the far end of his father's empty chair and sat back, waiting.

"Members of the board," Ahn Jung Ho said, smiling widely and addressing the room with open arms. "Thank you for granting my request for an emergency meeting."

Ahn Jung Ho continued, "In light of our director's health, we need to discuss some management changes."

"As chief administrative officer, I have naturally assumed many duties as our chairman has taken steps away from the company for his health. I believe we were all aware of this."

A murmur of assent rippled through the room.

Ahn Jung Ho smiled. "If it would please the board, I would like to request nominations for acting director."

Hyun Tae stood, sweat beading at the back of his neck. Whatever the board decided, it couldn't be Ahn Jung Ho. "I would like to address the board."

Ahn Jung Ho's smile froze, polite and steely. "Anyone object?"

No one at the table said anything. Ahn Jung Ho gestured to Hyun Tae.

"Thank you for allowing me to speak. I have discovered some discrepancies in the accounting procedures in one of our divisions, which may be relevant to our choice of acting director today."

"Excuse me," an older board member, Mr. Choi, said, clearing his throat. "You have not finished your studies yet, is that correct?"

Hyun Tae gave a quick, respectful bow of his head. "Yes. I will complete them this year."

"Continue," the older man said.

Hyun Tae straightened, brushing off the attempt to highlight his youth. "My education in America is academic at best, which is useful but not as useful as my experience. I have worked in and understood this company proficiently for many years."

The uncertainty remained on most of their faces. "More to the point," he continued, "I have evidence of the misuse of company funds—"

This time Ahn Jung Ho cut him off. "To the point?" He touched a hand to his mouth, as if unsure about his next words. Hyun Tae knew they were more calculated than his slush fund. "If we must discuss the point, Kim Hyun Tae, then how can we ignore your personal decisions of late?"

The board stared back at him, but Hyun Tae remained calm. "My personal decisions?"

"Yes. There have been some unfavorable rumors," one of the women said. She looked a lot like a steamed yam to Hyun Tae. Wrinkled and meaty at the same time. "We have a brand to protect, even if the rumors are not true."

Several others agreed.

"They are not true," he said.

"It's not appropriate," the yam continued.

"I agree," said another, nearly ancient board member.

A skinny, bald man closest to Hyun Tae, a man who had been loyal to Hyun Tae's father since the early days of the company, cleared his throat. "Hyun Tae...how will you answer to the scandal? It is a delicate time for our company."

Hyun Tae was stunned. His father's most loyal ally was questioning this.

The room fell dead quiet.

Hyun Tae tapped a finger on the table, going through the scenarios he had rehearsed in his head all day yesterday. If the company passed to Ahn Jung Ho now, he would never get it back. Not until Ahn Jung Ho had run it into the ground. He stood, his palms going sweaty. He had never been this nervous about anything. *Stay focused.*

Ahn Jung Ho came to Hyun Tae's side, putting a hand on his shoulder. "Now gentlemen and ladies, I think we are being harsh on our young Hyun Tae. He is new to this game after all."

People in the room chuckled.

Smiling, Ahn Jung Ho continued, "And undoubtedly this will blow over. I want what is best for this company, and with respect to Hyun Tae and Kim Sang Sik's wishes, I wish only to propose that I take on the director's duties until our director returns."

Several heads nodded in agreement. Hyun Tae was losing them. He jerked his shoulder out of Ahn Jung Ho's grasp. "With all due respect," he bit out, "I feel the best interest of the company does not lie with Ahn Jung Ho being given this position. He has abused what little power he has now. I ask that the board at least look at the reports I've compiled."

"Something we would be more than happy to sit down and look at," Ahn Jung Ho said, giving his toothy smile. "I am happy to improve, of course. But more pressing than clerical errors is the immediate future of the company."

Mr. Choi held up a hand. "I have heard enough. I think we all know what must be done here."

Hyun Tae had nothing. No leverage. Despite everything he had done, he had grossly miscalculated, and his family would lose control of this company in a matter of moments. His heart beat furiously in his chest, and it reminded him of Chase. Her clear blue eyes filled with betrayal the last time he had seen her. He clenched his fists at his side.

"A vote then," Mr. Choi said quietly. "All in favor of instating Ahn Jung Ho as acting director..."

The door flew open, slamming against the door stop as a small figure tumbled into the room.

Chase stood there in the doorway, blond, curly hair disheveled and falling around her face, cheeks flushed. "Wait."

Chapter Thirty-Four

One Hour Earlier

The morning sun shone through the window, a beam of light escaping through the gap of blackout curtains and onto the polished hardwood floor. The expansive apartment featured little more than one white couch, a glass coffee table, and a wooden chair in the middle of the living space. Chase sat still and straight on the crisp sofa with Joon Suh beside her. The man sitting across from them held a small glass of vodka in his hands, the half-empty bottle on the coffee table between them. Joon Suh had taken up the offer of a glass, but he'd only sipped it once and put it back on the coffee table.

"I understand Mr. Kim is in the hospital," Professor Kruljac said, his heavy-lidded eyes looking over at them, his Russian accent thick.

Chase waited, letting Joon Suh speak. She'd learned of the news last night, and though she'd wanted to call Hyun Tae, he had made it clear that she didn't belong in is life and she would let him believe that was true, for now.

Joon Suh nodded. "Yes."

Mr. Kruljac said, "My condolences to the family."

Joon Suh bobbed his head. "Thank you."

Chase curled her toes inside her shoes, stifling her impatience. They didn't have much time. Joon Suh had sent an email to Kruljac saying that they wanted to talk about the upcoming board meeting and what Ahn Jung Ho had hired Kruljac to do for KimBio.

The professor looked over at Chase. "I heard Mr. Ahn has been trying to retrieve the file from you."

"I didn't know what it was," she answered.

"I told him that. I also told him that if you didn't know what the file was, then you probably didn't care. And you if did, it was too late."

She'd been so caught up in all the drama that Ahn Jung Ho had inflicted on her life that she hadn't thought much about the professor's intentions. It might be useful to consider that. "Why did you agree to take the research in the first place?"

"I was working on the same research in a lab in Canada, but our investment money dried up. Bates heard about my work and offered to bring me on the team. Unfortunately, the head of the research wanted to approach it with a different method, one that I did not agree with. What could I do? It was not up to me. And then Mr. Ahn contacted me and offered me all the research money I needed and the authority to pursue my research at KimBio if I would give him what Bates had done. So I said yes. But I didn't tell him that the research is useless."

That was a new development. "The research Ahn Jung Ho stole isn't a breakthrough?" she asked.

Kruljac smiled. "No. It isn't."

"So it isn't going to help KimBio at all," she mused.

"No, it won't. However, the research path I am on is much more promising, but since Mr. Ahn threatened to reveal that I had stolen research from Bates, I have no intention of working with him. He has blackmailed me into silence, but he won't blackmail me into doing research for him."

Joon Suh spoke, his voice silky. "Would you like to be free of Mr. Ahn?"

Kruljac raised an eyebrow. "Is that possible?"

Joon Suh stood up. "Yes, but only if you come with us to speak with the board. They are meeting now. If you will come and tell your story, we can remove Mr. Ahn from KimBio."

Kruljac took a sip from his glass and put it down, his eyes cold. "Nothing would give me more pleasure."

As they crawled through traffic, Chase ran through all the worst-case scenarios in her head. If they arrived too late, and the board had made their decision, what then? It was over? Hyun Tae would lose everything.

The car pulled up in front of the glimmering glass building with KimBio displayed prominently on the outside. Sitting in the front seat of the car, Chase shoved the door open and hopped out, pausing only to shout to Joon Suh, "Bring him up! I'm going first."

"Room 2021!" Joon Suh shouted back.

She didn't care how crazy it made her look; she ran. Past the freezing mist of the fountain and straight through the heavy glass doors, she darted across the foyer and skidded to a stop in front of the elevator. She mashed the button half a dozen times, and then waited impatiently for one of the two doors to open. A woman in a suit eyed her suspiciously.

It dinged open, and even though it technically didn't save her any time, she ran into it, pressed the twentieth floor button and then rudely hit the door close button. There was a small crowd waiting to enter the elevator, but she didn't have time to stop at every floor they needed. She blocked the entrance. "Sorry! It's an emergency! Get the next one!"

The woman in the suit glared. The four men behind her seemed incredibly confused, but no one moved or said anything. As the doors closed, Chase waved. "Thanks!"

The ascent felt agonizingly slow. When had the meeting started? She pulled her phone out of her back jeans pocket. Nine twenty. Maybe it hadn't even started yet?

The elevator dinged, settled, and then finally opened. She jogged out of it, checking room numbers as

424

she went. 2005, 2007...the hallway reached a T, and she tried to guess which way to go. She veered right, and she sighed in relief as the numbers jumped up. 2017, 2019...

She heard voices coming from the last room at the end of the corridor. It looked to be a large conference room, and thedouble doors were closed. From inside, she heard a male voice saying something distinctly affirmative. It sounded like some kind of decision. Not thinking, Chase wrenched open the door, stumbling over the threshold, and shouted, "Wait!"

Chapter Thirty-Five

Hyun Tae stared at Chase, several emotions warring for control. He couldn't help the way his heart jumped, with both excitement and pain as he remembered how he had deserted her. His brain finally took over, and he tried to figure out what she was doing here. Was she going to try to blame everything on herself? The room full of distinguished-looking men and women stared in mute surprise.

Chase smoothed her disheveled hair, her blue eyes shining brightly in the morning sun that cascaded through the windows. She swallowed. "I'm sorry for interrupting."

In Korean, Mr. Choi asked, "Who is this?"

Hyun Tae had no intention of revealing who she really was, if they hadn't figured it out. He was sure some of them would start to remember the party and Ahn Jung Ho's disastrous announcement. For now, he told a harmless truth. "She's a student at an American university."

Chase looked at them for a moment and Hyun Tae explained. "He wanted to know who you were. I said you were a student. Some members of the board speak English, but not all of them. I can interpret for you. What do you want to say?" he asked, his eyes boring into hers.

"Please," Chase said, "If you'll wait just a moment, I have someone coming who can explain things." She seemed to gather her courage before saying, "Things that prove Ahn Jung Ho has been stealing research from other facilities."

Hyun Tae translated it word for word, dragging his eyes from hers, his mind reeling. *Did she actually manage to find him?*

The board stared in shock at the drama unfolding before them. The yam lady demanded to know who the girl was that she could make such outrageous accusations.

Ahn Jung Ho gave a giggle, bringing a hand to his mouth. "The antics of youth."

Chase smiled, though it was a strained, plastic attempt. "Please, just a moment. He will be here soon."

And so they waited in arid silence that sucked any warmth from the room. As the seconds turned to minutes, it felt as if gravity itself had increased.

Ahn Jung Ho heaved a heavy sigh, "Kim Hyun Tae, I appreciate the stress this must cause for one so young. And I appreciate your efforts at retaining the integrity of succession, but any momentary distractions will only delay the inevitab—"

The door opened.

Professor Kruljac walked through, a dark coat over his arm, his clothes rumpled in an academic way, his distinguished face showing amusement.

Hyun Tae couldn't believe Chase had found him. When had she done this? He regained his wits and gestured to Kruljac. "This is Professor Matthew Kruljac, a researcher for Bates University."

Ahn Jung Ho's complexion had turned pale.

Kruljac inclined his head. "Ladies. Gentlemen." Without any preamble, he walked to the table nearest to him, just to the left elbow of Mr. Choi, and reached into his jacket pocket. He held up a black thumb drive for a moment before gently placing it on the table. "My emails with Mr. Ahn." He retrieved another identical flash drive, lining it up with the first. "Account transactions." And then finally, he pulled a third from his pocket and placed in a neat row, shiny and black, with curved edges. "Phone recordings."

A chair squeaked somewhere in the room.

"Mr. Ahn contacted me to steal research on allogenic cell research from Bates University for KimBio. Which I did."

Ahn Jung Ho huffed. "A lie. I have done nothing but serve this company loyally. For two decades." He pointed to Hyun Tae. "His entire lifetime."

Kruljac shrugged, his hands in his navy blue slacks. "I believe the evidence speaks for itself. I have no fear

428

that your company will handle this correctly." He gave one of the board members a confident smile. "It's in our best interest, no?"

Hyun Tae didn't bother translating that. "Mr. Choi, would you be so kind as to verify this information?"

Ahn Jung Ho made a strangled sound of outrage. "The impudence of this. I have been framed."

Mr. Choi, ignoring the protest, opened his laptop and plugged in the first flash drive. He placed a pair of reading glasses on his nose as the information popped up on the screen. He read for a few silent minutes. Hyun Tae's heart beat loudly in his ears. Why did Kruljac come willingly to admit he was a criminal? He looked to Chase. She gave him a little thumbs up. Whatever it was, he didn't care.

Chase had not only saved the day, she had come back. For him.

Mr. Choi cleared his throat, clearly embarrassed. "It is as he said. We will need to have these authenticated but..." he trailed off.

Ahn Jung Ho laughed, incredulous. "How absurd."

The board members were silent, this time in a way that blared accusation. This sort of scandal was far more dangerous than a tabloid. Hyun Tae knew the police would never be contacted, and there would never be lawful justice, but it was enough to remove Ahn Jung Ho from his place. Even if he had succeeded in stealing research from Bates. Hyun Tae would never use it.

Ahn Jung Ho nodded, his features quickly morphing from incredulity to anger. He rapped his knuckles on the table, "If you think I will be silent about this, you are wrong. This man," he jabbed a bejeweled finger at Kruljac. "He is a liar."

The men sitting next to Ahn Jung Ho looked away from him, as if he were not there. Mute rejection.

As Ahn Jung Ho swiftly stalked toward the door, Hyun Tae realized he would have to pass through Chase to exit. He felt a sudden leap of fear.

But when he looked, she was already gone. Ahn Jung Ho swung the door open, and with a tight click, was gone.

Hyun Tae looked to the men and women of his company, all eyes glued to him. Every document would need to be assessed. Every phone conversation. Every account detail. And then they would wipe it clean, and he would deal with Kruljac however he felt necessary. It was going to be a long day, and although he was relieved to be rid of Ahn Jung Ho, he knew his mind would be elsewhere.

Chapter Thirty-Six

Chase rolled her foot from toe to heel, rocking the wooden bench swing back and forth in a slow tempo. The cold air chafed her ears, and the smell of something fried gnawed at her stomach. In her hand, the small lock had warmed to the temperature of her skin, and she traced the letters on its face. *CEB. HTK.*

She chewed on her lip as she stared at it, the sunset behind her casting a warm glow on the gold of the trinket. How long had he loved her?

The sound of crunching gravel made her look up.

Hyun Tae stood at the edge of the rooftop garden, his hands in a smart black wool coat with a high collar that hid his chin. And those dimples she loved. The cold had already turned his nose pink, and she wondered how long he had been standing there. There were benches all along the stone pathways, but she had chosen the swing at the edge, which was framed by tall palm plants that shivered in the wind.

She stood up from her seat, sliding the lock into her coat pocket as he approached. "Hey."

He gave her a half smile. "Hey."

Chase looked down and nudged a small stone off the path with her sneaker.

"Kruljac told me everything," he said. "Even if you hadn't offered him a job at my company, I think your persistence might have won him over."

She grinned, looking up. "Yeah?"

He nodded, taking a step closer. "Yes."

Chase cocked her head, "So you're not mad I said he could work on your team? What if he sells your secrets to Russia or something?"

He gave a silent laugh, a plume of white swirling from his lips. "Well, I think with you watching him, he might think twice about crossing us."

Us. Chase's heart did a somersault.

He stepped closer again, forcing Chase to tilt her head up to meet his eyes. "You stayed."

"I stayed," she said, her voice raspy. His eyes were so soft, so warm and inviting.

He reached out to her, and when she didn't move away, he slid his hand into her right pocket, grasping hers before his fingers hooked around the lock. He gave a little tug, pressing their bodies close together. "Chase." He leaned in close, for once, seemingly a little dazed himself. "Thank you."

She brought her left hand up, and cupping the back of his warm neck, stood on her tiptoes to pull his lips to hers.

He abandoned the pocket, and cradling her face in both hands, kissed her slowly, his lips molding perfectly to hers, the warmth from his body enveloping her as she melted into him. It could have been summer judging from the heat in her veins, and she couldn't have imagined, couldn't have ever dared to dream that another person would feel so right in her arms. She wanted to pull that thick coat off and feel if his skin was as velvety smooth as his lips.

When they pulled back, both of them short of breath, Chase said, "It was like that the first time, you know."

"Hm?" He asked, distractedly smoothing the skin of her cheekbone with his thumb.

"The first time you kissed me."

He smiled, pulling her into a tight hug and kissing her forehead. "I know."

"You know?" she asked, a little outraged.

"If your heart monitor didn't give it away, the way you kissed me back would have."

"Mm," she agreed, burrowing back into his arms. He felt so good. So solid and warm and perfectly shaped to hold her.

"Thank you," he said again.

"Did it all...I mean is everything okay now?"

"Yes," he replied, tightening his hug with a sigh. "It did. Or it will. You saved my company, Chase. You saved me."

She smiled. And then she laughed.

"What?" Hyun Tae asked.

433

"I just realized my mom is going to go nuts when she realizes I've gotten a Chaebol to fall for me."

He laughed, pulling away from the hug and taking her hand in his. "She might not laugh when she realizes our countries are on the other side of the world."

Chase shrugged. "I can be an artist anywhere."

He stopped, looking down. "You don't have to. I don't want you to give up on your dreams, Chase. I've already ruined the chances that have come your way so far. I don't want you to feel like you've chosen my dreams over your dreams if you choose to stay here with me."

She knew he couldn't go. Not now. They might finish out the year at Bates. Or he might transfer to another school to finish, but his company needed him. And she needed him, too.

"Chase, I love you. I love you more than I thought I could. Before we met, I thought I loved my company and my work, but..." he trailed off, looking down at their joined hands. "The way I love you is magnetic. I look for you when you aren't there. I feel you enter a room before my eyes can catch up."

Joy surged up within her, and Chase tightened her hold on his hand. "And yet you'd still understand if I stayed in California?"

He swallowed hard, nodding. "I would."

She gave him a smile, raising one brow slightly. "This is why I had to save you. You're such a martyr."

"I'm...I'm what?" He blinked.

"I do love my art, and my family, and my friends in California. But Hyun Tae, I stayed *here* for a reason." She took the lapels of his coat in her hands and pulled him close. "I love you more."

He stared at her, the joy transparent in his sharp features. "So you'll stay?"

Chase nodded.

With a smile tugging on his lips, Hyun Tae leaned in until they were a breath away from hers. "Don't slap me."

She laughed just before the kiss sealed her lips.

Epilogue

Chase sat with her hand in Hyun Tae's, looking down at the stage from the most expensive seats in the huge Seoul Olympic Stadium. Massive screens lit up the darkened stadium, as well as thousands of handheld LED lights with Hipstar's logo. A low bass beat thumped, and the screens showed close-up pictures of the band members. When Daniel's picture flashed on the screen, the entire stadium filled with screams. Apparently his fans had forgiven him, especially after he'd taken a brief hiatus, which had frightened them into thinking he was leaving their beloved Hipstar. The crowd screamed again as the music changed, and the five members rose up from beneath the stage, pyrotechnics exploding behind them.

Caught up in the excitement, Chase pulled her hand away, waving her Hipstar light and screaming, "Hipstar! *Saranghayeo!*" Hyun Tae collapsed in his seat, laughing at her.

A video of glass shattering played on the big center screen, the sound crashing through the stadium, and Daniel stepped forward. Eyeliner accented his eyes, which were lightened to a warm amber with contact lenses. His hair had been dyed platinum, and he looked otherworldly in the bright white lights.

"*Daebok*," she said out loud.

"I'm not taking you to any more Hipstar concerts," Hyun Tae said, laughing at her again.

She reached out and grabbed his shirt, pulling on it playfully. "*Oppa!*"

He stared at her warningly, and her cheeks flushed, but no one could tell in the darkness. There would have been a kiss if they weren't in public. He still made her knees weak just looking at her.

She looked down at her ring finger. A stray beam of light caught the large, round-cut diamond on her engagement ring.

The first few notes of Hipstar's newest song started, and Daniel sang, his light amber eyes staring back at the audience. The song was haunting, sweet, and hopeful, and Chase found herself staring back at him, remembering when she and Hyun Tae had seen Daniel backstage, right before the concert started.

He'd met them just outside the inner lounge, in a wide painted brick corridor. There were a lot of stage technicians dressed in black wearing headphones and microphones who were busy checking equipment and consulting with each other.

"*Hyung*," Hyun Tae said, and the two of them embraced.

"You look like a different person!" Chase said. Daniel wore slim black leather pants and a silk shirt with a long black jacket, elegant yet not quite something anyone would wear off a stage.

"That's because I'm wearing more makeup than you are. I like your shirt."

She'd worn a Hipstar T-shirt with all the band members featured on the front and Daniel's name on the back. "It's pretty great."

"Nervous?" Hyun Tae asked. This was the band's "comeback" performance for their new album.

"No, I wasn't, but thanks for making me think about it now."

Hyun Tae grinned, looking pleased with himself.

"You're going to be awesome," Chase said, pretty sure she would throw up if she had to do anything in front of thousands of people and wondering how he did it. Their choreography was difficult, and they were singing at least twenty songs tonight.

"Thanks," he said, and then bent his head, touching his earpiece. "Ah. Sounds like the guys are ready. Glad you came. Hope you have a good time!"

Hyun Tae grabbed Daniel in another hug and then took Chase's hand. As they turned to go, Chase looked back. Daniel's eyes held hers, the amber color making his eyes soft and strangely unreadable, like a mirror that reflected her own thoughts back at her instead of revealing his, and then he smiled and turned away.

About the Authors

Devon Atwood is the author of two YA fantasy novels, and has experienced both traditional, small publishing markets, and self-publishing endeavors on the road to authorship. You can find her on Facebook, Twitter, Instagram, and Google+, or, more likely, with her nose in a binder, washi tape in hand and eyes aglow with organizational bliss.

Alice Cornwall is a seasoned writer with an ingeniously useful "crap-o-meter" and a Bachelor's degree she doesn't really intend to use. She lives in Pennsylvania with her fancy cat.

They write a blog about k-dramas that can be found online at https://devonandcornwall.wordpress.com.

Printed in Great Britain
by Amazon